DEAR MILTON &

I HOPE YOU ENJOY.

"I say that we must learn from our past so that we do not make the same mistakes in our future."

General Drorkon, Two-Twenty-Eight Heavy Cavalry of Camia

ALL THE BEST

Dear Milton & Vivie,

Hope you enjoy.

All the best

Search of the Lost

The Knights of Ezazeruth Trilogy

Thomas R. Gaskin

Published by New Generation Publishing in 2015

Cover illustration by Jon Sullivan

Maps by Thomas R. Gaskin & Katie L. Gaskin

British Library Cataloguing in Publication Data. A catalogue record for this book is available from the British Library

www.thomasrgaskin.com

ISBN: 978-1-78507-163-8

www.newgeneration-publishing.com

ACKNOWLEDGEMENTS

This being my first book published, I have many people to thank and acknowledge for their support:

Firstly, to my mum and dad, who've stood by me and supported me throughout in so many ways; I got down a lot, and your words always picked me back up.

My amazing brother and sister who've done brilliantly in life, I will never tell you but I always look up to you both.

To my wonderful wife and children; I tried not to type when the kids were awake, and you always helped me find that missing word!

To Clare, who read my book when others wouldn't.

To Mary for her time in proofreading my story.

To Graham, for re-editing my manuscript.

To Jen, for your proofreading touch and encouragement, you have my deepest gratitude.

To Phil, thank you.

To Jon for your amazing artwork, thank you so, so much.

To Jenny for your help.

To Linda and the group.

To Paul, you've helped me on a really personal level and I owe you so much. I'm proud to call you my friend.

I am dyslexic, so this book also goes out to all those with learning difficulties. It's a hard world to exist in, but exist we do, and great things we can still achieve.

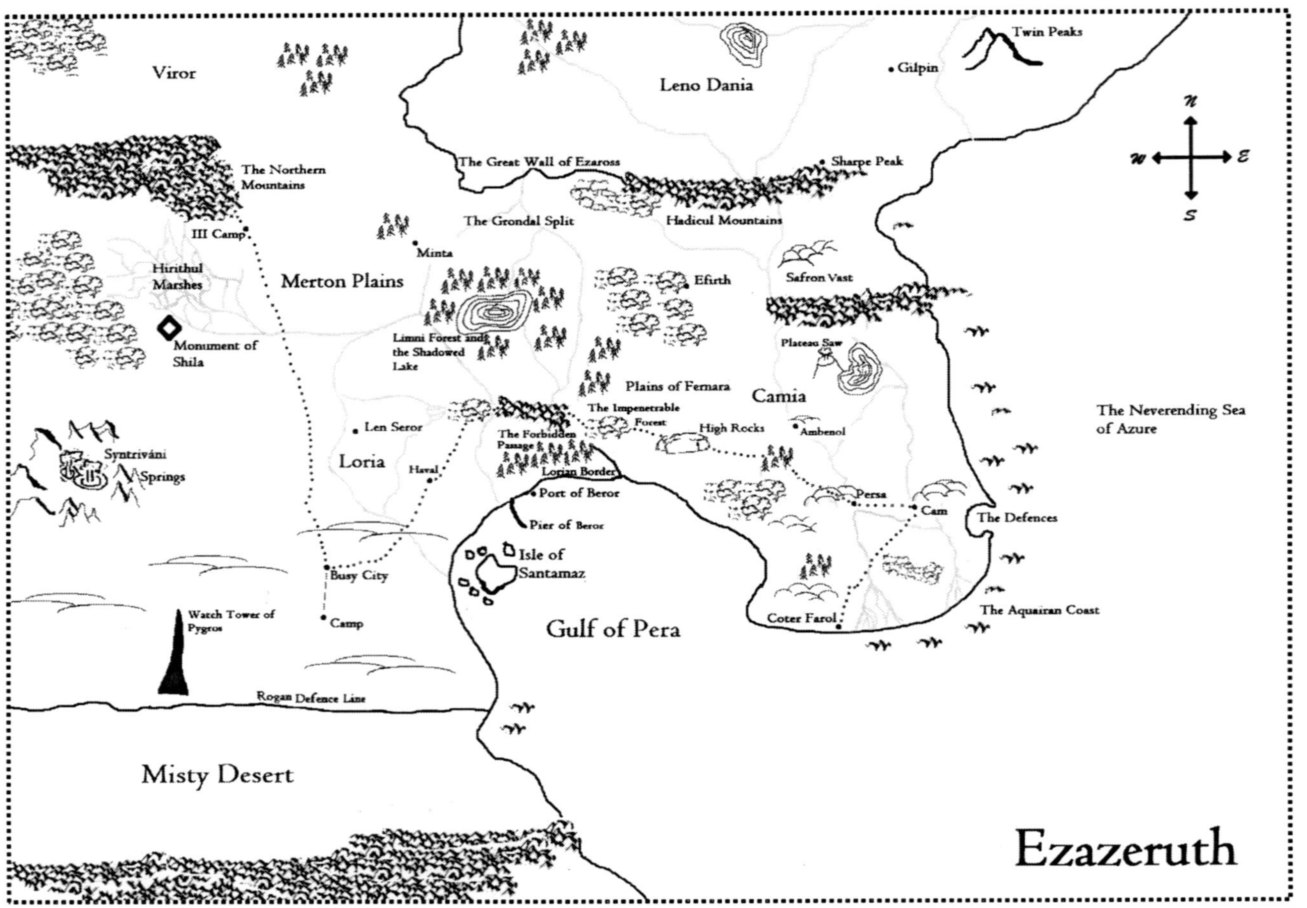
Ezazeruth
N
W
E
S
Viror
Leno Dania
Twin Peaks
Gilpin
The Northern Mountains
The Great Wall of Ezaross
Sharpe Peak
III Camp
The Grondal Split
Hadicul Mountains
Minta
Hirithul Marshes
Merton Plains
Efirth
Safron Vast
Monument of Shila
Limni Forest and the Shadowed Lake
Plateau Saw
Plains of Fernara
Camia
The Impenetrable Forest
High Rocks
Ambenol
The Neverending Sea of Azure
Len Seror
The Forbidden Passage
Syntriváni Springs
Loria
Haval
Lorian Border
Persa
Port of Beror
Cam
The Defences
Pier of Beror
Isle of Santamaz
Busy City
Watch Tower of Pygros
Camp
Gulf of Pera
Coter Farol
The Aquairan Coast
Rogan Defence Line
Misty Desert

For Stephen, Samuel, Isabel and Katie

Prologue

In the time of the Ninth Age in the world of Ezazeruth, on a clear spring morning with the wind calm and the sun bright, a dark ship arrived on the east coast.

It is not known where the ship came from: it appeared like a bird from behind the clouds, the sails black and torn, the wooden deck dark and rigid, and there was nothing aboard but a chest.

The ship sat alone for several days until two young brothers walking along the shore found it, with parts of the vessel damaged as it had collided with scatterings of rocks off the Aquairan Coast. The inquisitive children were able to climb through a large hole at the prow and boarded the ship to have a look around, and, in the centre, strapped to the main mast, they found the chest.

It had no lock, and was decorated with pure golden edging around its sides, patterns that seemed to form words in a language neither understood, etched into the wood. The children could not help but open it and take a look inside.

Instantly, a black cloud billowed from the chest and possessed the children, and they stood where they were, perfectly still, their eyes red and with menacing grins.

A day later, the parents and a hastily formed search party looking for the children finally found them on the vessel, but, when spoken to, in unison and in voices not their own, they said:

You banished me, you ridiculed me, I hate you!

Terrified, the parents tried to plead with the boys, but they repeated the sentence whenever spoken to. So the families consulted with their country's Ikarion: a mysterious, shape-shifting entity which humans worshipped as a god. No one really knew what they were or where they came from; they just appeared one day, a group of them, and each took a piece of land to help guide and protect all humans on that land, adopting the appearance of the native animals to help win over the humans' trust. Their reign was the closest thing to peace humanity had ever seen, forever being known as the Golden Age.

Soon, it arrived: a tall, white wolf, its fur pure as the clouds above, its eyes blue and piercing as a crystal sea on a bright day.

It studied the boys and grew concerned, concerned by a dark threat, long forgotten.

Telepathically it spoke to its people, and messengers were sent out across Ezazeruth to bring all the Ikarions in the land to the ship, for in fear of the boys' message the wolf wanted its kin's counsel.

Meanwhile, all were told to leave the vessel, and the wolf carried its protective gaze upon the children. But, as word of the possessed brothers spread, locals became fearful of them and saw them as demons. Soon local villagers arrived armed with farming tools or makeshift weapons, growing more agitated and fearful by the day. They did not advance on the ship, but surrounded it. One night they tried to set fire to it, when the paranoia became too much to bear, but a thunderous growl from the wolf scared them away, and so they watched on in fear at a distance, never wanting to take their eyes off the four red glows of the boys' eyes in case something happened. And, despite pleas from the wolf for them to leave, they could not.

Within a month, all the Ikarions in the land had arrived, and together they boarded the ship, with a now large gathering of humans from across the local regions watching on. But, as the last Ikarion came aboard, the ship, under a spell none could prevent, immediately left the shore taking the two children with it … and, despite the damage to the ship, it sailed away and the Ikarions were neither seen nor heard from again.

After they disappeared, the seasons started to change. The summers grew hotter; the winters grew colder; frequent lightning storms tormented the land. This caused the mood of men to escalate into madness; paranoia set in between kings and soon war broke out across the world.

Without the guidance of the Ikarions, man changed beyond imagination. The countries took up arms and fought and quarrelled amongst themselves, ruining the world that had given them so much.

Then one day, small groups of creatures attacked the land, menacing the inhabitants of the world, and, following them, a dark, dense cloud venturing high into the sky devoured the east coast.

Out of the black mist came the darkest of armies, with all manner of creatures and beasts. They advanced under the banner of a yellow serpent wrapped around a red star: the banner of the dark sorcerer Agorath, an evil and vengeful Ikarion who had been banished for treachery nearly a thousand years earlier, as he did not follow their ways of peace and kindness.

Some say he was deformed, others say that he was not truly an Ikarion: but, whatever his origin, he was cruel and brutal.

With him were creatures fiercer than humans could ever imagine, named the Golesh – like the servants of the Dark God Strok, an eternal being of devilish intent, from the religion at that time.

Mooring on the east coast, they mercilessly slaughtered their way across the land, and soon everyone had succumbed to the wrath of the dark army whom they had dubbed the Black.

Within days the Black tore into cities and villages without warning. Some nations rose up and fought against them, but with overwhelming numbers no one could repel the savage force that soon spread over the world like a plague.

Swarming cities like rain and devouring the land like fire, the creatures pillaged, massacred and destroyed Ezazeruth with utter savagery: no human was spared, no one received mercy, and *nothing* was left alive.

Throughout it all, Agorath stood and watched, his staff with a red jewel mounted atop of it always in his hand. He controlled his army with the staff, always pushing onwards and sure of the victory yet to come.

The remaining kings of the known world met at the monument of Shila, a rocky chasm deep within the earth to the west, and together they took up arms in a mighty alliance and marched on the Black.

On the plains of Merton they met, in a bloody campaign.

The battle wore on for days, with heavy losses on both sides. Agorath used his magic and earthquakes swallowed entire battalions; tornadoes of fire engulfed regiments.

Warlocks of the land could do little to stop his savage attacks, as he was too powerful. But the humans did not yield, and eventually the creatures were flanked, pushed onto the back foot and forced to retreat.

One man named Duruck, bloodstained and fatigued, raised his sword high in the air, and, in one last attempt to abolish the Black, rallied the remaining force of the alliance and pushed on to triumph.

Agorath tried to counter, but his creatures fled, unable to match the tenacious savagery that the humans fought with. They retreated back to the coast whence they came, the allies chasing them down giving them no time to regroup. They were treated with a cruelty equal to their own.

Eventually, the remaining Golesh got onto the craft they had arrived on and sailed away, leaving Agorath alone on the beach, full of a new hatred and animosity for his own creations.

As he turned to face the world he had tried to conquer, he was confronted by two figures. One stood dark and hooded and holding a staff, and the other was Duruck, with his bloodstained sword, slowly whetting it with a stone along the single-edged blade, snarling and digging into his reserves of energy.

Keeping their eyes on each other, Duruck and Agorath collided in a colossal duel.

Trying to use power and magic to his advantage, Agorath first had the upper hand against his enemy, but the hooded figure manipulated his energy by sealing the jewel within a spell, forcing the dark sorcerer to fight like a common man.

However, Duruck's skill was far superior to Agorath's, and, heavily wounded, he struggled safely onto a vessel and left the shore drifting out to sea. The shadowy figure broke off its spell and Agorath slowly sailed away, swearing violently that he would return.

And so the Battle for Salvation had ended.

Man had prevailed that day, but at a great cost. Many were left dead, few kings were alive and some races now ceased to exist.

With no one to stop them, the last of the kings declared which countries they wanted to conquer. The country of Camia in the north, the last strong force in Ezazeruth, came down and took over the south-east coast, the brash King Afthadus proclaiming that his armies would protect the world against the dark tide should they return.

But the King of Loria, an adversary of Afthadus, had a better idea. He said that there should not be one country holding the burden of responsibility for protecting the world, but an entire army that would protect *all* within. They would be called the Knights of Ezazeruth, and would not fight for one king or individual or personal conflict, but for everyone.

All the kings except Afthadus were in agreement, so, forced to concede to the Lorian's plan, Afthadus agreed on condition that they stayed within Camia.

Thus it was that each country gave its best men to the cause, and eventually three armies were created. Each was ten thousand strong and named for its particular skills: the Oistos being trained archers, the Ippikós expert cavalry, and the Xiphos, highly skilled swordsmen.

The strongest leaders, who had proved their worth in the Battle of Salvation, were set to command and guide them, and, following his courageous duel with Agorath, Duruck was proudly put in charge of the Xiphos.

And so they waited on the east coast, training every day in a regime that would turn boys to men. It was not for the faint-hearted.

But, after two decades, there was no sign of Agorath or his savage minions, and the knights began to die or become ill, old and feeble. Due to peace, few had the skill or experience to match them. Thus their unreplenished ranks started to waver.

To stop this, King Afthadus forced a warlock to curse the knights: never to age, never to become ill and never to die.

Trapped by this awful curse, the knights pleaded and begged for their mortal lives, but Afthadus refused. He was scared, and did not want to risk the lives of his people should Agorath return; and he had little care for the feelings of the knights.

The knights could not seek help from other countries: none wished to stand up to the Camions who were now too powerful to contend with. So, the knights threatened to exile themselves, never to return.

Afthadus, however, laughed and reminded them that they had taken up a blood oath and would have to adhere to it when the time came. So, in fury, the knights marched away from Camia and Ezazeruth, turning their backs on the world they once loved. And, for over two thousand years, few have known their location.

Now, in the present day, an old threat returns to a new world, a world still at war and not prepared to take on what will come. With enemies mixed with friends, and destinies that need to be fulfilled, the knights must be found and brought back to protect what they promised all those years ago.

The Knights of Ezazeruth are the world's only salvation.

Part One

Chapter One
The Born Captain

The captain sat high on his horse, with spears surrounding him. He could not make out which were his own men, and which were those of the unknown enemy who had ambushed them in the hills near the coast of Coter Farol.

"FORMATION!" he shouted, but his voice was not heard due to the deafening noise of battle and men crying in agony.

Before he could react, a broad, black creature like he had never seen before stepped before him; its skin was of greyish blue with veins protruding, its torso and head were covered in thick black armour, and it struck a thick, barbed spear into his horse's neck.

The horse reared with a scream and fell to the side, the captain landing with a breathless thud on the ground, covered by dirt kicked up by the fighting.

He lost his spear and helmet in the fall, so on all fours he drew his sword and stood up straight, his long, blonde hair twisting in the wind, sweat dripping into his eyes as he squinted and the vertical scar over his left eye creasing. He stood firm, a tall man with a square jaw, snarling with hatred at the ambushers.

He looked around at the battlefield before him, where his men were holding their rounded shields tightly against them with their spears balanced over the top, trying to rally into groups. He wasted no time in rushing towards them.

He gripped his sword tightly, his long but scarred arms telling of many battles.

A creature charged towards him, slicing with a heavy mace, its mouth open wide and fangs dripping with blood, red blood as if it had been sucking away at its victim, one of his men; and he gritted his teeth at the thought of such savagery.

The captain ducked as the mace sailed over his head, and then brought his sword up from his right, cutting deep into the creature's torso. He looked it in the eyes as the thing let out a high-pitched shriek he had not heard before. Wrenching his sword out, he pivoted on his heel and sliced the head from its neck, the body landing heavily and the head rolling away.

Hearing a shout, he turned to see one of his sergeants running towards him.

"Captain! We need to—," but the sergeant was cut down by a creature repeatedly slashing away at him with a dagger.

The captain quickly drew a knife from his belt, threw at the beast and ran to his sergeant's aid, but he could tell the man was dead, lying still with his eyes open looking up, and multiple wounds exposing his organs.

He had never fought anything like these creatures before; they were strong, and seemed to relish pain, fighting with an almost sadistic bloodlust to inflict agony. He feared them; many battles he had fought in, many wars and many creatures and humans he had fought, but this was the first time that he had been shaking to the core of his body. The battle did not seem decided, with man and beast falling to the blows of metal, and he knew he had to gain control quickly or he would lose a lot of men and the battle.

The dirt track they were on kicked up dust around him, making it hard to see what was happening, whilst the sun was shining over them, making out silhouettes as they fought.

He mustered as much breath as he could and bellowed with his rugged voice, "FOR THE KING!"

Spurred on by the fact that he was still alive, the chant followed around the battlefield and his men fought on with more determination to finish this foe. The creatures began to struggle in their wake as his men rallied against them.

The captain, however, had spent too much time concentrating on what was around him. He felt a sharp pain slice through his wrist ... a fallen creature lying on its back had hit him with a sword in its last dying moments.

The captain kicked the creature in the head, then stamped on its arm, pinning it to the floor. He then raised his sword vertically and brought it down one-handed into the creature's chest. Blood spilled out from its wound like a spring, and the creature coughed as life left its body.

The captain looked at his arm. Blood was dripping heavily from the pulsing cut, but all he could feel was a tingling sensation. He didn't feel squeamish at the sight of the blood; in fact he embraced it, and, holding his sword firmer and his wounded arm close, he darted forward and fought with his men.

As the enemy continued their charge, the soldiers started to mass together and a phalanx was finally created, with a line of overlapping bronze shields, the infantrymen crouching low and throwing the spears over, as step-by-step they paced forward, jabbing their spears into the black beasts. The soldiers on the outside of the phalanx waited for them to get close, and the wall opened up to let them in, and standing behind their brethren they pushed on. The edge of the battle was finely in their favour, but the beasts did not let up on their advance.

Nearby, on the outside of the phalanx, a young soldier in the thick of the crowd was holding his shield tightly as a creature battered at it with a heavy sword. Sparks flew from the pounding the shield was receiving, making him fall to one knee. In more of a reaction than an act of skill, he lifted his shield, pushing the enemy's sword away and skewering the beast in the gut with his own. He pushed forward all the way up to the hilt and stood still in shock for a moment. He had never stabbed anything before in his life, but it had tried to *kill* him, and this gave him a reason to kill it first.

But the creature was not done yet; it punched him in the face hard and he reeled in pain. Pulling his sword out, as he fell to the ground, he saw the creature looking down at him. He could not see its face, as a large helmet sat over it, but something about the way it was looking down at him made him feel that it was smiling.

Is this my time? he wondered.

He had always dreamt about being in battle, about the gloriousness of it, but he did not think it would end like this, and he intended that it wouldn't. He brought his legs back and kicked hard at the creature's kneecaps, feeling them break between the soles of his boots. The creature's head rolled back and it shrieked from inside its helmet. The soldier looked up as the creature fell on top of him – quickly he drew his dagger and held it upright at his chest in both hands, striking the creature at its heart.

It was heavy, it stank of rotted flesh, but the soldier shoved it off, continually stabbing it to make sure it was dead, its body jolting with every thrust.

Amongst the noise, he heard the war chant of his brethren as they pushed forward to where he was. Still on the floor, he looked across and could just see their feet marching towards him, the creatures falling before their wall of shields.

He should have stayed on the floor, but instead pushed himself upwards using just his dagger. But as he did so, he saw a white light appear right in front of him, and heard what he thought was the distant noise of thunder. And, all seemed to slow down as he stared intently at the white light for a moment. Then, as abruptly as it had come, the light vanished and a creature's face darted through it towards him, slashing violently with a hatchet.

The soldier slashed at the bare skin of its arm, thinking that he had severely injured it, but the creature stopped and simply looked down at the deep gash without concern. No blood came out; it seemed more like decaying flesh shrivelling in the hot sun, the exposed wound showing muscle and tendons tensing and flexing. Then slowly, as the horrified soldier watched, a surge of black blood trickled out of the wound like thick nectar.

The creature smiled and then continued to swing frantically at him as if there was no injury at all.

The soldier staggered back as the hatchet whistled past his nose guard with a hair's width to spare, but, seizing the moment, he parried forward, pushing the dagger firmly under its armpit and into its heart. The creature fell instantly.

Feeling something fall heavily into him from behind, he turned with his dagger raised, meeting his captain, also with his sword drawn ready. Their reflexes stopped them both, and back-to-back they fought on.

The creatures seemed fewer in number and less organized. The phalanx was now impenetrable, and the young soldier and his captain were just waiting for the creatures to be driven back so they could get behind it.

But the sun was shadowed as a broad and tall creature stood before him, much bigger than the young soldier and bearing a spiked mace dangling from a heavy chain … another appeared at its side and held a large shield with a serrated sword plastered in blood.

Armed with only his dagger, he dodged a mace blow but again it swung around and nearly hit him in the face. Taking advantage of his dropped guard, the other creature attacked the soldier. He slashed hysterically away at it to keep it back, but the mace came back around again and hit him in the shoulder.

A surge of agony caressed his shoulder and moved down his arm, and he staggered, trying to keep himself up and fight the pain. But he was in battle, he needed to fight! He needed to survive!

As the creature with the serrated sword advanced on him he gritted his teeth and, holding his dagger downwards, he stabbed down into its shoulder where it met the neck, and pulled its head into the path of the swinging mace, crushing its skull.

The soldier stepped back, breathing heavily, to be with his captain, holding his free arm against his captain's waist to tell him that his back was covered. But he became fatigued as the world around him started to spin, and the numbing pain in his shoulder started to spread across his body.

The mace-bearing creature pulled the mace back around and attacked the young soldier in fury. He stood dazed, fatigue finally settling in, unable to move from what seemed like the killing blow. Then, he was pulled back by his captain, who jumped forward and stabbed the creature in the throat.

The creature fell into the bodies behind it, and the soldier turned to thank his captain ... but saw something was wrong.

A look of disbelief had filled his captain's eyes, and blood was running out of his mouth. Behind him, a creature had buried an axe into his back.

For a moment time seemed to stop. The captain slowly looked up into the soldier's eyes, before he coughed out a mouthful of blood over his chest and fell to the ground with the rest of the victims.

The soldier quickly grasped his dagger at the blade and hurled it, hitting the creature standing behind his captain square in the visor. It was a perfect shot, and the beast fell.

The defensive line then met them, the chaos around seemed to subside and he looked down at the state of his captain. He took in a quick breath and fell to his knees.

The captain was lying on the ground motionless, but when the soldier put his hand out and gently pulled him over, he saw that the man was still alive, but only just.

The soldier pulled him up and held him in his arms. The captain did not move his head; he just looked up at him with sorrow in his eyes.

"What's your name, boy?" he asked, trembling as his body began to shut down.

"Havovatch, Captain," the young soldier replied.

The captain half-grinned and closed his eyes for a moment. Then he took in what lungful of air he could, coughing up thick lumps of blood as he did so, but just managing to speak, "Havovatch!" he said weakly, "the sergeant is dead; are there any other officers?"

Havovatch took a quick glance around but saw no one with a crest upon their helmet or any markings upon their armour.

"No, Captain, I can't see anyone."

"Then, I order you to take my command: you *must* report this to the King; you *must* tell them what happened here!"

Havovatch frowned; he had only passed out of training a few months ago, now he was instructed to take charge of a regiment? As much as he tried not to let it show, his mouth quivered.

"Don't worry," the captain said, putting a shaky hand on his shoulder, "from what I saw, you are a good fighter. I believe in you, you *can* do this, you *must* do this!"

Havovatch nodded gently; the captain smiled and then looked up to the sky and closed his eyes. His body relaxed and he was no more.

Havovatch's eyes began to water. Seeing death for the first time shook him, especially like this – no amount of training could prepare him for it. But what unsettled him the most was seeing someone dying in his arms that he could not save. He felt so helpless; he had joined the army as his father and grandfather before him for the adventure, for the courageousness, not for suffering. The reality of battle was far more disturbing that he'd expected.

He neatly lowered his captain to the floor, taking the sword from his limp grasp.

He stood up and regarded it. It was a kopis sword, with a firm guard and a single-edged blade that widened near the end; it was a bit shorter than his arm and curved slightly in the middle, very different to his current weapon, wherever that was.

Holding it loosely, he stared down at his captain. "May the Grey Knight of the soul come for you and guide you to the everlasting light." Havovatch looked down at the sword and, closing his eyes, with a hint of remorse, he said, "I will fulfil your orders, Captain."

He turned and took in a deep breath. He stood like a warrior should in the aftermath of battle: tatty, his blue tunic sticking out from his bronze armour, torn and waving in the wind, and his cuirass dented and covered in black and crimson blood. He had lost all his weapons in the fight and held only his captain's sword. Wiping the blood with a rag, he placed it in his scabbard and tried to think about what to do, the captain's message echoing in his mind: *'you must take my command'* – would anyone believe him? Surely there was going to be another officer around, and he looked desperately.

The noise of battle had subsided; victory had been late but a victory it was. Those that were left of these murderous, ravenous beasts were now fleeing towards the shore in the distance. Some of his brethren were running after them in a mad rage, whilst others were shouting for them to come back – they needed to regroup and could not risk becoming separated.

Some of the creatures lay on the floor half injured or maimed, shouting out mocking shrieks before soldiers maliciously drove their weapons into them, causing more unpleasant cries that sent a shudder down Havovatch's spine. He was concerned with what they were … he had never seen anything like them before and he knew that the attack was now a declaration of war.

He regained his breath and composure and walked through the midst of the battlefield, taking in the scenes in detail. Dirt still floated in the air; soldiers lay dead or injured around him, begging for mercy whilst their limbs lay next to them on the ground.

All around him men could be heard crying, some screaming in pain.

They had set out as part of a training mission to teach the new recruits what life would be like in the heavy infantry, only two hundred of a six-thousand strong regiment. And so they ventured to the south of Camia to protect the southern shores from pirates. What they found was something far more terrifying.

Havovatch wished that the rest of the Three-Thirty-Third, his regiment, were here with him; they were on stand-down until their captain returned, and he wondered how they would take the news that he wouldn't.

He knew little about his captain, but he did know that he had served in that rank longer than any other and had been renowned for his bravery. He knew the death was going to affect people back home, and it sent a shock to his heart that he was the only one who knew he was dead.

As he strolled through the grim scene, trying desperately to think about what to do, he came across his captain's horse, and, looking down, he found his captain's helmet.

Havovatch bent down and picked it up, taking it in both hands. He studied it in detail, stroking the markings on the sides of the helmet – two olive branches carved into the cheek guards, showing the insignia of a captain. He squeezed it between the palms of his hands to feel the firmness; it was incredibly strong. He ran his finger from the nose guard up towards the blue crest that went vertically down the back of the helmet. He admired it: a symbol, something to respect, something to honour.

He looked around to see if anyone was paying him any attention. But no one was. This was it: he knew if he put the helmet on then he was stepping into a world he did not know, and that when found out he could be subject to torment he could not bear to think of. Taking another look around, though, he noticed that there were no other leaders: no one taking charge, no sergeants or lieutenants, no order, no leadership. He had to take control, irrespective of the consequences, and get the men back to the city of Cam and raise the alarm.

Gently he put it on, as perfect a fit as his own.

He looked around, finding the helmet gave him a slight surge of confidence. Absent-mindedly he strode over the hill, his chin up and left hand resting on his captain's sword, and stopped when he saw Rembon sitting on a rock, stroking his head in stress. Havovatch knew him well; he had been the loud know-it-all in training, his nemesis, the boy who kept walking into him to show off to his friends, who would trip him up as they passed each other, who would mock him at every chance during the day. Now he was brought down to his knees in the reality of war.

Havovatch was different in many ways. During their six months of training he had been at the top of the class, disconsolate and determined and put in charge of segments of the unit during his training. Rembon saw him as a target for his jealousy.

"*You!*" Havovatch shouted, with a warm feeling of satisfaction in his stomach at being above him.

Rembon looked up instantly, as did everyone around. Havovatch suddenly felt panic grip him; he was about to bark out an order but now, with everyone looking at him he did not know what to say.

"Captain?" one of the soldiers ventured.

"Erm, th-th-this mess is not going to clean itself up! A-All of you, gather the wounded, leave the dead and bring some of these foul creatures with us, we return to Cam!"

To his amazement, movement began. They were obeying his orders.

He was amazed that no one thought that he was not their captain. He supposed that, with the neatly fitted helmet and the captain's sword in his scabbard, there was nothing to identify him as anyone else. After what they had just gone through, no one was in the mood to argue over small details; for most of them it was the first time they had been in battle and their mood was sombre.

He walked through the carnage, helping to their feet those who could walk and giving them words of encouragement. He tried to speak ruggedly to match how his captain had spoken, and it seemed to work. Most of them had not really seen the captain's face, and only the thin line of his mouth between the cheek guards and his eyes were visible, helping him with his masquerade.

Watching everyone getting their hands dirty made him want to join in, but he knew from his training that a leader needed to see more about what was going on so he could give instruction.

A million thoughts ran through his mind and he had to shake his head to clear it of the thoughts that kept resurfacing. To regain control, he walked away from the battlefield for a moment and looked at the lush green landscape around them: tall, steep hills surrounded by towering mountains in the background to the north, and the blue sparkling ocean to the south-west. A scene of natural beauty lay before him, whilst behind him was only pain and suffering.

As he gazed at the view, he noticed a stretch of long grass either side of the battlefield where the creatures had attacked them from, and a fearful thought struck him.

Turning, he saw a lieutenant striding past. He remembered him well, as he had been an instructor during training.

This was good, he thought; he could take off the helmet and hand control over to the lieutenant and be free of this new and frightening responsibility. But, before he could speak, the lieutenant approached and said, "Captain, what are your orders?"

Havovatch thought, with several of the men around all now looking at him, he could not reveal himself. He pointed into the grass and walked towards it confidently.

"Lieutenant Jadge, take a body of men into the grass on either side, check there are no more creatures lurking there and return to me!" he said as hoarsely as possible.

The lieutenant saluted and gathered a dozen or so men. They took shields and spears from corpses, even some from the dead creatures, and lined up in two columns on either side of the battlefield. Jadge stood in between the columns and gave the command to march, and simultaneously they ventured into the undergrowth. Shortly behind them, other soldiers joined and they went down the crest of the hill together.

The grass was so long that they were soon lost; all that could be heard was their trudging through the crunchy foliage and the sound of metal upon metal as they knocked against each other. They soon returned, and a few men from each column walked over to the lieutenant and reported their findings.

Whilst this was happening, Havovatch was watching his men empty a supply cart and put the dead bodies of the creatures that were not too badly mutilated into it. He approached one that was hanging over the cart and ripped its helmet off. Sneering with disgust at the smell, his eyes widened in shock, showing the whites of his eyeballs, as he stared at the face of a creature he thought to be a servant of the dark God.

It had gaunt cheeks, a long narrow nose and huge pointed ears, with rings of rusted metal along the edge. Its teeth stuck upwards over the top of its lips and were yellow and black with decay. It had long, white shaggy hair around the side of its scalp and past injuries were held together with metal plates and screws buried into its skull. Havovatch pulled his head away, grimacing, and, reaching out, he shoved the helmet back on behind him.

As the weapons were piled on to the cart, he looked at the horrific equipment and felt demoralized at the wounds they must have inflicted. They were not built for stealth or to inflict quick death, but to create the most dreadful injuries and as much suffering as possible.

He walked away to try to compose himself, but had to pause when he saw Lieutenant Jadge approaching. He avoided his gaze, and made it look as though he was listening but keeping an eye on the men at the same time. "Report!" he said with a slight stutter.

"Captain, the men report that there are flattened areas of grass where the enemy lay in wait; they went down further but found that the grass had not been touched. I am confident that we have fought the last of them off." Havovatch nodded. Jadge leant in closer and lowered his voice, saying, "Captain? What are these things?"

Havovatch did not know what to say: "Erm, ju-just get the men into formation, Lieutenant." He knew he was losing it; the stress was becoming too much to bear.

Lieutenant Jadge was taken aback at the sudden bluntness in his captain, but didn't question him. "Three-Thirty-Third!" Jadge barked aloud to the men, "we leave at once, set up a column and be on your guard!"

The soldiers gathered; they had now retrieved their spears, helmets and shields and stood ready to march. The dead lay on the ground as gulls scavenged. Havovatch hated to leave them there, but time was running short and those creatures had taken their toll on the men. They could not cope with another prospective battle.

The last of the men got into line; they held their shields tightly and their spears over their right shoulders and waited for the command to march. Havovatch stood at the side of the column; the men did not look at him, they just kept their gaze forward as they were trained to do. The carts were put into the centre to protect the wounded, and everything was ready. He pushed his chest out and shouted into the air, "THREE-THIRTY-THIRD! TO-YOUR-DUTIES!"

As one they marched back down the hill the way they had come. Lieutenant Jadge appointed himself as the forward pointer and led the column back north to Cam.

Havovatch watched as the column marched. He was intent on getting every single one back alive, and as the last of them passed he walked behind … then, at the last minute, he paused and turned around.

He looked back at the battlefield, at the sight of his *first* battle; all his life he had wondered what it would be like, but it was nothing like the glory he had imagined. These beasts and his men were sprawled over the ground or lying over rocks, spears and bearers bedded into the ground, swords sticking out of victims, some with their hands still clenched around the weapons.

He knew that experienced regiments would need to come here and fight this foe, and he only wished his regiment had left Cam at full strength – then they would have been a force to reckon with …

He gritted his teeth, muttered an oath to himself and strode with purpose to catch up with the marching regiment. He was keen to make sure that the sacrifice of the dead was not in vain.

But one question struck him as he marched. What was that white light he saw during the battle?

Chapter Two
The King of Camia

For the five days since the battle, Havovatch had marched the Three-Thirty-Third hard, with little time to rest. If the attack was the start of an invasion force, he was intent on getting back to Cam as quickly as possible. Havovatch was tired; he had slept little and kept going over what could happen to him when he got to Cam. He thought that when he got into the city he might be able to sneak into a shadow, throw away the sword and helmet and join the ranks and claim that it was a ghost that led them back. He had certainly heard of stranger stories.

Marching at the head of the column he came out of his dreary trance when he saw a light cavalry unit approaching from around a hill. He put his fist into the air and the marching stopped.

As the riders came into view, he saw that there were only twenty of them, wearing black tunics with golden body armour that was thinner than his heavy infantry armour. Tall, black peacock feathers sprouted out from the tops of their helmets.

He could tell which one was the officer; a lieutenant approached, elegantly decorated with fern branches adorning the breastplate of his armour and cheek guards of his helmet; clearly he had spent more money on making himself look good for his commission. He held up the palm of his hand in greeting, and Havovatch instinctively saluted in the Camion way – a clenched fist to the heart, and then a straight hand to his forehead – but then realized that he was acting the role of a captain, and the lieutenant should be saluting him, but he barely made a gesture towards him.

"Captain, are you OK?! You look like you have been in battle," he asked, clearly concerned.

Feeling slightly apprehensive, Havovatch did not really know how to respond. The lieutenant gazed at him, and then started frowning when it took him so long to answer.

"Captain?" the lieutenant prompted.

"Y-Yes … And no, we were attacked at Coter Farol. We need to report to the King as soon as possible."

The lieutenant whistled behind him and two riders from the rear of his cavalry unit rode forward. "Send word to Cam," the lieutenant said quickly, "we have an attacked unit approaching the city."

Without question they turned and galloped away as if their lives depended on it.

"Who attacked you?" the lieutenant said as sternly. Clearly being high up in society made him feel he was above most people, even a captain of the infantry.

"We don't know." Havovatch felt it strange that a lieutenant spoke down to a captain, but felt too nervous to challenge him, for he wasn't one.

The lieutenant flashed a quizzical look. "You don't know?" he said bluntly. "Well, what did their armour look like? What banner did they follow?"

Havovatch gestured over to the cart filled with the corpses of the creatures in the middle of the column. "Take a look for yourself; for they were not human, but beast."

The lieutenant stared at the cart for some time. Havovatch could only see the whites of his eyes through his helmet; they were struck with horror.

"Very well," he said, not tearing his eyes away. There was a long pause as the lieutenant came to terms with what he was seeing. "Cam is half a day's march; we will escort you back." He spoke differently to how he had started, as if his thoughts were elsewhere, for fear can affect everyone differently; the lieutenant was more scared than he had ever been.

He shouted out a command and the other eighteen riders positioned themselves along the column of Havovatch's men. He was too tired to shout out any kind of order and just gave a nod to the front row. They looked at each other, and then began marching down the path, dragging themselves along with what little energy they had left.

For the rest of the day they passed rolling hills, sporadic woodland, and weathered statues of past warriors and kings, set as markings of famous battles or fallen heroes, until they finally came into view of Cam.

It was an ancient stone and wooden city situated on the largest hill in the vicinity. Rising high up into the sky, it could have been mistaken for a mountain, but it hummed with the lives of a dense population within its walls.

At the summit of the city sat an Acropolis surrounded by large pillars, the drums wider than a giant tree trunk. At nineteen pillars long, it held up a solid black roof which glittered blue in the direct sunlight and could be seen from all around as a beacon of Camia's magnificence.

Below the Acropolis were two levels. The top level consisted of towering buildings, which looked over the surrounding landscape where the rich dwelt, whilst the working class lived on the bottom level, inside cramped stone, square, flat houses, markets and barracks. Surrounding the city were its impressive high walls, making it look impregnable.

The city had been designed by the best architects throughout its history, to be able to withstand the mightiest of sieges and the fiercest of battles. And even now, new designs were being set out to make it bigger, better and more domineering.

Inside the city lived some of the world's best military minds and, higher up in the city, the richest and most famous Camions were found. The city was wealthy and opportunities lay everywhere. That was why Havovatch had chosen to join the army of Camia; because of the prospects it offered and the city he would live in.

The Three-Thirty-Third column, along with their escorts, marched downward along the long, straight road that led down from a hill towards the giant gates, Havovatch marching at the front.

He wanted no one to be able to see his face in the column; it had been hard enough concealing himself as it was in the past five days. He had only taken his helmet off a few times at night when he knew no one was watching, and, as comfortable a fit as it was, it was still irritating not being able to remove it.

Tired and battle-scarred, the column marched on, relieved that the city was before them and that they could finally stand down in the safe haven. Standing on the battlements were soldiers, women and children who looked out to see them and cheered as they approached the grand gates, helping to lift their spirits.

As Havovatch approached the gates, he was captivated by how big and strong they looked. Standing at least a dozen men tall and a few feet thick, with sheets of metal hammered between each piece of wood to add to their strength, they never failed to make him gasp in awe, no matter how many times he had walked through them.

Standing guard at the gate were Cam's reputable watchmen wearing beige tunics and brown leather body vests, and holding blunted spears. They also held white oval shields with a gold boss placed in the middle.

The scouts sent to the city had obviously made them aware that the Three-Thirty-Third were approaching, as they stood in a tight line and pushed aside the curious crowd which had developed around the gates, allowing ample room for the regiment to enter.

As the Three-Thirty-Third approached the arched gate, the crowd's sighs of relief were almost audible. But, when Havovatch entered the main plaza behind the gates, getting ready to find his dark corner to hide in, he was dumbstruck at being greeted by two huge, very well-dressed Knights of the Palace Guard. He stopped and stared up at them; their presence seemed to create an inescapable field around him. After a moment, Havovatch saluted them, but they barely made a gesture in return, standing aloof, their cold, uncaring eyes giving nothing away. One of them regarded him coldly.

"Captain, we have heard of your coming. The King will speak to you immediately," he said, ominously.

Havovatch had only seen the King once at his passing-out ceremony, when he had been officially made a soldier; he shook his hand and received his helmet. He had heard so much about the King and remembered everything about him from that day. The King did not even look at Havovatch; he just gave him his helmet, said "well done", and glanced around as if he could not wait to leave. But he was fearsome to see; surrounded by his knights and other politicians, he was almost frightening to look at. He held so much power, but from what he heard, he did not do much with it and was not well liked by his people.

The regiment marched on. Havovatch swallowed, his heart pounding heavily from within his breastplates, and with a knight either side of him he marched towards the summit of the city.

The knights stood tall over him, huge, broad giants. They wore enormous, black shoulder pads decorated with golden edging, and though their breastplates were thick and solid, they moved with ease. In their right hands they carried long spears, with the blade a third of the length down. And on their left arms they carried a large square shield. They wore thick black cloaks that dangled down behind them and threw up the dust of the street. They looked respectable, but also terrifying.

All Havovatch knew about them was that they were said to be the ultimate warriors in Camia, and after proving themselves in battle were tasked with protecting the King. He found it unusual that the King saw it fit to take the best warriors away from the ranks where they were better placed, but he supposed they had earned their position, even if they had not fought in years.

Havovatch was terrified; he had never been escorted anywhere before, and now he had two of the finest warriors of Camia escorting him. He was wondering if they had found out that he was not a captain and had actually placed him under arrest? It would explain their attitude towards him.

He had seen many people being escorted around the city, but he had never been in this situation himself. Often during his training, he saw the Knights of the Palace Guard escorting all sorts of people, from the most senior of officials to weak, decrepit old men. He supposed that this manner of escorting was for a variety of reasons – to stop them from running away, to make sure they got to the King, or perhaps to protect them from anyone who did not want a message to get to the King. But he had not heard of assassins lurking in the shadows any more, that was ancient history ... or so he believed.

As they walked up the labyrinth of the active city, he took the opportunity to take a look at his surroundings, as he had not explored much when he was training.

At the bottom of the city, stone buildings surrounded areas closest to the walls, but as they progressed higher the buildings transformed mostly into those of wood. Havovatch thought that this must be part of the defences; as stone buildings could not burn so they were situated nearer the wall in case of a siege, but the wooden buildings were easier to construct and turn into interesting designs. These designs were not just square structures of wood, but each house had been turned into a building of magnificence, interesting patterns carved into the woodwork, and wooden statues and gargoyles sticking out from the roofs. Camions were renowned for their carpentry skills, but when it came to masonry, they were not as accomplished.

They eventually drew near one of the gates that led to the higher level; they were quite high now, much to Havovatch's displeasure. He was not a fan of heights, but did not realize how high up they were until he turned around and saw the city below him and the surrounding landscape. And, even though he was standing on a wide concrete street, he had to steady himself.

Above him along the parapet were clean, white and blue Camion flags waving violently in the wind, with knights standing between keeping watch upon the horizon, dark and disciplined.

As Havovatch and the knights went to enter the gate leading to the second level, which was much like a smaller version of the front gate, it appeared dark and intimidating to him; he grew fearful of passing through. But, with the knights by his side, he was pushed on.

There were no watchmen at the gate or in the upper part of the city, partly because it was far more civilized and they were not needed, but the palace guards were in plentiful supply and so were charged with acting as watchmen.

Havovatch had never been to the second level before; it was like stepping into a different city. The streets were immaculately clean; there was lots of room for people to pass by one another. No beggars lived in the streets, there were no market stalls and everyone who walked around wore long, very elegant togas and as much gold as they could burden themselves with. Most had servants, or their own personal guards, trailing behind them.

Havovatch could not stop staring – he was captivated by scenery that was too interesting to ignore, but he came out of his trance when suddenly the knights stopped, fell to one knee and bowed their heads. Havovatch could see something was passing them at a crossroads, but before he could see any more, a large arm from one of the guards came from nowhere and pulled him down to his knees. Havovatch allowed himself to fall … he had no idea what was going on.

Then a small, delicate group of women in white appeared. They looked soft and gentle and walked with such elegance that their bare feet could hardly be heard on the cobbled path. Everyone fell silent as the citizens bowed to them. The women held their hands up as if they were in prayer, and kept their eyes on the floor. Long, netted veils held thin golden tiaras to their coiled hair, which fell down their backs, the veils falling all the way past their legs to brush the ground gently behind them.

Escorting the women were eight guardsmen on either side, wearing beige tunics on which rested golden armour; on their heads were large, golden helmets, with wings sprouting from the sides like those of an eagle. They walked professionally, with their hands resting on the hilts of their short swords and their eyes constantly on the crowd, looking for threats.

In the middle of the group walked a lady, more glamorous than the other women. She had a gold tiara nestled into her golden, plaited hair; it had long, thin pieces of gold that entwined down her back, joined loosely with her bracelets and her belt. She was the most beautiful woman Havovatch had ever seen.

She looked up momentarily but all she saw was a dirt-covered, battle-worn captain staring up at her, and, on either side, two imperial knights of the King. She bowed her head and carried on, but unbeknown to anyone, a mysterious smile appeared on her face.

There was something about her that Havovatch could just not take his eyes off. He had lived in a solitary area growing up and did not really meet many women, but he felt there was more that he wanted to know about this one. He had only ever known his mother; rarely he would go to markets and see girls, but never had he interacted with them.

He felt a sudden shunt from his right as one of the knights pushed at him with a shield, and found they were now heading towards the left junction. He was high up now; it looked as if he could reach out and touch the fluffy clouds circling above, and soon he came into view of the magnificent white wall circling the Acropolis.

His heart started to beat faster, the reality of his cover being blown suddenly present in his mind. They turned a corner and he saw another gate in front of him, and he swallowed, trying to summon the courage to walk into the unknown. Yet again, as they approached, the knights at the gates stood to attention and then back at ease when they had passed by.

Just like stepping into the second level, he felt as though he had stepped into a different place on the other side of the gate.

He was shocked at the courtyard; it was not a grand display of wealth and affluence, but bare. Grey stone blocks lined the inner wall, with barrels to one side filled with spears, logs of wood stacked against a wall, with the Acropolis in the middle.

The narrow palace doorway had to be at least twenty feet tall, and as it opened it creaked loudly. There were no men opening the door, but with giant chains attached to it that went through holes in the wall into the Acropolis, it opened almost automatically in front of him.

The knights stopped and stood to attention facing each other as Havovatch continued down a long, narrow corridor alone. He looked behind him to see why they were no longer escorting him, unsure of what to do, but his legs kept walking as if separated from his body.

He could not remember the last time he had felt this apprehensive. He thought for a moment that he was going to be set upon. Suddenly his mind was filled with dread, plagued by worry and suspicious of what he could expect. Being mocked in the stocks, attacked or maybe even killed? He knew little about the law and was unsure of what could befall him.

Lining the corridor in alcoves were statues of kings from old and famous weapons hanging on the walls. Soon he approached the end of the corridor where two more doors stood, and they opened up in front of him.

As he walked in, he saw that the room was surrounded by ascending steps on which lords and ladies were sitting, some clustered in groups, others alone, all silent in his presence. Havovatch felt that everything he did was wrong somehow, as though he were breathing wrongly, walking wrongly…

He saw the King of Camia straight in front of him, sitting on his throne on a raised platform; a tall, thin man stood just in front and to the side, looking tired and bored. He had large eyebrows and a mole on his cheekbone. He looked like a servant or speaker for the King.

The throne was enormous, Havovatch felt it a bit pathetic, but it showed off the wealth and power that his king possessed. It was made from solid gold, with patterns of different trees shaped into it and jewels nesting on the golden leaves. At the top sat a bronze hawk looking over the hall, its wings outstretched as if embracing it.

Havovatch continued to walk towards him steadily.

The King sat tall and grand, both hands resting on the armrests. He looked very serious, his dark, large eyes surrounded by his large, brown, bushy eyebrows and beard. His face was so hidden by hair it was hard to tell how old he was. Huge, jewelled rings glittered on his fingers, his long, thick, brown hair lying flat over the top of his blue cloak. In front of the King, on the floor, stood a black cloud of palace guards, arranged in a semicircle. He wondered how the King had managed to get so many guards all of the same size and stature.

As he got closer he saw a glittering turquoise square on the floor, just before the knights, and wondered if he should stand there. He stepped onto it and no one seemed to protest.

"Captain Perlemos of the Three-Thirty-Third Heavy Infantry in the presence of King Colomune of Camia," an aide said formally, as he introduced the King to the guest of his hall.

King Colomune looked down at Havovatch and in a calm, deep voice said, "What word do you bring, Captain?"

Havovatch suddenly saw the two cavalry scouts standing to one side, wearing red ribbons upon their arms. This meant they had been chosen to perform the ultimate call, the most urgent of messages, perhaps that an outpost had been under siege or, in his case, that a regiment had been attacked.

Havovatch stammered at first, trying desperately to find the words – what do you say to a king? How do you say it? Eventually he managed to say, in a weak tone, "It was an am…ambush, Sire, we had a v-v-victory … but at a-at a c-cost." His voice rang with nerves.

As King Colomune frowned at Havovatch, he heard the lords and ladies muttering and giggling behind him. He had never felt so uneasy in his life – he felt full of fear and anticipation, dreading what King Colomune was about to say. Seconds seemed to take a lifetime to pass. He stood with one hand on the hilt of his captain's sword, the other straight down the side of his body, and he squeezed his fist tight, trying to take some of the tension away.

King Colomune leant on the side of his throne whilst he stroked his beard and looked at him with clear confusion. "You're a Captain of the realm, are you not?" he barked. "Remove your helmet at once!"

Havovatch shakily took his helmet, feeling his short, dark hair brush against the edge. He moved to put it under his left arm but realized he needed to rest his hand on his sword, so he quickly passed it to his right and stood up straight. Again there was more arrogant chatter and quiet giggling from behind him, but King Colomune looked up quickly with a stern face and easily returned the room to silence.

Havovatch was surprised that no one seemed to realize that he was not a captain, not even an officer, now he had removed his helmet; after all he looked too young. But with every worry he had, a million more branched off, and he could feel himself start to shake. He couldn't take this any more, he did not want to be a captain, he wanted to be back in the ranks with his friends. No – he wanted to be back home, and never so much had he wanted his mother.

As the King raised his hand in an elegant fashion and said, "Continue," Havovatch stuttered. He preferred the helmet on and now he could see everyone looking at him. This was it – he could not go through with the pretence any more … He fell to his knees and bowed to the King.

"Sire, I am no captain. The captain of the Three-Thirty-Third heavy duty infantry died in my arms after he saved me; the armour I stand in is mine." Havovatch drew his captain's sword and raised it in both hands as an offering to the King. "This sword and helmet belong to the man I honour, who ordered me in his last dying words to get the Three-Thirty-Third back to Cam and to report to you, Sire."

The hall was deathly silent. He could hear the wind banging against the windows outside and discreet gasps from behind him. He looked out of the corner of his eyes and then spoke again.

"I bring the bodies of our attackers back with us, my liege, so that you may see what ambushed us. They were nothing I have ever seen before in my life. They were great in number and strong in battle." He hoped desperately that the attention of the King would deviate to whatever this mysterious foe was, and perhaps forget all about him.

For a moment, there was silence, and the King just looked at him, his face stern and grim. For Havovatch did not know what to do or what would happen. He could feel his heart pounding the inside of his body armour with all the pressure. At least now it had all come out; it was done.

But he jumped when King Colomune waved his left hand at the knights, and in a deep voice he shouted, "Seize that traitor!"

Two guards strode forward and abruptly pulled Havovatch to his feet. The sword dropped from his grasp and landed on the stone floor with a loud, rattling clang.

They held him firmly in each arm, the tips of his toes brushing against the ground. Around him there was haughty chatter, some not managing to hold in their excitement and bursting into laughter.

With a face of terror, he stared at the King, wondering what was about to become of him. Now that Havovatch was under guard, the King rose and walked towards him, not taking his eyes from his captive.

"I find you guilty of impersonating an officer," he shouted. "I have no care for disobedience, and an example must be made!" As he strode towards Havovatch, the guards clustered around him.

Havovatch felt small and intimidated, but the King did not stop there. "But you have one saving grace! If your tale is true then you will be spared. If it is not, then you will fall, either to a lifetime of hard punishment, or death!"

King Colomune was a foot or so away from Havovatch's face, and his huge, black eyes were staring intently into his. "For now, though, you will go to the Heat Pit!"

There were no goodbyes after that; there was no explanation, the guards just hauled Havovatch away back down the long corridor. He tried to walk, attempting to maintain the last shreds of his dignity, but the guards' grip was so tight he found himself being dragged instead.

He had no idea where he was going, he did not even know what the 'heat pit' was, and the fear of what it could be made him close his eyes in sorrow, for he knew it was not anything good. As he was dragged away, he muttered a prayer to himself that he would be all right, or that he would not suffer.

When Havovatch had left, King Colomune sat back on his throne. "Get me a tea, Atken," he said to the man standing just in front of him.

Atken let out a long sigh – "Yes, Sire" – as if it were the twentieth time that day. As he walked off, King Colomune looked at the lords and ladies staring blankly at him.

"Fetch me a messenger," he barked out to the hall at large.

One of the high-ranking officers stepped out of the crowd, with a group of aides trying to stick close to him. He was a tall, muscular man with red, shoulder length hair and a neatly kept beard. He wore black armour that was fixed tightly to his broad, square shoulders; the hawk's head embroidered on each shoulder pad showed he was the commander of all military personnel in the land, and also the famous Knight Hawks, the special forces of Camia. He stepped forward with pride and honour, his chin raised and his helmet held firmly under his arm.

"Who would you like, Sire?" he asked respectfully.

"The best you have, Commander Thiamos."

"And for what mission?"

King Colomune grew impatient – he was a king, and expected people to do as they were told at a moment's command – well, so the colonel had always said. "Commander, I do not wish to justify myself to you!" he growled.

Thiamos took in a breath. "Forgive me, your Highness, I merely enquired, as the mission may call for a particular messenger with a special set of skills."

"Oh, well, very well. It is to go to Coter Farol to investigate these claims that this young soldier has brought back with him," King Colomune said, with slight anger clouding his voice. The commander was right, of course – there were hundreds of messengers in the city, and all of them different. He should have known this, however, and cursed himself for not remembering and for the commander making him look the fool in his court.

Thiamos passed his helmet to his aide, not taking notice of his king's anger, and continued to walk forward, his head down in deep thought. He put his hands together and raised his fingertips to his lips.

"If I may, Sire, wouldn't a light cavalry unit be more prudent? If they were attacked by an unknown force, a light cavalry unit would fare better in the ensuing struggle, whereas a messenger will be on foot ... and alone."

Again it was another good idea that Thiamos had proposed, but once again the King had not thought of it. He sat, seething with anger as he tried to come up with something that didn't make him look more of a fool.

"Commander!" King Colomune said after a moment's thought. "I have made my decision; why do you delay this mission with futile questions?"

There was little noise amongst the crowd ... most of them were ex-officers and agreed with Thiamos, but Thiamos's expression had not changed.

"We do have one man, Sire. He is a bit ... eccentric, but he is the best we have. He works alone and I have the utmost confidence in him. But I ask that you forgive his ways when you meet him, Sire."

"Yes, whatever!" King Colomune barked. "Just bring him in, damn it!"

Thiamos bowed at the waist and went to fetch the messenger. One of the knights picked up Havovatch's sword and helmet and put them in a cabinet on the far side of the Great Hall, and the lords and ladies kept silent in the hall, as a tense mood was in the air.

A short time later Thiamos walked in, a decrepit man trailing behind him. He was short and slender, as thin as a man could become; his hair was so thin that half his scalp was showing. He walked with a swagger, as if he was mad or drunk. A short sword hung loosely by his side and a small sack was sitting over his shoulder. It was clear to all that he travelled light and without much company.

King Colomune regarded him with some thought for a while.

"I hear you are the best?" he growled at the messenger.

"Oh, it does so please me to hear you say so, Sire," the messenger said, smiling. He had few teeth in his mouth, with a larger one sticking out over his bottom lip. Even when he closed his mouth, King Colomune could still see it sticking over his bottom lip.

The King felt uncertain. This man was filthy, and clearly lived rough; could he trust a mission as important as this to him? Nevertheless, he said, "Very well. What is your name?"

"Cathel, Sire."

"Cathel, you are to go south as quickly as you can. A skirmish arose near the shore of Coter Farol. I wish you to go there, then return to me and report your findings in detail. This must be done with haste!"

The messenger smiled and bowed his head, then opened his arms out wide and put one foot behind the other. In an unpleasant and slightly patronizing tone, he said, "Your wish is my command, Sire."

With a limp he hobbled towards the door.

When he had gone, the cart with the creatures' bodies was hauled into the hall by a large palfrey and placed to one side. King Colomune rose and made his way to the cart to examine the bodies, which were now being unloaded by the knights. Allowing the King suitable distance, the lords and ladies then rushed forward to try to get a good view of the bodies.

But, in the corner, a solitary man stood gazing out of the window at the messenger walking down through the city. The watcher was a well-dressed man, elderly but respectable. He was bald with a long nose and distant eyes, and he leant silently against the window, just gazing out, visions of his past appearing before him.

The man wore the armour and insignia of the heavy cavalry unit embroidered on his huge shoulder pads, a horse's head covered in chain mail. His own chain mail hung from neck to foot; a red robe was draped over his shoulders and fell down to the floor. Two short swords were strapped to each thigh and a long sword with a purple hilt sat in a scabbard on his back.

Under his arm he held his helmet, a gold coloured helmet that had black and white horsehair cresting over the centre and dangling over the back of the helmet in a long ponytail. This showed he was a general, the second highest-ranking officer in the Camion military.

He was not willing to get involved in inspecting the creatures. He didn't need to, because he had seen them before.

He muttered to himself in a low and solemn voice, "They will be needed," and then closed his eyes tightly, as if trying to block out the pain of his past.

Chapter Three
Return of the Black

It was scorching hot in the Heat Pit, situated in the very hill the city was founded on. Carved like a deep cave near the top of the city, it sat underneath the Acropolis.

Inside the Pit itself was a huge cauldron in the centre of a dark and miserable hollow, surrounded by men feeding a ferocious furnace below it. Just outside the Pit was a pulley system that went all the way down to the river Amura flowing past the outskirts of the city, where water was constantly fed up and into the cauldron.

From outside the city, labourers brought coal, wood and logs into the Pit for the slave workers to stoke the furnace. And at certain times of the day, when the water had reached the right temperature, funnels would open and the aqueducts in the second level of the city below would be filled with hot, clean water. It would be used to clean the streets, run into homes and bath houses, or even be used to pour boiling water onto besiegers. The tank was huge, spanning fifteen men long and ten men tall, and constantly steaming from the boiling liquid within.

The Pit was hot, with its only entrance being the mouth of the cave, and with small funnels that let the smoke escape in the ceiling and blow safely away from the Acropolis.

The only source of light came from the fire the workers stood around to keep burning, and Havovatch sweated with a heat he had never felt before. He clenched his shovel tightly, but the heat seemed to make it too hot to hold. In front of him was a large pile of coal which was constantly fed with more coal from the paid labourers, laughing mockingly as they walked back out to bask in the sunshine after dumping more on top for him to heave into the furnace.

Havovatch snarled – he hated being treated like vermin by them, he was better than this. They were dumping more coal on his pile than the others because he was closest to the entrance, and with it being so hot they wanted to get out quickly. But it made it look as though he did not shovel enough in the day.

But it was one of the best places to be, near the entrance; as it was so high up, a strong breeze would often blow in and tingle his skin. Just outside the entrance stood guards constantly watching them, too clad in armour to enter, for the heat was so intense.

Havovatch wore nothing but a filthy rag about his waist; his hair was matted and clogged up and his skin filthy from the soot. His sweat ran clean marks down his skin, making paths like a map. He had a Gracker tooth tied around his neck; a good luck charm his father had given to him when he was young, which he had never removed. It was said to be from a demon that lived beneath the waves of the sea in the far north, and could blow vast amounts of solid ice like a dragon would breathe fire. A serpent, a vicious sea monster. He had never seen one, only heard about them in stories, but his father saw the tooth at a market when he was in the infantry many leagues from home and brought it back for him.

Havovatch sighed. He had no idea how long he had been there; he went in before sunrise and came out after sunset, and had lost track of time long ago. It was an exhausting job, but fortunately being an infantryman he was able to cope with hard labour.

The heat though, he hated it, he always had as it made him feel uncomfortable. When he was cold he felt calm and relaxed, when he was hot he sweated and itched.

He looked around at the other criminals. They all seemed to keep to themselves and would occasionally glance over at him before muttering amongst themselves again. Everyone around him was a criminal of some sort; King Colomune believed in giving hard punishments and making criminals work for the country they had tried to turn their backs on. Most of them had been there for years and it showed. They had visible burn marks all over their skin, their hair was very long and some sported so much facial hair he could not make out their features. But they were well built; shovelling coal and heaving logs for so long had made them very strong and toned.

Havovatch noticed that it was nearly sunset outside. He could see the orange glow from the small amount of sky visible through the entrance. "Oi, Cretin! Get over 'ere!" shouted a slave worker at Havovatch. A huge tree trunk had been hauled in from a pulley system on the ceiling and was being placed on the floor.

The worker was covered in severe burn marks; Havovatch thought that he must have fallen into the furnace a long time ago, probably because of a fight. His face was disfigured and he spoke in broken Camion as his lips were too mangled to pronounce the words properly.

Havovatch hated being called a cretin, though, and was about to shout an insult back when he stopped. Taking a deep breath, he calmed himself, remembering that he was keen not to be noticed by the guards, to stay away from trouble as much as he could. Back in control, he went to lend his aid to the other condemned.

Half a dozen men unchained the trunk and placed it on the floor next to the furnace; they then crouched down and hauled it up and into the fire in one lift. As they did so, flames and embers flew from the blaze and onto their bare skin. Havovatch did not flinch any more; for the first few days he had done, but as time wore on the pain of the fire did not seem to worry him – he just got used to it. He was starting to worry that he was getting too used to the heat, though; he hated the heat and never wanted this to change. If he did ever get out of there and went back to camping under the stars on a cold night, he would be a very happy man and would never complain about the lack of comfort again.

He went back to his position and started to shovel more coal into the roaring furnace. He had contemplated his actions ever since he was thrown into the Pit. He was both proud of what he had done and also regretful about it; he often changed his mind as the days wore on. He kept saying to himself: *Where would I be now if I had not taken control? Would the regiment have deserted? Would we have been ambushed again? There was no coordination, and I was ordered to!* He had thought of nothing else but this scenario since he had been put into the Heat Pit. But what was done was done, and he had to live with the consequences despite what had happened.

Just then a man fainted; either because he was too hot, or, more likely, pretending because he was bored. He was taken outside and given water until he felt better. Havovatch could have done the same but he just wanted to keep his head down and get on with it; working hard could go in his favour ... he hoped.

He had no idea that a messenger had been sent out to confirm his story or if they would even return, but what King Colomune had said never failed to haunt him. If what he said were true, then that would be his only lifeline.

Another bucket of coal was thrown onto the pile. He shovelled more into the fire and again it roared at him as if it were alive. But this time, as he stared at the fire, he thought he saw something in the flames. It started out small but soon grew into a circular white light, beaming right at him. He took a quick look around, but no one else seemed to notice it, and, in the background, he heard the faint roar of thunder. The light was not in the fire, but a glowing white orb in the space between him and the flames. Absent-mindedly he reached out to touch it, but as he did so it suddenly vanished, and he was taken out of his trance by the feeling of his skin burning. Withdrawing his hand quickly and assessing the white pustules forming on his fingertips, he shook his head and put it down to stress and madness, although he did remember that he had also seen it during the battle.

He leant on his shovel and started to think about his future. He hoped he would get his honour back. That was the most important thing. He wanted to be back with his regiment; he had done what he was ordered to, and now he just wanted to get back to what he had always wanted to do – be a soldier.

He did not sign up for this! He signed up for loyalty and to serve his country. If anything, it felt as though his country had turned its back on him.

Suddenly, there was a crack of the whip and a sharp pain stung across his back. He had been standing still for too long and it had been noticed. He cringed and pushed his chest out to try to take away the pain, and reluctantly shovelled more coal into the fire, cursing under his breath at the pathetic guard who had struck him. The guard simply smiled and rolled up his whip.

Havovatch wished he had a sword so that he could get his own back. Instead he gritted his teeth and carried on.

***

Five weeks from the time Havovatch was thrown into the Heat Pit, King Colomune was sitting on his throne. Business was almost done for the day and he felt exhausted; he had been sitting all day long listening to how lords needed money for a loan, or soldiers needed help to secure their land, and after a while it grew tedious and tiresome.

All he heard were moaning and whining from people; rarely did a new lord who came into some money or knighthood come along and donate wealth to the throne. Such generosity or charity was seldom seen these days.

King Colomune felt stressed; nothing seemed to work for him. He often looked at the statues of his ancestors made famous by great battles or wars, or by bringing their country to greatness in their own way. *What would his statue be remembered for?* he always wondered.

He came back out of his trance to hear the end of a lord's request for more soldiers to be posted in an area west of the city, which had been plagued by unusual disappearances. As well as this, small villages had been ransacked by what they thought were wild folk from the barren wasteland to the north-west of Camia.

King Colomune rubbed his forehead and closed his eyes. "I will send the Two-Twenty-Eighth Heavy Cavalry out to scout the area. They will monitor on the situation and report to you. Now leave me!"

At the single wave of his hand, the lord bowed and walked briskly towards the doors, but just before he reached them they burst open and Cathel ran in. He was so fast that the knights guarding the entrance to the Acropolis were struggling to catch up. Cathel scampered into the hall with what energy he had left; he looked as though he had been running for days without rest. A red ribbon was tightly tied around his left arm. Everyone stopped what they were doing to look at him. The knights around King Colomune, in unison, moved swiftly from standing upright to battle stance, their spears pointing forward and shields brought to their chests. Commander Thiamos, who was talking to someone at the rear of the hall, went to obstruct Cathel, but he passed him too quickly.

The hall fell silent with curiosity, noting the deplorable state he was in. They had seen the ribbon on his arm and they knew there was something seriously amiss. As for King Colomune, he was now fully awake and looking at Cathel with excitement. He perched on the edge of his throne.

Cathel's attitude was completely different from when they had last met. He was no longer conniving, he was not smirking out of the corner of his mouth and his mocking expression had quite vanished. He was sweating, his clothes were torn and some strange black liquid was splattered all over him. His sack was missing and he grasped his sword in his hand tightly as if he were never going to let it go.

"SIRE!" he bellowed, petrified. "SIRE! THEY'VE ARRIVED!"

He fell to the floor, right in front of the black wall of knights guarding the King. The knights running behind Cathel caught up and pulled him to his knees. They tried to haul the sword from his grasp, but although Cathel was a skinny man and had little muscle mass, they still struggled to retrieve the weapon; he did not even seem to notice the firm grip they held him in.

King Colomune looked at him, baffled. "Who have arrived? Speak!"

Cathel started to tremble. After a moment he spoke in a very low voice, as if a demon were speaking inside of him.

"Sire, when I reached Coter Farol, I saw the remnants of battle, man and beast lying together in their last acts of war. But I heard noises." He paused, trying to come to terms with what had happened. "I saw things in the distance at the shore, so I approached." He began to sob uncontrollably. "I sneaked up to the cliff's edge. I was stealthy and hidden, and from there I watched them; small groups of terrible, dark, foul creatures landing from small craft, small enough to navigate through the shards of rock along the coast; their skin was as grey as a mountain face, their voices as hideous as a cave ghoul. I watched them in silence for a day and a night, but they found me. I don't know how, but they found me. I tried to fight them but they were strong and great in number. Eventually they tied me up and tortured me, along with several inhabitants from the surrounding area. I had to tell them … the pain was too much … I *had* to tell them who I was. And they released me … to send a message back."

Cathel paused for a minute, trying to muster up the words. It was as if they were so terrifying that just mentioning them would kill him. Then, in a high-pitched shriek, he screamed, "The Black are coming!"

Everyone in the Great Hall glanced at each other and started mumbling; even the knights moved from their immobile stance to look at each other's reactions. King Colomune sat there, still half on his throne, leaning on his right hand as he stroked his beard, not taking his eyes off Cathel.

He knew exactly what he was going to do, he was the only person in the room to feel excited, but he waited a minute to make it look as though he had thought all his options through. Then, in a firm voice, he ordered, "Muster the banners!"

Several of the high-ranking officers, some with a red ribbon already in their hands, put them around their left arms and quickly made their way to the hall door. Others picked up papers and barked out orders for the citizens to leave. A huge commotion started in the hall as everyone carried out the King's orders.

King Colomune rose from his throne and strolled through the centre of the hall with his knights mustering around him. Cathel sat on his knees; the guards had let him go and he watched his king approach, his face wet from crying. King Colomune looked down at him. "Go home and rest – you have done well." He then passed him without further thought, leaving him a quivering wreck. As he marched forward he barked, "Fetch me my armour; everyone to your battle stations, we are now at war!"

Horns and bells rang out across the city ... soldiers were running along the battlements filling up small barrels with arrows, spears were being put into holders for soldiers to use, engineers started preparing catapults and clearing out market places. It was something they had been drilled in for so long that now the time had come, they were more than ready.

Riders rode out of the city in different directions, towards the villages, towns and cities. They showed the banner of King Colomune, a white wolf on a blue background, and clearly displaying the red ribbon upon their left arms. They would ride through a town or village and on to the next. As people would see them, the men would run to their homes and dress in their war uniform and then return to their regiments. And so the bannermen rode out to their allies across Ezazeruth, summoning them to fulfil their oaths to the King.

King Colomune stood on top of the battlements of the courtyard looking down at his capital. *Perhaps,* he thought, *this will be my time.* He did not know who these 'Black' were, but from the manner that Cathel had returned in, it was obvious that they meant great harm to the realm. If he succeeded in defeating them, he would rise to glory. He smiled to himself as glorious thoughts came to him.

Just then a man appeared from the hall behind the crowd; a tall, thin outline, almost like a wraith stalking its prey. As he came into the light, a face full of lines and fatigue emerged, with long, drawn eyes and an almost grey hue to his skin. The insignia of a colonel decorated his shoulder pads; three silver fern leaves, all sitting and facing the same direction.

"War?" he quizzed the King, patronizingly.

"Yes – one of our regiments was attacked about a month ago. Remember? And, by the look of those creatures they brought back with them, we are dealing with something dangerous. They attacked us! And we will respond!" The King's attitude changed when the colonel appeared, the thoughts of statues and songs disappearing in an instant.

"A bit rash isn't it Sire?" the colonel continued. "Going to war over something we know little about?"

King Colomune started fidgeting, clearly uncomfortable in the presence of this man. "Well – what would you have me do? Those creatures sent a declaration of war to us; you can't expect me to ignore this threat!" he argued back, trying to stand firm but slowly losing his composure in the face of this man.

The colonel just stood there, seemingly mulling over his king's argument.

"Maybe you're right," he said after a moment. "However, as I said, we know nothing of this … Black, who're they? We only have the word of a street peasant to go on. And even if they do exist, what then? Where do we send our army? What are we supposed to be prepared for? We have no idea when or where they would attack. You seem very eager to go to war with an invisible enemy; only fools would consider such an action sensible," he finished, seemingly smiling as he said it.

King Colomune bristled at being called a fool; however, the colonel was right. He was *always* right, ever since he managed to attach himself to his side, always with the right suggestion or idea. King Colomune still didn't like the way he was spoken to, but decided not to say anything, as always seemed to happen with the colonel.

"What do you suggest, then?"

The colonel waved a hand dismissively at him.

"Why don't you start by searching for what this *Black* actually is – if it does truly exist? Meanwhile why don't you leave everything else to me? I'm sure I can manage everything without you having to get involved at all. You go and play with your little toy soldiers on that thing you call a map in your throne room," he said, with a cruel smile at the King's noticeable discomfort.

The King, however, was oblivious to the insult aimed at him, thinking of the task ahead. He hated studying, the endless searching through boring scrolls and books, all for pointless information that he couldn't understand or just made him tired. All he wanted to do was find the enemy and destroy them in glorious battle, coming home to a chorus of praise being showered on him, for him to be finally recognized as the legend he thought he was. However, he was no good at battle strategies, so the colonel's suggestion seemed a good one, despite the boring, endless hours it would produce for him.

As he came out of his thoughts, he looked up to see the colonel walking back the way he came, paused, then turned back to face him.

"There is another problem, though. The infantry unit that was attacked – they lost their captain, did they not? You may want to find a replacement, and soon."

The King thought for a moment. "I will send for someone to draw a list of candidates and pick one from there."

The colonel stood staring at his king at the suggestion, then a slow smile crept across his face and the King swore he saw an almost savage look appear. Then it was gone in an instant and the King shook his head, putting it down to the excitement of the day.

"Here's a suggestion,' said the colonel. 'Why not promote that boy who brought them back? He seemed to show some guts after what happened to them, and we need someone quickly to take over. He seems like the prefect choice."

The King balked at the idea of a normal infantry solider becoming a captain. Usually the higher ranks were chosen through high-born families, or a committee who chose those who had proven their worth and experience.

"Are you sure? He isn't even of high birth, plus I sent him to the Heat Pit as punishment for impersonating an officer."

"Then you'd better get him out of there."

With that the colonel turned and left, the shadows swallowing him up again.

King Colomune was not sure of the decision, but the colonel seemed to have left him with no choice. He turned towards a palace guard. "Fetch me Havovatch!"

The knight walked off without question, and Colomune turned to an aide. "Go to the scroll halls, see if you can find anything out about this … Black."

Atken then arrived with a cup of tea in an antique teacup. "Your tea, Sire; let me guess, you would like another just after?"

"Yes, thank you, A—"

Atken left immediately with a suave walk, his arms down by his sides, leaving King Colomune to look at the city below as the cavalry and infantry units left marching south, the find the Black.

A while later, Havovatch returned in shackles to the battlements surrounding the Acropolis, guarded by the one knight. King Colomune had not moved, but stood daydreaming about statues being made in his honour and children singing songs about him.

Havovatch was still only wearing the filthy white rag about his waist (though it was far from white now), his hands dangling loosely in front of him.

King Colomune turned to meet him; observing the way Havovatch shivered, taking note of the wounds and dirty rags still plastered to him. "Young man, I have been remiss. In all the years I have reigned I have never come across anyone like you. And … it is not often a king has to apologize for his orders, but I had to be stern in case you were lying." He gestured with his hand for Havovatch to follow him along the battlements. Havovatch was confused and so engrossed in the conversation he did not realize how high up he was. "You brought my troops safely home after an awful attack, and you tried to give me a message … that turned out to be true. These are the virtues of a leader and you have impressed me."

"Thank you, Sire," Havovatch replied, slightly startled. He had not been expecting this today.

"I have decided that I am going to award you the rank of captain."

Havovatch went still and wide-eyed, wondering whether it were true – his own father had not even got to captain.

The knight hit the back of his legs with his spear, pushing him to the floor. King Colomune drew his sword and rested the flat of the blade on Havovatch's head. He bowed and quivered slightly, hoping this was not some trick to actually behead him.

"I officially award you the rank of captain, Havovatch of the Three-Thirty-Third Heavy Infantry. May you lead with honour and justice, and fulfil your oath to me and the Kingdom. Now rise a captain and leave the man you were behind: go forth and fulfil your oath!"

Havovatch rose to his feet and the guard unshackled him. He turned to King Colomune, rubbing his wrists, and said, "I will fulfil the oath, my King." Although he did not agree with it, he had jumped what seemed five ranks without training in one step; now he had the responsibility of commanding an entire regiment. But it was Camion tradition that when a king gave you an oath, you had to accept it whether you liked it or not, and Havovatch knew that.

King Colomune glanced at him passively. "Havovatch, your regiment is on standby in the city until they receive further instruction. In the meantime, get to know your officers and your rank. The Three-Thirty-Third will be filled with new recruits to swell to eight thousand under the rules of war; I suggest you prepare them for battle."

With that, he went to leave, but turned and handed Havovatch a small knife. It was no longer than Havovatch's middle finger. It was beautifully decorated in gold and immensely sharp – as Havovatch found out as he touched the blade and blood ran out from a fine cut.

Havovatch was so engrossed, he did not even notice that the palace guard had gone too; he was standing alone on the battlements, not really sure of what to do, holding this small token from his king in his hands. As he turned to walk away, he was met by a group of dumbfounded officers who had been rushing to bring news to the King, and had just witnessed the promotion.

"What the ... !" said one.

"Did he just ... ?" said another, too speechless to understand the meaning behind promoting a boy.

"You worthless rekon, what did you do to get that?"

Havovatch didn't know what to do. He actually agreed with them – he was not ready to be a captain, he barely knew how to be a soldier ... he had only passed out of training a few months ago.

Hesitantly, he bowed his head and tried to leave the courtyard. He felt worse than when he had been in the Heat Pit; it added to his misery that he was semi-naked. But the officers blocked his path. One shouted, "I'll be damned if you think you are one of us; an officer is a gentleman, you're nothing but a filthy scoundrel in a rag!"

"Yeah, you worthless git!"

They started rubbing his hair as if he were a hound, and pushing him.

"Look!" Havovatch protested. "I just want to get away, please let me go!" In answer, one of the men kicked him in the rear and he fell forward, much to amusement of the officers. He scrambled to his feet and ran out of the gate clutching the knife in his hands, insults ringing out behind him as he ran.

Once he was in the first level of the city, he made his way through the labyrinth of streets and down to the lower borough, his heart racing. Keen not to be arrested for carrying what he thought looked like an assassin's blade, he tucked it into the rag around his waist. But it was far from comfortable, and the open blade kept cutting at his hip.

Around him everyone was going about urgent business: some standing around in curiosity about the sudden alarm; others were messengers running from house to house; some were just walking with friends trying to understand what was going on.

As Havovatch walked, he felt very out of place. He looked decrepit; he was still in his rags, soot covered his skin, his hair had grown long, he reeked of sweat and he had not had a proper wash since he had left on his first mission. He walked down the path deep in thought, but stopped as he felt something shove into him … someone had purposely hit him as he walked by.

Havovatch turned to see who it was, expecting an apology. But instead he came face-to-face with a sour-faced colonel, not one he had met before. He was short and slim with gaunt cheeks, and had silvery hair combed back. His wiry eyebrows were arrow-shaped, like the shape of a cat's ears, and the corners were twisted in a long tangle which showed he often played with them. He wore very clean, light cavalry armour which looked as though it had never been in combat – it had barely a mark on it. He stared at Havovatch with a disgusted look on his face and puffed heavily on a thick cigar.

In instinct, Havovatch saluted him. "Sir!"

The colonel looked Havovatch up and down and took the cigar out of his mouth, blowing smoke into his face.

"What do you mean … *Sir*?" he sneered. "Why do you salute me, peasant?"

Havovatch wished he had just said sorry and carried on; he was now feeling rather foolish. "I was promoted to captain just now by King Colomune, Sir," he replied, though in his state he could not quite believe it himself.

The colonel paused for a second, then tilted his head back and cackled with laughter. "My arse have you boy, you're a mere peasant! And you can't be much older than fifteen?"

By now, a crowd was starting to grow, and they were watching with obvious enjoyment.

"Eighteen, Sir," Havovatch corrected, again by instinct – he could not help himself.

The smile vanished from the colonel's face.

"Are you trying to insult me, boy? Trying to look good in front of all your friends because you think that you can talk up to an officer of the King?" He looked around mockingly, waiting for Havovatch's friends to come out.

"No, Sir, I am an officer." Again Havovatch kicked himself, and wished he could just shut up; he was getting in worse trouble the more he spoke.

The colonel's face went red. "You disgust me, boy – you live in my city, you feed from my food, the blood of my men keeps you alive and you can't even be honest! You deserve to be flogged!"

The colonel reached back without taking his eyes off Havovatch. A servant behind him quickly passed forward a whip; the colonel unrolled it and threw his arm back further, ready to beat Havovatch. Havovatch, standing still, closed his eyes and turned his head, but nothing came. Just before the colonel went to whip him a huge armoured arm came down from a godlike figure and grabbed the colonel's before he could throw it forward.

A palace guard stood towering above the colonel, and said in a deep voice from the mouthpiece of his helmet, "This man *is* the captain of the Three-Thirty-Third, I believe at your request, Colonel Sarka? So I think it would do you some good to check your orders next time before you behave in this manner. Do we have an understanding?"

There was pure rage in the colonel's eyes. He knew he could not talk back to a palace guard; the only one who told them what to do was the King, and the colonel had no authority over them. Calming himself with obvious effort, the colonel took a few moments before smiling up at the guard, the rage disappearing from his eyes.

He turned back to Havovatch. "Oh, I see – I understand now." His attitude was the complete opposite now the guard had appeared.

Havovatch was once again confused about the situation. Who was this man? Had they met before? Why would this colonel have recommended promoting him, and if so, why the hostile greeting? So many questions ran through his head as he tried to make sense of it all.

The guard's grip slackened and the colonel went to walk away. As he passed Havovatch, he stopped and whispered into his ear.

"This isn't the last you've heard of me, boy! Always remember the name … Sarka, Colonel Sarka! We *will* meet again." An object was thrust into Havovatch's palm. With that, he strode off, pushing people from the crowd out of his way whilst his servants frantically followed, trying to keep up.

Havovatch looked down at the object: a small knife, but not as glamorous as the one he had received from the King. The blade was blunt and heavy, the small handle black with no decoration except an 'S' carved into the handle.

The palace guard approached. "I noticed the King gave you one too?"

Havovatch pulled it out and compared them, whilst a red patch formed on the rag around his waist.

"Know what they are?" said the guard, seeing his confusion.

Havovatch shook his head.

"They are tokens; only the rich have them, as they're made by a specialist in the upper borough. The King gave you one of his as a sign of respect, and this means he has the utmost trust in you."

"And this one?" Havovatch said, holding up the colonel's.

The guard let out a sigh. "That one is a Vendetta, given to people to show that they have no feeling for them, that they are nothing more than an enemy."

"Great," Havovatch said sardonically.

"The rich offer them out as they need to. They have two sets each. The Vendettas are always black, plain and heavy with a blunt blade. The Respect knives are light, rich in colour and fiercely sharp. They have the colours of the person's house, with only the King having pure golden handles."

"What do I do with them?"

"Well, they're not much use in combat, so most put them into glass boxes or cabinets to show off to their friends who they're respected by. The black ones they hide."

"What if someone loses the respect of the person who gave it to them?"

"Then that person has to blunt it down like that one," he said, pointing at the black knife, "and if you gain their respect again then the Respecter will have it sharpened at their expense. One way or another, you have them for life."

"But why knives?" he quizzed.

"Because if you get a Respect knife, it is like saying I care about you and want you to have this to protect you. But if they despise you, they give you something that you cannot defend yourself with, basically saying they don't care if you die."

"Charming," said Havovatch, still a little perplexed at the items and wondering what he would do with them.

"The tradition goes back centuries; when tribes would meet to arrange trade agreements or a pact with each other, they would give each other a sharp knife to show respect. And if ever they lost that respect the tribe would demand the knife back, blunt it down in front of them and return it. Basically saying we don't trust you. However, it's far easier now to have two sets."

Havovatch stared at the knives for some time, and when he looked up again the guard had gone.

Taking a deep breath, holding a knife in each hand, he walked down the street. Keen to get correctly dressed, he once again (and now at a slight run) made his way to his barracks, hoping he wouldn't come into contact with any more mocking officers or spiteful colonels.

As he scuttled down the streets, he came to a junction where a crowd had gathered. Passing by were the woman in white he had seen when he had returned to the city. He had no idea how long ago that had happened now.

Everyone, no matter who they were, had bowed to her presence. Havovatch looked around and quickly realized that he was the only one standing, and dropped quickly into a bow with everyone else.

As the women passed by, one of them in the centre of the group, with golden hair falling behind her back, dressed in pure white and barefooted, paused. She stepped out of the circle of women and turned to meet him. He was sure he recognized her. "Ah, Captain," she greeted pleasantly. "Congratulations on your new promotion."

Havovatch looked up confused. "My Lady, how do you know I have been promoted? It happened just now."

The woman in white smiled. "News travels fast in this city," she said.

She reached her delicate tiny hand out and Havovatch leant forward to kiss it.

"My name is Princess Undrea," she continued. "I hope to meet you again soon, Captain." She spoke with a voice of sweetness and innocence, but Havovatch noticed a look in her eye as if she knew him, or knew of him, but he definitely did not know her; he had known very few girls in his life.

She turned to one of her guards and nodded. He stepped forward and removed his cloak, wrapping it around Havovatch's shoulders. Slightly surprised, he was nevertheless grateful for her generosity; too nervous to speak, he let out a wry grin.

With a radiant smile, she left, followed by her escorts.

Havovatch stood there, not really sure about what to do. Everyone around him got back to business as if he were not there, so, now clothed, he walked his way back to the barracks.

Chapter Four
The Mission

A week had passed since Havovatch's promotion, and he had been doing as he had been told by King Colomune, embracing his new leadership role. As instructed, his barracks swelled with new recruits who had not yet passed out from training; some had not even started yet, but had put their names down ready to join. He had to send three thousand of the more experienced soldiers to a support barracks outside the city, so that they were within easy reach at short notice but not taking up too much room in the city.

Other regiments also had an allocation of soldiers, but most were sent into the light or heavy infantry, as the cavalry did not have enough horses and the fleet could only hold so many on their ships.

Still, despite the measures that Havovatch took, the Three-Thirty-Third's barracks inside were cramped. The barracks consisted of four long, narrow buildings, each supposed to house a thousand soldiers, but they held far more than this. Each barracks had five hundred bunk beds, but some of the troops had to sleep on the floor or wherever they could find a space.

Surrounding the barracks was an eight-foot high wall, and there was one entrance. At the front of the barracks was a small yard – apart from small drills that took place in the yard, all the training was done at special training camps a few times a year.

The one luxury they had was that, when they were posted within the city, they had a lot of time to themselves. Despite this, most had to use their free time to keep fit; they had to drill once a day, practise battle manoeuvres three times a week, and conduct fitness tests once a month, to make sure they made, and kept, the grade of heavy infantrymen.

But the new recruits were not even close to being trained to heavy infantry standards, so Havovatch increased the amount of exercise done in the hope that the recruits could learn as much as possible before battle, much to the delight of the experienced soldiers who wanted to use their time in the city in their own way, mainly with women and wine.

Outside the city on the open plains surrounding Cam, Havovatch got his regiment lined up, with the new recruits mixed with experienced soldiers as they practised phalanx manoeuvres and small battle drills. Due to the demand for armour and weapons, the best Havovatch could find to equip the recruits were wooden shields made from the lids of barrels, and sticks to use as swords or spears, which would not even equate to the weight of real ones but would have to do. They had no helmets, no armour; they would only know the formations and how to fight off an enemy with a lump of wood.

A few positives did come from this training, though. Havovatch learnt how to command big formations, the single- or double-syllable commands to shout so that they could follow his instructions (mostly the sergeants or lieutenants would carry his voice down the line), and the populace from the west side of Cam would come and watch them from the walls, which built up their confidence.

But his main issue, by far, was getting his recruits equipment. As Camia was a military state, there was a high demand for regular armour and weaponry, and with the blacksmiths within Cam and across the country working flat out, there was still a long time to wait for any of the soldiers to get what they needed.

Traditionally, a Camion soldier would earn his armour and weapons in his six months of training. To start, they would do two months of basic training, and when their strengths were identified, the trainers would place each of them into different regiments: cavalry, infantry, physicians, fleet, engineering, archers and artillery, with different strengths of troops within each regiment, Havovatch had been put into the heavy infantry, and was happy he could follow in his father's footsteps.

During training, he had built up his equipment as he progressed through the six months; each time he completed certain stages he was given his own spear, body armour, sword and shield with the bronze helmet awarded to him at the end, and it had been the proudest moment of his life.

But now he was a captain, his helmet (which was recovered from Coter Farol) had been adapted with olive branches carved into the cheek guards and a blue vertical horsehair crest adorning its top. He could have invested in getting more of his uniform adorned in the same way, but he would have had to pay for it, and, despite him being a captain, money was tight.

However, Havovatch was finding that it was one thing to look like a captain but quite another to act like one. Being an officer was far more difficult than he had predicted. It was apparent to all that he had no experience. He found that some of the lesser ranks purposely mocked him and asked questions they knew he could not answer, in protest at his promotion. Whilst they had spent years training and rising from rank to rank gaining valued experience, aspiring to become a captain or more, Havovatch had overtaken them all in less than a year of training. They felt that he had broken the rules and had been rewarded for it.

He did not react to this jealousy, but rather, by using common sense and reading as much as he could, he caught up to his new tasks as quickly as possible. He was smart and did not allow himself to get worn down, but despite this, he found himself agreeing with them to a certain extent.

Despite the objections in the ranks, most of the new recruits seemed to like him, and eventually the others came around as well when they saw that he was willing to get his hands as dirty as the rest of them, and that he showed compassion as well as leadership.

The thing he detested the most was the workload. What with senior officers wanting statistics and new training targets being constantly reviewed, he was often bogged down. He gave most of the work to corporals, sergeants and lieutenants below him to help unburden himself of the pressure, but as soon as one problem was dealt with, two more came along. Havovatch had always had a quick mind for problems, always managing to find a solution. However, it still didn't mean he liked doing it very much.

Whatever little of his own time he had to himself, he spent studying so that he could understand maps and tactics at a glance. The one exception to this was spending some time with his childhood friend Mercury … they had reunited after training, and were posted into the same regiment, although Mercury did not march to Coter Farol as he had an injury and stayed within the city. Now that he had been promoted and the chain of command had changed, he was determined not to let it get in the way of their friendship.

However, some of the men noticed and it was clear they thought that Mercury got preferential treatment, so he tried to keep their friendship subtle. They often walked to another borough of the city to find a bar they could sit in where no one knew them. One time they saw a group of officers from the Three-Thirty-Third nearby and had to hide. To most people they looked as though they were up to no good, constantly ducking behind barrels, jumping over walls or at one point scurrying up onto a rooftop. The city watch were alerted on a number of occasions, when citizens informed them of their strange behaviour. They would then spend time having to hide from them as well, and would have to get back to the barracks without anyone seeing them. It would look a bit strange for a captain and mere soldier to be hanging around together, and sneaking around within their own city, but Mercury would always find the funny side, always managing to bring a smile to Havovatch's face.

Another three weeks passed, and Havovatch was sitting in his room, reading a letter from his father. It was a reply to his last one informing him that he was now a captain. Havovatch smiled as he imagined his father writing, "How the hell did you do that?" but also repeating how proud he was throughout. Havovatch had asked King Colomune during a quick meeting to stamp it, otherwise his father would not have believed him.

He put the letter down and sighed as he looked at the mound of scrolls on his desk that he had to read through. He wondered how his captain before him had managed to get anything done.

Picking some up, he looked at a new anti-siege weapon that was being implemented on the city walls. As far as he could tell, it was a log of wood that was hinged to the parapet, and when siege towers approached, they were thrown over the extended pieces of wood to stop the siege towers from getting close enough to drop their bridges. It looked complicated and needed some perfecting, and it meant the entire span of the city walls was covered in hinged logs, but he could see its potential. He just could not understand why the weapon had been invented in the first place – they were not at war with any countries that had siege towers, and few countries were as developed as Camia. There was no reason for anyone to invent this weapon in the first place. But with the new threat of the Black, all designs that had been previously rejected were being re-examined in case they could be of any use.

Despite all the commotion of the previous few weeks, with the fear of impending attack, it seemed that the Black situation was dying down. There were fewer reports of attacks on villages, and a Camion task force had hunted down the creatures near Coter Farol and annihilated them, leaving their corpses hanging on the cliff's edge as a warning to any others who thought they could attack Camia. But their race still remained a mystery.

He sat back in his chair and rubbed his face with both hands. Mercury would be joining him in a few hours, so that they could go out for the evening. They had a few things they needed to discuss, woman problems mainly … the problem being that no woman seemed to fancy Mercury.

Havovatch jested that it was his long, red hair and that he needed to get it cut short like his. But, unlike Mercury, Havovatch was not often one for jokes; he kept to himself, but having a friend like him (who was a comedy all by himself) made Havovatch feel as though he could have a sense of humour sometimes. Mercury was a well-built young man: with a square frame, he was a bit larger than Havovatch, and now, with his raw strength after training, he never let Havovatch forget it, sneaking up on him and bear-hugging him continually.

He awoke from his trance when there was a knock at the door. Sergeant Metiya opened it and a palace guard entered rather boisterously, not caring how he acted or if he had interrupted him.

"Captain Havovatch, you are summoned by the King!" he ordered.

Havovatch sighed. So much for his relaxing evening. Scribbling a note to Mercury about his delay, he stood up and followed the knight up to the Acropolis.

The journey went quicker then last time he came up; he had so much on his mind, he couldn't actually remember having walked there.

The knight took him through the gates as usual, but they did not enter the actual Acropolis; instead they walked around the side and down a slight slope. At the end there was no building or entrance and he wondered where he was being taken, for it looked like a dead end. In the corner were a few barrels and racks of spears, but otherwise there was nothing there.

Then, he saw that embedded into the side of the foundation of the Acropolis was a wooden, studded door. He wondered where it had appeared from – he was sure he had not seen it before. The knight opened it and stood waiting for Havovatch to enter. Behind the door was a small, torch-lit spiral staircase leading down. Havovatch entered as the guard waited outside; as he went down he came across another door facing into the Acropolis wall – *it must be leading to the Great Hall,* he thought. He walked for some time and soon came into a chamber; he thought that this was in the base of the hill and he was sure it was deeper than the Heat Pit.

Inside, King Colomune was awaiting him, with Atken standing presentably to one side. Atken had one arm behind him; the other was in front of his stomach, with a towel draped over his forearm.

Upon seeing Havovatch, he pulled a chair back for him to sit down; his serious, yet slightly bored expression remained unchanged.

Havovatch gave a nod of thanks, but Atken did not so much as grin to say he acknowledged it.

Spread before Havovatch was a large table, covered with a huge map of Ezazeruth that spanned the entire length and width of it. Placed around it were different coloured, different shaped statues, finely crafted from wood, representing the last reported whereabouts of regiments, kings or possible sightings of the Black.

Havovatch sat with his helmet on his lap, his shoulders square, looking ahead until he was spoken to. King Colomune carried on reading a parchment, but there was something about him that made Havovatch think he was just doing it for show. His eyes were not moving; he just sat there with his eyebrows raised, looking down at the parchment and murmuring under his breath as he appeared to read the words.

Havovatch tried not to read too much into it; he just carried on looking ahead, trying to look presentable; he was in the presence of the King, and it was daunting.

After waiting what felt like an hour, Havovatch started to peer about his surroundings as he got bored, his shoulders dropping as he could not hold his posture any longer.

The room was dark with a low ceiling, illuminated by a few lanterns on the wall and some candles on the table. He saw a set of double doors that were barred from the inside, a long plank of wood sitting across in front of them locking them in place. He almost jumped when he saw a very large set of armour sitting in an alcove, thinking for a moment that there was another person in the room with them. He stared for some time at the armour. *A huge man must have owned that once,* Havovatch thought in awe.

As he continued to look around the room he started to think he was in the King's private meeting place. It seemed so out of the way and secluded. It started to make Havovatch feel uneasy.

After a few more minutes of silence, Atken eventually let out a long sigh. "Are you going to keep pretending to read that parchment all day, or will you stop wasting the young captain's time and tell him why he is here?"

Havovatch was taken aback by how the butler spoke to the King. This was not the way anyone speaks to a king, especially not from a butler! Havovatch quickly turned his gaze towards the King, expecting the worst. Incredibly, King Colomune didn't move, not even a flicker of an eyelid. Instead he waved a hand and said, "tea, please, Atken; there is no other need for you to be here."

"Of course, after all I'm just a butler," Atken said sarcastically before exiting through the door Havovatch had arrived through.

King Colomune took in a breath, looked up at Havovatch and grinned. "Forgive Atken, his family has been serving my bloodline for many generations. But he's ... very unusual. You get used to him after a while, and he does make a splendid cup of tea."

Havovatch did not really know what to say, his mouth hanging open at the scene he had just witnessed. Being in front of the King, however, made him feel so intimidated that anything he said he thought would make him look stupid. He quickly shut his mouth.

"So, Captain, how are things?" he continued after he realized Havovatch wasn't going to respond.

"Very well, thank you, my liege." Havovatch thought it best to keep it short.

"Good! Very good. I am guessing that you are still curious as to what attacked your regiment over at Coter Farol?"

"Yes, my liege."

"Well, as you know, after the message we received the other week, the country and the world had war declared on them. So, obviously, we decided we must be ready!" He stood up, walked across the room and picked up some very old scrolls, and as he returned, he dumped them down in front of Havovatch.

Havovatch, rather confused, picked one up and tried to read it. The language was Camion but many of the words were slightly different from those he knew.

"My aides have been working tirelessly over the past few weeks to find out who this 'Black' are," said the King. "From what we have found in ancient texts, it is likely that the attack you encountered was the first of a dark tide heading our way. Even the way you were attacked by a small sortie appears to be the same way it was done thousands of years ago: small scouting parties approach the land to cause chaos and anarchy, then eventually a bigger horde will arrive. With this information in mind, I have decided upon your first mission." Havovatch swallowed. "I have been informed by my aides that there are three armies spread across Ezazeruth who are to be summoned if the world ever comes under attack," Colomune continued. "We know little about them, only that they are called the Knights of Ezazeruth, and each is skilled in different tactics. Your job is to deliver a message to those armies and summon them to my command."

Havovatch felt confused. "Sire, will this require my regiment? We are not exactly an exploring or scouting unit. Surely they would be better suited?"

"No, I need a commander I trust. Also know, this won't require your regiment, rather you will choose four men from your regiment and yours only. You will leave tomorrow at first light, but Havovatch, choose carefully, for the outcome of your mission may entirely depend on the men you choose."

Still feeling somewhat confused at this new development, Havovatch knew better than to question the King. Instead he waved an open hand across the large map of the world.

"Where are these … knights?" Havovatch asked.

King Colomune sat back, casually. "We are not entirely sure. As I have said, little is known about them; they vanished from history thousands of years ago. But we have information to suggest that one of them may be in a forest west of us, just before the Forbidden Passage. Go there first, and if you find them they should direct you to where the other knights are. Remember, Havovatch, the fate of the world rests upon you succeeding in this mission!"

Havovatch inwardly groaned, whilst keeping his eyes fixed on a scroll. Then he remembered his company and looked up at his king. "Yes, Sire," he said, straightening.

King Colomune bent down and produced a small, thin, leather pouch from under the desk.

"In this pouch are your orders for the commanders, leaving passes for the city, and maps. Go to the armoury once you have chosen your men tonight, and get whatever equipment you need; I strongly recommend light scouting uniform. You will be expected back here four months from today. Now leave me." He finished his speech with a wave of his hand.

Havovatch stood up straight and saluted. "Yes, Sire!"

Then he turned on his heel and walked out, leaving King Colomune on his own … or so he thought. As soon as he shut the door, a hidden passage opened in the wall and Colonel Sarka strutted into the chambers.

"You did well," he spat. He was biting chunks from an apple, sloppily and loudly.

He put his skinny, grey arm on King Colomune's shoulder and patted it with a heavy hand, then pulled up a chair and sat with his feet up on the table, still scoffing the apple.

"He's a new captain, he's only been in the army a few months, and I really don't think he is the best person for this job," Colomune protested to the colonel.

"Ha," Sarka spluttered with his mouth full. "It will be a good learning curve for him, trust me. He is the best person, or otherwise I wouldn't have suggested him." He paused to bite more of the apple, and spoke with his mouth full. "Besides, we need the experienced officers here in case of attack."

The colonel tossed the half-eaten apple across the room, leaving it to roll under a set of drawers, and rubbed his hands on his tunic. King Colomune frowned at the lack of manners, but otherwise said nothing.

Sarka walked around the table and leant on the end, looking at the miniature figures on the map. "Now on to other business; I think you should make an alliance with Loria and Leno Dania."

"But we are at war with them."

"We have not fought either of them in over five seasons or so, and besides we need every man we can get. The Black are coming and there is nothing we can do to stop that. I would have thought that someone like yourself, a grand king, a brave king, a … *mighty* king would want to make your mark in history because of this. So, be the bigger person and ask them for a peace treaty. Don't forget, they are allied with our allies, and so will be likely to want to help the world rather than oppose it."

King Colomune looked down at the map in thought and then nodded. "Make it so," he said reluctantly.

Sarka continued. "Also, we have found possible coordinates for the Black's homeland. When the last of the banners arrive, seize the opportunity to sail and take the fight to them! It will be the last thing they will be expecting, and children will be chanting your name for the rest of eternity."

This gave King Colomune goosebumps and his posture changed; he sat back stroking his big, dark beard in reflection of Sarka's idea as a cheerful smile grew on his face. "Hmm … your plan has merit, but will leave Ezazeruth defenceless. I should run this past the other kings before we go any further; it is their armies I would be taking after all."

Sarka stood up quickly in frustration. "The banners!" he spat. There was a pause as he tried to compose himself. When he did, his voice was slow and deliberate. "The banners answer to you, my King; you don't need to seek permission from anyone. You do as you please with their armies, but the longer you linger, the more time it will give the Black to mobilize their forces! You must act now!" He banged his fists on the table, making the statues vibrate in their places.

King Colomune thought for a little longer, whilst Sarka stared at him intently.

After a pause, Sarka spoke again. "If it pleases you, my King, I have another suggestion. Leave your own military here. Then, when you come back and have your army still intact, you can finally finish what you started and conquer your enemies, as they will have no force to oppose you!" He finished with a vicious grin.

Just then Colomune jumped as Atken entered the chambers with a small cup of tea. He was glad for the interruption, and upon seeing Atken, Sarka straightened himself up.

"Your tea, Sire, as you requested." He then turned to the colonel: "Would you like anything, Colonel Sarka? Tea? Wine? Poison? It would be my delight with whatever choice you want," he said with a straight face, his eyebrows raised.

Sarka just gave a hard stare and a grunt.

"Now, if you don't mind, the King has a lot to do and needs his rest," Atken said with a gesture of his arm towards the doors. He took the long beam off the double doors and held one open for Sarka to leave; before he did, though, Sarka turned and faced his king.

"Don't worry, my King, this will be your mark in history; this will be your moment!"

Then he left, as Atken pushed the door shut as hard as he could, to create as much noise as possible behind the colonel.

Colomune thought of Sarka's words. His plans had merit. Even if he did fail with the mighty force of the banners, he would still have all of his men left to defend his country. It seemed like a sound plan.

He sat there looking down at the statues; almost sulking. Apart from the Camion statues, he gathered them all up and placed them at the defences on the map. They made a good heavy defence and the Black would have difficulty getting through them, but the south would be left vulnerable. Most of Ezazeruth's armies would be with him soon; after all, his father's legacy was in building alliances, and he was going to use their armies now for his own purpose.

Atken resumed his position adjacent to the King and appeared to be sleeping. The silence left Colomune in deep thought.

He rubbed his eyes. He could send for Commander Thiamos, the highest person in command of the military second to Colomune himself. But he rarely spoke to him. Sarka always said he shouldn't, that he was going to give him bad advice and make him look stupid. In fact, Sarka said that about every officer. King Colomune thought this because Sarka was always bitter that the committee had never promoted him past colonel. He wondered if he could just promote him to general or commander, but the committee usually dealt with promotions and Sarka had never asked him to mediate.

But it made Colomune feel inadequate: whenever he thought something through and he went to make a decision or he went to speak, Sarka's face would then appear and he would withdraw his decision. Endless possibilities of being wrong would surface in his mind with the negativity that Sarka had given him.

Colomune shook his head and returned to the thought of Sarka's plan. Maybe he was right, maybe this was the best solution, to take the fight to them before they struck … He stood up and walked over to his father's armour. It hung up proudly in its alcove, the armoured arm resting on its grand sword. His father had been much bigger than he was, and he wondered if he had been a giant; the shoulder pads on the armour were hugely broad and the torso section looked as though a bear could wear it. His father had been a marvel to see to his men, and gained much respect. Despite the armour having been cleaned, Colomune fancied he could still smell the scent of his father's blood wafting from the breastplate. He had made his mark in history, and Colomune just hoped his time would come as well.

"Yes! Sarka is right: let's take the fight to the Black!" he found himself saying aloud, gripping his fists.

Atken awoke from his dream to look at his king, his vacant expression unchanged.

"Did you say something, my King?" he asked although more rhetorically than sincerely.

"When the banners arrive, prepare them to go to the defences with haste. Tell the Camion fleet, and any banners' ships, to meet there as well once all the regiments have arrived," he growled.

"Of course, as such messenger duties are also part of my job description," Atken said sarcastically and left.

Colomune felt jittery, filled with so much confidence that he was making the right decision. There was no alternative.

Returning to the table, he pulled all his military statues back to Cam, leaving all the banners at the defences and a small scouting statue for Havovatch's unit just outside the city walls.

Chapter Five
Recruiting

Havovatch walked back to the yard, feeling apprehensive. He was reflecting deeply on his conversation with King Colomune, and the more he thought the more worried he became. *Am I up to this mission*? he repeatedly asked himself. The fate of the entire world was resting upon him, and it made him feel overwhelmed.

He was taken out of his trance as he approached the yard and heard a commotion coming from inside. Echoing from there was a familiar chant he usually heard from the Camion stadium where they played Rowlg, a violent and deadly sport where armoured men with blunt weapons had to get to opposing sides of a hilly, sandy pitch with a ghoul's head, by any means possible.

He quickened his pace at the sound, and as he passed the gate he saw there were no guards manning it. Instead there was a large gathering in the centre of the yard, and the guards either were trying to get through, or, to his dismay, were joining in.

Havovatch stood there, dumbfounded at the chaos and lack of discipline that was going on within *his* regiment. He knew things were hard because the ranks had swollen, but this was absurd.

"Regiment!" he shouted, but no one heard him – everyone was shouting too loudly at whatever was happening in the centre of the crowd.

"Regiment!" he shouted again, but still no one listened.

He grew angry, his arms and head started to shake with fury, and, filling his lungs, he bellowed with a rage he rarely released, "THREE-THIRTY-THIRD!"

His voice echoed over the chant. There was instant silence. The group of soldiers parted out of the way, revealing a bloodstained boy still punching the stomach of an enormous soldier, who stood to attention and did not seem to feel the punches. Havovatch couldn't believe how big the man was, more solid and taller than any man he had ever seen. He was at least nine feet tall, his arms were like tree trunks and his muscles seemed to bulge with every movement. Havovatch had not noticed him in the last few weeks and wondered how that could have been possible.

The boy punching the soldier was one of the new recruits, and despite everyone around standing to attention he continued to unsuccessfully hit the giant in the torso, trying desperately to cause him some form of pain.

Havovatch nodded at two guards, who rushed forward and seized him. The boy looked angrily up, but the guards shoved him onto his knees, holding his hands firmly behind his neck. He could have been no older than fifteen.

With him restrained, Havovatch turned and addressed the rest of the regiment.

"You are lucky enough to be serving in the best infantry unit in the Camion army, and I come back after only an hour away to find that you have all disregarded your own duties!"

No one said a thing; they just stood there in full anticipation of what was to come. Havovatch turned to see Lieutenant Jadge just entering the yard. He marched in with one hand on his sword hilt, the other marching in time with his gait, and stopped to look around, astonished by what he saw.

"And where have you been during this mayhem, Lieutenant?" Havovatch demanded angrily; usually he felt uncomfortable shouting at soldiers older than him, but his fury gave him the confidence. Lieutenant Jadge swallowed, knowing that he had been in charge during Havovatch's absence and had left on a quick errand. He said nothing and instead waited for what was to come.

"Have this lot drilled until they need new boots and report these two to me," Havovatch said, waving his hand at the boy and the giant.

Lieutenant Jadge sighed, walked towards the main body of men and started barking orders. The couple of hundred soldiers ran into columns and sulkily began arduous amounts of press-ups and stress positions, whilst others who had hidden in the barracks watched on mockingly. Havovatch wanted them to suffer, mostly out of vindictiveness because of the sudden burden that was now upon him.

As he walked up to his chambers that overlooked the yard, he passed Sergeant Metiya, who was standing outside his door overseeing what had gone on.

"Do you know those two who were fighting, Metiya?"

Metiya was an old veteran, a seasoned soldier who could not cope with the normal everyday duties of heavy infantry any more, but could still stand on ceremony outside his captain's chambers, and did so with the utmost integrity. He had been in the infantry all his life and Havovatch was pretty sure he was going to die in it.

"The boy, no," Metiya said, "but the large chap, yes. His name is Buskull. He's just returned from assisting the Knight Hawks with a mission."

"Knight Hawks?"

"Special forces, Captain."

"Oh."

Metiya leant on his spear comfortably. "He's been in the Camion infantry about eighteen years now ... *very strong*! Never seen anything like it! He does not usually wear armour because of his size, he just wears what he wants and fights with an old relic of his."

"Relic?"

"Yes, Captain, a double-headed battle-axe, fearsome thing, I've been told that it is centuries old and never needs sharpening."

Havovatch raised his eyebrows. He had a good sword but even that needed a lot of whetting. The sergeant continued. "Not a lot is known about Buskull; he keeps to himself and rarely talks to anyone. He is a fierce warrior though, disciplined, adept, and his war cry is something you will never forget. But the curious thing is that he does not like fire."

"Really?" Havovatch asked. He was surprised that someone like Buskull could be scared of something as simple as fire.

"Oh yes, but that's all I know in regard to that. Oh, I also heard that he comes from a sort of lost civilization, a race of people who are naturally strong and gifted in other ways, too."

"What other ways?"

"Not sure, Captain. Buskull is a mysterious chap, but perfect for the heavy infantry. Oh, and don't call him Giant! He don't like it."

"Why?"

"No idea, but the last lad who said it to him ended up being thrown on top of a rooftop; he woke up a week later with a thumping headache and no memory of what happened."

Havovatch chewed on his lip whilst listening to the sergeant. "Thank you, Metiya, it was interesting to hear this. Make sure they both come and see me as soon as they have finished."

"Very good!"

Havovatch patted him on the shoulder and entered his chambers. It was dark inside, the room spotless and narrow. Along one side of the wall was a long window, with a wooden shutter and his bed just below it. A chair sat in the corner facing out of the window, where he usually read, and fell asleep with a book on his chest.

His desk was to his left as he entered, facing the doorway so that he could see who came in directly. He had rows of shelves, with his chosen God – Grash, God of Conflict – in the centre. Offerings of money, food and even a few drops of his blood had been placed before the small statue of a tall, armour-clad knight, holding a very long spear and a huge shield. Every soldier had some God they supported, with little shelves next to every bunk. With Havovatch being a solider, he went for Grash as did most of his comrades. It was a no-brainer: in war you hoped to fight well and die honourably, and supporting Grash would help them in their journey.

The rest of the shelves were crammed with second-hand books he was keen to read, since he had received his first payment. He spent most of his earnings on books to learn from, for even though he was a captain, his pay did not allow him to buy much.

Once inside, he slammed the leather pouch on the desk and sat down for a moment in silence, closing his eyes whilst he took in the day's events.

Sitting on the desk was a small, glass-fronted box with green felt inside, holding the King's Respect token, with space for five more.

On the top shelf was a damaged wooden box he had found in the yard, filled with Vendetta knives from people who protested against his promotion. Every one of the knives came from someone he did not know. He did as the palace guard had instructed: he hid them.

After a while, when he felt he could cope with looking at his orders, he reached over and took hold of the pouch. It was thin and small, and had two holes in the back for him to slide his belt through. *It should fit quite comfortably,* he thought. Carved around it were olive branches.

He opened the flap and took out the neatly folded parchments inside. The pouch contained a fairly detailed map. He had never really seen a map before, and this gave him his first look at the world. It was marked with all the rivers, forests, towns and cities in Camia. But as Havovatch looked at the different countries across the world, he noticed most of them lacked somewhat in detail.

It listed mountain terrains, deserts, danger areas marked with skulls, large rivers and the capital of each country, but no information about any towns or points of interest. He was surprised to see that to the north-east of Camia, before Loria, was a barren wasteland with skulls placed all over it.

He picked up his orders, which simply read:

Find the Knights of Ezazeruth and give them the parchments marked with an X. Do all within your power, give your lives to the cause, do not fail!
Signed King Colomune of Camia

Havovatch looked over the parchments marked 'X': there were just three small pieces of paper, and on each one was written:

You are to fulfil your oath

This is strange, Havovatch thought. Why had he never heard of the Knights of Ezazeruth? He rubbed his face tiredly – he could have done without that fight; it was just adding to an already stressful day. He felt hot too, so got up and pushed the wooden shutter wide open, allowing a nice cool breeze to fill the room. As it pricked against his skin, he suddenly felt calm, and he took in a deep breath. Looking out of his window there was not much to see, just the rooftops of a few houses and the back of the mighty wall surrounding Cam. He liked waking up to the window being open, though, seeing clear blue skies with Camia's often perfect weather.

Sitting down again, he looked at the map for the forest to the north-west before the Forbidden Passage. It was marked the Impenetrable Forest, and again marked with skulls. He frowned in thought. How could a *forest* be impenetrable?

He was still studying the map carefully when there was a sudden knock at the door. "Come," he said tiredly, and laid down the map.

In walked Sergeant Metiya followed by a guard, Buskull, the boy and another guard.

Buskull stood up in front with his chest out and chin up, staring over Havovatch's head. Now Havovatch saw him clearly, he could make out more of his features; he had a finely trimmed, blonde beard and a bald head, with a scar running down the left side of his face.

The boy was short and had thick dark hair; his eyebrows were large and seemed constantly raised, as if he were unimpressed by everything. His appearance was sloppy at best, and he slouched rather than stood to attention.

The guards waited behind them, holding their spears upright.

"Stand to attention, soldier!" Havovatch addressed the boy sternly.

"Why? You're the same age as me, why should I take orders from you?" the boy said, sneering.

Metiya moved forward to take hold of him, but Havovatch put out the palm of his hand to stop him. "No! He will be dealt with later."

He stared at the boy wondering why he was so angry, and how best to deal with him, "I like a disciplined barracks. Your behaviour reflects me and I will not tolerate rudeness in any way. Now, regarding today's earlier disturbance, what do you have to say for yourselves?"

Buskull spoke first; his voice was harsh and deep, like a blunt blade carving through wet wood. "My apologies, Captain – we accidentally tripped over each other's bootlaces in the yard and were brushing the dust off each other."

Havovatch noticed the two guards smirk. It was clear that Buskull was wise to the responses he should give. The boy, however, had obviously not been in the regiment long enough and hadn't caught on to what Buskull was trying to do.

"Sir, he pushed me when passing in the yard, I demanded an apology and he refused," he said in a weak and unschooled tone.

Buskull said nothing, just staring into space. Havovatch could tell that the boy was not being entirely honest either.

"What is your name, boy?"

"Boy?! I'm the same age as you!"

"Name!" Havovatch shouted slapping the palm of his hand on the desk.

He subsided. "Hilclop."

"How old are you?"

"Fifteen."

"We are not quite the same age, then, are we?"

"That's not what the others say!" said Hilclop, trying to carry on the argument.

Havovatch gave him a long and disdainful stare. "How long have you been in training, Hilclop?"

"Two weeks."

That explained it then. Havovatch was annoyed that he had spent six months of agony, stress, sleep deprivation and hardship, which turned him into a different person – a warrior – whereas Hilclop had only spent a few weeks. But now that they were at war, anyone who had signed up was instantly thrown into any regiment. In Hilclop's case, this meant that discipline and respect for rank had not sunk in yet.

"I feel you have a lot of growing up to do, Hilclop. May I suggest you take a long look around and follow by what you see, and the next time I give you an order you had better damn well obey it, or it will be the flogging pad. Do you understand me?"

Hilclop bowed his head like a sulking child, and said quietly, "Yes, Sir."

Havovatch slammed his hand on the table again, making Hilclop jump. "I hold the rank of Captain, and that is how you will address me!"

Hilclop sneered silently at him with animosity, as if he wanted to tell him exactly what he thought of him but kept it in.

"Two days' pay will be deducted from you both," Havovatch finished. "Now get out of my sight!"

Buskull accepted it and went to leave, but Hilclop tutted and started talking to himself about how unfair it was, and Havovatch had finally had enough. "Sergeant, take this miserable rekon outside and teach him some manners."

"Certainly, Captain," Metiya said with some delight, and, hitting Hilclop in the backside with the butt of his spear, he started shouting at the top of his voice, "HUT-TOO-HUT-TOO-HUT-TOO."

Buskull marched out when they had left, ducking under the doorway as he did so.

Havovatch sat looking into space for a while; then the dreaded thought of who to take with him on the mission started to dawn. He knew a lot of soldiers who had just come out of training, but he did not really know any of the experienced soldiers, and they were the ones he needed.

He took out a blank piece of paper, dipped his quill into a pot of blue ink, and titled it:

"Recruiting"

It had his name on it, and a blank space below. After some thought, he knew he needed someone he could trust, so Mercury's name was written down.

He really struggled – everyone he could think of were officers, but they needed to stay here, and the inexperienced soldiers, were too … inexperienced.

There was a knock at the door.

"Come."

Sergeant Metiya popped his head in. "Just to let you know that Hilclop has been dealt with, Captain."

"Thank you, Metiya, that was quick."

Metiya gave a wide grin. "After the amount of time I have been under the Camion reign, you tend to pick a few things up about how to discipline soldiers quickly … and directly."

Havovatch smiled, but he stared at the page, still in thought.

"Everything alright?" the sergeant offered.

"No, not really; I have a mission from the King, and need to leave tomorrow at first light, but I am to choose four men from the regiment and I cannot think of anyone. Do you know who would be a good idea to take?"

Metiya stepped into his office and closed the door.

"What sort of mission is it, Captain?"

"We are travelling across Ezazeruth to find three commanders, and deliver a message to them."

"Well, for his strength, I would, of course, say Buskull. He will come in handy in tight situations. There is a new soldier to the regiment who served in the Two-Twenty-Second light cavalry unit; he is a very good swordsman, and would be good in a melee – he's fit, strong, with good endurance, and I would strongly recommend him."

"What's his name?"

"Feera."

"Why did he leave the Two-Twenty-Second?"

"Well, all I know is that he was accused of a crime, and he was given the choice of imprisonment, or joining the infantry for ten years."

"The infantry isn't a punishment, Metiya."

"Try saying that to a cavalryman."

"But should I take someone who has committed a crime?"

"If I may, Captain, I don't know the ins and outs of his crime, but I know Feera. And he is the most noble, honourable soldier I know. And he will be an asset to your mission."

"Very well."

"Can I make another suggestion, Captain?"

"Fire away."

"The young boy, Hilclop: he is naïve and stupid, he has not learnt respect for rank or discipline. But I have been in the infantry all my life, and I have seen many soldiers come and go. In Hilclop's case, he has probably spent his whole life in one place and never seen the world, a simple messenger mission to three commanders could not be all that difficult, and all the fighting is likely to be done in Camia. Why not take him with you? It would do him some good, and keep him out of trouble here, where these young boys need to be turned into soldiers without distraction."

Havovatch chewed his lip. "He could put the mission in jeopardy, though."

"Yes, that is true. It was just a thought, Captain."

Metiya, with a wink, left his captain alone to think things over.

But as Havovatch looked down at his paper, he had absent-mindedly written the last three names: Buskull, Feera and Hilclop.

He sat for a while looking at the page, but he was overcome with a tingling sensation in his head, and before he knew it, he was asleep.

He woke a short while later but he did not think he had slept long. The shadows of objects and ornaments on his desk were still roughly where they had been before he had dozed off, but something was missing.

He lifted a few things up, trying to work out what it was, but everything appeared to be there. As he sat back, he went to play with his Gracker tooth around his neck as he always did when deep in thought, but it was *that* which was missing.

"Oh, no!" he said out loud – he was sure he had it on; he never took it off.

He looked all around his room, but it was nowhere to be seen.

There was a sudden knock at the door that made Havovatch jump. Mercury entered, a smile on his face, his noticeably long red hair sleeked back. "Hey, Vatch."

"Don't call me that, please!" Havovatch replied, as if this were not the first time. "It's Captain now, get used to saying that," he said, still stressed he had lost the most important thing in the world to him.

Mercury looked slightly taken aback at Havovatch's tone, but simply responded with, "Right you are, Captain, my apologies." He threw himself down in the chair opposite Havovatch's desk, followed by a short silence.

"Look," Havovatch said, at last noticing his discomfort. "It's just as hard for me, too. But if you say it in front of the others, it causes trouble. I have to be impartial." He felt a little guilty, for speaking down like that, but the looks he got from the other soldiers were too much to bear, and he had told him more than once not to call him by that name.

Mercury shrugged. "Fair enough, V…Captain."

Havovatch gave him a short, hard look, before standing up and guiding Mercury with him. "Come, let's get a drink. I need one after today." Before he left, he took one more look around, but the tooth was nowhere to be seen.

Havovatch returned to his chambers with Mercury quite early that evening. It was still slightly light outside … the sun could not be seen, but there was a faint red glow upon the horizon.

They had been to one of the recruits' bars, and although they had not had much to drink, the outside air was warm and muggy, and it started to make them feel a little merry.

As Havovatch came into the yard, he spoke to a guard standing at the gate. "Summon Hilclop, Buskull and Feera at once!" he said; his tone was half slurred, but he tried to stay professional. He finished by adding, "And bring some water as well."

The guard saluted and marched away. They continued to his chambers, and once in, Havovatch sat at his desk and Mercury sat opposite, both with their feet up on the table. Before too long, a lackey entered the room with two jugs of water, and stalled upon seeing a private sitting so casually in the captain's chambers. He quickly slammed the jugs on the table and hastily left the room. Mercury looked at Havovatch and smiled. "A bit nervous, don't ya think?"

Havovatch just raised his eyebrows, instantly taking one of the jugs and gulping the contents down.

"Mercury, there is something I need to tell you."

"Oh?"

"I have decided to take you on a mission."

"Great, where we going?" he said eagerly.

"Well, we need to discuss that when the others get here."

"Others?"

"Yes, have you met Buskull, Feera and Hilclop yet?"

"Nope. None of them."

Remembering Metiya's words, Havovatch thought it best to warn him of Buskull's size first, as Mercury was usually one to voice his thoughts.

"Whatever you do, don't call Buskull—"

Before he could finish, there was a knock at the door. Mercury jumped up from his chair and stood to attention in front of Havovatch's desk as he smartened himself up. He instructed them to enter.

Buskull and Feera marched in and stood to attention, their shoulders back and chins up, whilst Hilclop slouched and gazed around disinterestedly. Havovatch was not surprised that he now had two black eyes, but he decided not to bother looking into it. What went unheard he could do little about.

It was the first time he had met Feera: with eight thousand soldiers under his care now, he had barely met a handful of them.

Feera was fairly tall and thin, with dark hair and a wiry beard running along his jawline. He looked strong, but more built for speed and agility. He was pleased with Metiya's choice already, and looking forward to seeing what he could do.

He noticed Mercury trying to look out the corner of his eye as he saw Buskull for the first time. His eyebrows frowned and his jaw dropped.

"Blimey, you look like a giant!"

"Mercury!" shouted Havovatch. But Buskull did not appear to move. Still giving Mercury a hard stare, Havovatch put his hands together and leant on the desk, examining the four of them.

"Gentlemen," he started. "A mission awaits us directly from the King. I have been tasked to deliver a message to three commanders spread across Ezazeruth, and I must choose four men to accompany me. You are those four." He paused for a moment, to let this sink in. "As far as I am concerned, the less you know the better, but I have chosen you all for specific reasons. You will go to the armoury on Elmwood Road at once, where you will be given scouting uniforms. We leave at sunrise tomorrow. Any questions?"

Feera stepped forward. "Captain, will we be getting into any combat? Five of us may not be enough under the current circumstances."

Havovatch looked down at the map. "Some parts may be perilous, but most of the route is relatively safe. With any luck a small unit like us would be able to slip away from any trouble unnoticed. Any other questions?"

The three of them stayed silent but Hilclop spoke up. "Sir, what is our mission? Why can't you tell us all of it? Surely we have a right to know?"

Havovatch just gazed at him and said, "Dismissed."

The men turned and left, Hilclop two seconds behind the rest of them. Havovatch sighed; he was regretting his decision to bring Hilclop along already.

As Mercury left, Havovatch heard the sound of the wind being thumped out of someone, and knew instantly that Buskull had got his retribution, although it did seem cruel.

After the others had left, he realized that it was the last chance to write to his father. He pulled out a clean peace of parchment and dipped his quill into a pot of ink.

Dear Father,

I am going on a mission tomorrow, so you won't get a reply for some time. I can't tell you how difficult it is not to tell you where I am going, but rest assured, I will be OK.

I hope Mother is well and I look forward to seeing my darling brothers soon. I already have positions ready for them within my regiment. Wow, it sounds weird to say that!

I miss you all deeply, but when I get back from this mission I am sure I will be allowed some leave, and I will come and see you.

Miss you all.

Captain Havovatch of the Three-Thirty-Third

Havovatch went down to the armoury shortly after the others. It was on the other side of the city, but the walk did him some good – it gave him time to contemplate things. He had been thrown into a serious position now, and he had a lot of responsibilities.

When he entered the armoury at last, he was immediately struck by the heat. What with the roaring fires and the blacksmiths' aides banging away at armour and weaponry, Havovatch was starkly reminded of the Heat Pit, and he had to quickly compose himself, banishing the memories of those hateful weeks from his mind.

His head cleared and he saw the head blacksmith standing on a stool, trying to get a torso size for Buskull. He wore a heavy, grey apron, and had huge, bushy mutton chops.

Havovatch looked over his men. Buskull wore a new pair of big black boots (his feet twice the size of Havovatch's), dark trousers, a grey vest and a large, brown belt with a big buckle. Both Mercury and Feera were dressed in the same light scouting uniform – a dark green tunic, dark trousers, a strong, brown, leather body vest with a quiver attached to the back, and a long, hooded brown or green cloak. Feera wore two new swords that curved slightly near the tips; they looked impressive and Havovatch found himself feeling a bit envious. One was fixed alongside his quiver, facing over his left shoulder, and the other by his thigh.

As for Hilclop, he had just gone for the standard issue heavy infantry uniform of blue tunic, sword, shield, spear, dagger, helmet and heavy armour. All of these had been borrowed, as he had not earned them yet, and none of them fitted him either.

Havovatch felt like punching a wall, or better yet Hilclop – the boy just did not seem to show any common sense at all. "Blacksmith!" he shouted. "Can you get the boy fitted with the same as Mercury and Feera, please?"

The blacksmith sighed heavily, as if Hilclop had been uncooperative before Havovatch's arrival, but he obediently went over to him. Hilclop immediately started protesting. "Sir, I don't need it, I want what I've got," he said abruptly, obviously not reading the situation.

Havovatch lost his temper. He grabbed Hilclop by the scruff of his tunic sticking out from his armour, and shoved him to one side of the room. "Seriously, boy, learn to keep your mouth shut and do as you're told, or I'll make you carry Buskull all the way there! And if you call me Sir once more, I'll beat you solid! I am a captain! And that's how you will address me!"

Hilclop cowered under the threat, trying to retreat back into the wall as much as possible. Havovatch shoved him against the wall again, harder, and walked over to the others, who were doing very badly at pretending nothing was going on.

He looked at what Feera and Mercury wore ... they looked good, but Havovatch fancied something different. He had always been a keen knife thrower as a boy; it was a skill he had picked up from his father. He asked the blacksmith if he had anything of the sort. The blacksmith smiled.

"Oh, yes," he said pleasantly. "In fact, we have something new that needs testing." He went into the back room and returned with a leather vest. "This vest has thin metal plates made of Bygodiun steel sewn in between the leather, so that the owner can manoeuvre easily but still have a strong form of protection."

"Bygodiun steel?" questioned Havovatch.

"Yes, Captain, the finest, toughest and lightest steel in all the land."

Buskull let out a grunt, as if he knew dozens far better.

Havovatch took the vest in his hands. It was much lighter than he thought, and with a little adjusting on the hips and shoulders, it was a good fit. It had a wide dagger fitted upside down to the front of his left shoulder, which he could pull downwards if the situation called for it. It had five small throwing knives arranged on the small of his back, and three on the back of each shoulder. These were good throwing knives, with double-edged blades and brown handles.

He threw a few at a test target sitting on the wall with perfect accuracy ... they had good balance and not only hit the target but stuck in it. Mercury walked over and struggled to pull one out with both hands, but Buskull leant over and with one hand yanked it clear with ease.

The blacksmith also handed Havovatch a strap that went around his boot and held a collection of more throwing knives, and twenty spare knives that he rolled up in a piece of leather and attached to his carry bag. He was also issued with a new sword but declined, saying that he would stick with his late captain's kopis; it was frowned upon to use something that you had not earned. But his captain had died before his time, and using his sword in some way helped Havovatch to feel that he was honouring him with it.

The scabbard for his sword was already attached to the body vest. It was much more comfortable to carry this than to use a belt. It meant carrying everything on the body armour, and not on loose equipment. The body armour fitted so well to his torso that he carried the weight on his shoulders rather than his hips, but he still got a belt to carry a spare dagger and his pouch with his orders in. He felt a little heavy on the left-hand side from the weight of the sword, but it was all tightly fitted. He could move around, and everything stayed where it was and did not get in the way.

Havovatch looked at his unit; for a small group they looked impressive, almost elite. It was like his dreams as a child, leading a group of warriors on a perilous quest to save the world, and it struck him that they were. "We will still take our helmets, apart from you, Buskull," he said, noting Buskull didn't have one.

They finished their outfitting. Hilclop seemed nervous and quiet throughout, though, and did not join in any of the fun Mercury and Feera were having with each other, which mainly consisted of them loosening each other's straps on their vests, or trying to empty each other's quivers without the other knowing ... typical humour for infantry soldiers.

Just before they finished, the blacksmith left the armoury and went into an adjacent grocer's. He returned with stone bread, dried meat, biscuits and boiled rice. He handed the food over to the unit, who distributed it into their ration packs. They were also given waterskins, made from the stomach of a cow, with a stop in the top to carry their water.

Finally finished and equipped, they stepped outside.

"Go back to the barracks," Havovatch advised. "Get some sleep. We will be up at first light."

As they walked away, he could hear Mercury and Feera as they laughed into the night. Buskull was walking next to them – he could clearly see his silhouette – but Hilclop trailed behind, and Havovatch again felt suddenly doubtful about taking him.

Havovatch himself did not feel tired – on the contrary, he felt very awake with all the thoughts running through his head. He decided to make his way to the Holy Gardens for a bit of peace and quiet.

The Holy Gardens were a sanctuary for the Camion God of Peace, Dimiourgós. They were calm and serene, and full of life in the way of plants and the natural elements of the world, a proper offering for the gentle God.

It was always peaceful there, and he had often visited the place during his training. It was nice to have a place where he could relax and not be shouted at all day.

He walked along the cobbled street deep in thought, so much so that several people who passed him and shouted out greetings were completely ignored.

But something ominous did take him out of his trance: two figures ahead standing at a junction. They seemed dark and sinister, and as he approached he grew apprehensive, wondering who they were. But the candle lights from the street lanterns illuminated them and, although he had not seen them before, he realized he was staring at two of the legendary Knight Hawks.

One was tall, whilst the other was quite short, but both looked strong and well armed. They appeared to wear armour however they liked, with the tall one's left arm covered in steel but his right arm having nothing below the shoulder. The short one had armour from head to toe, but in thin plates to give him good manoeuvrability. They both had knives, short swords and long swords strapped to their bodies, and one of them carried what looked like a large, heavy crossbow, but not of a design Havovatch had seen before. What really struck him, however, were their faces: they had none. Their helmets were the same as his but darker, much darker. They had a small, dark orange crest going vertically back, but the gaps in their helmets, where their faces would have been, were just blackness. He wondered if they were human at all; it was like staring into the Shadow World.

The Knight Hawks appeared to be staring back at him, saying nothing.

Havovatch grew afraid of them, and, keen not to stay there any longer, sped up his walk to the Holy Gardens.

When he got to the gardens, he finally managed to calm down. Fireflies were buzzing around, illuminating the beds and spring. It was a relaxing sight. The gardens themselves were impressive: well kept, with a finely cut lawn in the centre, surrounded by an eclectic assortment of plants from all around Ezazeruth. In one corner was a gentle water feature, which trickled from a natural spring all around the garden to small pools in various places.

It was therapeutic, and for a moment Havovatch forgot everything and entered a world of his own. He sat back on a white bench with his arms behind his head, looking up. It was a clear night, and many stars were out.

He looked up at the constellations and the three moons above him, and thought how strange it was that he was sitting so far from home and yet everything looked as it did when he was hundreds of miles north at his home of Efirth.

But then he heard a noise which took him out of his daze, and as he looked to his right he saw a woman approaching him. It was Princess Undrea, alone.

As she approached him, she smiled pleasantly. "Greetings, friend," she said, her voice as sweet as the breeze. She wasn't as affluently dressed as he had previously seen her, wearing a minimal amount of jewellery and a pearlescent white toga. She looked just like an ordinary citizen.

Havovatch was so taken aback that he forgot to answer.

She frowned. "Is there a problem?" she enquired.

"My apologies, Ma'am." Havovatch stood up and saluted her.

"Please, Captain, you are off duty! Sit, there is obviously something on your mind. Would you care for someone to talk to about it?"

"Apologies, Ma'am, but a captain of Camia is never off duty."

Undrea smiled. "Nevertheless, you still have something on your mind, and I am a good listener." She sat on the bench, cupping her chin on her palm and making herself comfortable, looking up at him.

Havovatch sat down next to her, but not too close, for she was the King's daughter; it was as though there was a protective bubble around her that he dared not penetrate, or go near. He sat on the far end of the bench and threw one leg over the other, holding his hands close to him. "So … what makes you think I have something on my mind?" he asked, too nervous to say anything else and staring directly ahead.

"Very few people come here at night when the city is sleeping, and those few who do, come to get away from what is troubling them."

Havovatch half-grinned. "You are as wise as you are beautiful, Ma'am, but I do not feel it's appropriate to talk personal matters with the King's daughter. My apologies."

She reached over and took his hand; she penetrated the bubble and he visibly became uncomfortable, withdrawing to the edge of the bench and bringing his arm closer to himself even more so than he was, yet she still held his hand. "Many people say that to me," she said, ignoring his discomfort. "But they always end up telling me something or other at some point." She smiled at Havovatch, her bright blue eyes shining.

He grinned; he wanted to tell her everything, but would it be right to do so? He could tell she would not jeopardize the mission; it just seemed strange talking to someone in her position. He wasn't sure how or why he spoke, it was almost as if she had control of him. "I'm only eighteen, and I am a newly appointed captain of an entire regiment, do you know how big that is? Eight thousand men. Not only that, I have been given a very important mission by the King, your father. I'm not sure I can do this."

Undrea smiled sympathetically, as if she understood what he meant. "Well, the King would not have given you the mission if he didn't think you were up to it. He also would not have promoted you if he did not think you were capable. His actions reflect upon him as well, you know."

Havovatch sighed; he could not deny that there was meaning in what she said. "But why me? What made him choose me? There are dozens … no, hundreds of men better prepared and more experienced than I am, yet he chose me."

"Then realize that. He chose you for a reason, and in time that reason will become clear."

Havovatch thought this over. Perhaps she was right. It was something worth thinking over, at least. "Thank you," he said at last. "You have helped me to relieve some distressing thoughts."

Undrea smiled at him and gently patted his arm as if her job was done, and suddenly he felt in control again. As she got up to leave, Havovatch stood up and saluted, then realized something.

"Princess, if people come here when they have troubles, may I ask if there is anything you need to talk about?"

She turned and smiled. "No," she said softly.

She stood still for a moment, the pulled a cloth from inside her toga and walked back to him. She gave him a kiss on his cheek and handed him the white cloth. "In times of need, look at this, and *remember* me, Captain," she said, as if it were an order.

Havovatch took it, and, surprised at her affection, he put his hand to his kissed cheek. He examined the cloth she had given him, but as he looked up, he caught a wave of her toga leaving the entrance to the gardens.

He sat down and looked at the cloth. It was just a small, white piece of fabric, but he was suddenly filled with happiness – whether it was the kiss or the cloth, he was unsure. But he definitely felt different from when he had entered.

As Undrea walked out of the gardens, she instantly saw Colonel Sarka, walking alone through the city with his hands behind his back, holding a rolled-up whip.

"Ah, if it isn't his Highness's spawn," he said dirtily.

She looked back for Havovatch but he was out of her sight.

"I have no desire to speak to you, serpent," she said defensively, although her voice trembled with fear.

Colonel Sarka stepped into her space and started touching and smelling her golden hair. When he moved down to her neck, she pulled away fiercely. Sarka's expression darkened. "You're lucky that you're the King's daughter!" he snarled.

"I wouldn't threaten me if I were you, Colonel … I outrank *you*, remember? And it would do you some good to remember that I know the poison you wreak upon my father, and this city!"

She tried pushing him out of the way, but his face turned red with anger at her rejection, and he grasped her wrist.

"You filthy ..." he started. He threw back his arm, unravelling his whip, but before he could strike, a deep voice echoed from the shadows.

"Is there a problem here, your Highness?"

The colonel quickly let go of the princess, turning round to see the two Knight Hawks standing behind him in the shadows, their features just made out by a slight reflection on their body armour from the moons above.

"If you could escort me back to my tower, I would appreciate it!" Undrea said, with a tremor in her voice.

"Certainly, our Princess." They stood either side of her, but the colonel stood defiantly in front of them, forcing them to walk around him.

As they walked away, he spat on the floor after them and continued to walk down the dark street alone, looking for something to take his frustrations out on.

Chapter Six
Destinies Begin

A loud knock at the door awoke Havovatch. He sat up rubbing his face, feeling like he had not slept at all, just closed his eyes for a minute and, upon opening them again, found it was morning. "Come," he ordered groggily.

Sergeant Metiya stepped in. "Captain, you asked to be woken at dawn."

"Thank you, Sergeant."

Metiya left, shutting the door behind him. Havovatch walked over to his water basin and rinsed his face, then looked in the mirror and sank into deep thoughts.

He started to think of his home and how much he missed his parents, his friend and the quiet life he had left behind. He also realized his life seemed to have shot forward ten years within a few months. It was too much to bear, like a physical weight upon his shoulders. He would give anything to be fourteen again, making bonfires, fishing, hunting, listening to his father regale him with stories of his career as a soldier. Havovatch's own career was turning out to be quite different.

He was starting to dress himself when Corporal Malon burst into his quarters, panting heavily and trying to muster the breath to speak.

"Damn it, man, have you not heard of knocking?" Havovatch shouted.

"A…apologies Captain, but it's Hilclop," Corporal Malon said hurriedly. "He's gone!"

"Gone?"

"Yes, Captain, gone! His bed has not been slept in, and his armour lay where he left it."

Havovatch thought for a moment. "Get Buskull in here now! I want every man in the regiment searching the barracks. If he is not found in ten minutes – no! five minutes – sound the alarm citywide and let them know that we have a deserter!"

"Yes, Captain." Corporal Malon saluted and ran out.

Havovatch leant on the water basin and let out a long breath, then threw it against the wall behind him, shattering it into pieces. "Damn it!"

He took in a long, deep breath and tried to compose himself, then carried on getting dressed. It was too late to re-recruit for Hilclop's position; they would have to be a unit of four. He cursed himself for not having a backup. And he cursed himself for listening to Metiya.

He carried on getting ready; he adjusted the straps on his new armour, pulling them tightly against his body. He checked that he had all his knives on the length of his back and his shoulders; he strapped the knife set around his leg, then pulled down his sword, which was hanging up on the wall, and placed it in his scabbard.

Buskull was soon at the door, Metiya letting him in. He was already dressed for the mission and had probably got up hours before anyone else to prepare.

He ducked under the doorway. "You summoned me, Captain?"

"Yes, I know you had an altercation with Hilclop yesterday and he has now disappeared. I want to know everything that happened after you left the armoury!"

Buskull kept his gaze on Havovatch, speaking slowly in his deep and fierce voice. "Captain, we all walked back together. Hilclop was trailing behind us a bit, but he was following us nevertheless. He checked in at the front gate when we did; the last I saw of him was when he went towards his barracks."

Havovatch stared intently at Buskull. He was not a man to hold a grudge against one of his own, and he was certainly not one to lie.

"Fine, go and get Feera and Mercury and meet me at the front gates. I may be late because I need to report to the on-duty colonel."

"Captain!" Buskull saluted and walked out, ducking his head again as he did so.

Havovatch half-walked, half-ran through the city. He was angry – they should have left by now and all would have been well. Instead everything was going wrong, on today of all days.

The on-duty colonel's office was on the other side of the city, and all the city's folk were out and about in the morning air and getting in his way. It was hard going, and he had to abruptly push his way through a few people; he did not like to be rude, but needs must. He could not just leave with a deserter on the loose. Hilclop may be a traitor for all he knew, and could be taking a message to the enemy. Havovatch had to play it by the book – that was how Camions did it.

He got to the colonel's office, and knocked harder than he meant to on the small green door, but there was silence. Havovatch wondered for a moment if anyone was in. Then he heard a rumbling noise, the door seemed to vibrate, and a deep, rough voice emanated from within the room. Havovatch stared on in confusion, then noticed that there was a pink glow flickering around the sides of the door.

"Colonel?" he said with some trepidation, and knocked again.

Then the murmuring stopped, and the pink glow dissipated. He opened the door and peered into the room. A slim, short man stood hunched over a large, cube-shaped box. His hands were resting on the sides of the box, and he was doubled over as if in pain.

"Colonel?" Havovatch asked again. Then he noticed the skin of the slim man's hands, pale white with blue veins.

The man turned. It was Colonel Sarka, the colonel he had had a confrontation with shortly after he had been promoted. He was hoping never to meet him again. The colonel was sweating profusely, and looked white and shaken.

"Did I say you could enter?!" he shouted.

"A-Apologies," Havovatch stammered. "Are you OK? I heard a noise."

"Don't patronize me, boy! What do you want?"

"Apologies, b…but I have a deserter."

Colonel Sarka sat down at his desk and wiped his forehead with a cloth. He was panting, as if he had run a long distance.

"You have a what?" he snapped.

"A deserter, Colonel," Havovatch repeated. "One of my soldiers is missing."

"I know what a deserter is, you stupid rekon!" Sarka barked.

Havovatch bowed his head and gritted his teeth, keen to try not to let the colonel see his expression.

"Apologies, Colonel."

"Who is your deserter?"

"His name is Hilclop; he is no older than fifteen. He joined the Three-Thirty-Third under the rules of war and has not completed his training."

"Have you got men out looking for him?"

"Yes, Sir, the barracks have been checked thoroughly and I have put a city alert out. All the gates are closed."

"And what are you doing? You're in full armour. You're a little overdressed to be looking for a deserter."

"I have orders from King Colomune, I am on a mission that should have started over an hour ago. I am late due to this mishap."

Sarka's face changed with a cruel smile, remembering that it was his idea that Havovatch should go on the mission. "Well, I guess I will be cleaning up after you, Captain. Get out of my office, and pray you don't have any more incidents! We don't want to fail in this mission now, do we?" A smirk flashed at the corner of the colonel's mouth.

"Sir!" Havovatch saluted.

Havovatch had no care for Sarka's threats, having more pressing matters on his mind. He marched out and made haste for the main gate of the city.

When he got there, he found his unit huddled next to the wall, trying to stay away from the crowd that had mustered around the gates and were arguing with the watchmen about leaving the city.

"Right," Havovatch said decisively as he approached the others. "We are one less but have no time to re-recruit. We leave now!"

They approached the gate but a watchman stopped them. "I'm sorry, Captain, but we have closed the gates. We have a deserter."

"I know, he was one of mine. I have permission from the King to leave the city on a mission for any reason, though! Now let me pass or I will let you speak to him." Havovatch pointed over his shoulder at Buskull, who realized what he was doing and stood straighter, looking as intimidating as possible.

The watchman swallowed and took a step back, but nervously protested, "I have my duties as well, Captain."

Havovatch passed over the orders allowing them to leave the city. The watchman read for some time, but hesitantly allowed them to leave, much to the displeasure of the crowd, who disliked their detention there.

They left the commotion within the city, and walked into the plains and rolling hills surrounding Cam. It was a fresh spring morning; a slight mist hung in the ravines of the hills and the grass was wet with dew. A gentle breeze brushed past them as they walked. Outside the mighty walls, everything felt strangely still; it was a feeling of huge vulnerability, but also freedom. They had the whole world at their fingertips, and, although they were restricted to a mission, they were able to roam freely around the world of Ezazeruth. It was the first time Havovatch had felt this liberated since he had enlisted. He checked his map every few paces; he was so nervous that he kept forgetting what he had looked at and had to check it again.

They walked in a small group along the path without speaking. Now and again, people or carts rattled by on their way to the city, but otherwise it was quiet and peaceful. As they walked, something caught his attention to the west. Glancing sideways he saw the white light again, with the distant rumble of thunder. He stopped as the others carried on unaware, and squinted to see what it was. It was brighter and clearer than it had been before, and although it looked miles away, he found himself reaching out his hand to try to take it. As he did, it immediately vanished.

He heard Buskull shout out, "Captain?"

Havovatch glanced his way, feeling confused. This was all getting too strange, he thought. He started to grow concerned for his sanity. Shaking his head clear, he caught up with the others and carried on.

They soon came off the road and headed west, and as they got to the summit of a hill they set off at a slight run to keep warm and make sure that they covered a suitable distance.

With the incident of Hilclop left behind him, Havovatch tried to concentrate on his mission, but soon his thoughts ran on to the scenario from that morning. He wondered what Colonel Sarka had been doing before he entered his office. And what had he meant by that last comment he said?

"So, what do you think happened to Hilclop, then?" Mercury asked him, trying to get a conversation going as they ran. Havovatch did not answer, but he did linger on the question. Where had Hilclop gone?

***

As evening fell over the hills, Havovatch's thoughts turned to rest for the night. He had pushed the unit hard all day, and they had mostly marched up hills before running down them. It was a good way of maintaining their endurance and still making good ground.

He thought it best to cut across country and go in a straight line, rather than stick to the paths and roads. There was no direct route to where they were going, for most roads only led to key towns and villages.

From the many worries that burdened his mind over recent events, he also thought about how he was going to find the first commander of the knights. Perhaps, when they got to the area of this 'Impenetrable Forest', they might pick up some information in taverns or villages.

Maybe someone would even have created a story or song about them long ago that was still being told, Havovatch more hoped than thought.

As they walked over the crest of a sloping farmer's field, they came into view of a small farming town in the ravine of a valley. It looked peaceful; all the labourers in the area were returning from their hard day's work in the fields. The town itself had no walls or defensive structures, and many windows were lit up, thin wisps of smoke gently rising into the air from chimneys.

Havovatch and his unit walked down on a snaking path into the town, and as they approached they saw a wide street which, when they followed it, led the way to a main square with a circular fountain in the middle. As they entered the town, they saw above them an arched sign hanging over the street. 'Welcome to Persa' was written on it, in silver italics.

As they walked through the town, they noticed many townsfolk sitting at tables or on doorsteps in the cool evening air, smoking and drinking. They were not a very loud community, just happy to have the company of their friends, pipes and beer. Havovatch and his unit walked casually through the centre of the street, taking in what was going on and trying not to look too conspicuous. No one seemed to regard them very much, though a few glances were thrown at Buskull.

As they approached the end of the street, they came to a tavern. Inside, Havovatch could see the yellow glow from candles and fireplaces, and silhouettes of people moving around inside. It did not appear to be very busy, and he decided to have a look inside.

As he walked towards the doors, he looked up. Above him there was a sign of a farmer wearing a jumper made of hay, bearing the name 'The Farmer's Yarn'. It was swinging gently from side to side on rusted hinges.

"We'll stay here tonight," he said to the others. There was no protest from his men – they were happy that they could stay in some comfort and have a proper meal, and they knew it might be their last decent one for some time. They followed him inside.

When they walked in, no one seemed to pay them much attention. The barroom was wide with a low ceiling, and it was faintly lit by the amber glow of candles around the room and a small fire to one side. The ceiling was so low that Buskull had to duck, but he made no fuss.

They found a table in the corner away from everyone else. Havovatch and Mercury walked over to the bar whilst Buskull and Feera made themselves comfortable. The barman turned to meet them, a short, bulky man with more facial hair than Havovatch had ever seen.

"What'll it be, lads?" he asked, in a strange accent that Havovatch knew was native to farmers; it was so strong he almost did not understand what he said.

Havovatch handed him some papers. "I am Captain Havovatch of the Three-Thirty-Third Heavy Infantry. I am on orders from the King. We request that we stay in your facilities tonight. You know your generosity will be rewarded."

The barman let out a sigh. He clearly did not like the fact that he had to let soldiers stay without any upfront payment. It meant having to spend time and money getting to a city far away, and he could lose a day's time and money trying to do so.

"Very well," he said reluctantly. He knew he could not turn away soldiers defending his country.

"Plus three pints of your strongest ale and any non-alcoholic beverage you have please, bar master," added Mercury.

"Who's drinking non-alcoholic?" Havovatch murmured to Mercury.

"Buskull," replied Mercury. "Don't you know he doesn't drink?"

Havovatch raised his eyebrows but was not entirely surprised; Buskull seemed to possess many strange qualities that separated him from the other soldiers. Or even simply other people, come to that.

The barman poured them their drinks and told them that they would be staying in a large room, big enough to accommodate all of them, at the back of the tavern.

Havovatch was rather hoping for a room each; having his own quarters had made him feel more comfortable, being isolated, but he knew he had wound the barman up enough, and bit his lip to stop himself from asking for separate rooms.

When they got back to the table, Havovatch ordered them to go one by one to the room and take their equipment off.

When they had done so, they just sat at the table in silence. It was very quiet in the bar, which made it more peaceful for them. They wanted it to last as long as possible.

Although Buskull looked rather ridiculous – his huge frame sitting on a small stool was a sight to see – the unit knew better than to mock him, Mercury finding it the hardest to hide his grin and not say anything.

However, no sooner had the peace descended in the small place than the pub door flew open and a small group of merry women walked in.

The mood of the patrons seemed to lift as they entered. They wandered over to different tables and sat on the laps of some of the men, stroking their faces and making insinuating remarks about their arms.

Havovatch and the others knew exactly who they were and felt uncomfortable about it. Prostitutes were forbidden in Cam; the rich felt they made the place untidy, so they were banned, although it was always rumoured that there were brothels in the city, and that the rich themselves used them. But it could never be proven. The greedy rich often got what they wanted in Cam without being exposed.

The unit returned to their thoughts, ignoring the women in the bar. Feera, in fact, closed his eyes and almost seemed to be sleeping, although Mercury kept glancing over at a few of the women.

Havovatch just hoped the girls would not come over to them, but would stick to the men they knew. They were respectable soldiers of the King and they did not want any trouble. However, his wishes were in vain, as soon a young girl noticed them. She was thin, with blonde platted hair, and walked over to them with a big, false smile on her face.

"Well, well," she said sweetly. "New meat, I see."

She started to stroke Feera's face as she passed him but he pulled away, clearly not wanting her affection.

The girl gasped. "You don't want me?" She recovered a little. "Fine, I love playing hard to get." She reached over and put her hand on Buskull's enormous shoulders.

"My," she said, her voice squeaking, "never have I felt such hard … shoulders." For a moment she almost seemed shocked at the inhuman and deformed bone structure, then she shrugged it off and bent down to put her arms around him.

Without warning, Buskull leapt from his stool, kicking it behind him. Turning, he picked the girl up, leaving her feet dangling off the floor. He said nothing but his eyes did all the talking – they blazed with fury that she had touched him against his will. Fear seemed to grip the girl, and she hung there silently, looking deep into his eyes, seeing a rage that she would never understand.

Silence filled the room, making Havovatch glance around. Every pair of eyes was on them, and some of the patrons were beginning to stand up, slowly but hesitantly. Havovatch, Mercury and Feera looked around, bracing themselves, and slowly rose to their feet.

Buskull put the girl down gently, not taking his eyes off her, the anger slowly subsiding in his eyes as if the look of the girl brought back a painful memory. She quickly turned and ran towards a much larger woman sitting on the far side of the room. Hugging the traumatized girl and looking at the unit with disgust, the woman stood up.

"You pig!" she shouted. "You-ugly-horrible-pig!" She turned her attention to the rest of the room. "Get 'em, boys!"

At her command, all the men in the room rose to their feet, some grabbing bottles and others taking antique weapons off the walls or picking up chairs or stools.

Havovatch opened his mouth to plead with them, dropping his guard to a more diplomatic one, but before he could say a word, the men ran forward, pushing them backwards into a corner.

One old man shouted to a group of young lads in the corner.

"Boys, get the giant!"

Buskull's ears pricked at the word, and, roaring in a way that made everyone jump, kicked the table towards them, flattening them all. Building up a huge breath, he shouted even louder and dashed straight into the melee.

Havovatch and Mercury pulled their chairs up and smashed them over the heads of two others. Feera deflected a rusty sword away with his hand by the flat of the blade, then palm-struck the man in the jaw, making him drop the weapon and clutch at his face in agony.

Buskull stood with his arms wide and ran into the melee, knocking back a group of drunks and crushing them into a pillar. As he turned, two more men holding either side of a bench ran into him … the bench hit him in the stomach and snapped in two, but Buskull did not seem affected. Instead, he grabbed each end of the broken bench, which the two men were holding onto, and swung them into each other.

One of the drunks scrambled onto the bar and jumped onto Havovatch's back, screaming as he did so. But the patrons did not seem to realize that they were dealing with heavy infantrymen, well-versed in hand-to-hand combat, so instead of panicking, Havovatch put his hands behind the man's neck and pulled him over his shoulders, hauling him heavily down onto the wooden floor. For good measure, Havovatch kicked him in the groin to make sure he did not get back up.

Meanwhile, Mercury and Feera were almost standing back-to-back, with their arms raised in a defensive stance. This was no battle; they were not looking for weaknesses in their opponents nor trying to kill them, just kicking and punching at the drunken fools, trying to get them to back off.

Buskull was picking men up with one hand and throwing them out of windows or into other groups as if they weighed nothing at all, before turning around and punching a man so hard he flew backwards and landed right through the floor. A young boy who fancied his chances ran at Buskull and whacked a chair over his back, but he did not even flinch. He turned to meet the boy, and with one hand he lifted him up by his throat and slammed his head hard into the ceiling, knocking him out. It was the first time Havovatch had seen him fight properly … he seemed a different man, wild. It was as though nothing could stop him at all.

Despite Buskull's best efforts, the unit was still outnumbered, and they were fighting the locals who were too numbed by alcohol to notice some of the pain they were receiving. Other people from outside noticed the commotion and flooded in to help their fellow villagers.

Mercury ended up on the floor in a headlock whilst two others were kicking him in the stomach; another started repeatedly slamming a stool down onto him. Feera and Havovatch could see what was happening, but they had their own duels to contend with.

"BUSKULL!" Havovatch shouted at last. "HELP MERCURY!"

Without hesitation, Buskull ran in his direction, knocking everyone down, then grabbed hold of the attackers and pushed them through a wall. They all landed heavily in the next room, Buskull purposely landing on top of them to break his fall. He promptly got up, leaving them groaning, then brushed the dust off himself and walked back into the bar. Straight away, he brought his fist down onto the head of an unsuspecting man trying to fight Feera. Feera, in turn, elbowed another drunk in the face, then pushed his fingers into the man's larynx, making him choke and step back, gasping.

As one man came at Havovatch with a decorative sword he took from the wall, he dodged the blade, then followed this with a heavy punch to the man's nose and an open-palmed slap across his ear. The man's eyes started to water and he clutched at the side of his head, crying out in agony.

It was clear that these men did not often fight – they were strong from labouring in the fields all day, but they did not know combat.

Finally, the bar fell silent.

Men lay all over the floor, or slumped over tables or through windows, most groaning and some even crying. The barman was sunk behind the bar in terror, clutching a towel and looking around at his once perfectly quiet establishment. In the middle of the room, Havovatch and the others were the only ones standing. They stood in a square facing outwards, ready to take on anyone. The women were silent; some of them lay in the corner of the room clutching at each other in terror, and others were holding some of the injured men. All of them were completely shaken by their ordeal.

Just then, the door burst open and a group of soldiers ran into the tavern. They were not battlefield soldiers but the town's watch, so they were armed with wooden cudgels and clothed in thin armour. At first they ran in, suspecting a normal bar brawl, but as soon as they saw the state of the tavern, they stopped on the spot to take in the situation.

Havovatch withdrew with his unit to the back of the tavern, whilst the watchmen stood in the middle, amazed by what had happened and unsure of what to do or where to start.

A seasoned watchman pushed his way through the gathering and looked around. He was tall and broad, with short, white hair and a white beard, and scars all over his face. He wore medals on his chest, so Havovatch knew he was an ex-military man.

"What has been going on here?" he demanded, in a rough but well-spoken voice.

He looked at the unit. "Is this a result of you? Who are you!?"

Havovatch stepped forward and saluted him.

"Sir, I am Captain Havovatch of the Three-Thirty-Third Heavy Infantry. We were set upon by these drunken fools and had to defend ourselves in response."

"I am Commander—" He stopped and looked at Havovatch more closely. "You don't look like heavy infantry, or old enough to be a captain. What business do you have here?"

Havovatch moved to produce his papers from his pouch, then realized that he had put them with his uniform in their room at the back of the tavern.

"Sir," he said, "I am a captain; my papers from the King are in our room at the back of the inn. But I can assure you that we did nothing to provoke this!"

But the older woman who had started the fight, and who was now holding an unconscious man in her arms, shouted, "Yes, they did! They hit one of our girls!"

The commander had had enough. "Captain, this is a quiet and peaceful town that does not often have bar brawls; now you come here and that all changes. As a result, I am placing you and your men under arrest."

Havovatch stepped forward in protest. "Sir, we are on an urgent mission from the King; we have no time to waste being under arrest!"

The commander clearly did not believe him. "That's as maybe, Captain, but you have committed an act of criminal violence. For that I will see that you are made to pay!"

Havovatch looked back at the others. Mercury's face was swollen; he was hunched over with one arm holding at his stomach and Feera trying to prop him up. Havovatch knew that there was nothing any of them could do right now; they could certainly not take on armed men, and they were battered and bruised from the brawl. Reluctantly he conceded, and raised his hands.

The watchmen instantly surrounded them, taking hold of their arms, though with Buskull three watchmen merely pointed the butts of their spears at him. Then they were all escorted to a cart outside, taunted by an angry mob of villagers.

Chapter Seven
A Man and his Demons

Fandorazz looked out of his chamber window at the city below him as the sun set. Because of his late family's fortune, he had one of the highest apartments in the city, second to the King, and it overlooked the whole north side of Cam.

As a result, it had one of the best views too; on a good day, it was clear for leagues with no towns, villages or hamlets in sight. It was rumoured that rich folk paid an enormous price so that no settlements would be erected within their view. Instead of creating jobs and tilling land to help feed a quickly developing and overpopulated country, it was felt that the rich wanted the northern countryside left as it was, just so they could enjoy the pleasures of the natural world. But whenever this was challenged, it always hit a suspicious dead end, as did most things involving the rich in Camia.

Fandorazz looked down at the goings-on within the city: children running around in the streets, soldiers on the battlements smoking, chatting or standing watch. Beyond the wall, low hills covered in lush green grass surrounded Cam, its winding rivers painted amber by the setting sun. Sporadic woodland covered some hills and valleys, made up of different kinds of trees, some pointed and thin, shooting high up into the sky like a rack of spears, and others large, their trunks wider than the columns that held up the Acropolis.

The sun on the horizon glowed behind the hills, turning the clouds orange and merging with the pale blue sky above. The three moons were just coming into view. Peril The Guardian looked the closest, and was visible all day long, but Merta the Watcher was faintly appearing, and the slight hint of Seagorn the Herder was starting to show its rounded shape.

He turned to look back into the dark room and saw his late family's portrait hanging above the fireplace. It had tilted slightly. He gasped and dashed over, and with a deep breath and focused delicacy, tilted it back into position, touching it as if it were very fragile.

He stood back and put his hand on his chest, his eyes beginning to water. He looked closely at his son and daughter; they were both being hugged tightly by his wife, who stood behind them with her arms around them. He stared at his wife's gentle smile of happiness, then at his past self, standing tall and proud behind them, his chin up and chest out and his face alight.

He wished that they were still with him now. His wife would be cooking dinner, his children would be playing outside with the other children and he would be in his study, surrounded by the matchstick models of his buildings and shelves crammed with scrolls of his thoughts, ideas and prints for buildings.

Despite the cramped room, it was very tidy, and he had kept it that way, professional to the highest extent. But now, five years later, the room was locked, as were his children's and the room he once shared with his wife. Instead, he spent every day in the dark and deathly silent living room. It held only a firm couch, a desk, a few shelves with books on; all were covered in a noticeable layer of dust.

Most things had been left as they were since that terrible day five years ago, when an accident had left his family dead. He had been taking them away to live in a new place on the other side of Ezazeruth, so he could follow his dream and complete his ultimate project, the building and design of an entire city. But, along the route, a freak rockslide had buried his family whilst he had watched helplessly. The last thing he had remembered was calling out his wife's name, Sharna, and seeing her face wrought with horror, his children clutching her ... and then he had only seen rubble.

He had trouble going to sleep, and any time he managed it he would often wake up a few hours later. Most of the time, he fell asleep on the floor drunk. Sometimes he would wake up and find that he was on the sofa, but his sleep was no more comfortable.

He closed his eyes for a minute as haunted voices came back to him. "Traitor," they cried. "Failure, pathetic, cretin … murderer!"

Tears formed in his eyes and ran down his face at the words, and he frantically shook his head to make them stop, his neck aching. He had given up trying to find out where the voices were coming from; he accepted that he was insane.

"It was not my fault!" he usually argued out loud, but the voices would argue back, laughing as they did, and every time he lost.

"Shut up! Leave me alone!" he shouted this time into the deserted room. But the laughter grew louder, as if more voices were joining in, and his tears flooded his cheeks.

He had been the best, the best architectural engineer in all the land and arguably in the world. His ability ran through his bloodline, right from the very birth of the city of Cam where his family had created designs and techniques that no one else could seem to master. But now he had been brought low; he had not designed anything since the death of his family. A shrine had been built in their name in the Holy Gardens, but it was not enough.

Fandorazz walked over to a table in the corner of the room, where his half-completed model of a castle lay. It felt strange for him to walk, he often did little movement. His body seemed to come alive as he paced forward.

The castle was a unique design that he had been working on before his family were killed. It was meant to keep watch over the west. Eight years on, he was no nearer to completing it than he had been.

He looked at it for a moment and knew there was something about it, something in the back of his mind, which he could just not grasp, something about how to complete the foundation for the battlements ...

It felt so obvious when he looked at it, but there was a mental block preventing him from solving the problem.

He let out a long breath and walked back to the window, gazing out again at the natural beauty around him. His mind was telling him to just crawl out onto the ledge and jump; he would close his eyes and leap to meet a new fate, and finally he would be with his family. And the pain and voices would go away. Several times in the past he had tried it, but just before he jumped, his wife would appear smiling down at him and holding out a hand to help him back in. He sometimes tried pushing himself to the edge, just so he could see her smile. She always had a smile on her face that made all his troubles fade away. She could smile to armies and kings, and it would turn their minds from battles and war and towards peace. But her smile was hard to remember – the last look on her face had been one of shock and terror.

He glanced over at the battlements of the matchstick model city again. He was not sure how, but something caught his eye ... then it clicked inside his head. The particular design he had in mind would give superb strength to the defending garrison! He walked briskly back over to his model on the table, took a bit of the castle off and put another bit on underneath it, then put the battlements back on top again. No glue was needed; it sat there securely without it. He even pushed down on it slightly and it held. It was strong, despite being made out of thin bits of wood.

Weeks had passed since he had had another breakthrough, but recently they were coming more frequent. And, now he had finally completed the task he had set out to do for that particular structure of the castle, he felt a slight feeling of achievement. But as soon as he moved to do the next bit, the block came back again. The grin fell from his face, and he let out a long sigh of frustration and rubbed his forehead. Slowly he walked back to the window and gazed out again, putting his hand up onto the side of the window and resting his head against it.

He started thinking about getting ready to go to a meeting that evening. Usually he wouldn't – he couldn't even remember the last time he went outside. But this was one he had to attend: all the architects in the land were meeting with the head of their council to discuss what they could do to help in the current affairs of the state, which was now under 'the rules of war', meaning that changes were to be made to everyday life, to prepare to defend the country. Fandorazz knew that it was more about them using this opportunity to get money or success for themselves.

His friend Hembel would come by soon, and go with him to the meeting. He put on his finest clothes and waited until the knock came at the door. The clothes did not fit him any more; although he did not exercise, he also did not eat. He drank, though, and paid for a porter to fill up his wine rack every week. His finest clothes hung on his skeletal body – he had been a slim man; now he was indescribable.

He sat in his chair looking into space, depression gripping his heart with every beat. The more he thought about his family, the worse it became, and in some strange way he felt that he was enjoying it. Maybe happiness was just not worth it.

A knock came at the door but Fandorazz did not notice it at first; he just sat there with his eyes tightly shut. Then another knock came, much louder and harder. He opened his eyes and moved to get up, but Hembel let himself in, half hanging on the door.

"Ready?" he asked, his manner friendly. He was dressed in his finest clothing as well, wearing a green tunic buttoned up to his chin and carrying reams of scrolls under his arm. Hembel wasn't a particularly famous architect – far from it. But he had been a good friend to him in the past few years. Before the accident, Fandorazz had barely spoken to him – he had had no need to. He was the best at what he did; he had a wonderful family and the best chambers in the city. *Why would I need to consult with lesser men than myself?* he'd thought at the time. The last thing he needed was another architect trying to get into his spotlight.

But, the day after the accident, Hembel had been there, and nearly every day since, trying to support him where others used the opportunity to rise to greatness in his absence. They were welcome to it, he thought. He was content to wallow in his own self-pity for the rest of his life.

They walked out of the door, but Fandorazz forgot to lock it, and Hembel had to stand by the door and shout for him to come back. Fandorazz felt awkward; he could not seem to remember to do the simplest of tasks, and day by day things were only getting worse.

They both walked slowly down the winding, cobbled streets, Hembel speaking about his life and things he thought were amusing to try to cheer him up. "So, I said to her what can I get you? Spirits? Beer? Whatever your poison …? She then rolled her eyes up at me and left." He laughed out loud, thinking that Fandorazz would think it would be funny.

But Fandorazz was, as always, in a world of his own. He just stared at the floor, not taking anything in, the sheer burden upon his heart weighing him down. And unbeknown to him, Hembel kept looking him up and down as if trying to find his secret, hoping that he would reveal his mastery of engineering, and as he did so, his eyes narrowed in reflection of his wicked act.

Chapter Eight
A Shadow in the Trees

Havovatch was bitter and angry. *What else could I have done?* he kept asking himself. It was the first day on his first mission and he was already behind bars and helpless. His unit were black and blue, and their weapons and uniforms had been confiscated.

They were all in different cells in an underground prison block underneath the watch-house. He was sitting in just his tunic, wet in places from blood, none of it his own.

He perched on a solid wooden bench whilst staring into darkness, contemplating what had happened at the bar. Now and then his thoughts were interrupted by a rat scuttling along the floor in the dark abyss. The cell was small, with no windows, and if he lay down on the bench he could barely stretch out. He was cold, but he liked that. There was a pile of hay in the corner, but it had the unmistakable, unpleasant smell of months-old vomit that had, instead of being cleared up, just had more hay dumped on top of it.

The cell door had a small window with three bars installed in it. Havovatch peered through now and again to see if he could see anything down the corridor, but it was too dark. Even when the door at the top of the stairs was opened, no light came from it, and only the amber glow of the torch showed that it was a couple of guards bringing a drunk in for the night. They taunted Havovatch as they passed.

"Not so tough now, are yer?" one shouted, hitting his cudgel against the bars, the other guard laughing as he did so.

Further along, in a cell nearby, Buskull was feeling worse, as he knew this was all his fault. He knew that he could easily kick his cell door down, but he did not want to make the situation any worse than it already was. He sat up on the bench with his legs pushing against the opposite wall, continually banging his head against the brickwork. The physical pain dulled away the burden of the evening's events.

Feera, in another cell, stood up and went to the tiny, barred window on the door. He put his arm through and stretched down but the lock was way out of reach. Instead he took deep breaths of the cool clean air emanating from the corridor, trying to replace the dank humidity in his cell, the soldier within him working, trying to find a way out. He felt along the corners of the floor and ceiling with his fingers, he tested the solid cell door for weaknesses, but he was locked in tight.

Havovatch could hear him moving around. "Get some sleep, you lot," he shouted into the darkness. "You'll need your energy tomorrow. Don't worry, we will get out of this."

Even though he was unsure as to how they were going to get out, he was hoping a night's sleep would do them some good.

Feera sat down on the edge of the bench upright, closed his eyes and placed his hands on the bench either side of him. He thought back to a time in his life when he first sat on a horse, and galloped off on his own whilst his family stood amazed that a young boy could naturally ride so well. Riding was his passion, and remembering that moment helped him to relax and focus. He didn't realize, but he was rocking back and forth as if he were actually riding a horse then. But, as he pretended to grab the reins, he held his fist too tightly and a pain shot up his forearm, a pain brought on by a punch upon a man who deserved it, the man who put him in the infantry, and his knuckles went white with the image of his face in the blackness.

Mercury could not sleep. He had been the worst affected in the fight; some of his teeth were loose, he had cracked ribs, his face was bruised and swollen, he couldn't feel his left arm and he was pretty sure his nose was badly broken. He lay on the bench staring up at the ceiling at first, but soon had to sit up as he could not breathe.

Every time he moved he was in more discomfort and pain, but he tried hard to not let anyone hear. The night would be a long one for him, and he was desperate for a drink. He felt the damp walls and even tried to lick them to get the moisture off, but it did not satisfy – he could just feel his throat swelling up. He felt as though he was constantly about to swallow his tongue.

He lay back down on the bench, one hand supporting his head and the other across his body, trying to compress the pain. Slowly, he started to get a tingling sensation inside his head as his body gave in to the agony and shut down, allowing him to sleep, though instead he entered a world of suffering in his dreams.

As Havovatch lay in his cell, he thought he could hear thunder outside, but he knew it was not the season for it. He knew that the darkness was playing with his thoughts, making him think he heard and saw things that weren't there, but nevertheless he could not help but feel that he was not alone in his cell. As he dozed off, he cast his thoughts into the blackness and was sure he could see someone in his mind's eye. The vision was blurred and wavering, but he could see a tall, thin man dressed in white, shrouded in a purple haze. Again he shrugged it off, putting it down to concussion or sleep deprivation.

Thoughts passed through his head as he dozed. He thought about home, the wooden shack located in the middle of a valley of trees near Efirth, two hundred miles to the north of Cam, just below Hadicul Mountains, smoke pluming from the chimney as his mother cooked dinner; his father outside cutting logs, fish from the river hung up on the side of their shack ready to eat, and pigs snorting in their pen.

The area he lived in wasn't a palace. It was a clearing in the woods in a small ravine of two hills. Most of it was boggy with mud, as all the water from the valleys funnelled through their ravine. But his father and grandfather had created a dam, trailing the water away from the house; it was still boggy, but this gave a surplus supply of water for growing food.

His mother was a keen gardener, and had her own fields growing all sorts of fruit and vegetables from all over the world. No one was allowed near them; she put all her effort into growing them and became very protective. Havovatch smiled to himself when he remembered when he sneaked into the crop patches for a dare, and got caught. He was more frightened of his mother telling him off than of anyone during his training. She was a kind woman, though, loving and fair, and always put people in their place. He did not sign up to the military when he was sixteen like other friends he knew, as his mother made him wait until he turned eighteen. He hated the two-year wait, but now his training was over he understood to a certain extent: it must have been hard for his mother to let her child go off and not look after them – she had done so for the past eighteen years, and hearing the experiences of his father probably added to her worry.

But as he thought of her, he remembered her face, and his father's. They were both fair-haired whilst he was dark, but he remembered that his uncle on his father's side was dark, and his aunt on his mother's side was dark-haired as well; his brothers were also different from him. They were both younger. Hamrilar was stocky; he liked growing his hair and had not cut it in years. He was five years younger than Havovatch, and wanted to join the infantry as well one day; he too was inspired by the stories told to him as he grew up by their father in the evening by the hearth.

Harrowgan, however was completely different. He had red hair but often shaved his head, and he had grown a goatee when he started to grow stubble. He was much like Havovatch in that he was quiet, but he did not enjoy an active life. Instead he was a keen artist, and often wandered off on his own to draw. Once, Havovatch and Mercury had found him sitting on the side of a cliff with his legs hanging over the side, looking around at the beautiful landscape, and drawing frantically on a scroll with a piece of graphite. He was not sure what he wanted to do in life; he never showed any interest in the military and he rarely spoke.

As Havovatch dreamt on, his pain became a distant memory and his mind wandered into happier places. For that second, whilst he was far away from his responsibilities, he could feel an almost real sense of freedom. It was something he had never felt before, just thinking of his life years ago, and how badly he wished he were there now, whereas then he wanted nothing more than to grow up and be a soldier.

Morning seemed to come slowly. Havovatch had more strange dreams and awoke in exactly the same position he had been in when he had tried to doze off, just lying on his back and staring up at the ceiling.

He thought it was morning because he could hear commotion from outside the cell door, and beyond that the noise of street carts rattling along pavements and the faint call of birds, but inside it was still as dark as it had been hours before.

Suddenly the cell door at the top of the corridor swung open heavily, clanging on the stone wall and making him jump. It seemed different this time, not the noise of guards bringing a drunk down the stairs, but more ominous than that. Lots of heavy boots were stomping down the steps with clear purpose.

Havovatch got up, wincing at some of the bruises that had started to set in, and made his way to the cell door. He peered out of the window, trying to catch some glimpse of movement.

He heard a deep voice shouting at someone, but it was slightly unclear what they were saying.

The voice became louder, and eventually he heard a shout, "Open that door, you bloody cretin!"

Torches suddenly appeared and the stone corridor was lit up, but it was not the guards holding the torches. It appeared to be what Havovatch thought were Camion heavy cavalry soldiers. He squinted as he tried to adjust to the light.

The gaoler, who was quite old, decrepit and hunched over with long grey hair, came into view. He was desperately reaching for his key chain to open Havovatch's cell. He looked rushed and panicked.

The door eventually opened, and the old man was pushed out of the way whilst a large officer with a big, shaggy, brown beard bowed into the doorway and looked down at Havovatch.

"Captain Havovatch?" he boomed.

Rather curious, Havovatch just nodded.

"Follow me!" the officer simply responded, turning back into the hallway.

Havovatch stepped out just as the officer was demanding that the old man open the other cells. One by one the doors to the other cells were opened and out walked Buskull and Feera, but when Mercury's cell was opened, he did not come out. A soldier peered in and then entered. He returned shortly, supporting Mercury, whose free arm was clutching at his ribs.

The other detainees in their cells, thinking that it was a jailbreak, started shouting for them to be released in their drunken state, but all were ignored, and the unit were led upstairs where they grimaced at the natural light coming in through the windows.

As they walked, Havovatch noticed that their entire route was lined with cavalry soldiers standing to attention at the sides of the hallways. Two of them were holding a rather burly watchman against a wall with his hands behind his back. Havovatch caught a look at his face; he was scarlet red and foaming at the mouth with anger.

Havovatch wondered who they were ... they were too far away for a message to have got to Cam and back in the time that they were imprisoned. And, judging by the attitude of the guards, they were there to protect him and his unit.

They were led up more stairs to the top of the watch-house, and came into an open-plan grand office. There, the commander from the night before was sitting behind a desk, neat piles of paperwork spread before him, which he had probably spent the night writing incriminatingly about them.

Stood in front of his desk was a cavalry general, holding his helmet under his arm, his other arm resting proudly on his sword. The commander of the watch looked angry, as if his remit had been stripped away from him; he was biting his lip and more red in the face than the man being held downstairs.

The general turned to them. He was not very tall – in fact, he was quite short – but he looked judicious and battle-wise. He was bald, and his armour was immaculately clean and shiny, but still dented and scratched (the sign of a true leader, Havovatch thought), much like the rest of the cavalrymen around him. Havovatch's attention, though, was drawn to the sword strapped over the general's back; it had a small, purple hilt. He had never seen a hilt that colour before.

"Ah, Captain, good!" he said. "I believe you have more pressing matters to attend to than rotting in a cell in the middle of nowhere?" He raised an arm, guiding them back out of the door. "Your equipment is waiting in the next room; my second here will accompany you out of the village ... Can I suggest that you make all due haste?"

Havovatch stood still, startled. "General, with respect, may I ask who you are? And how do you know what duties I have?" He was keen to learn who else knew of his mission.

The general turned back to him. "You may ask, Captain, but I shall not tell you. I am asking you to trust me. Now, with every second that passes you are delaying your mission!" He clearly spoke as if he knew how vital it was to summon the knights.

Havovatch wanted to know more about the mysterious general, but he was right, he had to get moving, and turned to leave.

"You will know more in time, Captain," added the general, making him pause again. "Go and get ready, and we'll escort you out of this pathetic town."

The comment seemed to anger the commander even more, and Havovatch heard his knuckles crack as he clenched his fists. With reluctance, he saluted the general, and the unit walked into the adjacent room and put their equipment on. Mercury had the most difficulty; when he took his wet, bloodstained tunic off to put another one on that the cavalry had given him, Buskull noticed the bruises and went to assess him.

Mercury winced and pulled away. "I'm fine!" he said, waving a dismissive hand and giving that one sided smile he always gave, Buskull knew he wasn't, but he shrugged; he could not treat Mercury if he did not want to be treated.

When they stepped outside, the whole street was lined with cavalry. However the townsfolk were about too, still disgusted with the way the unit had come and disturbed their peace. Word had travelled quickly around the town and all the people were out to see the men who had caused such frenzy. The large woman who had set them up the night before was still there, surrounded by her girls, all of whom were looking at the unit with grim faces. Havovatch and his men put their helmets on in defiance, kept their chins up and marched through the street, followed by the cavalry either side of them. As they marched, they noticed that some of the townsfolk had come with rudimentary weapons, some holding table legs with a spike through the end, others with farming tools and other implements. They were obviously keen to get their retribution, but had thought better of it now that there were some two hundred heavy cavalry around.

When the unit had left the town, they were escorted for a mile further until a corporal trotted up to them. "Captain, you should be fine from here onwards. I wish you luck!" He saluted, then turned and galloped off with the others. Havovatch looked around for the general, keen to speak with him, but he was nowhere in sight. He must have left in a different direction.

All alone and with nothing else to go on, they all carried on down the path to head west. The only upside was that they were up earlier than they would have been if they had slept in the tavern, and could cover some good distance today. Nevertheless they were hungry, thirsty and aching.

Havovatch was angry with the way they had been treated by the town's commander. He was keen to press the matter with the King on his return, and, what with the bruises he was feeling, he was keen to make a big deal about it too. He had not felt like this since his first week in training, and with the pain clouding his judgement, he did not realize the state Mercury was in.

***

As the day wore on, no one spoke to each other – they just bowed their heads and stumbled along, their enthusiasm wavering.

Mercury looked the worst off. He had a split lip and bruises all over his face, and dragged himself behind the others, trying desperately to keep up, his breathing irregular and heavy. But he wanted no one to know of his condition, and, with his helmet on, they could not see the state of his face.

There was tension amongst the group. Feera and Mercury occasionally glanced at Buskull, who was the only one who did not appear to be injured. They did not hate him for what he did – they just wished they knew the reason behind his ways. It was strange how serious he was, how he never liked to be touched by women, how he did not like fire … but they were wise enough not to ask him.

Eventually they came to a brook in some woods, and Havovatch told them to stop and rest for a minute. As he took off his helmet, he looked around and finally could see the tension in his unit. Feera and Mercury were sitting by a tree stump with their backs to Buskull, clearly displaying some annoyance. Buskull was standing still, resting on the hilt of his axe and looking in Havovatch's direction, waiting for an order.

Havovatch was the first to speak. "Look, it was no one's fault what happened last night, I want you all to know that. Irrespective of the situation, if one's in, we're all in, all right?"

Feera and Mercury shrugged and nodded in agreement and looked up at Buskull; he looked down at them in turn.

"Thank you," Buskull said quietly, breathing a sigh of relief that they had finally talked about it.

Immediately, it seemed like a weight had been lifted from the unit, and Buskull relaxed a bit and stretched, his joints cracking loudly. "I feel like a cave ghoul."

The others looked at each other.

"What's a cave ghoul?" asked Feera.

"You know? The creatures from the Hadicul Mountains?"

They all looked baffled and shook their heads.

Buskull tilted his head in confusion. "So you have never heard of a cave ghoul?"

Again, they all blinked at him.

"Well, you must have heard of Ninsks?"

Their confusion doubled.

"The guardians of the Rogan Defence Line," Buskull pressed, "the human spiders?"

"I've heard of dwarves," Mercury said, stammering from his swollen lip.

"Well … yes, but they're human."

Each glanced at each other, wondering if they were being led on by Buskull.

Frustrated, Buskull threw his arms up and walked away, muttering to himself, leaving them to wonder if he was mad.

Bending down by the edge of the brook, Buskull drew a curved blade from the back of his belt and started cutting something that he had found in the water. Then he walked back to the others and picked up two smooth pebbles. Putting the substance between the stones, he started to grind them together until whatever it was became a mushy, green mess. Taking the stop from his waterskin, he poked the green mush into the end and shook it well. He then turned to the others and handed it to Havovatch.

"I warn you, it will taste foul, but if you keep it down it will help to heal your wounds. Trust me!"

Havovatch flashed a look of trepidation at the others, but took a swig and handed the waterskin to Mercury.

He felt fine: it tasted like water, and he swallowed again, clearing his mouth. Then he smiled and looked at the others. Mercury took a long swig; Feera sniffed the end and took a small sip, then shrugged and finished the rest off. Then, Havovatch's face changed – he started to taste something. "Oh, no!" he said. At first the taste was subtle, but it grew in its intensity, and he ran to the side of the brook, followed by Feera and Mercury. The taste was setting in their mouths, and whether they spat it out or threw up it would not change anything. It tasted like rotten vegetables, mixed with horse manure, and the entire ocean's worth of salt. It was the most disgusting thing they had ever tasted.

Havovatch retched over and over again, but nothing came up; his stomach tensed so much that his abdomen started to ache. Then he sat on a rock briefly, hunched over whilst the plant digested in his stomach. He could feel it working quickly, almost straight away; sudden pains he could not ignore faded away, but the bruises and cuts were still visible.

He leant back to recover, constantly sipping water. He tried to take his mind off the sensation he was experiencing, and the foul taste in his mouth, and began to wonder as to who the general was. How had he known where they were and the mission they were undertaking? Havovatch thought their mission would be top secret, but maybe the general was just privy to it in some way and happened to be passing by the town at the right moment?

Whatever the reason, it just seemed too much of a coincidence, but he was glad that they were out and on their way again, because whilst he had been in the cell, he had had no idea of how to get out.

After a while, they all put their equipment back on and set off again on the path west. The plant remedy that Buskull had made was working well, and even Mercury was getting back to his normal witty self, popping off jokes and keeping the mood of the others up as they went. But the taste still lingered.

It was early afternoon. Havovatch walked at the front of the unit, frequently checking his map and occasionally making some notes on the back of it with a thin piece of graphite. He kept drinking more than he wanted too, sipping continuously at his waterskin, as the taste of the remedy that Buskull had given him still remained. Mercury and Feera were talking to each other and Buskull walked a little distance behind the group, constantly wary of his surroundings. Havovatch tried not to get too involved in their conversations … he wanted to be seen and respected as a leader, not for the personal views he held.

They had walked for some hours, and the sun was high in the sky with barely a cloud in sight, so Havovatch decided it was best to walk through the woods so that they would not get too hot or burnt by the sun. It would also mean that they would not draw too much attention towards themselves.

They followed a path laid out by locals. Every so often they came across someone and they would step to one side, letting them pass, or if they had enough time they would hide in the shrubbery, but they did not interact with them. If they came to a hamlet or small village they would walk around it. Havovatch wanted as few people to see them as possible for various reasons: word might have got to them about the altercation at Persa, or some people might inadvertently give information to unwelcome ears about a group of four well-armed soldiers prowling the area.

By early evening they came to a stream and Havovatch turned to the others. "We'll rest here for a bit."

The stream was calm and wide, leading to the river Amura in the east. The water was deep and very transparent, it flowed nicely, and the sound of the rushing water was peaceful.

The unit broke out their waterskins and refilled; it was customary to fill your waterskin whenever you came to a river, for you never knew when you could refill it again. It was especially important in the heavy infantry – with all the weapons and armour they were carrying, and all the marching they did in a day, they had to stay hydrated. Afterwards, they ate some of their rations whilst resting against a tree stump or rock.

Buskull even found a raspberry bush, and started filling his enormous hand with pickings and offering them to the others.

Feera and Mercury started licking bits of seeds from their teeth and pushed their helmets just over their eyes so that they could get some sleep. "I could get used to this," said Mercury.

Buskull went and sat about twenty paces away, keeping an eye out in the direction that an ambush seemed most likely to come from. Havovatch could almost see his ears twitching, as if he was listening for anything untoward. He sat down cross-legged, and put his axe on the ground. He could not see his face, but his shoulders suggested he was breathing slowly, as they rose and relaxed ... it appeared as if he was meditating.

Havovatch himself sat on a rock, removed his boots and began massaging his feet. With his new boots, he had accumulated some large blisters, so he put them into the water. It felt good to let cold water flow between his toes and clean the blisters and sores that had formed.

He pulled a knife from his vest and sat twisting it and throwing it in the air, catching it perfectly by the handle. It was a way of calming himself, and he smiled; ever since childhood his father had taught him how to wield knives, and he felt as if they were a part of him. His hands showed it as well, with many thin scars and calluses from the constant use.

He missed his father; he was glad he had got a letter off to him before leaving Cam. His father would then know what he was doing and not to expect a reply for some time. But a thought struck him: *would they be OK?*

After all, he was marching across the world and far away from home, and could not protect his family, whereas if he were fighting in the east of Camia, he would feel that he was protecting them. He just had to remind himself that his family were near the north of Camia – thousands of soldiers stood between them and the defences. They would be fine.

After a while of thinking of his family, something in the air seemed to change, shaking Havovatch out of his playful trance. Suddenly on alert, he started searching around, looking for whatever seemed to have disturbed the peace. As he looked down the river, he thought he could see a black object lying in the long grass next to the brook. It was not too far away from him, and as he looked it turned out be a satchel, but there was a familiar feeling about it; then it struck him. It was the same military satchel that he was given as part of his kit. But the owner was nowhere to be seen. He looked about ... Mercury and Feera both seemed asleep, Buskull meditating, but he could not see anyone else. He continued to look around, casually trying to see if there was anything out of the ordinary, but it all seemed fine. Then, something caught his eye.

What looked like a dark figure hiding behind a tree was looking at them, peering between leafy branches, trying to be inconspicuous. Havovatch kept his gaze away as if he were looking at something else, and tried to make out if the shadow represented a threat. However, Havovatch wasn't very good at being inconspicuous either, because after a few minutes of this strange exchange, the surreptitious figure realized it was also being watched. In one quick move, the figure turned and ran into the woods.

Havovatch immediately sprang to his feet and started running barefoot after it. He turned as he ran and shouted over his shoulder, "On me!"

The others were startled out of their own states, but immediately jumped up and followed him, leaving behind most of their equipment. Mercury's injuries, however, got the better of him, and he eventually fell back.

Feera saw the figure and quickly passed Havovatch. They all ran as quickly as they could; after the ambush at Coter Farol, the unit were not willing to let any suspicious activity go.

Feera gained ground rapidly and grabbed the figure at the top of a steep slope, but they were both running so quickly that the momentum caused them to roll down the hill. As they did so, they punched and kicked each other, Feera having the upper hand, stronger and clearly a better fighter than this masked stranger.

When they reached the bottom, the stranger tried to get up and run again, but Feera jumped on top of him. Hitting him in the back of the head, he then rolled them over and pinned his arms down, then pressed his knee on the stranger's sternum. A groan echoed from behind the sack that was obviously supposed to hide the stranger's face, and it sounded male.

Havovatch and Buskull then slid to the bottom of the slope where they lay, whilst Mercury stopped at the top of the slope and looked down, his arms caressing his rib, panting heavily. Havovatch drew his sword and pointed it at the neck of the figure.

"Who are you?" he demanded.

Feera pressed his knee on the figure's chest harder, the figure whined and winced in pain, and Feera pulled the sack off his face.

They all stared in shock.

"Hilclop!" Havovatch shouted. "You fool! Do you know what you've done? Do you know how much trouble you have caused?"

Hilclop tried to get his breath back and speak out, but with Feera leaning on his chest it was difficult. "F-Forgive me, Sir, I just couldn't do it."

Havovatch wanted some answers out of him, but knew this wasn't the time or place. Taking in a breath, he said sharply, "Buskull, tie him up – he comes with us!"

Havovatch turned and walked back up the slope towards Mercury. Feera pulled Hilclop up and shoved his arms behind him as Buskull bound them.

"Where were you?" Havovatch said sternly to Mercury when he got to the top, then lowered his tone so that others could not hear. "I'm counting on you to cover my back, why did you think I brought you on this damned mission?"

"Sorry, I tripped," Mercury said, wincing, still trying to hide the obvious pain he was in.

Havovatch tutted and walked away, shaking his head.

"Vatch," Mercury shouted after him. "Vatch, wait! We can't go back to Cam, let the boy go! He will be caught anyway at some point or other."

Havovatch turned and glared at him directly. "No! It's a hanging sentence for desertion, and he might be a spy! He comes with us; we will explain it to the King when we get back. We have a mission; we cannot ignore it!"

Havovatch turned and went to walk away, then turned back to Mercury again. "And stop calling me Vatch – it's 'Captain' now! Get it into your damned head!"

Mercury flinched as if he had been stung; in a low tone, he said, "Yes, *Captain*!"

Havovatch stopped for a second, realizing that he had let his friend down, but he did not turn or say anything; he just carried on walking.

When they got back to the stream, Havovatch put his boots back on and made sure he had all his equipment. Hilclop was brought back, the rope binding his hands attached to Buskull's belt, his face wet from crying. Feera walked behind him.

Havovatch walked over to Hilclop. Hilclop was looking down at the ground, but Buskull leant down and lifted his head up by his chin.

In a firm voice, Havovatch said, "Boy, I will say this once, so try to listen. If you run or do anything, *anything*, that puts the lives of this unit in danger on this mission, I *will* kill you! Do you understand me?"

Hilclop swallowed but said nothing; he just nodded his head, looked down at the ground and started to sob.

Havovatch turned to the others. "We leave now!"

Chapter Nine
At the Hands of the Black

Four days had passed since they had found Hilclop. He behaved well and said little, but his cumbersome and lazy ways impacted on their advance. Often walking behind, he was more dragged by Buskull than walked by himself, and his sulky attitude seemed to be washing off on the rest of the unit.

They spared little of their own rations with him, and made him drink from rivers rather than waste their water. Havovatch knew he was being hard, but he was not really sure who Hilclop was. He showed no pride in his country or himself; he knew a lot about what they were doing and for all Havovatch knew, he could be a spy – the real reason for his desertion. He certainly had a lot of qualities to confirm it.

The thought of coming across other regiments in the meantime, though, was becoming very attractive … then he could hand Hilclop over to them. But even so, there was a nagging feeling at the back of his mind that said it was wrong.

As he walked he pondered over it; he was almost glad that they had found Hilclop in some ways, because it helped solve unanswered questions that kept badgering him.

Mercury staggered near the rear; Havovatch thought that he was keeping an eye on Hilclop but actually knew nothing of his suffering. Constantly walking put stress on Mercury's aching body, but he refused to speak up and fought on through the pain.

As the unit slowed whilst walking out of a forest, Mercury approached Havovatch, who was again deep in thought.

"Va … Captain."

Havovatch did not notice and Mercury called out again. Havovatch looked up, startled, his face plainly showing there was something wrong.

"What's on your mind?" Mercury asked quietly, hoping that he had forgotten about the quarrel they had had the other day.

"With respect, my friend," Havovatch said, sounding tired, "it's best that you don't know." Mercury nodded and tried to think of something to change the subject, desperate to rekindle some warmth between them.

Havovatch did not want to tell him too much; if they were captured, then the less Mercury knew, the safer he was, especially because soon they would be passing into Loria, a country with which Camia was technically at war, as it would not see Camia as a superior power. The last thing he wanted was for them to be caught and give over information about their mission, and for the Lorians to use the Knights of Ezazeruth to their own advantage. He knew little about Loria: it had been drilled into him since as far back as he could remember that its people were savages, and nowhere near the sophistication and intelligence of Camions.

They continued to walk down a dirt track, with visible signs of cartwheels trailing in the mud. There was a slope on their left, with thick woodland spreading along their right-hand side.

Mercury continued talking about life and how he missed home, trying to come up with his quick-witted jokes and hoping it would bring a smile to his friend's face as it used to.

But Havovatch's attention was elsewhere; he could sense something amiss in the air. He could smell the faint scent of charcoal, something burning, and he knew that, somewhere, something awful had happened. He walked away from Mercury whilst he was still talking, and scrambled up a slope.

Buskull sensed it too and was already ahead with Hilclop, half asleep and dragged in tow. Mercury realized that Havovatch was not with him and sighed, thinking that something irreplaceable had changed between them. Nevertheless, he followed.

When they all got to the top of the slope, they saw it. The scene that greeted them was one that would live with them for the rest of their days. Each of them stood there in disbelief, and Buskull fell to his knees in shock. The rest did not even notice, as they were so taken in by the sick sight before them.

They were looking down upon a small village – or what was left of it. The whole village had been burnt to the ground and dead women, children and men lay scattered around the burning ruins. Buskull rose to his feet, snarling, and drew his battle-axe. The others followed suit, each drawing their own weapons. They slowly advanced down the slope towards the grim scene, Buskull gritting his teeth, rage barely contained in his body.

In a column, they slowly walked towards the village, careful not to disturb the scene. The wounds on the bodies suggested that the villagers had been running away when killed. There were injuries found on the victims' backs, lacerations and crossbow bolts sticking out from them, some still bearing the weapon that had killed them. Rivers of blood had run along the ground, with red tributaries collecting in a small puddle at the base of the hill. They could see the white of the victims' bones sticking out from their skin, and found one woman with her skull caved in, and her brains sprayed over the ground before her. There was no sign of any attackers anywhere, yet they proceeded with caution, walking mere feet away from the corpses of their kin.

Hilclop struggled to take it in; he walked wide-eyed and shook visibly at each step he took. He had not really seen death like this before, such butchery of innocent people, and he started to panic.

"Who ... What could have done this?" he said, terror starting to build in his voice.

Havovatch turned to shush him, and Buskull pulled at the rope and put his finger to his lips, but Hilclop couldn't help himself. "Please unbind me!" he begged. "Give me a weapon! Let me go!" – his eyes still on the dead bodies around him.

But a firmer tug from Buskull, which brought him right up to his face, and a slap from the back of his hand, shocked Hilclop back to reality.

They walked into the centre of the village. What had once been a small, quiet, working village was now little more than charcoal ruins of houses and barns, with carcasses hanging from windows and doorways. In the centre was a small well, with a man lying hunched over it. Havovatch checked his pulse, but there wasn't one.

"It could not have happened too long ago – the embers are still hot," said Feera, peering all around him, as he tried to make sense of all this savagery. They could feel the heat from the fire of the buildings as they stood there.

"There is no evidence of them defending themselves, Vatch. There are no bodies of their attackers," said Mercury, standing upright as he momentarily forgot about his wounds.

"Perhaps the attackers took their fallen with them?" murmured Havovatch, mostly to himself.

Buskull was still deathly silent, his shoulders visibly rising with every breath he took, desperately looking around to find something to vent his anger on.

They stood on the spot, Feera and Mercury looking at Havovatch for an order. But he did not really know what to do. '*What do you do with something like this*?' he asked himself.

"Captain?" Feera said. "What are your orders?"

It was then that Havovatch noticed Buskull's distraction. "Buskull," he said, but Buskull did not seem to be in this world, and Havovatch thought he could see a tear running down his face. "Buskull!" he said more firmly.

Buskull looked at him, his eyes ablaze with rage. His arms tensed as he gripped his axe with white knuckles, and veins protruded from his arms.

"Unbind Hilclop and give him your dagger," ordered Havovatch, looking him over, confused. "If he runs, let him go."

Havovatch turned his attention to Hilclop. "If you run, you're on your own, and trust me when I say that at the moment it is better to stick with us!"

Hilclop swallowed. Buskull drew his dagger and, with a single slash, cut through his binding and gave him the knife. Hilclop looked at it, not really knowing what do to with it.

"Mercury, Feera, go as a pair and scout south of the village. Buskull, you and Hilclop go east."

They all nodded and started to fan out. "Stay close, laddie," Havovatch heard Buskull say to Hilclop as they left, anger somewhat gone now he had some orders.

Havovatch stayed in the middle of the village and looked around the debris, studying the area carefully and looking at every possible thing. Someone or something could jump out at him at any moment and he wanted to be ready.

Peering into a barn, he was confronted with a hanging corpse swaying from side to side; he covered his mouth from the stench, and the sight. The victim was hung upside down, and appeared to have been used as a game, with multiple stab wounds and whip marks all across his body, blood still dripping onto the floor below.

Thankfully, Havovatch turned to hear Buskull shouting; he was glad for the interruption. He ran over to join them, followed shortly by Mercury and Feera, and found Hilclop on all fours, vomiting. Buskull was leaning on his axe and looking down into the long grass, his warrior composure back to normal. Havovatch thought it strange how quickly he'd changed from the shaking mess he'd been before.

Havovatch looked down before where they stood, and in the long grass he saw a creature lying dead; it looked just like the same thing he'd fought a few months ago at Coter Farol. It had greyish-blue skin and its nose and ears were very long. It had a huge laceration to its gut, and its killer, a farmer holding a scythe, was lying not too far from him, with a crossbow bolt protruding from his head.

Its stench was unforgettable – it stank of rotted flesh. The putrid smell was so strong in the air they felt they could chew on it. Havovatch covered his face with a rag.

"Well, it seems they are still attacking the area," said Buskull.

"There have been no reports in weeks; I heard the war had ended and everything was going back to normal," put in Feera.

"That was wrong. It is very much still here … what we fought was just the beginning, a test, and there will be more to come," Havovatch said, not taking his eyes off the corpse; then he suddenly realized he had said too much.

"How do you know that?" asked Mercury.

Havovatch flushed at the sudden slip he made, so tried to change the subject. "I think they must have moved on – they would not have a reason to linger. We are still in Camia, and cavalry units will soon be in the area and see the smoke. We must stick to our mission."

He began to walk back to the village. Mercury stared on, dumbfounded by the decision. "What! Leave? Leave this scene?" He threw his arms out. "There's been a crime of horrific proportions and you want to just *carry on*?"

"Mercury!" Havovatch snapped. "Remember your place! There is nothing we can do here. We have our orders and we must to stick to them!"

He turned and walked back to the village.

Feera looked down at the corpse, then reached down and picked up a mattock from the grasp of the creature, putting it through a loop on his belt. He looked up at Mercury. "When the time comes, we shall give them a taste of their own weaponry!" he said as a promise. There was conviction in his eyes. Then he too turned and caught up with Havovatch.

Havovatch entered the village, and looked around to see if there was anything they could salvage which would assist them with their mission – food or any water. But everything had burnt to the ground. He was not sure how he was coping with the scene before him; he had seen things he never wanted to. But his mind was elsewhere; he knew what he saw, but his mind was pretending it was not really happening.

Buskull and Feera joined him, Mercury dragging Hilclop by his arm and waiting behind them. They all looked at Havovatch as if they did not want to leave, they could not leave. And Havovatch noticed.

He had a thought. He had not read anything about preserving a scene like this just after he was promoted, but he did remember reading a diary about a massacre a cavalry general had once come across. The general had another objective and knew that he needed to stick to his mission, but for the sake of his men (who were clearly shaken by the ordeal), he knew he could not just walk away from it. So the general told his men to start a perimeter search, looking for any survivors or the perpetrators of the monstrous act.

Though the scene had been checked thoroughly, no survivors had been found. So the general told his men that there was nothing they could do, and to stick to the mission at hand. But they could take solace that they had done what they could, rather than leaving it as it was, and so pressed on. And it also gave his men purpose; when he got to his mission's objective, his men fought with a sadistic blood lust, taking their anger out on their enemy by any means.

Havovatch knew this would help his unit, and give them purpose in a mission they knew little about.

"Okay! We will do one more sweep of the area," he said. "Look for any signs of life, good or bad. If we find nothing, then we will move on, no discussion! Those are my orders!"

No one said a thing; Mercury stood playing with the hilt of his sword in his hand, Buskull and Feera just giving a nod in response.

"Very well," said Havovatch. "All four of you go together, start where we came in and work your way around the outskirts of the village. I'll meet you at the west bank."

They left, with Buskull putting his arm out to give Mercury some moral support. Havovatch went towards the west bank, checking the wreckage of some of the houses.

As he turned behind a wall and knew that he was out of sight of his unit, he suddenly put his hand out to lean against it and doubled over, his stomach wrenching so hard he felt he was going to cough out his guts. He sank to the floor and, leaning against the wall, removed his helmet and sobbed. He then hit his head against the wall, harder and harder, clenching his teeth and finally cradling his head in his arms, crying in a way he had never done before.

Afterwards, he sat there in silence, his face wet, staring blankly.

As he looked along the open plain before him, the clear blue sky became cloudy, with dark clouds forming. Then purple thunder started to shoot down, at first small strikes, then bigger and more fearsome.

Then the same white light appeared that he had kept seeing. Havovatch was suddenly overcome with a sense of peace; his body was numb and he wanted to jump out and grab the light, but he didn't. He sat there, simply looking at it, and the white light started pulsating beams of light at him, every beam making him feel more relaxed.

He thought he heard his name. "*Havovatch*" – the voice was distant and calm. "*Get up, you can do this, get up*!" it echoed around him.

Suddenly, in the blink of an eye, it vanished, and he blinked a few times. He sat up and saw that the sky was blue with no clouds. He rubbed his eyes, thinking once again that he must be going insane.

He grabbed his waterskin and gulped the contents, then splashed some over his face, and wiped his eyes with a rag. He still felt sick, but also felt more able to deal with it. He put his helmet back on and composed himself, then took out his map, drew an 'X' where he thought they were, and wrote next to it 'burnt village'.

For a while, he wandered into the field and waited for the others. He was standing upwind and was able to take in some fresh air for a moment.

The unit were doing a very intricate search, hoping to find some reason for them to stay, and even Hilclop was doing his best, but eventually they reached Havovatch empty-handed.

No one said anything, and, giving Mercury another look of disappointment at the little support he was getting, Havovatch walked on.

The others followed him. No one said anything: they just carried on walking north-west, and did not turn back to look at the grim scene.

***

The land turned to hills with deep crevasses and steep slopes, with no trees or rocky areas in sight. Havovatch knew that any day now they would be wandering into unclaimed territory, a place so bleak it could not be lived in, with some areas desert, few rivers, nowhere to till the land.

The only people who lived here were outsiders who did not want to be under the flag of any nation. Havovatch thought that they almost had a good life in certain ways; they did not have to pay taxes and they lived by their own rules, but because they did not belong to any given country, they had no support, no protection and no one to turn to. He knew there were only a few of these people around, and that they kept to themselves. They were known as Emiros, an ancient word for people who did not belong anywhere.

Havovatch knew that this could be a prime place to be ambushed, though, either by Emiros or the creatures, so he ordered Mercury to go up to the highest point and keep lookout whilst they walked in the ravines. He also thought that giving Mercury some time alone would help him get himself back together; he needed his friend back. But, after what they had seen that morning, he wasn't so sure.

Night was approaching and the sun started to fall below the horizon, so Havovatch decided to camp where they were. No fires were lit; they just rolled up in their cloaks and rested on the side of the hill. Mercury came down, keeping his gaze away from Havovatch, trying to pretend to the others that everything was fine and he was back to normal, but he did not hide his feelings well.

All was still and quiet, but Havovatch knew that all their thoughts were still on this morning. He decided to take the first watch on top of a hill with a rocky edge. He sat against the rock, staring around at the land lit by the moon's reflection. It was mostly quiet throughout his watch; although it was a clear night, it was also cold, and he was shivering. Holding himself tightly, with his knees brought up to his chest and his cloak wrapped around him, he tried to warm up, but he wondered if perhaps the shivering was due to the fact that he was finally away from the village, and the reality of what had happened was starting to sink in. He tried to take his mind off it by quietly singing songs or reciting poems to himself. He was not a good singer, far from it, but it helped him to calm his nerves and distract him from the unpleasant thoughts that kept resurfacing. One feeling he couldn't seem to shake away was regret: regret that he had not done more, regret that he had not pushed the unit harder and maybe got there in time so they could make a difference, maybe save them.

The one thing he could just not understand was why the Black would attack farming folk. They were no warriors: why would anything attack unarmed and peaceful people? The images of the children were the worst for him. But it made one thing clear: the true extent of the hand of the Black. And as he sat there looking up at the sky, he muttered an oath that he would make them pay, he would get retribution by any means.

Eventually the third moon came into view and he went to swap with Feera. Feera was still awake and went to watch obediently. Havovatch lay between Buskull and Hilclop and wrapped his cloak around himself. He knew most of them were still awake, and he did not blame them.

But Hilclop appeared to be sleeping, breathing slightly heavier than he was comfortable with, but he let him carry on, for he was asleep and not talking or whining.

Now lying down, he kept thinking he was hearing things, noises that seemed distant at first, almost intermittent. But Feera hadn't moved or said anything, so he closed his eyes and tried to sleep, finally drifting off into his own world.

He soon woke when he felt something tugging at his leg … it was Feera.

"Follow me, but be quiet!" Feera whispered.

Buskull was already sitting up on one knee with his axe in hand. He reached over and nudged Hilclop, who groaned and wrapped his cloak around himself tighter.

On their stomachs, Havovatch and Feera pulled themselves up to the crest of the hill and peered over. Buskull sat below, waking Mercury and then giving Hilclop another shove.

Feera and Havovatch looked down at an army of creatures marching in an unorganized rabble over the hills. It was too dark to see them clearly, but they were walking in scattered groups not far from them … fortunately not in their direction.

Their stench was familiar, just like the vile beast at the village, the smell still present in their nostrils. They made no attempt to hide their noise, with some wailing, others grunting and their armour clinking together. Two of them even broke out into a fight, the others watching on and cheering, howling into the night sky. The fight soon ended, with the victor tearing limbs off its victim with its bare hands, then holding them up like a trophy.

A sudden chill went down Havovatch's spine as he felt vulnerable and scared. It was dark, they were outnumbered, and if caught they would certainly be no match for the creatures.

"Two, two-fifty strong?" Feera whispered to him. Havovatch said nothing, just hoping that they would pass by unnoticed. He looked down at the others and gave hand signals for 'enemy threat', 'be quiet' and 'stay low.'

Buskull responded with a flat hand on his left shoulder, saying that he understood, but Hilclop did not know the signals, and asked what was going on, tugging at Mercury's cloak.

Buskull noticed and put a huge hand around his face, purposefully covering his mouth. But Hilclop jerked up onto his feet and tried to scurry out of Buskull's grasp.

Surprised by his actions, Buskull did not have a firm enough grip, and Hilclop stood up and shouted, "What the hell are you doing?"

Havovatch and Feera looked down at them in disbelief, as Mercury and Buskull jumped on top of him, covering his mouth. Feera and Havovatch looked back at the marching horde, and their worst fears were realized: they had been heard.

The creatures were advancing towards them with their weapons drawn, all of them shouting, howling, trying to intimidate their unseen enemy.

It worked. Havovatch's jaw quivered, he felt light-headed, he struggled for breath. Feera pulled at his tunic, and they jumped up and ran down the hill. "Run! They're on to us, run!" shouted Feera to the others.

Without hesitation Mercury and Buskull leapt off Hilclop and ran after them. Hilclop scrambled to his feet and tried to keep up.

As they sprinted over the top of the hill, Havovatch tried to look around to find woodland or a cave. The moonlight shone on the tops of the hills, but as far as he could see there were only hills for leagues around. There was nowhere to hide.

They ran to the top of the next hill just as their pursuers got to where they were camping. Sprinting was a difficult task in any situation; they could jog for miles, but sprinting was different. Their lives depended on it, though: the creatures had started to gain on them.

Running up hills was getting too much for them as well, and fatigue started to wear in.

"What do we do?" Hilclop shouted in an exhausted panic.

Havovatch thought quickly; he dreaded it, but there was no choice. "Split up!" he ordered. Just as they moved to obey, Buskull slowed down. He saw Mercury and Feera heading one way, Hilclop trying to keep up, and Havovatch another.

He snorted, muttered a quick prayer to himself, and then turned with his battle-axe in hand. As he walked towards the charging enemy, he was calm and pulled a book from his bag. Reading a few passages to himself in a language only he knew, he finished with a kiss to his hand and raised it to the air. Then taking a breath, he was ready: this was it.

Putting the book away, he held his battle-axe and stood on the spot; bending his knees slightly, he let out a roar they should have been able to hear in Cam, his tremendous shout crying over the vile beasts' onslaught. And he charged.

He ran down the hill with extreme rage; no man could stop him. He continued his battle cry, echoing in the hills around him, then he raised his axe and, with every step, stomped heavily into the ground, which was left with deep imprints of his boots.

When the others heard Buskull's war cry, they turned. They were all still in eyeshot of each other, and noticed that Buskull was missing. It took no discussion; they all raced after him except Hilclop, who stood clueless on the hill, trying to muster the courage to move.

Havovatch knew how important the mission was, but he was not going to desert a friend. He drew his sword from his scabbard, as did Feera and Mercury, and they darted over the hill to see Buskull with his axe in the air, facing the tide of creatures head-on and alone. It was magnificent valour, and it warmed their hearts to join him.

Hilclop crawled to the summit of the hill and peered over, but couldn't bring himself to go forward.

He looked on as Buskull crashed into the first few creatures, sending them flying. At first, he only met a few of the faster ones trying to get to them, but the main body of the horde were working their way towards him, their thunderous approach echoing in the night sky, just under Buskull's shout.

But Buskull was like a force of his own; swinging his axe in every direction, he cut through the armoured creatures with ease before bringing his axe down again to keep on, and he carved a way through the centre of the horde. But just as they started to surround him, Havovatch and the others joined him and covered his rear.

Havovatch threw a knife from over his shoulder at a creature that was just about to hit Buskull in the back. It sailed through the air quickly and embedded itself in the creature's skull, the creature going still and falling to the ground.

Mercury and Feera cut their way through with heavy blows, although Mercury was lacking in strength from his injuries. Feera swung the mattock he had stolen from the creature, and embedded it into their skulls, torsos, anywhere he could inflict pain. He fought with the dedicated anger he had been mustering all day; they all did. He did not see the creatures' faces as he cut into them; he just remembered the faces of the children lying on the floor in shapes he could only hope to forget.

Buskull swung his axe at every moving object, cutting clean through shields, armour and flesh, and Feera and Mercury stood either side of Buskull, hitting hard and low into the creatures coming down the hill, whilst Havovatch stood with his back to them, protecting the rear.

Havovatch's anger had been building, since Coter Farol, since the village and the fury of being arrested. The creatures were not prepared for it, and the unit carved a path through them, much to their surprise as the unit were becoming enclosed, and it would soon be a fight till the death.

Hilclop could not look any more. He pushed his way back down the hill and then lay with his arms wrapped around his legs wishing he could do something. Again he began to cry, and then he heard Havovatch calling his name.

"Hilclop!"

He squeezed his eyes shut and began to rock himself, praying that he was not there, trying to come away from reality and be somewhere else.

"Hilclop, we need you!"

"I don't want to be a soldier any more, I want to go home," he said out loud, sobbing, hoping that it would come true.

"Hilclop!"

But he just listened on, hoping that it would all be over and he could go home.

"Hilclop!"

Chapter Ten
Delusion

King Colomune sat at his desk writing notes about the day. He found it therapeutic to write; what went well and what went wrong. He thought reflecting on himself and others he had observed would make him a better king. Although he did not write as much as he used to, ever since Colonel Sarka had found his reflections and told him off for monitoring others.

He tried to protest against him, saying that he was a king, and should not be spoken to by a colonel in such a way. But the colonel reminded him that he had looked after him ever since his father had died, and that he should show some respect.

He closed his eyes and leant back on his chair. Rubbing his face to relieve the tension, he started to feel a little better and almost went into a slumber. Soon he was dreaming that he was back as a child running in and out of the courtyard to the palace, seeing his father sitting at the throne, so mighty, so powerful. Guards followed him everywhere he went; everyone in the city bowed to his presence or cheered; they loved him, they respected him.

But tears came to his eyes, as he received no such worship from those within his city, no such respect from his people. Once someone even tried throwing an egg at him – he was not entirely sure why. They shouted 'traitor', chanting songs about him.

He could still remember them to this day:

The King of Camia
The coward, the traitor
The man who's swayed
By the smallest of men
To do as they please
Rather than what's best
The day will come
When Colomune is done
And Camia will be perfect
Once again

He could remember every verse, and it hit him like an iron hammer.

But how could I be a traitor – I am their king, he thought, *they should love me*! – clenching his fists and going red in the face. He hated them, he loathed them, his own people below him in the city, and around the land. He hated everyone for not loving him.

The feelings brought back the image of another wretched day, remembering when he was just fifteen, and Colonel Sarka approached him telling him that his father had been killed in an ambush, and the frightful image behind Sarka as his father's body was carried slowly through the city.

The city had been quiet for months after; the air seemed to change, the world changed. His father was an important man, maintaining peace between all the nations in Ezazeruth. King Colomune had never found out who was responsible for his father's death.

And now, since his coronation, the world went back to ruin, tensions escalated, and before he knew it he was signing battle plans and sending regiments off to fight across the world. He was not even sure why he was doing it, Colonel Sarka drafted all the plans and brought them to him to sign. Sarka had always said that he knew what was best, but Colomune doubted it.

He thought so many times about standing up to Sarka, and in his head he imagined himself so powerful and mighty, and brimming with confidence. But when he saw Sarka, his presence, his ill look, his deep eyes, his gaunt face, Colomune would begin to tremble and any strength within him would fade away.

There was a knock at the door, which took him out of his slumber. He was relieved by the interruption, as he found himself visibly shaking. Colonel Sarka put fear into him even in his dreams.

He rubbed his eyes. "Come!"

Atken entered. "Sire, we have messengers back from the sea defences."

"Excellent, I will be up presently."

Atken said nothing, and left, closing the door.

King Colomune put on his thick, blue cloak and looked into a giant mirror, higher than he was tall, and wider than his arm's width. He was a king, a king of the most powerful country in the world; he reminded himself of how much power he had at his fingertips. He smiled.

He turned on his heel and walked up the long, spiralling staircase to the Acropolis.

As he entered the hall room, he noticed that there were a lot more people there than usual. Not just the lords and ladies of Camia who were usually there, but messengers and ambassadors from other countries answering the banners' oath, all bowing to his presence.

Atken, as usual, was standing on his usual spot on the step of the platform in front of the throne.

He saw tribes from Viror in the north, dressed in their thick animal skins, dark-skinned men from the south, heavily clad knights from the west, sailors from the islands in the Gulf of Pera. It was a diverse group, all bringing huge bodies of soldiers to his aid ... and his smile grew wider.

He walked over to his throne, his chest out, chin up, letting the people before him stay down a little longer: he felt that he needed them to show the proper respect.

Before sitting, he stood and looked around the hall room, then opened his hands out gracefully and said, "Rise, my friends."

He put as much emphasis and power into his voice as he could and sat on his throne, looking around. But the first thing that struck him was that Colonel Sarka was nowhere in sight. He was always there, usually standing to one side but within view, presenting hand gestures indicating whether to say 'yes' or 'no', or 'we'll discuss it later'.

The captain who had been sent to check the sea defences to the east of Camia stepped forward onto the blue square to present himself. He took off his helmet and stood presentably. He was an aged man, square shoulders and well built, but not very tall.

"Captain Seer, of the Three-Thirty-Sixth Heavy Infantry, in the presence of King Colomune of Camia," addressed an aide to the hall. Although a thought struck the King that he should have sent a cavalry unit rather than an infantry unit, as he would have got a report much quicker, he decided to not voice this.

"Captain, report your findings," said Colomune, quickly trying to distract himself from the thought.

The captain stood to attention; he tilted his head back, putting his chin into the air, and spoke with a deliberate tone. "Sire, the defences are in a state of disrepair: parts of them have eroded away or collapsed, or locals have taken the brickwork for their own use. In my professional, tactical opinion, if we were attacked now, we would not be able to defend the east coast!"

King Colomune sighed in deep thought when Lord Vitel strode forward. He was a tall, slender man, well dressed in long blue robes that brushed against the floor; a nobleman, and probably the most noble and honest in his standing.

"If I may, Sire, I live at Baysen, very close to the defences. I walk upon them often and they *are* certainly in ruin: there are solid great lumps of concrete sitting broken; there is no protection for any garrison. If the Black came now, they would simply moor to the side and gently step off. The soldiers will be sitting on masses of uneven concrete with no protection, and I agree with Captain Seer: they will *not* prevent an invasion force!"

King Colomune leant on his right arm, as he usually did when he was in thought, stressed whilst he tried to think of what to do. For once he wished Colonel Sarka was here. *Where is he*? he thought, still looking around. Suddenly the pride and power he had felt started to waver, and he was trembling again, and sweating.

"How have they come to be in this state?"

No one in the hall answered; they were not even sure who the question was directed at.

The silence continued, until Commander Thiamos stepped forward. "My King, I believe it is because we have never had use for them. They sit in a cove and defend a stretch of coast where there is nothing but water for leagues before it. No land has ever been found to the east of the sea. So, over time, the defences have been left to crumble."

The King then addressed Captain Seer again. "Can they be repaired?"

Captain Seer looked confused. "With respect, Sire, I am a mere soldier, and I have no knowledge of engineering."

Thiamos then stepped further forward. "If I may again, Sire, I took the liberty of summoning several groups of specialists to this council, some of whom are the best architects in the land. I trust you received the message?"

King Colomune hadn't, but was impressed with the initiative and nodded. But before Thiamos could carry on, there was a sudden uproar. The ambassadors from other kingdoms stepped forward, all arguing about their countries, asking why their architects had not been invited.

They started quarrelling in front of each other, with some bringing up old scores or irrelevant disagreements, just as an excuse to belittle each other or to start a conflict.

King Colomune knew he had to get this under control, so he did the only thing he could think of. He slapped a heavy hand down onto the armrest of his throne, the gold metal of his rings echoing around the hall. Immediately there was silence.

"My friends, some of you have come from afar. We are at a time of imminent attack and I suggest we leave old matters aside. As it is, the architects of Camia have been summoned, and I will hear no more of it!" he said sternly.

He felt content with his speech. Usually Colonel Sarka would intervene, or tell him to be quiet so that the arguments would escalate. He would never tell Colonel Sarka, but he enjoyed having control for a change.

Commander Thiamos gestured for the architects to be brought before King Colomune. Suddenly there was a huge rush from all around as the architects made their way down from the ascending steps or from the back of the hall, to make sure they were seen by their king. Fandorazz was amongst them, hunched down near the back, trying to stay out of sight, but was dragged by Hembel, who was almost on tiptoes with a wide grin on his face, his arm hanging down as he tried desperately to prop Fandorazz up.

All the architects were wearing their best clothes, standing proudly with scrolls of designs wrapped up under their arms. It was the moment they had all been waiting for. They had probably been practising their speeches with their wives so that they would stand out.

King Colomune regarded them. He knew what was coming: hours of debate and discussion, as each one put forward their ideas. *No!* he thought; with his newfound confidence, he turned to his aides sitting to one side of the hall, two very old, feeble men with scrolls shaking in their hands, stacked before them on the desk and crammed into shelves behind them.

"Who is the best architect in the land?"

After a short time of shuffling papers, whilst the architects were almost all on tiptoes with wide grins on their faces, hoping that it was one of them, one of the old men put a shaky finger up and stood up, hunchbacked. "Fandorazz of the house of Vimeon," he said in a frail voice.

Fandorazz's heart sank, and there was an audible sigh of despair from the other architects, who knew full well of his current capabilities. They all turned, looking for him, their posture very different from what it had been.

Fandorazz tried to cower down so he could not be seen; he felt panic gripping him, his heart boomed inside his chest, his hands started to sweat and every noise was magnified.

King Colomune looked at the group. "Fandorazz!" he bellowed.

But Fandorazz was still not willing to step forward, and cowered down, ignoring the call. Hembel tried to lift him up, but he acted as a dead weight.

Commander Thiamos stepped forward. "Fandorazz, you have been summoned by your King, now show yourself!"

Fandorazz opened his eyes and saw the architects around him part out of the way, with King Colomune now staring directly at him.

He stood up and walked forward, his legs feeling like jelly. He felt he could not move properly; he had never felt this inadequate.

"Y-Y-Yes, my King," he quavered, trying to get the words out, the architects behind him sniggering. Hembel looked on straight-faced, annoyed that Fandorazz had been picked, clenching his fists and gritting his teeth, thinking: *All the help I have given you over the years; why are you not bringing me forward with you?*

King Colomune looked at Fandorazz with some confusion. "So … you're the best?"

Fandorazz did not answer, almost feeling mocked by the question.

King Colomune had no time for this; he was said to be the best by his aides and he went with it. "I order you to go to the defences and repair them with haste; the Forty-Eighth, Three-Twenty-Ninth, Three-Thirty-Sixth and the entire workforce of Camia will be at your aid. Your orders are to repair them as quickly and strongly as possible, ready for battle."

Fandorazz closed his eyes; he felt light-headed and was not really taking in what was being said.

Seeing an opportunity, Hembel rushed forward and seized his arm. "Yes, Sire, apologies, but he has been taken ill. I will accompany him and we will begin following your instructions post-haste!" he said, with the most noble pronunciation he could manage.

Colomune gave a nod at Hembel as he pulled Fandorazz to the door, whilst everyone around him sniggered under their breath, the other architects looking on angrily.

As they left, King Colomune realized that he needed to tell the emissaries of the banners about his plan and tactics for their armies. But one of them stepped forward before he could speak. He was a large man, with dark skin, a black beard and an enormous stomach upon which he rested his hands; he stood very tall, probably the largest man he had ever seen, bigger than his father even. He towered above the crowd. He thought that he must have come from the deep south, probably Everost or Santamaz.

"Sire, we have all been called here, some of us from afar, but for what reason? What proof do you have of a threat of this proportion?"

All the other ambassadors nodded in agreement and stared intently at King Colomune for an answer.

Commander Thiamos stepped forward. "Thank you for your question, Chieftain Framlar. One of our regiments was attacked by a force we have come to believe are called the 'Black'. Our aides have looked into this further and found the attackers are part of an ancient power, an old dominion keen on conquering the world."

"And does anyone else know of this ... *Black*?" Framlar said, addressing the rest of the hall. He was not a friend of Camia, but a forced ally, someone who had gone to war against them and lost, and had to swear allegiance or risk being annihilated.

A few people muttered, but no one stepped forward.

He turned his attention back to King Colomune, pointing with his fist and raising his voice harshly. "Why is it that we should travel *so* far and give *so* much at the request of a king, who tells us little in return?"

There were noises of agreement from most in the hall – pretty much anyone who was not a Camion.

"Watch who you insult, Framlar!" Commander Thiamos said, stepping forward angrily.

Framlar, pleased that he had caused some doubt in the minds of the others, surrendered by showing the palms of his hands, and, with a smile and a bow of his head, sank back into the crowd.

Commander Thiamos, keen to clear any doubt, raised his voice. "We are facing an imminent attack! Little is known about this mysterious force, but what we do know is that they want to rule Ezazeruth, and you are part of it, regardless of whether you want to fight here or in your homeland. Either it will be today with us, or you are to stand alone."

The words seemed to sink in, and no one had anything to say.

King Colomune sat watching the drama cease, and thought it the most appropriate time to tell the hall of his plan.

"Thank you, Commander. I must add that, yes, we are facing a fight for salvation, and my council and I have come up with a plan that will maintain the peace of this world once and for all!" He clenched his fist for added drama, and everyone looked on intently. "I will be commanding your armies, and not waiting here for the Black to come to us, but taking the fight to them. It will be the last thing they will expect, we think we have found the coordinates for their land … and soon, we … the mighty alliance of Ezazeruth, will sail to a new destiny … a new salvation … and it shall be *they* who quiver as they hear the mighty armies of Ezazeruth sail across the sea, and end their regime once and for all!" he shouted, raising a fist in the air.

He expected cheers and shouts from the hall, and for them to think him as a god.

But what followed surprised him.

Silence, disbelief and shock; then, an uproar of anger followed. Messengers leapt from their seats to head back to their kingdoms; the ambassadors all marched forward, raising fists into the air in protest at this appalling act.

The palace guards circling King Colomune lowered their spears and stepped forward to push back the angry mob. King Colomune sat bewildered, staring at them, as they cursed his name. *This is not how it is meant to be!* he thought.

He grew angry … he was *their* king, their ruler, and they should love him, no matter what decision he made. "Get them out!" he boomed, his anger getting the better of him.

Amongst the shouting and chaos echoing in the hall, Atken turned to his king, and said calmly, "tea, Sire?"

Colomune was so angry, though, he did not hear him, and gripped the sides of his throne hard, making the wood creak.

The knights went about pushing people out, with no care for how they did it. They removed all non-Camions out of the hall; more knights came funnelling in from other doors, and pushed them outside and into the second level of the city.

King Colomune turned to his people; they were quiet.

Then Duchess Imara stepped forward, her blonde hair in a style that would be deemed exaggerated elsewhere: it was enormous. Her face was so covered in powdered make-up, he could barely make out her features. She was a large lady acting with an arrogant manner. In a very posh tone, she asked, "And what of our armies? Will they be going too?"

King Colomune despised her; she was nothing to Camia: she only had very wealthy ancestors and deemed herself more important than anyone else in the world. She even spoke down to him.

"No – the Camion military will be staying here to protect the city."

She showed great satisfaction in this, as did the rest of the hall. As long as they were protected, they didn't care about anyone else.

King Colomune looked to Commander Thiamos, who stood there clearly startled by the decision and trying to come to terms with it.

"Thiamos, is there any point in rebuilding the defences if we are taking the fight to them?"

Thiamos took a moment to speak; clearly he thought the attack was futile, but he could not bring himself to say it. "What ... ? Oh, yes, my King, God forbid that you fail on your ... magnificent quest, but we must be prepared!"

"What are the chances of them even attacking the defences? Couldn't they go south into Loria?" shouted a retired colonel in the crowd.

Again, Commander Thiamos stepped forward to answer. "It is unlikely; if the coordinates are correct for the Black's land, then the defences are the closest place for them to land such a large force, and from what we know about them they are not tactically skilled; their way of fighting was to take as much ground as they could, with little care for how many losses they had."

This started to settle in a bit more, and even the arrogant lords and ladies felt a shiver travel down their spines. One of them stepped forward, very slim, possessing an ill look. He had bony cheeks, his thin hair slicked back. "Thiamos!" he said as if it were a dirty word. "If your theory is correct, then why did they land at Coter Farol?" he said mockingly with a smug grin, turning haughtily to look at his friends.

Commander Thiamos turned to him. "That is an excellent question, Lord Fennell. Coter Farol is part of a cliff's edge to the south of Camia. It is easy for small skirmish groups to land without being seen, and for small craft to navigate between the shards of rock along the coastline. I'd imagine that they have landed as a scouting party, but for the mass bulk of an army that is coming, the only place will be the defences. Loria is too far, and they have to compete with strong tides and jagged rocks all along the south sea," he said calmly, trying to deliver himself well.

The smile from Lord Fennell's face completely vanished, and he sank back into the crowd under the mocking gaze of the others.

King Colomune became restless with their debates, and so rose from his throne and walked over to the large table with the map of Ezazeruth spread across it.

He started to feel lost without Colonel Sarka. He needed him to be here; again he looked around, hoping to see him, but he was still nowhere in sight.

But then thoughts of his daughter crowded in, as he noticed one of her guards standing to one side of the hall. He could not remember the last time he had seen her, let alone spoken to her, but in his absence her protection was paramount; if he were to fall in glorious battle, she would be the one to take up the Kingdom.

"Thiamos, who is your best swordsman?"

Without hesitation he said, "Pausanias, serving with the Knight Hawks, but he works very well with his brother Andreas, a skilled bowman."

"Good, they are now to guard my daughter … they obey her orders and go where she goes!"

"Yes, my Lord. Can I suggest that she be taken to Ambenol? It is an isolated fort, with good defences, and we can reach her quickly if she's in trouble."

"Yes, good idea – make preparations for her to leave immediately!" Colomune started to like the fact that people were freely shouting out ideas, and they were good ones too. *Why did Sarka always think this was a bad idea?* he thought.

General Drorkon suddenly appeared at the back of the hall. He stepped forward, pushing quickly through the crowd who were shocked at the sudden appearance of the general. "If I may, my King, with the current circumstances, might it be prudent to send a heavy infantry unit along with her to make sure she has added protection? Say, the Three-Thirty-Third?" he said, shrugging his shoulders and raising his hands as if it were a random selection. "They are, after all, the best regiment in Camia, and the best protection for your daughter."

Commander Thiamos spoke up. "General? I thought you were roaming the lands to the west?"

"You are correct, Commander, pardon me, my men are still doing so; I just came by the city to personally see an errand through and thought it best to see how things were going."

Just before Thiamos could challenge him as to what this errand was, King Colomune interrupted. "Excellent suggestion, General! Thiamos, make it so!"

Thiamos was startled. He wanted to speak up about sending his best regiment on what was effectively a babysitting mission, and was keen to press where General Drorkon had come from, but with a direct order he bowed and walked out of the palace, followed by his two personal guards. Drorkon again sneaked to the back of the hall, where he often stood looking out the window, when the lords pressed with their own matters, keen to get them out before Colonel Sarka returned and stopped them.

Standing in the corner of the hall, he looked around, but only saw the backs of people's heads, and slowly sneaked out of a secret door in the wall. It led down a small underground passageway through the hill the city was founded on. As he descended, he came out into a maze of tightly packed alleys and hidden doors through to the bottom of the city, towards the Three-Thirty-Third's barracks.

As he emerged from a secret door in the wall, and into a narrow alleyway in the slums of the city, five vagrants were sitting drinking. He walked towards them.

Startled by his sudden appearance, two of them stood up, half-leaning against a wall; one produced an old knife and the other a broken bottle. Drorkon was an elderly man but not a weak one, and he disarmed them with ease, leaving the others to sit back in fear as he stepped over them.

He carried on at a slight run, keen to get there before Thiamos, but he had to stay away from public places, making his task all the more difficult.

Suddenly, striding into a street, he pulled back and hid in a doorway, as he saw Colonel Sarka pacing past him. He looked stricken, clearly sweating, with fear and distress in his eyes.

He was walking from his office. Drorkon was not sure what had happened to him, but knew he could fall down and die for all he cared, for he knew of his contempt of his country, and his king.

When Sarka was out of sight, he again started running towards the barracks, the journey all the longer for having to take a detour. He eventually came in view of it.

He knew it would not be long until Commander Thiamos would arrive, and he had to act quickly.

The guard stood to attention when he approached the gate. Drorkon saluted and covered his face so that the guard could not tell it was him, and walked straight in.

Acting Captain Jadge was standing to one side of the yard, speaking to one of his corporals. When they saw Drorkon approaching, they saluted and stood to attention.

"Corporal, leave us!" Drorkon said abruptly.

The corporal scurried off as Drorkon took a quick look around to make sure all was clear from prying ears, and then stared Jadge firmly in the eyes.

"Captain, what I am about to ask you will go against all your morals, but you must do so for the sake of Ezazeruth, and *your* Captain!"

Jadge looked on ominously, wondering what was about to come out of the general's mouth.

"Your captain is in danger; he needs his regiment. You are about to be asked by Commander Thiamos to escort the King's daughter to Ambenol, but afterwards you must go and find your captain!"

Jadge stood perplexed for a moment, not saying anything about the fact that a cavalry general was asking him to desert. Almost with a laugh at the surreal order, he said, "Apologies, Sir, but are you asking me to go rogue?"

"I am!"

He gasped. "Sir, if I am instructed to by the King, or my commander; General Drakator, I will, but my allegiance is to them. I cannot break that."

Drorkon thought it was too much of a long shot to think that he would, and General Drakator was not nearby to speak to. He stepped closer, just staring deep into his eyes and almost touching his nose; removing his gauntlet, he put his hand on Jadge's face. Jadge went to pull back, but Drorkon spoke quickly and directly. "After you have left Ambenol, you must go to—"

As Drorkon removed his hand, Jadge stared vacantly, his eyes glazed white. Drorkon put his gauntlet back on. Just then he heard Commander Thiamos talking to the guard at the gate. He stepped back into a shadowed area between a hut and a wall, out of sight of Commander Thiamos. As Jadge woke from a trance, he looked at Drorkon hiding in the shadowed corner with nowhere to go, then turned to see the Commander approaching him, and then looked back at where General Drorkon was; in his place was a hazy, purple apparition.

Chapter Eleven
A Jovial Atmosphere

Hilclop lay curled up in a ball on the ground, no longer hearing Havovatch shouting his name. He lay there trying to move but couldn't; he could feel the messages from his brain going to his arms saying *pick up your knife*, but there was no reaction. He just lay there with tears streaming down his face. He could not muster the strength to move. He started by trying to open one eye, but it was as if he was not in control of his body.

Thoughts of his home and his family took over his mind. He hated his family, but they gave him the closest thing to love he got from anyone. He didn't want to be a soldier any more; he wanted to be home, and the sudden shock of reality gripped at his chest. His family hated him at home, but at least he was safe.

He slowly moved his hand around the ground, trying to feel for his knife, but he did not know where it was, just the soft feeling of the long green grass caressing at his body, and then it started ...

He remained trembling where he lay; the ground was shaking. *This is it*! he thought.

The rest of the creatures were now on their way to finish him off, and this would be how he would die: a coward, a pathetic human unworthy to exist in the world, and as much as he hated it, he accepted it.

The tremors got more frequent, then he could hear shouts and battle cries, but they were not coming from the direction of the creatures. They were coming from the bottom of the hill he was on. He looked down quickly in surprise to see three battalions of cavalry charging towards him in the dawn light, and he jumped up and stood there, astonished. Where had they come from?

They galloped straight past him and over the summit of the hill in several triangle formations.

As they passed him, Hilclop ran over the hill and looked down at Havovatch and the others. They were completely surrounded, and alive, but only just.

Fighting back-to-back, they were just swinging their weapons, trying desperately to keep the creatures back, and he could tell they were exhausted. Their blows were cumbersome, and their faces showed pain and fatigue. Buskull was the only one who did not appear exhausted, and anything that came within his axe blows met its fate.

The charge of the cavalry was tremendous, their hooves thumping into the ground, the cries from their riders echoing in the hills; but the creatures were so intent on trying to kill the unit, they did not even realize they were being charged by three thousand mounted soldiers. When they looked back and saw the onslaught, however, they instantly retreated as fast as they could.

Buskull, Feera, Mercury and Havovatch either fell to their knees or hunched over with exhaustion, and tried to regain their breath. Buskull was covered in sweat. It was steaming off him, his vest dark grey from the moisture, his shoulders rising with each breath.

The cavalry passed them and ran up the hill, cutting and stamping the beasts down as they went. When the cavalry passed it became clear how many the four of them had killed. There were at least fifty bodies lying on the ground, though it was hard to tell, as some of them were so badly maimed it was unclear what were complete corpses and what were not.

Hilclop nervously approached them, trying to put on an air of innocence with a weak smile, trying to look impressed by their accomplishments. The others had nothing to say to him, though; they stared at him, panting with sheer rage. The first thing they learnt in their training was that they always stood by each other – it was their code.

Havovatch stood up straight and walked towards him, staring intently. He stopped for a moment, staring into Hilclop's eyes, trying to find some justification in why he did not help them, but left them to die. But there was none, and he walked away, followed by the others.

Just then an elderly man trotted over the hill, with eight heavily armed bodyguards around him. At first Havovatch did not recognize him, but as he approached, he noticed that it was the general who had freed them back in Persa a few days earlier.

Havovatch walked over to him and saluted, as did the rest of his unit except for Hilclop, who was standing behind them wiping his face with his sleeve.

"We must stop meeting like this, Captain," the general said with an amused expression, "you certainly took a beating here."

"Yes, thank you, Sir, we are glad that you came when you did!" Havovatch said, still panting heavily.

The general laughed loudly. "We had scouts out following that very group. We were tracking them as we wanted to know where they were heading, but soon as you were being chased our scouts returned and naturally we came to your rescue."

"Well, Sir, you have our gratitude, and if you ever need our help we will be happy to oblige!"

The general regarded Hilclop and pointed with his head towards him. "What about him, the boy? He was lying on the hillside during your attack; is he one of yours? He looks remarkably like the deserter we have on the run at the moment."

Havovatch had every intention of saying that he was. He was happy to hand him over to them. He could then be rid of the inept boy who could be taken back to the city to stand trial, and he could get on with his mission absent of any more delays.

But when he went to open his mouth to say yes, he couldn't.

"No ... Sir," he said uncertainly; his unit shot him a baffled look. "He is a mere peasant we found in a village not far from here; we told him to take cover before the attack."

The general kept his gaze and nodded, "Very well. Are you talking about the village that was burnt down, east from here, about twenty or so leagues away?"

"Yes, Sir, the town had been set upon by creatures which we found evidence of."

"We came upon that terrible sight as well, and we tracked the group, only to find it was your attackers."

Havovatch sighed. "Are the banners not protecting the area?"

The general let out a sigh. "The King has them all heading for the defences, so we are patrolling this area instead."

"Why are they all going there?" Havovatch demanded, a bit more forcefully than he had intended.

"At this moment it is no business of yours, Captain – concentrate on your current affairs!" the general said sternly. "I am General Drorkon of the Two-Twenty-Eighth Heavy Cavalry, by the way." He held out his hand to take Havovatch's in a warrior's grip.

Havovatch took his wrist and was surprised at how firmly he held his arm. He retrieved his parchments from his pouch and passed them to him. "These are my orders, Sir."

Drorkon showed him the palm of his hand. "I have no need to see them, Captain; they are your orders, not mine."

Havovatch thought it strange that he did not want to see them. He was told that he always had to show his orders to those above him; he was sure that he *must* know of his mission, but he wanted to know more. Maybe he could be able to shed light on these mysterious knights.

Drorkon regarded Hilclop again. "Do you wish for us to take the peasant from you? It would assist you in speeding up your mission."

Havovatch looked over at Hilclop who was standing there silently, his face still wet from crying. It was a very tempting offer, but, as stupid as Hilclop was, he felt there was something in him. "No, thank you, Sir," he said. "He has family in a village along our route; I swore to get him back safely and I'd rather stick to my oath personally."

"Very admirable, Captain. You must be exhausted from your ordeal. May I offer my tent to you and your unit? We will lend you some horses tomorrow to help speed you along your way, and I won't take no for an answer!" General Drorkon said with an expectant smile on his face.

Havovatch liked the idea, apart from the horses ... he hated riding them. He purposely failed his cavalry training so he could get into his preferred choice, the heavy infantry. But, looking back at his unit, he saw that they were still panting and eager to rest. Turning back to General Drorkon, he said, "We would be delighted, Sir!"

Drorkon's face lit up. "Splendid!" He spoke to one of his guards, who trotted away in the direction they had come, they shortly returned with four already saddled horses. They all mounted up, with Hilclop sitting behind Buskull and keeping quiet. Feera jumped up with ease and made himself comfortable. Havovatch took a breath and made a poor attempt at getting himself up, but no one noticed Mercury, holding his ribs tightly. He punishingly pulled himself onto his saddle, wincing at the excruciating pain. But, once on, he did not want anyone to know about it, and fought off the urge to show the anguish on his face.

At a canter, they rode north with the might of the Two-Twenty-Eighth around them, and they went off into the dawn of day.

It was an interesting sight: three thousand men all camped around fires or lying under carts in the ravine of two hills. Their horses were tethered to sticks hammered into the ground. Red tents were erected close together in columns along the side of the hill; most had candle lights inside, showing silhouettes of soldiers reminiscing with their comrades or reading.

They had spent the day finding a decent place to make camp. Havovatch was horribly saddle-sore, cursing anyone who rode horses, and horses themselves.

He stood outside his tent, trying to get the feeling back in his legs, and regarded the cavalry regiment around him. They seemed different from the infantry; no one seemed to have quarrels or problems, and they all laughed and joked together. They seemed to be in a joyful and blissful mood, accepting orders without question from those in authority and fulfilling them to the best of their capabilities.

They seemed to dedicate all their energies to even the most minor of tasks they were given regardless of praise, and others who were not even part of the order would help without question. If anything, these were the perfect soldiers. And Havovatch chewed his lip at trying to think of a way to make his regiment as efficient.

He noticed that Feera looked uneasy around them, though, standing to one side with Mercury and looking uncomfortable. The Two-Twenty-Eighth was not his old cavalry unit, but Havovatch knew that it must be hard for him to be surrounded by the very people he wanted to be a part of. He thought how Feera should really be up on those beasts fighting the good fight, as he was born to; and swore an oath to himself that when this was all over, he was certainly going to see what he could do about that.

The perimeter of the makeshift camp was guarded constantly with scouts riding out into the darkness of the hills, with tall torches set upon their saddles like bearers. He could see them off in the distance, like fireflies fluttering about in the darkness. Sentries were posted at the highest points of the hills on lookout, and stood with notched arrows, constantly scouring their surroundings. The perimeter consisted of men patrolling and hammering torches into the ground, twenty or so yards away from the edge of the camp.

Buskull was given a tent, but he erected it at the very edge of the encampment, away from any fires or other tents, isolating himself. The sentries, without judging, set themselves further around him, although he went around and asked for their torches to be put out as the flames seemed to irritate him. Havovatch noticed his face for the first time as Buskull looked at the flames. He stared at it for a moment; it was a very short moment, but his eyes closed and he looked away. Sergeant Metiya was right; he did look pained by it.

Turning, Havovatch saw a neatly dressed officer approaching. "Captain, the general is ready for supper, and he requests your presence."

Havovatch nodded, and shouted over to Mercury, Hilclop and Feera, "Mercury, go and get Buskull; I'll meet you in the general's tent."

The general was in a far larger tent, set at the centre of the camp. When they entered, they saw that he was sitting at a long, solid, wooden table with a lot of officers crammed around it. All were laughing, drinking and swapping stories of their past experiences.

As they entered, everyone stood up and fell silent. The soldiers playing waiters for the evening brought chairs over for them, and the officers made space. It was a very jovial atmosphere.

General Drorkon told everyone to sit, and stood with one hand holding his pipe and the other holding a goblet of red wine.

"My friends," he said cheerfully to Havovatch and his unit, "may I introduce you to my men? They are fine cavalrymen, but I dare say don't play cards with them because you can hold a full suit and they will bring out a fifth."

There was sudden uproar of laughter, cheers and applause from the merry men. But the laughter died and Drorkon started to introduce his officers. "These two large fellows either side of me are Gwerob and Plinth; they're my commanders. Plinth has recently just had a baby boy, who we are looking forward to having in the ranks soon." Again there was thunderous applause and shouting as they all threw their tankards into the air, splashing their drinks, and patted Plinth on his huge shoulders. One officer even shouted, "At his age, he would be a better officer than his dad as well," and, despite Plinth's serious expression, everyone laughed. Havovatch also recognized him as the officer who had entered his cell to get him out in Persa. He thought the name 'Plinth' was fitting, for his build held the shape of a plinth and he could probably hold a statue on his shoulders, he was so big.

Drorkon then pointed to three thinner men sitting to the right of the table. "Those fine fellows are Captains: Minch, Hereson and Avort; they're in charge of a battalion of a thousand, man and horse each."

They toasted, giving a nod.

"And we come to the lower ranks, my lieutenants." He pointed to eight men spread around the table. "My Second Officers." Three men stood up and raised their mugs. "My sergeants." Ten men stood up and toasted towards them. "And we have three new additions to my regiment." Three young and nervous-looking boys stayed seated but nodded over at them.

"Every evening I have my men dine with me so that I can get to know them; we alternate each day," he said proudly.

Havovatch had not really been to a function this formal before, and was not sure what to do or say; sitting with his arms under the table, he looked at the fine men around him.

"I thank you all for your hospitality, and for saving our lives earlier this evening."

"Cheers!" They all shouted throwing their drinks into the air again before he could finish.

Just then, Buskull and Mercury wandered into the marquee, and both sat at opposite sides of the table where space was made for them.

Everyone tucked into eating the enormous buffet in front of them. There was no snatching or squabbling. One man would elect himself, carve some meat, and feed all around him with generous portions before putting anything on his own plate.

The waiters continually refilled everyone's drinks when they got below half-full.

One of the captains, in a lull in the conversation, peered over at Havovatch and made eye contact. "Congratulations on your early promotion, Captain Havovatch – it took me eight years in the infantry before I could get a promotion to corporal, five further to sergeant, then another six before the young general here saw my potential and took me on as captain, skipping lieutenant all together, and into the cavalry of the Two-Twenty-Eighth!"

Suddenly everyone stood, including General Drorkon, and raised their cups into the air. "To the Two-Twenty-Eighth!" they bellowed in unison before sitting back down to carry on eating.

"Thank you, I must admit it was a shock, but a pleasant one at that," Havovatch said when all had quietened down.

General Drorkon sat across from Havovatch. He had a generous portion of everything on the table on his plate, but he just sat with a smile on his face and one leg slung over the other, happily watching his men around him, and sipping from his goblet.

Havovatch remembered something that was bugging him. "General, I hope you don't mind me asking, but how did you know that we had been arrested in Persa a few days ago?"

The whole table fell silent as all looked at General Drorkon. Most of his officers looked at him, startled, as if he was hiding something; it added to Havovatch's suspicions.

General Drorkon kept his smile. "Well, we were passing through the town, I went to see an old tavern friend of mine and he was clearing up rather a lot of mess. I asked the old boy and a few others in the tavern what had happened. I must say that many unpleasant things were said about yourselves, but I instructed my men to go about asking the surrounding neighbours, and we got some different explanations as to what had gone on.

"I went and spoke to the Commander of the town's watch about the reasons you had for defending yourselves and the fact that you were on a mission from the King! But, to my dismay, he refused to release you, so I pulled rank and let you and your fine fellows out of the murky dungeons in which you were kept," he said toasting the air. Again, all the men, including Buskull, who seemed to be aware of their customs, threw their drinks into the air and cheered.

Havovatch was pleased with the strange coincidence, but he could not help but think there was a lot more to it than he realized.

As the dinner wore on, Havovatch felt much more relaxed, and everyone was joining in conversation with the people sitting next to them, whilst a talented young soldier played the flute in the background.

There were no disagreements amongst the officers ... everyone thought on the same wavelength and, despite their ranks, each got on amicably with the next.

Now and again a scout would enter the marquee and report to General Drorkon, who would listen intently and again have that pleasant smile on his face. He would touch the scout's arm and give praise, and then dismiss him.

Havovatch wondered how a man could be so positive all of the time; it was no wonder his men were all in such high spirits. Credit was given for the smallest of tasks, and in return they wanted to make sure that they honoured and respected their general.

Havovatch spoke to one of the sergeants sitting next to him. "Bren? Why does everyone keep toasting and cheering?"

Bren spoke with his mouth full of bread. He was a friendly man, but he did not look it, with scars on every exposed bit of skin, battle-hardened and strong. "It is our custom, and a bit of superstition. Being heavy cavalry we often ride into unpleasant areas, get surrounded and have to fight our way out. A lot of men die. So, when there is good news, we toast and we cheer, to recognize the good news and keep our spirits up, and in hope that it will bring good fortune."

"I see," said Havovatch. He had not noticed anything like this within his regiment, and he wished they did the same.

"But ..." said Bren, continuing, "we also have a symbol of pride; whenever one mentions the regiment, we have to respect it!"

"In what way?" asked Havovatch.

Bren grinned. "What is the name of our regiment?" he asked in a way as if he had forgotten.

Havovatch looked confused. "Well, the Two-Twenty-Eighth!"

Suddenly everyone stood, their chests out, drinks in the air and they shouted in unison, "To the Two-Twenty-Eighth!" before sitting back down and carrying on as if nothing had happened.

"I see," Havovatch said, grinning, whilst Bren coughed out his bread with laughter.

Over the course of the rest of the evening, most of the officers gave their goodnights, or left to inspect their men. They helped each other drunkenly out of the marquee; Havovatch could still hear them laughing as they made their way into the night.

Soon it was just Havovatch and his unit with Plinth, Gwerob, Drorkon and one or two of the captains and sergeants. Drorkon did not seem tired, but still kept talking with his officers and soon caught Havovatch's gaze.

Havovatch thought it a prudent time to bring up how he seemed to know things about their mission even though he did not read his orders. "Sir, I couldn't help but notice that you seem to know of the quest we are undertaking. Were you present when the King came up with the idea?"

Drorkon lent forward. "Yes, certainly."

He stood up and looked at his officers. "Gentlemen, thank you for your hospitality tonight."

The officers knew this was his polite way of asking them to leave, and they all did so without question. As they passed the unit, they all shook hands firmly.

Havovatch noticed that Feera was in his element; all seemed to want to say an extra goodnight to him. He was certainly going to have words with the general about a transfer for him now!

When they had all gone, Drorkon walked over to a large, wooden chest with golden edges. Havovatch couldn't help but think he had seen a chest like that recently, but could not place where.

Mercury and Buskull went and sat next to the others, so they were all sitting together, waiting for the general to return to the table.

He brought over a very old animal skin; Havovatch thought it to be mountain wolf or maybe snow tiger. It was so old that it was faded almost beyond recognition. As he unravelled it, there was an old delicate parchment that was unrolled within. Words of some sort were scribbled over it in strange patterns.

General Drorkon leant on the table and looked at each of them intently. "Gentlemen, what I have here few people in the world have ever seen or heard about, and I beg for your discretion." The five of them nodded without question.

Satisfied with their response, he picked up his pipe and stood up straight with his other hand behind his back. "History," he began, "is very easy to forget, especially for we Camions, who are so intent on evolving and looking ahead, we tend to forget to look back at our own past. Even the most important things in history have been forgotten, without a care in the world as to what happened to whom, or who saved whom from what. I say that we must learn from our past so that we do not make the same mistakes in our future!" He finished by toasting the air with his pipe and closing his eyes, with a slightly solemn expression on his face.

He then sat down, delicately put his hand on either side of the parchment and squinted. "Apologies, gentlemen: nearly forty years I have been in the army, and now has come a time when my eyesight is not what it once was."

He took a few moments to read and then took in a deep breath, smiled and rolled up the parchment. He leant back on his chair, crossed one leg over the other and respectfully put his hands together, holding his knee. He looked at the eager men before him, but he mainly fixed his eyes on Havovatch.

A long time ago, after tales become riddled and history was too long ago to be passed down the generations, a mysterious new entity came to the land; it is not known what they were, where they came from, or what they wanted.

Shape-shifting into beasts and creatures of their choice, they watched over mankind with fascination, about how we thought and lived.

But, at the same time, they were sickened by other parts of our existence: fighting, killing, war, destruction, and callousness towards one another! Eventually, they had had enough and intervened.

They took possession of the native creatures for each country, and they spoke to us telepathically and expressed their wish to help us.

To help win our trust, they used small amounts of magic to help grow crops, to form clouds to rain in drought regions, and to help passages of ships to safely get to their destinations; and we accepted them. And some humans, in return, became their students, and were taught magic and became warlocks and witches, helping shape the world with them.

They were seen as gods, and we worshipped the animals they possessed in their honour, and as such, named them Ikarions after the gods in Ezazeruth at the time, as man thought that they had descended from the heavens and appeared in physical form.

The Ikarions helped to guide humans and settle their differences with logic and reason, and in turn this led to the closest thing to peace in Ezazeruth since time was remembered.

But not all of the Ikarions were of good will …

One, named Agorath by his human followers after an evil creature of folklore, broke away from the peaceful ways of his kin, and, taking the shape of a scaly demon of his own design, took upon humans who did not share the ways of living through good and kindness, and set about to control all of Ezazeruth.

With sickened men, deranged women and an abomination of creatures he created, war was wreaked upon the human race!

But his lust for power was insatiable, and he knew that he would not be able to fight against his own.

With his scaly form, he sought out an ancient legend from the deep, and, sinking into the ocean in the Gulf of Pera, he searched through the depths of the sea, and after seven long days he eventually found the misty blue stone he was searching for: Beriial, said to contain a power no one can reckon with.

With it mounted upon his bladed staff, he led his mighty armies against the world.

Alone, the Ikarions tried to stop him as he attacked their countries, but with the Beriial he was far too powerful.

So they resorted to other means, and, uniting all countries together into an alliance, they rallied as one in the hope of destroying Agorath and his following.

But Agorath was cunning, causing madness and manipulating disagreements between kings and leaders; and with friction now between themselves war was deflected from him and Ezazeruth quickly plunged into chaos.

The Ikarions could do nothing to stop his savagery … except for one thing.

Joining together in a powerful force, they fought on the tops of the northern mountains against Agorath, and, after five days of ferocious battle, the Ikarions won.

Agorath was crippled; the stone was snapped from his staff and disappeared from legend. The blade was blunted and melted down, with the metal used to make four mystical weapons, called The Castion Swords, said to contain a power that would pass mystical abilities to their owners.

As for Agorath, well, he lost his form … he lost his will … and what was left of his armies were scattered south into the Misty Desert.

What was left of this crude abomination was cast onto a decrepit ship and forced to leave the land, the Ikarions casting a spell on the vessel so it could never return.

Agorath lay on the decking of the ship, paralysed and alone; he could just see the land become a thin line on the horizon before it disappeared. Constantly looming over him were storm clouds following him wherever he went; he went mad with the dull wetness, and for months he could do nothing to stop it.

Peace was once again restored to Ezazeruth, and man enjoyed the pleasures of the natural world together, and the threat of Agorath was a distant memory, not to be heard of again.

Or so we thought …

Agorath trapped the Ikarions and took them from Ezazeruth. But, soon after, a force so dark and powerful came to the land, in which no one was prepared for it, and Ezazeruth fell to the mercy of a dark army, called … the Black.

One by one, each country fell to their savagery.

Women, children, animals, crops, cities – everything was destroyed.

But, eventually, the last kingdoms in the world settled their differences, and took up arms together in an alliance bigger than has been seen, neither before nor since.

And they marched on the dark storm crossing their lands.

Narrowly they came to victory, but at a huge cost to the diverse world, with uncountable races, environments, tribes and civilizations wiped out.

Ezazeruth was left in ruin.

Unfortunately, Agorath escaped once again, and the world was still fearful of his threat.

So, to stop him, three armies were created to protect the world, and named 'the Knights of Ezazeruth'. Each was ten thousand strong and named for its particular skill: the Oistos, who were the finest archers, the Ippikós, fearsome cavalry, and the mighty Xiphos, the best infantry you will ever see: and they waited for the dark sorcerer to return.

But he never did, nor the hateful creatures he created, and over time the knights began to die.

So the then-King of Camia, Afthadus, forced a warlock to curse them with everlasting long life, and, unable to change Afthadus's mind, they left and scattered themselves across the world.

Few have met them, and those who have would not know of the pain and torment they have had to endure; they live on to this day, hateful of everyone within this world, for they let it happen, and could not stop them from being cursed. They do not want to be found, and do not want to fulfil their oaths.

The five of them sat motionless, staring at Drorkon in awe. This was one of the most perplexing but interesting stories they had ever been told, and their mission was to help this legend come to pass.

No one knew who should speak first, or what to say; there was a deathly silence in the marquee. It began to rain outside, and the gentle patter of raindrops was the only noise in the still tent.

Havovatch had never heard a story like it; it seemed so exaggerated, more like a myth or something of fantasy.

"S-Sir, if these stories are not known, then how do you know of it?"

General Drorkon smiled and looked down for a moment. "That is a story for another night, Captain."

Then Hilclop spoke. "Sir? I have seen little with regards to magic, a coin appearing from behind my ear, maybe, or a simple card trick, but are you expecting me to believe that men are living today that are thousands of years old … and that they cannot even be killed?"

The others naturally got annoyed with the manner in which Hilclop asked his questions, but he did bring up a valid point, and all stared intently for an answer.

"Listen, young man: anyone can be killed, you just have to find their weakness. The knights are cursed with immortality but they can still be killed in combat. There is no spell that can stop that, but they will not die of disease, age or illness."

"But the magic?" Hilclop pressed.

"There are some things in this world beyond our understanding, but anything is possible, and I tell you that this legend is not a folk tale made up for children to keep them in their beds at night. This is a true story about courageous men and women who live on to this day."

They sat still, deep in thought, trying to process the story, so many questions going through their minds. Even Buskull, who always wore the same serious expression, seemed to be inquisitive.

The general broke the silence, staring directly at Havovatch. "These are not just mere fighting men, Havovatch: they are the most elite warriors the world has ever seen, and they will not be easily or readily persuaded to fulfil their oaths, but know this: if you fail, Agorath will win this war … and he has already started!"

Havovatch, suddenly burdened by an almost physical feeling of responsibility, did not know how to answer. He felt his head nodding, but thought that it was just his natural military way of taking on instructions he was given; inside, he felt as though he was being ripped apart.

"And what will happen if Agorath wins this war?" put Hilclop.

"Death," General Drorkon simply said. "The world as you know will become unrecognizable. The carcasses of men will line the roads, the sky will dull from blue to grey, trees, birds, wildlife, it will all go, and what will be left will be complete and utter chaos. Any man who is alive will be a slave to his vermin, put through horrific rituals, and will beg for death."

Hilclop shuddered.

General Drorkon yawned widely after the deeply emotional story, and went to conclude. "All of you, I know this is a lot to take in, but you must understand that fate has brought you all here. You will all be playing a part in history to stop this evil from prevailing."

He then stood up. "Gentlemen, I can tell you no more. My men will give you the best horses we can offer tomorrow morning, and they will see to your weapons and replenish your ration packs. Can I suggest that at mid-morning you leave in the direction of the Impenetrable Forest, and whatever you do, do not mention to the commanders that you have spoken to me! For I fear it could cause more problems than you already have."

Filled with even more questions, Havovatch stood up, followed by the others, Hilclop slightly behind.

"Sir, thank you for your hospitality tonight, and thank you for your words of wisdom; we will do our best!"

Drorkon smiled. "I know you will." He then turned to one side, left into a compartment of the tent and closed the flap.

Havovatch quietly motioned for them all to leave, but he took one last look at the chest and realized that it was the same as the one in Colonel Sarka's office.

Drorkon paced around inside for a moment, rubbing his forehead; a tear ran down his cheek as he thought to himself: *By Gods, it's been too long; I hope this boy can do it! For the sake of this world, for the sake of those men and women, for the sake of every innocent soul, I hope he can do it*! – his body language fitting with his thoughts, clenching his fist, wanting to take his frustration out on something. So long he had waited, so long he had had to plan and do things against his will, all up to this point. He just hoped he had done enough.

He got into bed, despite still wearing his armour, and he fell into a deep slumber almost instantly … whilst unbeknown to him, a bright, white light appeared over his head, and the sound of thunder rumbled in the distance.

Chapter Twelve
Make for High Rocks

Havovatch woke late in the morning, in a narrow red tent. He was given sleeping clothes whilst his were cleaned before he turned in. It was the most comfortable sleep he had had in a while.

At first he did not even remember the night before, and took a few moments to adjust.

The sun shone through a thin gap between the flaps of the tent entrance, and a warm, gentle breeze passed through, tickling his skin. It made him feel more awake and relaxed at the same time.

As he sat up he saw his tunic hanging from the beam near the entrance; on the floor by his feet was his armour, with his helmet sat atop of it, as if mimicking a soldier inside.

He smiled to himself, grateful for the help he had received from General Drorkon, and he started to remember every detail about what he had told him the night before. He sat up on one arm and rubbed his face; the burden of being captain and looking after an entire regiment was not on his mind any more, but the responsibility and pressure was now upon him to complete his mission for the sake of the world.

He got dressed quietly and stepped out into the warmth of the summer morning. There were few clouds in sight, with blue sky as far as his eyes could see; the sun was shining brightly in the sky, illuminating the green hills around him. The rain from the night before had long since evaporated, and the clean smell of pollen was in the air.

Across the camp, men were grooming horses, sharpening weapons or on lookout, some even still sleeping. He saw Buskull pacing around the perimeter of the camp, dressed and ready to go. He started to wonder if he ever slept at all, for he never saw him go to sleep, nor saw him wake up.

Stretching, he went to wake the others but heard someone shout his name. He turned to see the general approaching. "I hope your sleep was pleasant?" he said cheerfully.

Havovatch grinned. "Very much so, thank you, Sir."

The general smiled and patted him on the shoulder, but Havovatch still had questions.

"Sir, I really am grateful for what you have done for us. I just hope I can do what is expected of me."

Drorkon put his arm around Havovatch and walked him along the tents. "My boy, we all have hard times ahead, but focus on the present, and take each situation as it comes."

Then he nodded with his head at Hilclop's tent, leant closer to Havovatch and whispered, "The boy ... he has good in him, and he will shine one day. You have shown the virtues of a leader by sticking by him, so don't let him go!"

Havovatch looked into the general's eyes and saw his wisdom, and knew that he knew all along that Hilclop was the deserter. He nodded; Drorkon grinned back and thrust an object into his hand, and, patting Havovatch on the back, he walked away.

Havovatch looked down and saw a small knife with a red and golden handle. Again the blade cut his finger as it rested within his palm. He placed it in the pocket of his body armour and opened the tent entrances to wake each member of the unit. He then sat in front of his own tent whilst his men got ready and read his orders. After speaking with the general, his orders seemed obsolete now, and after looking at them for the two-hundredth time from when he had received them, he took in a breath and looked around, as if the answer would jump out at him. He had to think of a different strategy for confronting the commanders, but remembering his history was even worse. To think that his own country had betrayed the men who swore to protect them! He grew up learning how amazing Camia was, and that it was the best country in the world because of the ways the Camions lived and ruled, unlike the rest of the savages who lived within the world. This was the other reason he joined the infantry: to protect their name and stop the world from defying them. But what he was told went against all that, and hearing the truth about their past, covered up by centuries of corruption and deceit, made him feel sick.

Buskull approached ... he had been given a new grey undergarment with a golden stitching around the edges; it pulled tightly against his frame.

"Captain, I have being doing my checks, we should have a clear run west ahead of us, and I sense no problems." Havovatch started to wonder what his senses were.

Mercury and Feera appeared, not only looking smart but also like soldiers: presentable, equipped and fearsome.

Hilclop was the last to get up; the others were standing in a huddle talking as he approached.

They looked up at him; he had been given a scouting cavalry uniform, a chain-mail vest with leather body armour, a long spear with a straight blade and a short sword, and a small bow with a few arrows. He beamed at them with his new appearance. He now felt like someone, someone who was important, and walked with a swagger as if he finally felt his part in life. He also had a lot more admiration for Havovatch, who had stuck up for him the night before.

Havovatch knew that General Drorkon had done everything he could to help them now; it was up to them to fulfil their purpose.

But, every time he thought about it, his heart missed a beat, and before he could dwell on it any longer an officer approached, gesturing gracefully at some horses being brought by five soldiers.

Five beautiful horses. One was white, two black, one grey and one brown; they were all ready to ride. One of the black horses, much bigger than the others, had been given longer stirrups for Buskull so that he could sit more comfortably.

"When you have no need for them, they will find their own way home. Just let them loose," said the officer, running a hand up its face to its poll.

Havovatch nodded; the officer raised his hand to shake his, and that of each man in turn. "Good luck, gentlemen."

A little perplexed at the attention they were receiving, they all mounted.

Havovatch did not sit down, but stood up on his stirrups, as the pain between his legs was too uncomfortable to bear, but he knew that with this new mode of transport they could at least cover some good distance, and get ahead of schedule.

He looked at his map and checked the route they wanted to go, north by north-west.

Then, he kicked his heel into the horse. At first the horse did nothing. Feera was the only one who was moving.

Havovatch sighed, and again dug his heel into the beast, but there was still no reaction.

"Move, you filthy rekon!" Havovatch shouted.

But, as Feera passed, he smacked the flat of his hand on the horse's rump and it set off at a trot, a bit too quick for Havovatch, who looked rather cumbersome as he was jerked around, taking a while to get used to the ride … and the pain in his legs.

As they did so, the Two-Twenty-Eighth stopped what they were doing and gathered, lining the route out of the camp in praise of the unit.

At the end of the camp, General Drorkon was mounted on his magnificent grey steed. He said nothing; standing back straight and helmet on, he saluted Havovatch and his men.

"Eyes right!" Havovatch shouted as they returned the gesture of respect. And, as they cantered away, the Two-Twenty-Eighth cheered and shouted words of encouragement at the unit as if they were legends riding off to their destiny.

For two days they had ridden along the Plains of Fernara – a nearly barren wasteland, claimed to no flag and no nation, it acted as a good wedge between Camia and Loria, which had been at war for years.

Emiros, the lawless folk who lived in Fernara, were said to prowl the area, although the unit had luckily not come into contact with these dangerous folk during the last few days.

Much of the land was covered quickly with their steeds, and they had left the hills and border of Camia far behind them, now travelling along flat plains as far as the eye could see. There were sporadic shards of rocks with small caves or caverns, but mostly the area was filled with yellow grass, mud and the occasional river that ran a murky brown, and put them off filling their waterskins. They came across a stone fortress and some derelict houses, long since abandoned, weathered and falling apart. But they steered clear, in case there were Emiros hiding within.

It was so desolate, Havovatch could see why Camia and Loria had not claimed the land. There was nothing here that would benefit either of them, and so they let the Emiros have it. But he knew that, if ever they wanted it, the Emiros would be no match for the strength of the Camion army. He smiled to himself at the pride of being part of it, but the corners of his mouth fell as he remembered their dark and dirty past.

As they rode along, Mercury and Hilclop were talking to each other. Havovatch could not tell what they were saying, but Mercury said something to Hilclop, who grinned and kept looking behind him at Buskull.

Then Hilclop reined in his mount and waited for Buskull to catch up. He said something to him as he passed but Buskull ignored him; then, as he caught up with Mercury, one of his mighty arms came up and punched him in the stomach.

Feera burst out laughing, and for a moment Havovatch turned to hide his broad grin.

Mercury stayed on his mount and tried to gasp for air.

Feera seemed to be enjoying himself. He sat with a perfect posture and almost pride as they rode along, his chest out, chin up and holding onto the reins with one hand whilst his other held at his waist.

Mercury regarded him, and, keen to move on from his humiliation, coughed out a sentence. "Did I hear that you were in the cavalry once?"

Feera's entire composure changed at the question. "Yes!" he said solemnly.

"Why did you leave?"

Havovatch was about to turn and tell Mercury to mind his own business, but Feera spoke first. "Some things in this world you cannot control, and for me it was one man, and I hope that one day I will have more control over him than he had over me."

"Who's that?" Mercury said fascinated.

"Mercury!" Havovatch called over.

But Feera carried on. "Sarka!" he spat. "Our paths will cross again one day, and the next time the blade will be in my hand, and I won't be sticking it in his back … I want him to see my face!" he said in a low quaver.

Mercury went to say more, but saw Havovatch mimicking his head being cut off with his hand, and realized he was pushing into unwanted territory.

It was too awkward to say anything else. They all rode on in silence, keen to let the dust settle. But Havovatch wondered if he should challenge Feera, as he had just threatened to kill a senior officer. He did not have much feeling for Colonel Sarka, but he felt he could not let insubordination go. He had quite come to like Feera, and decided to sit on it for now, but if he said anything again, he knew it was his duty to stop it.

At midday, four days after leaving General Drorkon's camp, Havovatch slowed his unit to a canter.

He kept checking his map to ensure they were going in the right direction, and thought they were nearly through Fernara and would soon be approaching Loria. He knew its borders were heavily guarded by a long wall spanning from the coast at the Gulf of Pera, up to the

Plains of Futor. But he was heading for the Impenetrable Forest, which was before the wall.

He started to relax, far from the goings-on in Camia. He started to think of back home again, and suddenly thought of how he and Mercury had explored their surrounding forests with sticks in their belts as pretend swords every day, making up their own adventures, their own stories. His favourite was the one of two young brothers protecting a village from the evil Toshka, a vile race his father told him about around the fire, by themselves. They would venture down from the mountains and take all the children. He remembered how they would hit the trees pretending they were Toshka monsters. He rested his hand on his captain's hilt at the thought, which put a warm feeling in his stomach.

All his life he had wondered what it would be like: wearing armour, holding a genuine sword, going on a real adventure. He never really got to appreciate it in his training, but now it was all over he actually thought back to how that strange little boy acted, and now he felt grown up. He was living the dreams he had had when he was young, although it felt far less glorious.

The thoughts went on until Buskull shouted, "Captain! There's something approaching from the south!"

They all stopped, and Havovatch looked over; he took off his helmet to help his vision.

Off in the distance, a dark line could be seen along the ridge of the horizon. There was no mistake: it was moving towards them, with gaps of light appearing amongst it, and, as soon as it became nearer, lots of tiny dots could be made out, jumping like fleas along the terrain.

Havovatch did not want to dawdle to find out who or what they were; any suspicious activity was a threat.

Quickly he looked at his map, desperately looking for somewhere they could seek refuge. A couple of leagues away was an area marked 'High Rocks'. He did not know what it was, but it was better than sitting on an open plain.

"This way!" he shouted.

They galloped after him, but whatever was following them was travelling much faster than they could, and was gaining on them.

The unit hung to their reins to keep themselves steady, and pushed the horses as hard as they could. The horses galloped with a speed Havovatch did not think they were capable of, as if they had been reserving a burst of energy or were controlled by some spell. It took him by surprise, and if they had not been being followed, he would have dismounted and walked. He cursed with every bump, closing his eyes and longing for the journey to be over.

High Rocks soon came into view; they must have been closer to it than he realized. It was a high rise, with huge boulders on top. He could see small cracks in the rock that they might be able to squeeze down, only accessible from an incline in front of them, with a sheer cliff face on either side.

Havovatch looked back to see if he could see what was chasing them, and his mouth dropped.

They were monsters: huge, dark, grey beasts with muscular bodies, large manes surrounding their necks, and powerful legs pushing into the ground; tearing up the soil as they did so.

They had tails longer than their bodies and huge, outstretched wings catching the air as they glided, but they were not flying. The monsters pushed into the ground, springing high into the air with their powerful legs, and, with their large wings, cascaded back down to earth, gliding long distances as they did so.

Riding each of the beasts were half a dozen of the creatures that Havovatch had kept meeting over the past months, howling at the tops of their voices at their gain and brandishing their weapons. He shuddered at their squeals, and closed his eyes in frustration that he had to battle them again.

"How'd they know where we are?" Hilclop shouted in a panic.

"What makes you think they're looking for us?" Feera shouted back at him.

Havovatch, though, knew Hilclop had brought up a valid point@ out of everywhere in Ezazeruth, why did they keep running into them?

Feera began edging ahead, but controlled his horse to stay with the others. Buskull rode at the back of them, already with his axe in hand.

"Fire some arrows!" Havovatch shouted over his shoulder.

Feera produced his bow and notched an arrow, clutching his legs around the horse's body he turned, aimed high and fired; the shot fell short with the beasts just out of distance, but he notched another arrow and fired again.

Mercury's bow was not strung. Trying desperately to string it, as well as holding onto the reins, caused all sorts of problems; then he dropped it. Hilclop just concentrated on getting ahead, and made no attempt to grab his bow.

High Rocks soon loomed above them. As they raced up the rise towards the giant boulders sitting on top, there were sporadic shards of rock slowing their approach, causing them to weave between them, allowing the creatures to gain.

Havovatch turned; the beasts were now nearly upon them; they were jumping as if to leap over the shards and land right on top of them.

Leaping from his horse, near the mouth of the closest passage, Havovatch shouted to the others, "Leave the horses, we fight these filthy rekons here! Quickly, into the passage!" before following Mercury, who had already entered.

Feera was the last one down, and cared too much for the horses to just leave them.

With Feera shouting and smacking their rears, they quickly galloped back down the slope. He watched as the beasts approached, but they ignored them, and were darkening the ground as they covered the sun above him, just about to land where he was.

He smiled, knowing the horses were safe, but then realized his own safety was jeopardized and that he was alone.

Drawing his swords, he rushed into the crack, moments before a great beast landed, making the ground tremble as it did. As he turned to look behind him he saw the beast push its way into the narrow passage, but the monster was too big to fit, and, snarling, with its salivating fangs, it tried to reach out, with its paw scratching chips off the stone. Its eyes were black with blood-red lines, and seemed to show nothing but rage.

Feera's eyes went wide: he had never seen a monster like that before, and fell over backwards.

Scrambling to his feet, he ran down the passageway, keen to get away from the savage animals.

The passageways forked out in many different directions, and in the panic he was soon separated from the others.

Havovatch and Mercury had to run sideways most of the way through the passage, as it was so narrow; soon they came to a small opening, and when they turned they realized they were alone. There was a step to the side of the rock face, which they used to pull themselves up onto a ledge, and caught their breath.

"What do we do now?" Mercury whispered, trying forcefully to calm his nerves.

"Looks like we fight," Havovatch said, resting his sword on his forehead whilst muttering an oath.

The creatures' shrieks were unsettling, and echoing through the maze they could be heard in all directions. Havovatch looked at Mercury, both of them thinking, *friends together, die together*. Nodding silently, they braced themselves.

The creatures were not discreet; they made as much noise as they pleased.

Havovatch started trembling; he knew how to fight, he knew how to kill, but waiting for them to come made him feel vulnerable ... and scared. They needed a plan.

Realizing it was the first time they had been alone together, Mercury opened his mouth as if to say something, but was not sure where to start.

"Captain," he said softly.

Havovatch looked up at him, and for the first time since his promotion he saw Mercury, and he saw his friend's face as he knew it before they enlisted.

"After what the general told us the other night, I...I finally understand the importance of this mission. I'm sorry it's taken this long for me to realize." He put his hand on Havovatch's shoulder; Havovatch put his hand on Mercury's arm as they grinned like the old friends they were. "Till the death, I'll look after you." Mercury smiled in earnest.

Havovatch sighed hard. "I've been distant and run-down recently, my friend; I should have believed in you more than I have done."

"Let's not get too sentimental – we are being hunted by deadly creatures."

"Ha." Havovatch looked around, trying to think of the best plan of attack.

The creatures were approaching as they howled from all directions. But after their moment the two Camions felt quite light-hearted, with a tense tie between them removed.

As Havovatch looked over at the other side of the rock face, an idea struck him.

He leant close to Mercury and whispered, "I'll leap to the other side of the rock. When they come into the clearing, I'll jump down and attack them; when they come at me, jump down behind them and kill as many as you can."

Mercury nodded.

Havovatch got up quietly, bringing himself close to the edge. He took in a breath; he was about fifteen feet up and, with the weight of his equipment and his slight panic, it started to dawn on him that he might not reach the other side, and he could fall.

Perching on his tiptoes, he leant forward, and, arms outstretched, he leapt.

It was further away than he had thought, and he landed heavily against the side of the rock, taking the wind out of him. His arms were desperately scrambling for something to grab hold of; only the friction of the rock against the skin of his hands and forearms was keeping him up.

He took in a deep breath and prayed that the creatures hadn't seen him; he was not sure how close they were, but their cries were getting closer. He scrambled, trying to find his footing, but there was nothing.

He had to be quick for the ambush to work, but he was starting to fall, the weight of his kit dragging him down, and he was starting to sweat, making him lose his grip. But, grabbing a throwing knife from his shoulder, he wedged it into a crack in the rock; sturdily it held, and he pulled himself over and stood up to catch his breath.

Mercury was standing up on the other side, looking helpless, but relieved he had got up.

Havovatch gave him a nod, and staggered to where he was going to jump down. Just at that moment, the creatures arrived.

They did not seem particularly intelligent ... if they had looked up they would have seen their enemy looking down at them. They just looked around with their ugly faces, sniffing at the air.

As Havovatch looked down from his high point, he thought, one false landing and he would break his legs; but he took in a deep breath and when they had all entered the opening, six in total, he jumped. Breaking his fall with a forward roll, he drew his sword, and as he sprang to his feet he slashed at the first unsuspecting creature across its throat, opening up its jugular.

The others instantly descended on him and he braced himself, being pushed back against the wall.

Mercury was on cue, jumping down behind them, and began striking heavy blows at their backs to get them away from his friend.

The creatures turned to see what was going on, and Havovatch parried forward, cutting another's arm off.

In the confusion, the group was soon brought down, and maimed corpses lay between the two soldiers, splashes of black blood smeared over them and the rock face.

Standing panting, Mercury regarded the bodies. No more howling seemed to be coming their way. "These are not like what we fought back in Camia," he said, breathing heavily.

"No," Havovatch agreed. "Their armour is thinner and weak, their weapons are not long and heavy but short and to the point, they're dressed more like … assassins."

They examined the corpses. "You think they were sent after us?" asked Mercury.

"I don't know what to think."

"But what if they were? Who knows what we are doing?!"

"I don't know! But the one thing for sure is that they can die, now let's find some more!" Havovatch said, lusting for more action as strength flowed through him.

Buskull stood atop the High Rocks' highest peak, looking down onto a long, narrow path. He could see a large group of advancing creatures approaching. They were a dishevelled group, all howling … in fact shrieks could be heard echoing all around the High Rocks. It wasn't a particularly big place, about two or three acres, but with so many passages, caves and different heights of rocks to run around, it was a warren. But he focused on the group below him, and his eyes turned red with rage and started mumbling in a foreign language as he prepared himself to fight. There were a lot of them, and the only grace was that they could only fight in ones or twos due to the limited space of the passage.

He looked up at Hilclop, who was leaning against a giant boulder, perched on the side of the rock they were on. Hilclop had his spear in both hands, ready to try to do something with it, but he was clearly not sure what. The spear was rattling as he shook visibly.

And Buskull had a better idea.

With no time for pleasantries, he shoved Hilclop out of the way just as the creatures were below them, and began to push the huge boulder as hard as he could. The creatures heard the noises of grunting and cracking rock, and looked up in wonder as to what was going on.

Buskull's entire body tensed, showing enormous, bulging muscles over his shoulders and back, as he strained and mustered all his strength to push it over the edge.

Hilclop saw what he was trying to do, and, pointing the butt of the spear at the bottom of the rock, he pushed into it, lifting as hard as he could. The boulder started to edge forward.

The extra strength did it, and the rock toppled down and crashed heavily, taking some of the rock face with it onto the creatures below. The creatures could do nothing, so many of them were in the way. Some tried to run, but none of them could move in time; they were all flattened, with the sound of crushed metal and black mist emanating from the base from where they stood.

Buskull panted slightly but regained his composure; picking up his axe and giving Hilclop a smile, he rubbed his hair as he strode past him.

Havovatch kept running through the maze. Up ahead he could see an opening, so he ran towards it. At the same time, more creatures came running at them from the other side.

Without hesitation he threw a knife, striking the first one in the eye. The creature stood there with its mouth open and then fell to the ground, its face hitting the floor and pushing the knife further into its skull so that it protruded from the back.

Havovatch then hammered away at two others with clenched teeth, bringing his arm up and down in a crossing motion. Due to the shape of his kopis, it felt like wielding an axe with the end bent and heavier, but with its slick thinness it had the agility of a sword.

Mercury took on another with his straight sword in the same way.

In such close proximity, the creatures could not surround them, but Mercury yelped, clutched his ribs and fell to one knee as an old injury opened up. Beneath his armour, blood pulsed out, from an exposed wound he had received from the bar brawl.

Havovatch heard and looked over. The creature before Mercury smiled and brought its sword up, raising it up to strike him.

"No!" Havovatch shouted. But he could do nothing with two more fighting before him.

Out of nowhere, Feera jumped down from above with his two swords in a cross, cutting the creature's head clean off.

In the sudden surprise, the last two creatures looked over, giving Havovatch the time he needed; he struck one, whilst Mercury lifted his sword up and struck the next.

Havovatch quickly bent down to Mercury. "Are you OK? Have you been stabbed? Where does it hurt?" he said quickly.

"I'm fine, really! Look," said Mercury, pretending to put weight on himself and hit at his ribs with his fist. "See! I'm fine." He tried to smile, but Havovatch clearly saw through him.

Nodding appreciation at Feera, Mercury asked him, "Where have you been?", trying to steer the discussion away from himself.

"Lost!" he said, breathless. "I've been trying to find you! Buskull and Hilclop are elsewhere."

Their conversation was cut short at the sound of more approaching yelps. They collected themselves and went further into the labyrinth.

"Run, they're behind us, run!" shouted Feera, trying to push them on.

They eventually burst into a clearing in what appeared to be the centre of the warren. They turned and pressed their backs against the walls they had just emerged from, and the unsuspecting creatures met their blades coming at them.

No strength was necessary; the creatures ran so hard into the weapons they impaled themselves.

Drawing their weapons up, they faced the opening, expecting more to come out.

"Coshta!" someone shouted.

Looking behind them into the clearing, they saw five burly men, with long, black hair and strong arms, holding swords and spears. Their clothes and armour were from different nations from all around Ezazeruth, one wearing the green tunic of a Camion archer, but the pointed helmet of a Leno Danian.

They stepped towards them, suspiciously.

"Emiros!" Feera spat.

They were not sure which was worse, the creatures or the savages. The unit braced themselves. The Emiros were hefty men, strong and fearsome, and did not appear to be civilized or speak their tongue.

"We cannot take them *and* the rekons behind us!" Mercury whispered.

"Well, we sure as hell can't run away!" shouted Havovatch, and charged forward at them, slashing away.

Buskull was kneeling down and resting on his axe, perched on the edge with his eyes closed and smelling the air. Just then, he tensed up and grabbed his axe as a group of creatures curiously appeared below them.

He looked at Hilclop with a grin and winked, "See ya, laddie," and jumped down with his battle-axe, shouting out with a voice so fierce it seemed to vibrate the rock, and overtook any echoes of shrieks from the creatures in the entire area. Hilclop pressed his hands to his ears; he was sure that he could have been heard twenty leagues away.

When Buskull landed, it seemed to make the ground shake, and, shouting with vengeful rage, he swung his axe from left to right, cutting clean through the creatures with one arm, and using the other to merely pick others up and throw them.

The surprise attack by the mighty warrior gave him the edge, but the creatures soon went on the offensive and, with their blades drawn, they attacked.

Hilclop looked down in astonishment. He knew this time he could not hide away, his palms were sweating, his arms were weak, but seeing Buskull so gallantly taking the creatures on his own put spirit into him.

Gripping his spear, he pointed it downwards and jumped.

He had never jumped from a cliff before, and the momentum was enough to strike his spear through two creatures, but he had an undignified landing on top of two others, which broke his fall.

Quickly scrambling to his feet, he clumsily drew his sword and stuck it into the back of the first creature he saw, more out of reflex than of skill.

Hilclop was proud of his performance and realizing that it was easier to kill than he thought; but the creatures turned on him, and that was where things went wrong. He started to tremble as they turned, falling back and trying to scramble as far away from them as he could.

Their faces shining with malice, cruelty and satisfaction, they moved towards him, sensing an easy kill in him.

But they were swept aside, their bodies cut in halves as they heavily hit the rock face. Buskull kept sweeping his axe like an unstoppable force, taking them down in twos, threes or more. Hilclop just decided to swing his blade from side to side as Buskull did, and it seemed to work. The creatures were withdrawing, and trying to defend themselves rather than attack.

Hilclop almost found it fun, but Buskull finished the job before he could really get stuck in to this new feeling. Despite the victory, Buskull still had anger in his eyes, and Hilclop kept his distance, retrieving his spear and, putting his boot on top of one of the creatures which whined as if it were barely alive, he pulled it back through with some force.

As Hilclop was retrieving his spear, Buskull heard another battle being fought on the other side of the rock face, and instantly scrambled back up to the plateau.

When the spear was out, Hilclop sneered at the blood dripping thickly down its shaft, and held it between his finger and thumb as if it were the most rancid thing he had ever seen. But as he looked up to see where Buskull was, he realized he was alone.

Hearing more shrieks approaching, he scurried back up the incline leading to the top of the rock as quickly as he could, not wanting to fight anything on his own.

Havovatch, Feera and Mercury were fighting their own battles as creatures were funnelling out of three exits to the clearing on one side, and the Emiros on the other.

They had killed two of them, but trying to fight man and beast at the same time took its toll. An impressive amount of bodies started to litter the floor around them, and the skill of the Camion soldiers showed.

Havovatch had thrown most of his knives; Mercury had both swords in his hands, as did Feera. Mercury seemed to be filled with so much adrenalin that the pain he was feeling was momentarily absent.

Luckily, because of the narrow openings, few attacked at once, but it was continuous.

Slashing at the leg of an Emiro, Feera kneed him in the face before turning to meet another creature. He stood sideways, fighting the half-fallen man with his left hand and the creature with his right. But as the creature fell, he heaved the sword from its chest, and another one came running out with a barbed spear. He parried backwards, and the creature drove it straight into the Emiro's chest.

Feera slashed upwards, severing the creature's arm, and then across, striking the long of his blade right into its chest, making it fall back with a vile wound.

The Emiro groaned and looked at the spear within him and, trying to pull it out, he looked up at Feera, said a word he did not understand (but he knew it was an insult) and fell to the floor.

With the constant attack from the creatures, the three soon became overwhelmed and started to edge backwards.

It became not a fight of skill, but a frenzy of throwing blades at everything that moved in front of them, in the hope that it would all stop.

But then they heard it: the cry, the shout, the noise that made their enemies tremble and their hearts glad; five creatures came flying backwards from the top of the rock face and landed on their brethren below.

Buskull stood on top of the plateau like a silhouette, the sun behind him turning his outline tall and grand, and, raising his axe, he jumped down and joined the fight.

Two Emiros were left, and one shouted and charged at him, but simply met his end with a hefty axe blow from Buskull. The last one disengaged from Havovatch and ran into a passageway on the other side of the clearing.

But Buskull did not notice a stealthy creature approaching behind him holding a rigid dagger, crouched as if it were about to pounce onto his back.

It raised the dagger, a menacing grin on its face, and within arm's reach it went to jump ... but Hilclop landed on the creature with his spear, snapping it into two, and Buskull carried on his attack, bringing the fight to an end.

But the fall had crippled Hilclop. Landing awkwardly, he lay on a pile of rocks, looking up at the sky with his limbs in misshapen positions.

No more creatures were left, no more shouts or howls ... they had won.

Panting, sweating and covered in black blood, they checked that they were OK, but something was amiss.

They looked over to the rock's edge and saw Hilclop lying on the ground in an unusual position. Havovatch ran over to him. Hilclop was still conscious and holding onto what was left of his spear, but it was clear from the rest of his body that he was in a bad way.

"My ribs hurt," he whispered.

Buskull picked him up carefully. Hilclop winced, and they walked towards the other side of the clearing and through the passageway, Feera leading the way with his swords ready in case they met any more Emiros.

Eventually they emerged on the other side, where they astonishingly found their horses waiting for them, but no signs of the beasts anywhere.

Mercury turned to Havovatch. "I thought they made their own way home?"

Havovatch too looked confused. He then looked at Mercury and said, "Maybe they know their task with us is not yet complete?"

Buskull pushed between them and laid Hilclop on the soft grass, taking his waterskin and producing a blue cube from a pouch on his belt. He put it into the bottle and shook it hard; then, bringing Hilclop's head up, he poured the liquid into his mouth.

Hilclop coughed it back up at first, but Buskull held his nose and mouth and forced him to swallow it.

Hilclop's eyes shut, and he went into a kind of slumber. The others stared on in wonder, trying to think if there was anything they could do to help.

Without warning, Buskull took hold of Hilclop's limbs and snapped each one back into place firmly.

Mercury retched against the rocks, Havovatch winced at the noise; Feera knelt down and held Hilclop's head, but he was out cold.

To distract himself, Havovatch looked at his map and took a few paces away. "The Impenetrable Forest is not far from here; we'll head in that direction and see if we can find help."

Mercury came back to them, looking white and wiping his mouth.

Buskull looked up. "He won't wake up for some time, but when he does he will be in a lot of pain. I suggest we get him there, and soon!"

Buskull held Hilclop in front of him and mounted his horse, and before the others could join him he was already off and galloping in the direction Havovatch had pointed out.

The others followed, constantly looking around in case the beasts or any more creatures returned.

Chapter Thirteen
Preparation

It was a calm day, the waves of the sea gently brushing against the stone wall that diagonally sloped into the water from the ground, and a gentle breeze blew in and past Fandorazz's face, making his skin prickle. The air was fresh around him; he could smell the salt in the air and feel the breeze push against him as he stood. He had not seen the sea in years; he had not felt like this in years either; getting outdoors was making him feel refreshed and unburdened.

Sunlight reflected over the ocean in the distance, making blue crystals glitter on the horizon. It was a pleasant sight and strangely made him feel calm for the first time since he could remember.

He turned and assessed the defences, standing aghast as he stared at them for the fourteenth time that day. He knew he had his work cut out.

The defences sat in a small cove and spanned just over a mile, with sheer cliffs on either side. It was the only part of the east side of Ezazeruth that was approachable from the sea. The entire coastline was littered with huge shards of rock sitting just above and just below the surface of the water, making it too dangerous for ships to come near.

It had been more than a thousand years since the defences had been built, and they had not been maintained since; some of the stone had corroded away, leaving huge chunks of concrete missing. Other parts had been demolished, or stolen by local villagers to build houses or fences. Other parts had huge gaps where the terrain had expanded, leaving a deep hole between the wall and the earth. What was worse was that the sea had hit against it, eroding the soil and making the holes bigger … creating further erosion of the wall, resulting in it becoming weakened in places.

One thing Fandorazz did remember: stone and fire would damage the defences like a blunt axe hitting a log. But water over hundreds of years was a far bigger destroyer.

He looked along the wall, to where soldiers and engineers were busy trying to repair the damaged areas with large logs of wood. It would work well as a breakwater, but it was useless in stopping an invasion force.

He rubbed his face, but as he pulled his hand away he saw something; he was not sure what, but something different was there. But as he focused, it vanished. He was used to being insane and ignored it.

So he turned, but again he had another vision; again he was not sure what he saw but something was standing before him. But this time he did not focus his vision, but let the object stay there.

He saw a structure – no, an illusion of a structure in front of him. It was an archery tower, and a good, solid one that could quickly be erected as well. Studying the area, he also realized it was a good place to put it.

He looked down at his sketch pad; he had a thin piece of graphite in his hand, and, slowly, as if it were an action not of his own, he began to draw, and, looking up at the misapprehension before him, he began to draw faster and with superb detail.

When he had finished he regarded his drawing, but something caught his eye. Looking up at the top of the cliff, he saw another illusion, seeing a wooden wall that archers could hide behind and places for catapults to be dug in. He tore away his previous drawing, letting it fall to the floor, and was sketching his next vision frantically on the page. He would look up for a moment, but only for a moment, to get a glimpse of the terrain, and he immediately looked back down to get the drawing onto paper before he forgot it.

Before long, pages littered his feet, of dark shades and structural designs as he looked around and put graphite to paper in a frenzy, in order to get these ideas that kept coming to him one by one. If anyone who knew him had looked over at that moment, they would have noticed that he was smiling slightly to himself, and that he appeared happy, an emotion he had not felt for a long time.

"Fandorazz?" He jumped as Hembel approached. Hembel's appearance was different; he slouched, and his face was long and drawn; he had done very little in the last few days.

"Yes?" he said hurriedly, so he could get back to his drawings, not taking his eyes away from the pages.

"What are you doing?" Hembel said.

"Umm, not sure really," he said distractedly.

"I have not seen you so …" Hembel stopped as he grew nearer and noticed the drawings around Fandorazz's feet, and turned away murmuring, kicking away loose stones as he did so.

Fandorazz was oblivious to the fact that he was gone. But, as he quickly looked up, he saw Captain Seer walk through one of his illusions.

"You!" he shouted.

"Yes, Sir?" Captain Seer said politely.

"There is a forest a few leagues south of here; get your men to start cutting the trees down and bring them here post-haste. It has to be a continual chain … oh, and see if you can get a message to Cam for more men, we shall need them!"

"Yes, Sir; can I ask what you need them for?"

Fandorazz let out a long breath. "You *can* ask, Captain, or you could do as I say and get it done! That way we can get these defences up and ready for the attack *as* per the King's orders!"

Captain Seer said nothing, slightly taken aback by the way he had been spoken to. He turned to get away before he could retaliate.

Hembel was looking at Fandorazz from a distance. Sitting on a rock, pulling a bit of grass apart, he gazed furtively at him. Fandorazz looked around whilst drawing, and noticed him. Despite the episode he was having, he knew that Hembel had been a great help to him over the past few years when others did not care, and thought it best to get him involved.

He approached whilst still drawing. "Hembel, my friend, could you help me?"

"Like you care?" he said, sulking, not looking up at him.

"What?" Fandorazz looked up sharply.

"As if you want *my* help!" he shouted.

"Hembel, I don't know what I have done for you to act like this, but …"

Hembel grunted and rose quickly to his feet, shunting past Fandorazz as he did so.

"Hembel, please talk to me. I need your help," Fandorazz shouted after him. But he said nothing, and carried on going.

Fandorazz did not really know what to do; he certainly did not know what he had done that was so cruel for him to be treated in that manner.

Cradling his portfolio, he turned and looked north along the edge of the defence wall. He was on a slight rise, with illusions of all sorts before him: repairs to the walls, trenches, buildings, structures; he feared there were too many to remember, and so his hand became a blur as he drew.

Fandorazz was not a strategist, but he could see how enemy ships would need to land. The likely thing would be for them to charge against the defence wall and crash into it, and, en masse, the army would pour onto the wall. Any slow attack would give too much time for the defenders to take them down or keep them back, so he needed to slow them down.

He noticed the tide was starting to go out and he had another idea.

Captain Seer passed him again, grunting. "Oh, Captain, good! Your timing is impeccable," said Fandorazz.

Captain Seer said nothing, just looking at him angrily in expectation of an apology.

"When you bring the tree trunks back from the forest, spike the ends, we'll need as many as you can, also, are we near the village of Brinth?"

"Yes!" Captain Seer said, hissing the 's' out.

"Good, I have an old friend there. He is a mason by the name of Groga; tell him I sent for him and to bring all the help he can muster at the order of the King."

Captain Seer went to walk away.

"Oh, and Captain … apologies about the way I spoke to you previously."

Fandorazz turned back before the captain could say anything, and kept drawing. He was not sure how long it would be before the Black arrived, but what he had in mind for them was certainly going to be a surprise, and with the proper support and resources he estimated at least seven days before he would be ready.

As graphite went to paper, he smiled to himself, as he imagined his family's happy faces in his mind … he wanted to impress them.

Chapter Fourteen
Strangers

Hilclop was in a bad way. Buskull had done what he could, but he was in a worse state than some simple remedies and bandages could cure.

As they cantered over the plain, they tried to make good distance. Still unconscious, Hilclop was now strapped into his own saddle, with the horse being guided by a rope being held by Buskull.

Havovatch had noticed a change in Buskull's attitude towards Hilclop; maybe this was how he always acted when a friend was in need?

The sky turned orange as the sun fell beyond the horizon, and eventually tall trees came into view. Havovatch started to feel relieved, but then thought about the next step to finding civilization; *And there may not be any,* he thought. Suddenly he was overcome with another feeling of dread.

The land changed as they approached the forest. It became hilly, but the woodland was hard to miss ... so staggeringly tall, it was the only visible thing for miles around.

As they approached the forest's edge they met a solid wall of verdant trees; it was so dense they could not see through.

"So that's why it's called the Impenetrable Forest?" Havovatch said to himself.

It was clearly no ordinary forest: dark and sinister, with strange, unnatural noises coming from the canopy, and with the sun beyond it cast a dark and intimidating shadow over them.

Looking up, Havovatch saw skulls hanging from the canopy, and he shuddered, for he could not tell what skulls they were, with many showing different shapes he could not recognize.

Dismounting, he drew his sword whilst Buskull stayed next to Hilclop. Mercury and Feera dismounted to follow Havovatch. They walked towards the trees with weapons bared. Havovatch first stabbed at the tree wall, but his sword just seemed to deflect away. Slightly baffled, he raised his sword and fiercely cut at the branches, but the sword rebounded off and came back at him. Falling to the floor, he sat up, shocked, and rubbed his aching arm.

"Please tell me you saw that?" he pleaded to the others.

Mercury and Feera cautiously hacked away and succumbed to the same fate, and sat before Buskull, rubbing their arms.

Becoming frustrated, Buskull dismounted and approached the trees. Raising his axe, he hewed through the trees with the driving momentum of his body pushing on, and, carving his way in, he disappeared into the forest.

Shamefully, standing perplexed, the others looked into the cavity being created and caught a glimpse of Buskull's grey vest fading into the shadows of the dark, murky wood.

When he was out of sight, they could still hear the sound of branches and vines being cut down by Buskull's mighty axe, but, to their astonishment, the hole began to close as the branches slowly started to grow back, closing the gap.

Havovatch turned to Mercury and Feera. "Get Hilclop and carry him through, quick!"

They both ran to Hilclop and together they cut at his bonds, and, as delicately as they could, carried him through. Havovatch checked the horses for any equipment they needed. But, as he went to hit them, they seemingly knew it was time for them to go and, in unison, cantered away.

Havovatch was surprised but did not dawdle, and, carrying the unit's helmets, he ran into the hole after them.

As he ran through the narrow path, he heard deafening noises behind him. He turned to look down the tunnel and saw the forest starting to close up fast, and the light from where he had come dissipate.

He ran with all his might, but with some difficulty due to the burden and the closing gap around him.

Suddenly he burst into a ravine and fell heavily on the ground, spilling the helmets with a clatter. Buskull stood, sniffing the air; Hilclop had been lowered to the floor, and Mercury and Feera were looking around at the astonishing sight of the unnatural forest around them.

The gap closed up, and Havovatch turned onto his back and looked where he had come from. "What the hell?" he said, still not believing what had just happened.

All except Buskull stood in wonder at how he had managed to do that. Buskull caught their suspicion and raised his axe. "This weapon has special abilities."

Calming themselves, they looked around. It was clearly not like any woodland they had seen before: the trees shot up higher into the sky than they could see, with trunks of all shapes and sizes. Some were as wide and thick as the defensive wall of Cam, others thinner than their little fingers, yet these grew taller than the others.

The forest floor was strewn with living plants and foliage that none of them had seen before.

Mercury helped Havovatch up and stood looking around in wonder, but Hilclop let out a groan and they remembered why they were there.

"We need to find help. Split up and check for any signs of civilization, footprints, dying fire, dead animals … anything!" said Havovatch.

Still bewildered by their surroundings, they hesitantly set off, with Havovatch and Mercury going right, as Feera and Buskull went left.

They ran for a while, Mercury holding his waist the whole time. Havovatch noticed. "You OK?" He stopped to move Mercury's arm.

"Yes! I'm fine, it's an old injury, it's better than it was."

"You sure?"

"Hilclop is the one who needs help, not me!" Mercury argued back, and continued to run with a slight limp. Havovatch quizzically carried on after him.

They ran, jumping over fallen trees and giant roots spread across the ravine.

Eventually they both stopped and succumbed to exhaustion. Havovatch put one hand against a tree to steady himself. "This is hopeless, what are we going to do?"

Standing up straight, he tried to shake off the burning pain in his legs, desperately trying to think. He felt so helpless; it was as if there was an idea in his mind but he could not grasp it.

Slowly turning, Havovatch was confronted by the white light. It was pulsing waves of energy at him with distant rumbles of thunder; all seemed to slow down, and he felt calm. But Mercury was oblivious to it. Havovatch had been waiting for this moment, and, striding forward, he went to touch it. It was yards away, now feet; he reached out his fingertips almost far enough and, just as he went to touch it, it vanished.

He blinked, sighed and crouched down, rubbing his face; tears were almost forming in his eyes and he could not understand what was happening to him.

"Did you hear that?" Mercury said, raising his ear in the direction they had come from.

"You saw it too?" Havovatch turned, astonished.

"Saw what?" Mercury said quizzically.

Havovatch's face fell. "Never mind, what did you hear?"

Far off and faint, they heard shouting, and it was clear who it was.

Quickly glancing at each other, they drew their swords and ran back the way they had come; suddenly Havovatch forgot everything as he surged forward.

As they got closer, they could hear Buskull's unmistakable war cry and started to fear the worst.

They came upon several tall, hooded figures that burst into view, standing with bows, aiming at Buskull and Feera, who were standing back-to-back with weapons raised.

But Hilclop was nowhere to be seen; as Havovatch and Mercury confronted them, more masked figures appeared from behind them, almost as if they were a part of the forest.

Perplexed and outmatched, Havovatch lowered his sword and took off his helmet, and, opening his hands out freely, he turned to the strangers.

The figures had black scarves across their faces, revealing just their eyes, and large hoods with dark cloaks; tucked into their uniform were vines and branches.

"Lower your weapons," Havovatch said to his unit, but Buskull kept his grip whilst looking around untrustingly.

Havovatch addressed the strangers, "I am Captain Havovatch of the Three-Thirty-Third Heavy Infantry of Camia. We need your help."

Not one of them moved or spoke, looking emotionlessly at their targets.

"We mean you no harm! Please – we desperately require aid."

A muffled voice came from all around the forest. "If you're a part of the heavy infantry, Captain, then where is the rest of your regiment?"

Havovatch looked around but could not see anyone; the sound seemed to come from everywhere.

"Please show yourself; we have no quarrel with you." Havovatch tried to sound reassuring.

Then a figure appeared from nowhere; whoever it was, they were slim and a bit shorter than the other hooded figures.

Havovatch could not see their face as they too had a scarf covering it. He assessed them quickly, he knew they were left-handed, as they had a quiver full of arrows over their right thigh. They also had a sword that was strapped to their back and reachable over their left shoulder. It had a long handle with a large, emerald-green hilt; shaped slightly like a spider but with only four legs, and bigger than Havovatch's head.

The stranger stood with their arms folded, clearly interested and feeling confident in dominating the situation.

"We mean you no harm," Havovatch said again.

"Huh," the figure laughed, "then why do you bring weapons here, cut through our home and threaten us on our own soil?" Their voice was muffled due to the scarf over their face, but Havovatch could tell that they were female.

He looked at Buskull and Feera and gave them a nod to lower their weapons; they did so with some reluctance.

"Apologies, but we needed aid for our friend. Can I ask where he is?"

"Being given aid."

"Then may I ask who you are?"

The stranger walked forward, her arms still folded. "No, you may not. As far as I am concerned, you are trespassing. We have no liking for outsiders, hence the reason why it should have been impossible for you to enter our domain. The only reason as to how lies with the Boldaring steel," she said, taking a look at Buskull's axe.

Havovatch followed her gaze.

"Please, the young boy you have taken, he is in a bad way. Please promise me you will bring no harm to him," he pleaded.

She shot him a cold look. "I have promised many things in the past, Captain, and that's why I live here! You don't make demands of me!"

Something seemed to click in Havovatch's mind. "Are you the Oistos?" Havovatch asked, quizzically, hoping to get some resignation from her.

Before he knew it, she drew her sword and pointed it at his neck within a heartbeat. The move was too quick and graceful; Havovatch could barely react. He cursed himself for putting his sword on the floor, and, tilting his head back slightly from the point of the sword, looked along the long double-edged blade into her eyes.

"Well, Captain of Camia, can I suggest you follow me," she said between gritted teeth.

"Please do us no harm, we are but simple messengers."

"You just said you were an infantry unit? Any more lies you have for us, Captain?"

Havovatch said no more, realizing he was digging a deeper hole. With his hands on the back of his neck, and all their weapons confiscated, they were escorted away deeper into the forest.

Chapter Fifteen
Pushing Limits

Havovatch sat on his knees with his feet crossed over, bowed forward with his hands secured behind his back. A sack covered his head, yet he tried to use his other senses to learn about his surroundings.

He could smell the unmistakable scent of a dying fire. There was someone pacing around behind him, maybe two … he could hear their breathing, and the soft sound of their feet stirring the earth within the tent. He was sure he was in a tent; he could hear wind hitting canvas, and rattling with every gust. The ground was not of wood or stone, it was dirt. He could feel his knees shifting it around beneath him.

He had been there for at least a night. It had been entirely dark for a long time, but now spots of light could be seen though the fabric of his hood.

He was thirsty, and could not feel his hands. He had not rested since before the skirmish at High Rocks the day before, and his body felt numb from being in the stress position all night.

"Can I have some water, please?" he called out, politely.

"Silence!" a stern voice responded.

But Havovatch needed to move, and, stretching his body, he leant up and crooked his neck, but two firm hands on his shoulders put him back to how he was. "You were told *not* to move! Do it again and I will remove your thumbs!"

The voice was fierce and provoking, as if he was goading Havovatch into moving again so he could do it.

Sighing heavily, Havovatch accepted it, but the stretch helped a little.

Suddenly there was another presence in the room, and then someone took hold of Havovatch's arm and hoisted him to his feet. He was taken outside, where he heard the natural noises of the wilderness: wind in the trees, birds singing.

He staggered for some time, being pulled in several directions as he got the feeling back in his numb legs. He tried to keep pace of the way they were going, so he could remember his route. But he lost track of the number of turns he had taken.

Eventually they stopped and he was let go; his hands were unbound and the hood was removed.

Squinting, he tried to adjust to the light. Looking up, he saw sunrays beaming through the canopy, and before him sat Feera, Buskull and Mercury, with their backs against a giant tree, looking up at him.

They were not tied up but had marks on their wrists, showing they had been. Havovatch looked at one of the guards, who gestured for him to sit down.

"No talking!" the guard said, his voice different from the one who had threatened him, but just as angry. Havovatch could only see his eyes, frowning and looking as though he wanted to kill them.

Sitting down and massaging his legs, he studied his surroundings now he had his vision back. There were children running around happily. Men and women were pacing to and from vegetable patches in a giant clearing in the distance, or gathering up livestock. They seemed aggravated by their presence, muttering as they passed and giving long, distasteful looks, the women pulling their children close and trying to hurry them away as they gazed at them.

The men, though: they were tall and seemed strong of arm. They walked with a certain integrity and honour about them, their clothes barely dirty or creased, and all of them carried swords by their waists.

As he surveyed the area he saw an approaching unit of men walking in two columns towards them. They were dressed in long, brown or green cloaks, each carrying a huge bow. They walked in unison, their eyes shadowed by the tops of their hoods.

The rest of the unit noticed them too and braced themselves, all of them eyeing every direction for some sort of escape route.

One of the men spoke. He appeared to be the leader and had a set of feathers on his shoulder. Havovatch was not sure, but thought that this must be their insignia, that he was an officer or something similar.

"You are summoned by our commander."

Looking at each other cautiously, they all went to get up, but the man put the palm of his hand out. "No! Only you," he pointed at Havovatch.

Giving a reassuring nod to the others, Havovatch walked towards the stranger, who also was masked, and carried the same look in his eyes as the others. The two columns of men surrounded him and they marched off.

As Havovatch walked, he took further note of his surroundings; it was a place he had never seen before, not like a normal forest. It was more than that: mystical, like a fey's world in a fairy tale.

He saw trees of different colours: one had blue leaves, and appeared to be changing colour before his eyes, slowly, in a waving motion, switching from blue to brown, to green and back to blue, its branches waving in the wind calmly and elegantly. But it suddenly turned red, and the tree tensed up as if it had just noticed Havovatch's appearance.

He looked away quickly, but another tree caught his eye; it was huge, like a giant oak tree, its trunk stretching high into the canopy, the branches spread out wide with all sorts of birdlife within the leaves. He was not sure, but he thought that it was singing to him. He could not make out the words, for the voice was soft and distant and in another language, but hearing it made him feel calm.

He didn't know why, but he could not tear his eyes away from it, as if fixed in a trance. He wanted to, so that he could see if it was some maiden singing, but kept staring with fascination at the enchanted tree.

But soon the tree was out of sight, as was the singing.

He took in a deep breath, puffing his cheeks. He wondered if he was in a dream or enchantment, but all his senses told him that it was reality. He could smell the sweet scent of flowers; he could taste them. He felt the wind fly past him; he could hear the soft sounds of birds chirping in the tress, and the sound of his and the guards' marching feet on the wide gravel pathway.

But his eyes! He could see so much, but it was the one sense he did not think he could trust at that moment. With so much magic about him, how could this be real, when it was so different from his world?

A shunt from his right took him out of his daze as they rounded a corner on the path. The path was wide, and consisted of white gravel, lined on either side with large, grey stones.

As he noticed the floor, he wondered how immaculately clean it was. There were no leaves on the ground, which he thought was strange considering where they were. The stones were well kept; some areas had grass, whilst others had soft bark surrounding the trees. The grass was trimmed, with flower beds flowing in different directions.

The whole place appeared properly maintained, the path branching out in different directions. Anyone walking about stuck to the path and did not dare venture onto the grass, as if there would be a curse on them. But they had no need to: the path was wide enough for carts to pass each other in some places.

After what seemed like a long time, he came to a lake – not a particularly big one, but he noticed the entire lake had lots of streams running out of it, all flowing *in*to the forest. To one side was a large hut, out on stilts over the lake, although he was not sure what it was for.

There were piers stretching out into the water, with small boats moored up. One part of the shore was like a beach with a sandy area, with children of all ages playing, digging holes or making sandcastles.

There were giant rocks to another side, just like High Rocks, and jumping from them were older children, only a few years younger than him, diving into the pure, blue water. Along the other side, in the distance, he could see people fishing.

Soon the sound of splashing and laughter was left behind, and he came to what Havovatch could only think was a community.

There were huts, all in tidy, long columns – some large, some small. Tree houses were situated high up in the canopy, bridges spanning from hut to hut, treetop to treetop. There were tall ladders stretching up to balconies, steps carved into dead trees, and some large trees hollowed out and turned into houses. But only dead trees appeared to have been damaged in order to make houses or steps; the living trees were not touched. It was clear that nature was respected here.

He could see why the inhabitants lived here: it had all the pleasures and wants of a community, but they shut themselves away from the outside world.

But the niceties he had seen came to an end. They approached an area that was blocked off, so that no one could accidentally make their way into it, with a tall palisade spanning as far as he could see into the undergrowth, and units of guards in groups of four, pacing up and down along it.

Stopping at a guard's post, the leader of the column presented some papers to the guard. They spoke in a language Havovatch could not recognize, and soon they were allowed to enter.

The wooden gates were opened, and they walked inside. Every now and again Havovatch saw mannequins or targets at different angles, hanging from trees or on the ground. All had the visible signs of arrow holes, whilst some were dressed in armour, and posed in a fighting stance.

He came across some of the trainees, standing up straight in columns of ten or so. Much like in his training, they were split up into small groups and each given instructors to teach them.

They stood proudly in their uniforms, consisting of green, brown or red hoods, leather body vests, a quiver at their backs or thighs and a bow in their hands.

But none of them had swords, not even training swords. Havovatch wondered if they had to earn them by stages like he had had to in his training.

Again, the instructors spoke out in a language he did not understand, and the young recruits obeyed with fierce responsibility, not misbehaving as some of his fellow recruits had during his training.

He saw a group firing arrows down a range, hitting with superb accuracy, moving butts that were connected to a rope and pulled by two men.

But soon it all came to an end; they had reached another palisade with a gate. The leader again showed some papers to the guard and spoke, and they were allowed to enter.

On the inside was a small crater in the earth, and situated in the middle was a wooden longhouse. Leading to the longhouse was raised decking, as if stepping off into the earth and mud was perilous. Havovatch was led along the decking towards a set of double doors.

As he walked into the dimly lit room, there was a long table with dozens of chairs around it. The room was neat, but it had very little in it, apart from a few weapons hanging on the walls; only one masked figure sat in the middle of the room. He also noticed that his pouch with all his orders was on the table in front of the stranger, and their equipment laid out to one side as if it had been examined.

"Good morning, Captain Havovatch," said a feminine voice from the masked figure, "I trust you had a pleasant night?"

"Yes, I did, remind me to return the favour when you seek out our hospitality," he said sardonically, as the thoughts of his burning body came back to him.

She laughed. "You entered my domain, with force I might add: I will treat you as such until I know what threat you bring here."

"All you had to do was ask."

"People lie, Captain, and a great many people here count on me not trusting strangers, and if you got to know us, you would understand that trust is something we don't give away freely."

Havovatch said nothing; he still wanted to get out alive but understood to an extent what she meant.

"You were not short of words yesterday, Captain."

"All I ask is for aid for our friend and we will be on our way."

"Really? Is that all you want?" She had an edge to her voice as if she knew more about his presence.

"He was injured, and under my charge he was, and still is, my priority."

The stranger stared up at him but said nothing.

"Is he OK?"

She remained quiet.

"What do you want from me?" he said a little more forcefully than he had meant to, but impatience was getting the better of him.

"I think the question, Captain, is what do you want from us?"

She pushed one of the orders on the desk over so Havovatch could read it.

You are to fulfil your oath!

Havovatch stared back at her. "So, you are one of the Knights of Ezazeruth?"

"Hard to believe, isn't it? We are the Oistos."

Havovatch suddenly felt light, as if a problem from his mind had disappeared.

"Well, that's great, we have found you, and you can fulfil your oath," he said, quickly forgetting his composure and smiling broadly.

"You think so?" she said coldly.

"Well, you will, won't you? I mean, you took up a blood oath – you have to adhere to that."

She grunted. "You surprise me, Captain."

"*What*?" he said, aghast, as if she had just said the unmentionable. He suddenly thought of his father, always telling him to tell the truth and be noble. "You cannot turn on an oath, especially a blood oath!"

"You're rather naïve, Captain, probably because in this day and age your country promotes young boys to a rank of a man who needs more experience."

"I know enough."

"That's a boy's answer!" she said sharply.

Havovatch was getting impatient. "What do you want from us? We gave ourselves up to you, we have told you we bring you no harm, yet you treat us like criminals."

There was a long pause, then she got up and walked over to a table with a jug and two goblets. She poured water into them both, handed one to Havovatch, then lifted her hand up and pulled her scarf down, revealing her face.

Havovatch was dumbstruck and stood with his mouth open. She was ... beautiful. He expected someone who was two thousand years old to be covered in wrinkles and furrows, their face long and drawn. But she had smooth, pale skin, with dark brown hair falling down from her hood, just covering part of her face, and deep, dark eyes.

She drank from her goblet, looking over intently at him. But he still had not taken the goblet, and, forcefully, she pushed it into his chest.

Havovatch took it and sipped the water, feeling the cold liquid go down his dry throat. "May I ask something, then? We are both soldiers, and, as such, maybe we should act like them. Can I ask your name?"

She looked at him for a moment before responding. "Garvelia."

"Now, can I ask of your intentions of me and my men?"

"Let's just say that few, very few, have ever come into our domain uninvited, and those who have, have never left."

"The world needs us, Garvelia, me and my men! We need to leave!"

"That's not a decision for you to make, Captain."

Havovatch let out a long breath, getting annoyed with the half-answers.

"Very well, so where do we go from here? A hangman's noose or the beheading block? If you don't mind, I'd rather something quick; I've had kind of a bad week," he said sarcastically, not wanting to play her game anymore.

Garvelia returned to her seat, and sat leaning on the desk, her face clearly unimpressed. "Captain, do you know of our story? Of what and who we are?"

Remembering the story told to him from General Drorkon, he could only reflect on the negatives with the way he was being treated.

"All I know is that you swore an oath."

Garvelia slammed her goblet on the desk. "Don't think you can mock me, Captain! You know nothing about me, my men or the pain and torment we have had to endure! So ... in my domain, I would appreciate a bit more caution before you speak!"

Havovatch said nothing; he knew he had overstepped the mark but still wanted answers, and he was not getting them quickly enough.

"Now, what is happening in the world for us to be recalled to service?" Garvelia said, calming herself and sitting back with both hands resting on the arms of her chair; it was unusual for Havovatch to see a woman in such a way, but it stirred up an attraction for him.

Composing himself, he spoke as if he were addressing one of his own officers.

"About two months ago, I was on a mission near the south coast of Camia. We were ambushed by a unit of heavily equipped black creatures, something I have never seen nor heard of. Before we know it, something called the *Black* has decided to invade us. The world is at war, and I am before my King, tasked to search the world to find three armies and deliver a message."

"Very well, Captain – was that so hard?"

Havovatch said nothing; there was a long pause whilst Garvelia sat looking out of the window.

After some time, she then turned her attention back to him. "Captain Havovatch of the Three-Thirty-Third Heavy Infantry of Camia," she said officially, "you and your men will be spared: you will be blindfolded and led out of the forest, but if you *ever* come back, you will be killed, and there will be no warning or second chances next time." Havovatch went to protest but Garvelia carried on. "We will not fulfil our promise to the land, for the land has nothing to offer us, but due to the fact that Agorath has returned, I know that Ezazeruth will need every good soldier it can get, and, despite your manners, you do seem to be a good soldier."

Garvelia put the orders back into the pouch the way she had found them, except for hers, and handed it back to Havovatch.

"With respect, Ma'am, I have been told of your betrayal, and I do empathize, but I beg that you do not punish the people of this world for someone else's deeds from many centuries ago. We need you!"

Garvelia said nothing; she looked as though she was thinking it over for a moment, but looked up and said, "I have made my decision, Captain; there will be no more discussion."

Havovatch bowed his head in shame.

"Your friend, Hilclop, will be ready to leave by this afternoon."

And, with a wave of her hand, the guards escorted Havovatch back to his unit.

When Havovatch returned to the others, they all got up and huddled around him.

"We have to leave. They will blindfold us and take us to the edge of the forest. Don't give them any trouble, let's just get out of here. Hilclop is better and will be joining us soon."

"Better?" Buskull queried. "His injuries were severe, he won't be better for months, maybe never."

"That's all I have been told."

"Are we at one of the knights' camps?" Mercury asked in excitable anticipation.

"Yes," Havovatch said in a low voice, seeing their faces frown with his solemn expression, "but we'll discuss it later."

They all sat down and relaxed with their backs against the giant tree trunk, able to have some rest for a change, and soon started to fall asleep in the tranquil environment.

Waking up a few hours later, they found their armour was in front of them. They got ready but found that they did not have any of their weapons back. Even some of the hidden knives Havovatch had had within his body armour were missing. They had been checked methodically to make sure they had nothing on them that could still cause danger towards the Oistos. He couldn't believe how professional they had been during his stay.

Soon a group of soldiers arrived and covered their heads with hoods, then tied a long rope around their waists and led them away.

Chapter Sixteen
Despair

There is a presence around me, four. Two to the right of me, two to the left. All male – I can tell by their sweat. No one else is around. The wind tells me that we are facing west. I can smell stone, granite off to the left, and trees to the right, I can smell its sap, its fern. But the one thing for sure, is that we are alone.

Buskull lifted his hood; his senses were correct. They were standing on the perimeter of the Impenetrable Forest. The sun was setting over the hills in front of them. But he had noticed that they were not where they had entered; the terrain was completely different. They were at the bottom of a slope with rolling hills before them; on one side was an opening of a stone valley, and on the other side were steep slopes with patches of tall fern trees.

Either side of them he saw Havovatch and the others standing still with their arms by their sides, and sacks covering their heads.

"OK, they've gone – take off your hoods."

They all did so; below them they found their weapons and, turning, they saw Hilclop, who looked well – slightly pale in the face and dark around the eyes, but he did not look broken.

"Are you OK?" Havovatch asked.

Hilclop just nodded.

"What did they do to you?" asked Buskull.

"Not sure really. I don't remember much; the main thing was waking up in a … in a tree. I was surrounded by branches, and as I peered over the bed I saw that I was high up. I was told to put this hood on and to hold a rope, and now I am here."

"How are you feeling?" said Feera.

"Fine, to be honest. Why?"

"Do you not remember the fight at High Rocks? You had some nasty injuries."

Hilclop shook his head, puzzled; Buskull approached him, lifted his arm and assessed it, then pressed at his ribs and looked at Havovatch. "It's as if he was not even injured at all!"

"Amazing!" said Havovatch, incredulously.

Feera stroked his face with both hands, to revive himself and relieve some stress. "So, what did the Commander say, then?" he said, addressing Havovatch.

"Well, they're still bitter about what happened to them. They said they will not fulfil their oaths."

"So, what do we do now?" asked Mercury, exasperated after everything they had been through.

Havovatch let out a long breath. "I guess we head back to Camia – there is nothing more we can do."

"But we have not completed our mission!" Mercury said sharply.

"We don't know where the other commanders are; it's futile carrying on."

The unit were solemn at the news. Everything they had done to get here, after everything General Drorkon had said to them, and they had failed before they had barely started.

But Buskull went suddenly alert.

"What's wrong, Buskull?" asked Havovatch.

"I'm not sure, Captain – there is something amiss in the air."

They all looked around but saw nothing. "It's probably something you are sensing from the Oistos?" Mercury put in.

"No, this is something familiar!" he said, peering intently at their surroundings; and, lifting his battle-axe into a defensive stance, he took a few steps towards the fern trees, almost sniffing the air.

They slowly drew their weapons and kept their gaze around them, but nothing could be seen.

Eventually, Hilclop abruptly holstered his sword, and sat on a pile of rocks, rubbing his neck. Due to the ordeal in the forest, Mercury and Feera did so as well and relaxed, but Buskull was still alert about something.

Havovatch thought it best to leave him to it; he would let them know if there was a threat.

"We might as well camp here tonight, and then make our way for Cam tomorrow; we will then get together with the Three-Thirty-Third and prepare for war," Havovatch said, yawning.

"Why have they let us out here?" said Feera, looking around.

"No idea," Havovatch said plainly, thinking it was done as some wicked trick; he did not even know which way he had to go to get home.

He yawned, his face long and his eyes drawn; he slumped to the floor and, taking in some deep breaths, he reflected on his conversation with Garvelia.

He sat for a long moment, gazing up and looking at the shades of the sky, changing from purple to orange in the evening air. His mind was not on the sky, though, but on Garvelia, his boyish fascination thinking about the woman and her beauty. He had never thought about a woman in that way before and it felt kind of frightening; he did not know what to feel, but he could not take his mind off her.

Strangely, he could not remember word-for-word what had been said between them; he thought it was because he was tired. He remembered the conversation as a whole, but that seemed like a distant memory. The thing that really struck him was how beautiful she was. He could not get the image out of his mind from when she had pulled the cover down from her face, revealing a beauty he had not seen since meeting Undrea. She had lit a fire in his belly; she was dangerous and a warrior, but stunning to look at, and he wanted to see her again – if not to satisfy his lust, then to get her to fulfil her oath.

"Captain!" shouted Buskull. He was slightly distant, and as Havovatch peered over the rock he was leaning against, he saw Buskull was alone, further into the valley near the foot of the hills and fern trees.

Getting to his feet, although somewhat sluggishly due to being tired, Havovatch drew his sword, and the others followed to where Buskull was.

But, before they got to him, drawing from around a corner of trees was a sortie of black creatures, assassins like the ones they had met at High Rocks. They had barely any armour on again, and their weapons were short swords or knives.

They were more than an arrow shot away, about twenty or so of them, but, strangely, they did not howl as they advanced. They walked slowly, as if assessing their targets.

"Shall we run?" Hilclop said, a tremble in his voice, whilst standing at the rear of the unit.

"No – they'll catch us! Prepare to defend yourselves!" Havovatch shouted. He looked over at the forest. "Garvelia, we need you!"

But there was nothing, just the chilling silence of knowing someone was there who was not coming out to help them.

"Garvelia! Please help us!"

But again there was nothing, just an eerie silence.

Then the creatures charged; it was unexpected considering their unusual ways.

There was nothing for it: they were going to fight, and, raising their weapons, the unit rushed at them.

Splitting up, Buskull pulled Hilclop right whilst Mercury and Feera ran left, with Havovatch running head-on into the rest of the sortie.

The spreading out made the creatures split up. There was no organization amongst them: they were so intent on bloodlust, they just attacked whatever target was closest.

Five ran at Havovatch, the few faster runners nearly upon him, but just before they clashed he ducked to the left as a blade passed by over him. Lifting his sword up, he slashed backwards, severing its head; not wasting any time, he brought the blade back and slashed across the throat of another.

It was easier fighting these creatures than the ones at Coter Farol: with more bare skin visible, there was plenty for him to hit at. But they were stealthy, fast and agile.

Feera and Mercury were attacking the left flank. Feera, with a sword in each hand, ducked, parried and thrust his blade into each creature with superb skill. It was hard to think he had once been a cavalry soldier – he was more of a scout. He was light on his feet, and had superb manoeuvrability, with his swords dancing in his hands. One second he was holding them up in his grasp; then, spinning round, he suddenly held them downwards and thrust into the creatures' bodies.

Mercury defended himself well, considering his weaknesses; he stood on the spot whilst using his long sword as a defence and using his short sword as an attack. But a small creature got within his guard and brought a small mace up, hitting into Mercury's ribs, doubling him over. Feera saw what happened and threw his sword at the creature, striking its back before it could bring its mace down onto Mercury's head.

Mercury dropped his short sword and clutched at his ribs, desperately fighting back the pain.

Buskull's war cry was tremendous, ringing out into the valley; he crashed into the creatures with Hilclop behind him, who was slashing violently but with little skill. Creatures fell around them, as Buskull cut through them.

Havovatch kicked a creature between the legs; just like all males in the world it seemed to be a soft spot for them, as the creature grabbed its groin and went cross-eyed. He head-butted the creature in the nose; the face guard of his helmet was sprayed thickly with sticky, black blood. He could taste it, bitter and foul like mouldy water with the hint of flesh. He spat it out, the creature before him with its nose clearly broken and a huge laceration across its face.

But, with so many creatures attacking him at once, Havovatch grabbed at its shoulders, kneed it again in the groin and threw it into three others. It did not kill them, but it gave him the time he needed.

A majority of the sortie attacked Feera and Mercury, and they soon became separated. Mercury panted heavily as pain rushed through him. Wounds from the last few weeks opened up and new ones were created. He soon became fatigued and his defence sloppy, desperately slashing wildly with his sword to keep them back, but, like animals sensing an easy kill, even more preyed on him.

Havovatch tried to find him in the battle, but in his own contests he could not tear his eyes away to see. One last beast stood in his way, but he was able to see over the creature's shoulder to Mercury, who was standing alone, being viciously attacked by two creatures, with Feera too occupied to help.

He knew he had to get to him.

Finishing his foe, Havovatch ripped his sword from its gut and ran towards him, but a shadow passed in front as a huge creature stood in his way, holding a heavy sword with a serrated edge, and in its other hand gripping a large, spiked knuckle-duster. It appeared to be in charge, with more armour and vastly bigger than the others.

It blocked Havovatch's path and, raising its sword into the air, it brought it down heavily.

Narrowly it missed him, and the blade cut deep into the earth with a tremendous thud. Bringing his sword up, Havovatch cut into its side, but it had no effect apart from making the creature angrier.

As it punched towards Havovatch with the menacing knuckle-duster, he fell out of its path. Desperately he tried to get to his feet, but the creature kicked him to the floor.

Looking up, he saw Mercury fall to one knee, his helmet off and clutching his ribs; he could do little to defend himself, visibly in pain.

"Mercury!" he shouted, but as he went to get up, the creature trod on his back, pushing him down. It then kicked him in the side, rolling him further away from Mercury. Turning onto his back, Havovatch looked up at the creature standing with its feet either side of him. It held the crude blade in both hands above its head, and went to bring it down. But Havovatch gritted his teeth and threw a knife, hitting it under the chin, then another in its neck, and another into its clavicle. The creature shrieked with pain and staggered back, trying to clutch at the multiple injuries; taking another knife he threw it at its knee, making it fall down.

Havovatch got up and, picking up his sword, grabbed the front of the creature's rag. With his arm pulled back, he thrust heavily into its chest as he brought the foul beast's face to his own, snarling as he did so. He then cut up with all the might he had, his forearm protruding veins with the strength flowing through him. He tore through the creature's ribcage, blood gushing down its front; the life faded from its eyes and it fell to the floor heavily.

Havovatch turned to see Mercury. He had managed to kill one of the two attacking creatures, but the other kicked him in the side and stood behind him, staring sadistically at Havovatch.

"*Mercury*," Havovatch whispered in disbelief, running the distance between them, pushing any other creatures out of his way. Mercury tried to spin around and stick his blade into the creature, but it grabbed his arm and bent it, breaking his wrist. Dropping the blade and crying out, Mercury was helpless.

Havovatch fought with little skill or regard for his own defence, in sheer panic to get to his friend, but there were too many creatures in the way.

The creature smiled at Havovatch; it picked up Mercury's sword and rested it in front of his neck.

Mercury did not look scared but exhausted, and just gave Havovatch a reassuring look and a slight smile.

Havovatch hit heavily into another creature and darted with all his might towards him; reaching for a knife, he realized he had no more. "Nooooo!!" he screamed.

The creature, with a brutal smile, slowly cut through Mercury's neck, holding his long hair in its other hand. Mercury's eyes looked up and blood poured down his front.

In a crying rage, Havovatch's teeth gritted and he pushed through the remaining creatures, not slowing his pace. Sword raised, he took on the creature as it fought with Mercury's sword.

Every slash Havovatch threw was personal and hard. The creature still held Mercury's head by his long hair and began using it as a club. Havovatch ducked under its blow and slashed, severing the arm holding Mercury's head, which rolled down the hill.

The creature obviously felt the pain, but, still snarling, it fought on with its free arm. Havovatch was not intimidated, though, and, using every limb, he thrust out at the foul creature, slashing its wrist. It dropped Mercury's sword, then cutting across the top of the creature's legs with his Kopis, the beast fell to its knees.

At first wide-eyed, the creature looked up at its victor, but grinned with its yellow fangs and chuckled unpleasantly.

Havovatch picked up Mercury's sword, and, resting them in a cross on the front of the creature's neck, and not taking his eyes off it, he forced them apart, severing the head clean; the body then slumped to the floor.

The deed done, he turned and looked at Mercury's fallen body. It did not look right; not long ago he was speaking to him, now he was not all there. Falling to his knees, and tears streaming from his eyes, he took off his helmet and fell onto all fours.

The others had finished with their skirmishes and slowly approached the grim scene, distraught and shocked.

Except for Buskull, who had lost friends before. Resting on his axe, he bowed his head and muttered a prayer, "May the Grey Knight of the soul come for you and guide you to the everlasting light."

Hilclop put his hands on his head, stunned and Feera, falling to one knee in despair and regret, buried his face into the crook of his arm.

Havovatch knelt, looking at the floor, seeing his tears visibly making clean marks in the grass; then, tensing his body, he gripped his sword and approached the woods of the Oistos, throwing it into the foliage. He heard the loud clatter of the sword falling from branch to branch and finally landing on the floor. "Cowards! You pathetic cowards, you swore an oath!!" he shouted, his voice echoing around.

But there was silence, and the others, looking on, saw that they were alone in the valley.

***

Havovatch laid the last of the rocks on Mercury's grave. He crouched down next to it, staring at Mercury's sword sticking out from the top, with his helmet resting on it.

Buskull, Feera and Hilclop had put all the creatures into a pile and burnt them, and were now sitting to one side, letting Havovatch have his moment.

Buskull sat with his back to the fire as he looked up at the stars. Feera had his sword out and rested his forehead against it, spinning it whilst in deep thought.

Hilclop was curled up in a ball on the floor with his cloak wrapped around him. He was not asleep, but was deep in thought too.

"I'm so sorry, my friend, I'm so, so sorry. I should never have brought you on this quest," Havovatch, said starting to cry, and rested his head on the top of the grave, his arms embracing it.

Feera felt worse: he had been fighting with him … and should have saved his life. Watching on, he could not take the guilt, and so got up to try to clear his mind. As he stood taking in the air, something caught his eye. He saw something twinkle from the firelight in the grass not too far from him.

He walked over to it, bending down to pick it up. "Oh, my Lord!" he said in shock, his guilt momentarily forgotten.

Buskull noticed that he had found something and wandered over. "What's the matter?"

"I found … something." He passed it to him.

Buskull examined it at arm's length, he wasn't a man to show his emotions, but this time he raised his eyebrows; he almost seemed scared, and gave it back to Feera.

"Put it away – it's not the time to burden the captain with any more issues, we'll tell him later."

Feera put the item into a pocket of his leather jerkin.

Just then, a noise came from the direction of the Impenetrable Forest. They drew their weapons and looked at what was happening.

From out of the shadows, Garvelia emerged into the clearing, finely dressed from head to toe in steel armour, with her breastplate the same emerald green colour as her sword. Two quivers were sitting over her left shoulder, and another two by her right thigh, her unusual sword reachable over her left shoulder. A griffin was embroidered on her breastplate, with the visor of her helmet up. She was dressed very differently to his heavy infantry armour. She was covered from head to toe in brazen steel, and still appeared to be able to manoeuvre easily.

She stopped in front of the unit. Suddenly, behind her could be heard a large gathering of metal marching in tow, its armour clattering together loudly, the stomping of feet in unison making a noise terrifying to any enemy advancing on it. And, from out of the forest, as if the trees had parted out of the way for them, a mass of steel-clad soldiers marched into the clearing.

"I guess you have shown us that we do have a duty to perform. I am sorry about your friend," she said, trying to sound sympathetic.

Havovatch said nothing, just stared at her with disgust.

Garvelia looked to an aid behind her, who passed her something, and she gave it to Havovatch. "I believe this is yours?" she said, handing him his sword.

Havovatch took it abruptly and put it back into his scabbard, then, turning with his unit following, they walked away.

Garvelia shouted after them, "Captain, not only one army can be summoned. It is the law of the land that we must all be summoned together; it is up to you to convince the other two commanders. If they do not come, we cannot fight!"

But Havovatch said nothing, and continued to walk away towards home.

"You will find the other commander to the south-west, in the desert; look for the city … Good luck, Captain," she finished; she then put her visor down and marched on with the rest of her men.

Havovatch stopped, looking over at the grave of Mercury then back at his unit.

"Let's go," he said eventually with a reluctant sigh, and set off due west towards the mouth of the Forbidden Passage.

Buskull looked at the valley's entrance and grew fearful; looking up, he saw gargoyles carved into the stone, facing down with their fangs out, as if howling, or warning any visitors to turn back. Not liking the sense of dread that was emitting from it, Buskull shouted after Havovatch. "Captain!"

But Havovatch kept walking, either ignoring him or too depressed to hear. "Captain!! … Havovatch!!"

But he did not stop, and, followed by Feera and Hilclop, Buskull took a deep breath and cautiously ran to keep up.

Garvelia watched them as they walked away, as one of her officers approached her. "Commander, what are your orders?"

Garvelia turned to look at Mercury's grave, and, waving the palm of her hand before it, there was a sudden ripple in the air and her sword glowed slightly; Mercury's grave then disappeared from view. "The death of that young man will haunt many, but at least he is at peace, and hidden from the world to look over this beautiful sight for the rest of time." She turned to the officer. "We march to Shila, we wait until the others are summoned."

"And if they're not?"

She let out a long sigh. "Then let's hope there is mercy out there … somewhere."

"And what about them? Do you think they know where they are going?"

Garvelia watched the unit climb over the large boulders and down into the mouth of the valley.

"The Algermatum will take care of them."

Chapter Seventeen
The Forbidden Passage

It had been two days since the unit had entered the Forbidden Passage. Much to Buskull's surprise, they had not come across any signs of civilization, although he grew more cautious with every step.

Havovatch had been quiet the entire time. In a depressed slump the whole way, he more staggered than walked, with his head bowed, not speaking a word or showing any signs of leadership.

At night, he sat separated from the others. He was constantly awake, his chest heavy, rethinking that desperate moment where he could have tried harder to get to Mercury … but failed. He walked on, thinking through every scenario of how he could have saved his life, but then reality would strike him and the burden of Mercury's death would become real again.

Buskull walked at the back of the unit. He was more than aware that his captain was struggling with his friend's death and took on a part of Havovatch's failing leadership role. Every so often, Feera and Hilclop turned to look at him, and he gave a nod of reassurance or a quiet instruction.

Feera was glum. He had lost friends before, but this time he felt responsible for Mercury's death. As he walked, he kept letting out heavy sighs, cursing as he did so with the anger and contempt he felt for himself.

As the sun rose, the valley became well lit; it looked as though rain had not touched the landscape in centuries. Surrounding the Forbidden Passage were acres of verdant forests and grass. But the passage looked as though it was cursed, as though it shouldn't be trespassed upon. It was a place that few people ventured into, but the reasons why were unknown to most of the world. It was just one of those places that no one went to. Local people thought it to be plagued and that no one could survive here, and so never went near. But stories from further afield became more fictitious. They said that the land was cursed, and demons were said to hide within the passage and take your soul, leaving your lifeless body to wander around the world like an aimless corpse.

Buskull was one of the few people in the world who knew the truth about the passage, and he kept his mouth shut, keen to get out before anything could happen. But he knew they were watching … he could not see them, but he knew they were there.

As he took in his surroundings, constantly vigilant of everything, he grew suspicious at the large number of potential ambush sites. They walked along the bottom of a valley on an endless snaking path, where he had to hold his breath behind every corner in case of attack. Although they had not come across anything so far, he hoped that he would, just because the stress of the unknown was too much to bear. It was like knowing something was going to jump out at you, but not knowing when. He tried to use his senses to scan ahead, but he could not get a reading … he felt blind going forward.

Suddenly, there was a disturbance in the rocks above them, a shadow flickering out of the corner of their eyes. Unexpectedly, a scree slope appeared to have been disrupted, with stones falling towards them.

Feera approached Buskull, trying to keep his voice low. "What do you think?"

"About what?"

"The captain? About this place!"

"He will be fine; just give him a day or two."

"We don't have that long. I know it's hard for him, it's pretty hard for all of us too, but we need him to snap out of it. I don't like it here."

Buskull said nothing. Suddenly, there was another movement and he caught sight of a shadow, suspiciously shaped like a human, just as they disappeared behind a rock.

"Think it's a threat?" Feera asked, obviously showing that he too had seen it.

"No." Buskull did not take his eyes off the spot, but showed his concern.

"What is this area? I've heard that people enter but they never come out."

Buskull swallowed, trying to keep his face placid; he did not want to answer the question.

Havovatch walked ahead with his thoughts, unaware of the situation.

The sun was high above them now; there were no clouds and the heat was becoming intense. The valley was reflecting the light so much that they had to squint to look around.

"How long do you think this path will go on for?" Feera pressed.

"I don't know, but let's up the pace!" Buskull said, more sharply than he had intended.

Hilclop suddenly drew his sword after a small boulder landed just before him.

"No!" Buskull whispered, abruptly.

Hilclop looked at him in alarm.

"Put it back; if they see us draw our weapons they will assume we are an enemy."

Feera shot him a suspicious look. "*They*?"

Buskull ignored the question.

They carried on precariously, with more noticeable and frequent disturbances occurring. Havovatch snapped out of it when a scree fell, covering his feet. He turned to look at the unit, who were standing tensely, looking up at the terrain. It was the first time he had actually looked at them in the last few days.

Buskull noticed his attention. "Captain, I suggest we run!"

Not really understanding, but noticing Buskull's grave face, Havovatch nodded; he looked to the others. There was no argument and they set off.

Behind them, boulders, scree and rocks fell, as if the valley was imploding on itself. The path was suddenly covered, and a deafeningly loud bell rang out. It was so loud it did not seem real. They clutched at their ears with the deafening ringing.

Buskull, the only one unaffected, holstered his axe on his back and grabbed his comrades, chucking Hilclop over one shoulder and dragging Havovatch and Feera by their belts. He ran, keen to get away from the avalanching rocks behind him and out of the passage. Veering around a corner, he saw the path disappearing into a forest at the end.

The distance was about a third of a mile, a straight path with high rises on either side. It was a death trap; he could not turn back, but going forward seemed just as perilous. The bell constantly rang, and his companions screamed in agony for it to stop.

He sucked in a breath and ran, instantly gaining ground and sprinting towards the forest's edge.

Instantly the valley around him fell apart, boulders crashing down, smashing into small, more dangerous shards. Some stones hit him, drawing blood along his shoulders and the top of his bald head, but he did not slow his pace. His rage built up and, turning red, his teeth gnashing and foaming, he let out his war cry.

The sound of the bell became hidden under his voice and he shouted louder and louder, sending a message that anyone who came at him would meet their end, but it almost meant that he was preparing for his.

A boulder larger than he had ever seen came hurtling down to block his path. He had no choice. Dropping the unit, he retrieved his axe; holding it far back and holding his other arm forward for balance, he put all the rage he could muster into its swing and hit the boulder with all his force.

The sound of rock shattering echoed, and the bell noise stopped. The boulder not only fell to pieces but flew out of their path and hit the other side.

The ringing finished; the unit staggered to their feet, although still holding their ears and delirious.

They kept slumping over and, looking up, they saw the passage swirling, with the thunderous ringing still within their heads, their vision swirling in a dizzying pattern.

Buskull pulled them on, using his body to shield himself from any other debris, the mouth of the forest now an arrow's shot away.

Then, a chanting noise was heard – the sound of men stamping rock upon metal whilst shouting in a foreign language.

Everyone except Buskull fell back to the floor, desperate to lie down in their dizzy state. Looking up and around him, lining the cliff's edge above, appeared dark figures, silhouetted by the sun behind them.

Although having a human appearance, with arms, legs and skin, they were much more frightening. They stood at least two feet taller than any man, and wider. Like small giants, with their long, huge arms, looking as though they could crush a boulder in their grasp.

Upon their heads they wore stone helmets, and they wore little garb, just leather belts going around their shoulders or torsos. Rags covered their waists.

In their hands they all held a crude weapon, longer than they were tall, with blades on one side as a big as a man, a spike or bludgeon on the other. At the bottom of each weapon was a spike or ball, and they held it in one hand. Although it was obviously heavy, they thudded the ground with their chant, holding it in one hand.

Buskull's chest was breathing hard; holding his axe in both hands, he looked up at them, and, filling his lungs, he bellowed "RECASHA! EMIDIAL, SARAFA!!"

Some of the chanting died at hearing the words, but not all. He had told them who he was; he knew they would understand their fate, he knew they feared him. Using the distraction, he gathered up the others and bundled them into the forest.

With some of their senses returning, they were able to push on, holding their hands out for support and guidance. Buskull was behind them, shouting words of encouragement, but with the tinnitus in their ears, he was barely heard.

As they ran, branches hit and whipped at them, but their momentum did not subside. Travelling light, they got ahead quickly. But the chant behind them grew loud again; they were being chased.

Running into a clearing, they came upon a drop before them, and again slumped to the floor.

Havovatch started to regain his hearing, although he had a throbbing headache.

He looked up at Buskull. "WHO'RE THEY," he shouted sluggishly.

"The Clup'ta!" he said, his voice low and full of hate.

Havovatch pulled himself up, leaning against a stake in the ground on the edge of the canyon, but, as he looked, he noticed it was the stake that had once supported a bridge across the river.

Below them were gushing rapids, waves crashing against the cliff's edge sending spray and water droplets into the air. Some of the heavier crashes sent water cascading over them, and it helped revive them slightly.

Standing up, they quickly sought an escape. The bridge looked as though it had been cut down from the other end, as if keeping something on this side of the river.

The current was strong and the water white, and as they looked to their left they saw a huge waterfall with vapour misting into the air, jagged rocks edged along the top of the fall, with the water caressing them as it fell with tons of force.

"What do we do?" Hilclop shouted, panicking, his uniform soaked through.

"Run!" Havovatch shouted, and he pointed down river.

Few trees grew on the side, giving them some space, but it was still hard going. Running in single file, they stayed close to the trees' edge, trying not to get too near to the water, with Buskull at the back keeping his eye out; but his weight was too much, the narrow path crumbled, and he fell towards the river, just catching some roots as he fell.

Havovatch turned and, running towards him, he gripped his forearm tightly. Feera came back to help, but there was no room for him to manoeuvre. Buskull gritted his teeth as he held on. "Go! Don't stop for me, go!" Buskull shouted.

"Never!" Havovatch muttered through clenched teeth, as he held on to his friend for dear life.

Feera looked up, and the Clup'ta emerged from the trees. He looked back at Hilclop, who was selfishly trying to get onto the rocks on the edge of the waterfall, ignoring their attempts to save Buskull.

"Captain!" Buskull said, seeing the threat, "Captain! Let me go." But Havovatch ignored him, "*Havovatch*!" he said again, "you-need-to-let-me-go!" he said with a reassuring gaze.

He shook his head, "I've had already lost one friend, I'm damn well not going to lose another!"

Heaving with all his might and mustering strength he did not know he had, he lifted Buskull slightly, and, bringing his axe up, he cut down onto the base of a tree; screaming, they pulled him up.

They had no time to linger, and, running, they joined Hilclop. As they peered over the falls, water cascaded down, colliding with the river and rocks below. The noise was deafeningly loud, with mist rising up to create a dense fog.

"They fear the water; getting across is our only chance!" Buskull shouted.

Feera jumped over with Hilclop, but the rock was too small for anyone else; they needed to move to the next one and, grabbing Hilclop by his tunic, Feera jumped, hauling the inept boy with him. On the other side, he pulled his bow free and notched an arrow.

Havovatch then jumped over and turned to Buskull. The first of the chasers reached him, screaming as he ran. The man did not slow his pace charging at Buskull, but Buskull ducked down, hooked his arm under him and threw him over the cliff. Then, holding his axe by the bladed end, he hit another, with the handle knocking him into the falls and over the edge. Then, turning, he jumped onto the rock with Havovatch.

Havovatch jumped to the next, followed by Buskull.

Feera fired a shot; he was clearly not a good archer, and the arrow sailed way above the Clup'tas' heads. Nevertheless, he kept firing.

Turning, they were met by the charging mob, which were standing still, looking ominously at them.

It was strange that they did not dare follow them across. They just continued to stare in a still and emotionless state. Soon a horn rang out from back in the valley and, as if they were the undead, they turned and walked away slowly, not looking back.

The pressure off, the unit moved over to the middle and relaxed a little, but the thick mist was soaking their uniform and night was approaching. They needed to dry off and get some shelter.

Feera pushed Hilclop onto the next rock, but it was only big enough for all of them to stand in single file.

Hilclop was at the front, and Feera tried to encourage him to move on, but he was too afraid. Visibly shaking, he hunched down and clung to the rock as if he were not in control of his actions.

"You need to move!" Feera shouted.

Hilclop just shook his head frantically.

"You can do this!" Feera tried to reassure.

Hilclop closed his eyes, trying to take deep breaths. "This cannot be happening!" he pleaded.

Feera put his hand on his shoulder. "It is happening, and I know you can do this."

Hilclop looked again at the rock. It wasn't very far, he knew he could jump the distance easily, but the sheer drop of the waterfall added to the huge fear building up in him.

He bit his lip, built up some courage and, standing up, he leapt, landing on all fours, desperately clinging on for dear life. But he had done it, and, looking back, he smiled.

With shouts of praise from the others, he then went for the next one, and the next, with the others following, until they eventually got near to the other side with one more rock to go.

Taking his sword, Hilclop poked into the river to see how deep it was, but he could not feel the bottom, just the sheer brutality of the force pulling his weapon from his grasp.

He pulled back, and they stood there looking at the last rock. It was about three men's span away. "Shall we take a running jump?" Hilclop suggested.

"No!" said Havovatch. "You could slip and fall to your death. We will have to find another way across."

"There isn't another way, Captain. If we turn back, they could be waiting for us. We have to cross here," said Buskull.

"Then what do you suggest?"

Buskull handed him his axe, which Havovatch dropped due to the weight. He waded into the river, keeping his body in front of the rock on the edge of the fall. Keeping an immense grip, where a cracking noise could be heard as if the rock was breaking under his grasp, he pulled himself towards Hilclop. As he got near enough, without warning, he picked him up and threw him over to the next rock.

Hilclop screamed as he was thrown, but he landed with plenty of space, the breath knocked out of him. He lay on his back for a moment to regain himself.

Feera knew what was coming, but before he could think about it a heavy grip took hold of him and he went over to join Hilclop, landing on top of him.

Havovatch, seeing what had happened to the others and not wanting to join them, shouted, "Go and find a dead tree, anything so that we can get across!"

They quickly made their way up a clay slope of the shore and straight into the woods.

It did not take long for them to return, carrying a fallen tree. It was more than long enough but looked quite unstable, looking just a little rotten; it was the best they could do. Placing one end on the rock, they held it upright and let it fall, landing on the rock in front of Buskull and Havovatch.

Buskull strolled over quickly; it seemed strong enough. Not fond of heights, Havovatch knew that this would bring him right to the edge of the waterfall, but, with his men looking on, he shook it off and quickly ran across.

However, the wood was more rotten than he had anticipated, and Buskull's weight made it crack underneath him. Without warning, he fell into the water and straight over the waterfall, disappearing from sight.

It happened so quickly that the unit did not even realize at first. They turned in astonishment, rushing to the edge of the cliff and peering down at the river below, desperately trying to search for him.

The unit turned and ran up the slope and along the tree edge, following the river, looking intently and trying to find a path down.

Havovatch could barely breathe; the water was filling his lungs and the weight of his weapons was weighing him down. To add to the misery, he still felt weak from the deafening bell attack in the valley.

Entangled in his uniform, he tried to release himself, but the current pushed him further down river. Light faded as he was pulled deep and then brought back up again, gasping heavily for air; he would then be taken under again before he could get enough.

Just as he got a grip on the clasps for his body armour, he crashed into a rock; with the mix of cold water and trauma, his fingers went numb and he lost his grip, again being sucked back under.

He brushed past close to the shore, and felt the riverbed underneath him. Trying to scramble to his feet, he slumped over again and was carried away by the water.

He knew this was it. He was exhausted, he could not breathe and he knew the others were not with him. Slowly he started to black out, letting his body relax; he started to see circles around his eyes, and then, overcome by an emotion of peace, he saw the white light that had been haunting him for the past few months, and, gently smiling to himself, he opened his arms out to embrace it.

But two arms appeared through the light and grabbed him. Being pulled by his body armour, he was hoisted from the water and slumped onto the shore.

Coughing up a lung full of water, his stomach retching, he lay face down on the soft soil. As each of his senses came back to him, he started to return to reality. The water clearing from his ears, he heard that the river was calmer around him, and he was away from the waterfall.

He was cold, trembling from the ordeal. He did not know where his helmet was, and was not sure where he was or what had happened. He felt heavy pats on the back, and with each one he coughed up more water. When his breathing slowed down and he started to get some strength back, he rolled over and looked up at his saviour. He saw the outline of a tall, broad figure kneeling over him, '*Buskull*?' he thought.

But there was something different about this person.

He tried to pull himself up, looking up at the stranger who was kneeling in front of him, but he just saw a blur. As his vision cleared, to his shock and confusion, he saw a man he vaguely remembered. The figure had the heavy infantry armour of Camia adorning his body, the crest of a general's symbol embroidered in the middle of it. The general held out his hand to help Havovatch to his feet.

Havovatch tried to sift through his memories to remember who this person was, or where he knew him from. He was still trying to remember when he heard shouting behind them. They both turned and, looking up at the cliff's edge on the other side of the river, they saw the rest of his unit looking down at them. Buskull was there, waving his arms trying to get their attention. He then pointed further downstream and they started to move.

Havovatch turned to the unknown general. "Thank you, Sir," he said exhaustedly.

The general gave a nod and started to stride down the shoreline, with Havovatch trying to keep up.

But the general stopped, and, looking into the river, he waded in up to his knees and retrieved something out from between two rocks. Turning back to Havovatch, he handed him his helmet with weeds covering the crest; he looked unimpressed, as if he should be keeping better care of his equipment.

Havovatch knew what he meant – there were no excuses in the army, especially in the infantry, and with a nod of gratitude he wiped the weeds away and fixed the helmet back on.

They joined the others as the terrain flattened out and the river broke away into smaller tributaries. As the others approached them, they stopped in surprise. They weren't expecting a general of the Camion army this far out of the country, especially at a time of impending war. Havovatch was still trying to find a name to introduce him, when Feera helped him out.

"General Drakator, what are you doing here?" he blurted out in confusion.

Havovatch almost kicked himself. Of course it was him – he had met him a few times during his training and his passing-out ceremony, and around the city. He also remembered that the general was mute, which had been the subject of much talk during his training. Havovatch mentally cursed himself for forgetting such a person.

Ignoring Feera's question, the general crooked a finger towards the lands of Loria.

As they looked on, as far as they could see were different shades of greens and yellows over the angles of fields, and in the far distance were faded shades of mist as the land met with the horizon. Beyond that was their destination, and although Havovatch felt he could simply reach out and touch it, he knew he would have to walk for miles and miles before they would even get close.

As they stood looking out at the beauty, the general was already off down the hill. Turning back, he waved a hand for them to follow. Still very confused, and wanting answers as to what he was doing there in the first place, they reluctantly set about walking down the hill, and the next stage of their journey began …

Part Two

Chapter Eighteen
The Departure

Fandorazz stood with a group of engineers clustered around him, looking at a plan of the defences that showed the superb detailing of his ideas. Sprawled out over a table were his sketches, and he stood over them, pointing with an architect's stick, made from a Gracker rib. His father had passed it down to him before he died; it went back generations. He could not remember the last time he had used it.

He directed where he wanted people to be, what they were doing and at what times, with the finely detailed map inside his head so as to get exactly the best results from the resources he had available.

"I don't care for your insolence, Cordor! You do as I say, not what you think is best. If those archery towers are not erected by tomorrow morning then you are clearly not capable of doing the job you have trained so long for."

Cordor bowed his head in shame. He had only given a suggestion on some designs he had in his head for the archery towers, but they had been shot down for being too expressive.

Fandorazz knew he was being harsh, but he couldn't let such things slow down the work: they only had a short time to complete this seemingly impossible task, and he knew he was right without being questioned. He was only like this when he was working. *When the job is done, I will go back to being human,* he had always said to himself.

"Men's lives depend on the defences being completed as soon as possible, and I am not going to fail in this task whilst I am in charge."

The defences were now a different sight to when he had arrived. A framework of archery towers lined the shore behind the wall. Lines of trenches were dug for the catapults that would be built within them. Storehouses were built at the base of the cliff a hundred yards or so behind the wall itself, and protruding from the top of the sea were spiked tree trunks to puncture the hulls of ships. Digging them into the seabed had been the most difficult task, as they could only do it at certain times of the day, when the tide went out. But the sea went out for over half a mile at knee depth during this time.

Fandorazz's friend Groga had arrived, a heavily built man with a bald head and large, rough hands, old enough that his skin was starting to wrinkle. He was said to be so in touch with stone he could talk to it.

Groga was the finest stonemason in Camia for two reasons: firstly because he was one of the few stonemasons in Camia, and secondly because he had an abundant amount of stone around him. The rock he used to live on was now a quarry, sending out rock all over the world.

He had brought all his workforce with him, some hundred men, along with huge blocks of Ieesa stone to replace the broken defences. Ieesa stone was far easier to construct with than other materials. It was not often found in many places, but it was lighter and stronger than other natural stone.

The ancient blocks that formed the defences were too big and heavy to move, so the Ieesa blocks were used to build around the damaged ones, with raises now and again along the wall.

Every man was labouring in the hot sun, and from a distance it looked as though a group of ants were colonizing the wall. Even the guards on watch were forced to work, knotting ropes, helping to assemble structures or digging, much to their dismay.

But still there was more to do. Fandorazz looked up continually to make sure no one was slacking; now and again, another idea would come to him and he would produce his book pad and start drawing.

But a call came out from a lookout on top of the cliff: "SHIPS!"

Everyone stopped and looked. The noise of the workers was replaced by an eerie silence, just the sound of wind and waves. Then, all the soldiers who were working broke away from their jobs, ran to positions and grabbed their spears and shields, some happy that they could do something they were good at instead of labouring. Horns rang out, and all the labourers ran up the hill out of sight, wanting to get away from the impending fight.

Fandorazz stayed where he was, clutching at his pad, and looked at the many ships approaching. Captain Seer came to his side, panting heavily from the exhausting labour.

"No, NO! Everyone back to work – they're ours!" he bellowed to his men whilst unfastening the strap on his helmet.

"What are they doing here?" said Fandorazz, somewhat annoyed that he had not been notified.

"No idea," said Captain Seer, not caring to talk and wandering off.

The workers made a slow walk back to their duties, clearly using the time to gather their breath, but they heard marching, heavy marching, and looking up to the tops of the cliffs, where all the labourers were now running back down … but not because they were returning to work.

Following them were hundreds, thousands of men marching down to the defence wall.

Heavily armoured and all ready for war, the diversity of soldiers from all around Ezazeruth marched towards the defences.

Small crafts arrived and docked by the wall, their crews using ropes to pull themselves up to stand on the battlements with white flags in their hands and guide the ships in, avoiding the timber trunks sticking out from the water.

When the ships finally approached, they came along sideways to the wall, with the following ships pulling against them; they made a long line of tethered ships, bobbing up and down with the waves, although not quite in a line, as they positioned themselves around the spiked trunks. Fandorazz could see the captains on the ships were more than disgruntled about it.

The marching soldiers wasted no time, and began to march onto the ships by large ramps, marching all the way to the end ship. When it was finally full, it broke away and waited in the open water for the others.

Fandorazz stood wide-eyed, wondering what had happened to his perfect working area. Everything was going so smoothly, but these army ruffians had ruined it.

Suddenly, King Colomune appeared, riding down with his escort of fifty palace guards. As he passed, everyone bowed down to his presence. He rode with the palm of his hand out to them and his chin in the air, holding on loosely to the reins of his magnificent white steed, and a slight grin of pleasure and confidence on his face.

Meanwhile, the constant marching of now tens of thousands of men continued behind him: heavy infantry, bowmen, cavalry, even catapults and machinery of all shapes and sizes were being mustered aboard.

King Colomune approached Fandorazz, who was still clutching his drawing book. Captain Seer, crouching next to him, tugged at his trousers, and he suddenly realized he had not bowed yet.

King Colomune took off his gauntlets. "Rise, architect!"

Fandorazz stood up. "M-M-My name is Fandorazz." Suddenly his confidence was washed away. Captain Seer, who was still bowing down, hit him on the side of the leg.

"I mean, your Highness," Fandorazz quickly added.

"I only have use to remember the names I need to know. I will address you by your job title," Colomune said coldly. He regarded the area and the work that had been done. "I heard this place was a state; it looks as though we are now ready for whatever they may bring?" he said, looking around, slightly impressed.

"With respect, Sire, there is much to do, but we are coming along well."

"Well, you will have no need. We are taking the fight to them, so tell your men to stand down."

"Stand down, Sire? With all due respect, what if you fail?"

Colomune shot him a furious glare at being spoken to in such a way. "Fail?!" he roared. "It's not a word I recognize in my book, Fandozz! Also, you should remember who you are talking to, architect – I will not have my plans or motives questioned by you!"

"I-I-it's Fandorazz Si—" – again, he was punched by Captain Seer. "My apologies, your Highness; I wish you luck on your mighty quest, but please may we continue? I hate to leave my work unfinished, and it may be of use in the future."

King Colomune thought it over for a moment. "Very well," he said, "I suppose we could use it as a deterrent to anyone else who thinks they can take on the might of Camia." He boomed with laughter as the excitement of his quest took hold of him. Forgetting his anger, he thumped Fandorazz on the shoulder, the heavy slap making him stumble forward.

"Tea please, Atken," he shouted to his butler.

"Yes, Sire, I guess all that walking has made one tired." He looked at the horse: "Would you like one too?"

Atken then turned and walked away, leaving Colomune's mouth dangling open. He then looked at Fandorazz and laughed out loud. "Carry on, Fandrizz," he chuckled, strolling off to one of the ships, and met the captain on board.

Fandorazz rubbed his shoulder, unhappy with the common assault, and Captain Seer stood behind him. "Wow, you still have your head?" he asked in an amusing tone.

"He hit me!" Fandorazz said in astonishment, still holding the shoulder and not liking that the King had got his name wrong after all.

Captain Seer could not help but laugh.

Fandorazz started to get angry at the captain. "Where's he going?" he said through gritted teeth, trying to keep his anger in check.

"My guess is that all the armies in the world are marching onto those galleons of the fleet except ours. He is going to war against the Black."

Fandorazz shook his head in disbelief. "But that is ridiculous! What I have in mind should prevent all that. He will just waste lives. Why make us do this in the first place?!"

"Waste or not, architect, he is the King and he has made his decision. We do not dare question him." He still chuckled at the treatment Fandorazz had received from the King as he walked away to sit on a rock nearby, taking a long gulp of water and dabbing his head with a cloth to absorb the sweat.

Fandorazz looked on, shocked, as vessels at the end began to undock once they were full, and to filter out into the open sea. He felt a chill run down his spine, as he could not help but notice that there was something terribly wrong about this idea, and that hundreds of thousands of men might not return.

Chapter Nineteen
The Good Samaritan

It was another hot day as the unit walked into the continuing hills of Loria, and the further west they went, the hotter it became. There were no clouds in sight, and there was nowhere to walk in the shade to try to keep cool. Bruises from past events were starting to wear off now; however, their bodies still ached from the constant walking.

Havovatch's armour was rubbing against him … he had to shift about to make it more comfortable, but before long he was uncomfortable again, with sores opening and oozing bodily fluids. But emotionally he felt better, now that his general was with them, and leading them.

Havovatch had not spent much time with General Drakator, nor been this close to him, but he admired him for the fine warrior he was known to be; an unstoppable swordsman who would fight armies single-handedly, holding flanks together. "A remarkable man," the tales said, and "a legend in the military". He had heard of him before he had joined, with his father regaling him with stories about his greatness when he was in the military. Every infantryman wanted to be him and saw him as their idol.

But Havovatch did wonder how old he was, considering that his father served had under him when *he* had been in the infantry, and it had been just over a decade ago that he had retired.

As they walked, Havovatch looked at the uniform he wore, for his own was light scouting uniform, which was still a burden, and Drakator wore far more than that.

He had thick, bronze body armour on, with his broad shoulders holding a long, blue cloak that fell down behind him and rubbed along the ground. His huge helmet had a vertical blue crest tailing down the back of his cloak, and big shoulder pads, with forearm and shin guards also included. The only things that were missing were the shield and spear of an infantryman. Only two short swords were strapped to his hip, plus a huge sword strapped to his back. Yet he showed no sign of fatigue or unease as he moved.

The sword on his back looked remarkably familiar, but Havovatch could not place when he had seen it before. It was a single-bladed weapon with a small hand grip and a purple hilt. Gold was edged around the grip where it met the blade and at the pommel.

Turning his attention away from the unrecognizable sword, he thought about the warrior himself. The word 'warrior', Havovatch thought, was defined by Drakator.

Not much was known about him in terms of his personal life, only that he was the best soldier in Camia, and that he could not speak. His acts of bravery in battle were notable; when other men would run he would stand his ground and carry the day. And, therefore, he had been promoted to general and put in charge of all infantry regiments in Camia.

He was a marvel to look at, an inspiring man, but Havovatch thought it just a bit odd that he was a general who was mute. Most leaders he had heard of were known for their speeches before battle, words of wisdom or shouting down to put others in line. But Drakator was known for his capabilities in taking on vast numbers single-handedly.

Havovatch noticed how he was constantly alert, his helmet shifting left and right, scanning the surrounding areas or reacting to every noise. Havovatch was certain that he was hearing things that he couldn't.

As they continued their journey, they noticed how deserted Loria was. There seemed to be no evidence of people, little farmland, just wild grass with sporadic rocky areas and old fieldstone walls lining the landscape, with unattended livestock milling around.

As Havovatch kept tabs on his map, he noticed they were also going an unusual way westwards towards the desert. It was not the way he would have gone. He would have taken the long way round staying north, keeping well clear from towns and cities, whereas they were currently heading straight for them, through the centre of Loria.

But he was not going to question the general. He had heard many good things about him, so there must have been some reason that he was here with them, some reason why he was leading them in the direction they were going, and so he followed.

Suddenly Drakator reacted to something. Drawing his purple-hilted sword, he held it in his right hand, his arms outstretched. Buskull looked around, but though he could not sense anything, he drew his axe, and the others followed.

Drakator threw his hand to them as if to halt their weapons.

The unit looked at each other quizzically: Drakator was ready for combat, but he was telling them to put their weapons away?

Then suddenly, out of nowhere appeared a vast sortie of black creatures from behind a hill, at least five hundred strong.

The unit went into a defensive line, Buskull licking his lips and snarling, ready to fight.

But they were well outmatched.

The creatures had not seen them yet, fortunately, hidden between two hills; the creatures were just appearing, but marching their way.

Drakator stood with his sword in one hand, and cast his other hand before the creatures, whispering in not a voice, but an echo, as if a demon or monster were speaking inside of him.

"Cover me," he let out in a low voice.

Suddenly, above them, a small grey cloud in the otherwise cloudless blue evening sky appeared.

Again, but a bit louder, Drakator said, "Cover me."

The storm cloud grew darker, almost black, unlike anything Havovatch had seen. He had seen dark clouds before, but not this dark.

There was the distant rumble of thunder, and again, louder, Drakator said, "Cover me," his chilling voice long and distant, sending a shudder down Havovatch's spine.

The creatures were coming into full view of them now; they were going to be seen. It was time to either run or fight.

Havovatch went to make a decision.

"Cover me!" Drakator shouted louder and firmer, his voice echoing into another dimension.

Havovatch thought that if the creatures did not see them, they were certainly going to hear them.

"Cover me!" even louder.

Then a strike of lighting from the cloud struck down and hit Drakator's sword.

"Cover me!!" he shouted, his mystic voice filling the air.

Another bolt came tearing down.

"COVER MEEEEE!" he screamed, his voice not stopping, shouting out in a continual flow.

Then bolts of lightning struck, tumbling down in a continuous current.

But the creatures did not seem to notice the sound of the lightning, the shadow above them of the now huge black cloud, or even the vision of the unit standing startled before them.

There was a wavy motion in the air between them, and the vermin passed by, oblivious to their presence.

Havovatch looked at the others, all confused and startled by what was going on. They were now in full view of the creatures, but the creatures did not react. They walked on by, hissing and snarling, some looking their way, but none of them responding; they just walked on in an unorganized rabble, not taking any notice of them at all.

Drakator didn't move; he stood with his arms aloft, his sword raised. Little could the unit see that his eyes were glazed white, still ringing out his scream.

The creatures soon went out of view and Drakator dropped his guard and fell to the floor, exhausted. As the unit raced to his aid, he turned to them, and signalled to take cover. He was breathing heavily and looked weak, blue veins visible on the skin they could see.

As soon as he stopped shouting, the thunder ceased, his sword glowing as if it were red-hot, but glowing purple rather than red. The clouds dissipated and all was normal again.

They all ran down the bank into a ravine and sat down calming themselves, all shaken and looking to their general.

"I thought you couldn't speak?" Hilclop said, astonished, the first to speak up about what they had seen.

Drakator looked his way for a moment, then turned back to keep an eye over the hill.

They all wanted know what had just happened, but, sensing Drakator didn't want to speak about it, they kept quiet and waited for their next orders.

Three days had passed since the mystic incident, but they still had not discussed it.

They had come across a small gathering of woods now and again, and been able to set up small fires and shelter from the wind blowing openly across the hills.

They had found some farmhouses and hamlets for livestock, but all were abandoned, as if left in a rush, and not long ago.

At night, Buskull would often sit with Drakator, neither of them saying anything to each other, just enjoying each other's company: two of the finest warriors Havovatch had ever met happily sitting together, enjoying the peace. He wondered if it was something to do with all the killing they had done – when times were quiet, they appeared to cherish it.

Then a thought crossed his mind: *Have I ever seen Buskull sleep*? He saw him lying down now and again, but he had shown no signs of snoring or heavy breathing. He had also never seen him yawning or tired.

Havovatch sat on a rock, playing with a bit of long grass, delicately stripping it into smaller pieces, then again with another piece. Feera lay on the floor with his helmet sat just over his head covering his eyes.

Hilclop sat hugging his knees. He had taken off his armour, leaving on just his tunic. It was not a particularly cold night, but Havovatch noticed that he was trying to comfort himself. He thought it must have been the stress of the last month taking its toll. Hilclop had been subjected to more than most soldiers would go through in a career, and Havovatch thought that if he had known the venture they were going on, he would certainly not have brought him.

But, with any luck, it might start changing him into a better man now that he was here – the man he should be in the Three-Thirty-Third, certainly doing what his training would have done if he had completed it.

Havovatch looked up into the clear night sky: stars filling up the blackness, the three moons, Peril, Merta and Seagorn in the distance. He didn't know what made him speak out, but said, on impulse, "Beautiful, aren't they?" while continuing his gaze.

Hilclop did not move his eyes from the fire, but gave out a slight grunt.

Havovatch decided to try to get something out of him, find out whom the person inside Hilclop really was. "Here's a question: which moon is bigger?"

Hilclop looked at him puzzled for a moment, trying to work out what sort of stupid question he had just been asked.

"Well, obviously that one." He pointed to Peril just set in front of them, looming on the horizon.

Havovatch grinned. "There's no need to be sarcastic."

"Well, which one is it then?" he said abruptly.

Havovatch sat himself up and shifted his sword back to make himself more comfortable. "To the eye Peril looks the biggest, but have you not thought though that just because the others look small, it doesn't mean to say they are?"

Hilclop looked up at the other moons. "They could be further away?"

"Exactly!" Havovatch smiled, brimming with great satisfaction that the most incompetent person he had ever met had learnt something from him. "Just because something looks big, it doesn't mean to say it is; it's about deception. For all we know, Peril is the biggest, but don't always be so sure."

Hilclop returned to hugging his knees and staring into the fire again. He did not look so serious now, his face a bit more relaxed.

They said nothing for some time, then Havovatch tried to speak to him again. "Why do you always get aggressive with people? Why not try to get on with them?"

Hilclop looked at him with almost hate in his eyes. "You would never understand."

"Try me."

Hilclop did not move or answer; Havovatch even thought he could see a slight tear appearing in the corner of his eye – obviously he was pressing into areas where he was not welcome.

Havovatch leant forward. "Listen, we have—"

"No – you listen!" Hilclop cut in. "Don't think that with your riddles, your amazing outlook on life and your belief that big moons hover over you gives you the right to press into my life! I like being quiet, and I certainly don't want you prying in, so just shut up and leave me alone!"

Havovatch gritted his teeth. Hilclop had spoken loudly enough that Feera woke up and lifted his helmet. Drakator and Buskull turned to see the commotion.

There were so many ways he could have dealt with him just then … some captains would have had him flogged in front of the entire regiment by each man.

But Havovatch was not like that. Hilclop turned over, showing him his back. Havovatch stood up and wandered over to Hilclop. Feera sat up, bracing himself in case Hilclop turned and hit him.

Standing over him with clenched fists, Havovatch bent down, then covered his cloak over him then wandered back and sat down. Hilclop did not remove it, but Havovatch could hear a slight whimper from him and thought it best just to leave him be for now. Tomorrow was another day.

He stood up and stiffened his back, arms and legs, then cranked his neck. Despite all the walking he did not feel tired, just physically numb. There was nothing he liked more than a good stretch; it seemed to make his body feel able again and relieve all the physical burdens upon him.

Mercury was still on his mind. He had thought about him a lot in the last few days, but not in grief. He felt past that now.

Standing up and staring off to the south, he looked as the reflection of the moons lit up the countryside on the clear night and, putting his hand in his pocket, he felt something, and pulled out a cloth.

It was Undrea's handkerchief. He smiled and, as he touched it, he was again overcome with a sensation of calm and happiness.

"Well, well, you have finally thought of me. I must say, Captain, I am a little insulted."

Havovatch almost dropped the cloth on the floor. He started to frantically look around him. "What? Who is that?" he said, startled.

Feera looked at him, confused.

"Tut-tut, Captain, I thought more of you than this! Obviously you have not thought about me at all, after all the help I have given you!" the mysterious voice said cheekily. It sounded like a slight echo, but clear inside his head. Havovatch grew fearful; he looked at the others.

Feera leant up, frowning. "Are you OK, Captain?"

"Do not be afraid – it is me. Your friend, Undrea."

Havovatch relaxed slightly, but still felt worried, what with the white light and now a voice inside his head, he did not know what to think. He looked at Feera. "I'm fine, something startled me, but … don't worry, go back to sleep."

Feera turned over, but stayed alert.

Whispering, Havovatch played with the cloth in his hand. "With all due respect, could you tell me what is going on? I'm a little confused, I can hear you but I can't see you."

"The cloth I gave you, Captain, will help us to communicate. No need for whispering, though."

"How? Are you some sort of witch?" he whispered again, not really grasping how to speak inside his head.

There was loud laughing, as if Havovatch had just said the funniest thing she had ever heard. However, he could not see the funny side; there was a voice in his head and he thought he was going mad, no matter who it was.

"Hardly – I am more of an alchemist. I am skilled with potions and used the rag to help you."

"In what ways?"

"Well, when you hold it we can talk. Well, not talk, it is more like reading each other's thoughts, but we are in control of what we want to say to each

other." Havovatch felt a sigh of relief at this; he started to think she had been spying on his mind all this time. *"It also means I can track you, and guide help to you where needed; and, one of my favourites, is that when you touch it, it will instantly fill you with peace. Even if you are on the verge of madness, it will help you to relax."*

"That's very impressive, I did not know such things existed. It sounds very … make-believe, though." Havovatch spoke for the first time in his head; it felt strange, but just as simple as talking out loud.

"Yet you are on a quest to find two-thousand-year-old soldiers, Captain. I don't like to be vain, but as I said, I am skilled in this art." He could tell by the way she was speaking that she was smiling.

"How does it work?"

"Well, you need to have something that is personal or close to both people. It can be anything, but cloth works better as it absorbs better; other materials may take longer." She spoke very clearly; she must have had a good teacher, for it sounded as though she was reciting everything she knew from a book. *"And you have my handkerchief. It was my mother's, and it is all I have left of her."*

"OK, so what of mine do you have, then?"

There was a slight pause before Undrea answered.

"Erm, I hope you will not hate me, it was your Gracker tooth necklace. I had to send you to sleep and I sneaked into your room and removed it."

Havovatch stayed silent, remembering the anguish he had felt when that had gone missing in his office; he had felt lost without it ever since.

"I am sorry, Captain, but I could not find anything else that would work; it was the only thing and I was short of time. You will get it back when you return, I promise!"

"Hmmmm … I forgive you, as long as I do get it back. It is very close to me."

"It is in good hands."

There was a moment's silence, as Havovatch stood wondering what to say to a princess? *"So, how are you, your Highness?"*

"I am very well, thank you, Captain. How are you?" she said formally.

"I am well," he replied, but his voice did not mean it.

"Come now, Captain, I am not a Ninsk, treat me with the intelligence I deserve. What is bothering you? If you remember our last meeting in the Holy Gardens, I am a good listener!"

"Yes, you are, my Princess." Havovatch took in a breath. *"My friend Mercury,"* he said bluntly.

There was a slight pause. *"I am so sorry, Captain. It must be so hard for you right now."*

"Well, yes, the last few days have been hell: Mercury's death, I nearly drowned and nearly lost my hearing. But I am pressing on, and remembering him as best I can."

"Oh, Captain, I really am sorry! I did not know you lost one of your unit, especially your friend, I know it's hard for you, but you must push on! We believe in you, I believe in you."

"We? Who else is there?"

"Just General Drorkon and General Drakator."

"Oh. So he is helping you?" Havovatch took a look at the warrior.

"I think it is more that he is helping you, Captain."

"So it was you who told them that I was in prison?"

"Yes, I figured since the scent went weak it meant you must have been underground, and on my map you were in the watch-house at Persa."

Havovatch smiled to himself. *"I owe you more than you know. You really don't realize how much I owe you!"*

He heard gentle laughing, not mocking laughter, but happy laughter.

"What's General Drakator doing here?"

"Helping you, but he will be leaving soon."

Havovatch felt slightly solemn at hearing the news.

"Why?"

"He has business elsewhere."

"Oh. How long can we talk for?"

"As long as you hold the cloth, Captain, but I think you should get some rest, you still have a long way to go."

"I like talking to you, but I guess you are right. Maybe we could talk tomorrow?" he said hopefully.

"I will always be watching, Captain: just tell me when you need help and I will come, just tell me when you want to talk and I will listen. But don't lose the cloth! For then, I will not know where you are, or be able to talk to you."

Havovatch looked at the cloth, cupping his hands, holding it within as if it would break.

"What if I get it wet or burnt? What if I go too far and you cannot see me?"

"Wet? You have nothing to worry about! Burnt though, try to keep it away from fire! I was short of time and could not mix the concoction to stop that, and its range is pretty long, so I will always watch over you."

"You sound like a guardian."

Again there was loud laughing in his head. *"I am your guardian for now, Captain, but when this is over, I want you to take me somewhere quiet and buy me a drink. We can then chat normally and not in our heads."*

"It's a deal," Havovatch said with a smile. *"Goodnight, Princess."*

"Goodnight, Captain."

Havovatch tucked the cloth into his armour at his chest; it was tight, and the best way to avoid losing it. Sitting upright with his legs and arms crossed, he began to doze off, and went to sleep.

Undrea sat in her tower at Ambenol with a map of Ezazeruth sprawled before her on a diagonal desk. Around her were stacked plates and goblets that had not been picked up or cleaned. She had barred the door behind her, locking herself in the room; she wanted no one to come in and compromise Havovatch or his mission and so just received food and drink through a hole in the door.

She looked down at the map, where a small, blue crystal dot marked where Havovatch was, a gold one for Drakator next to him, and a red one to the west of Camia where General Drorkon was. They had burnt a small thin line from the routes they had taken on the map.

She dried her tears at hearing about Mercury's death via her cloth. She did not even know him, but she knew it would be hard on Havovatch, and she held the Gracker tooth in both hands at her cheek to comfort herself. All the aristocrats had wooed her with marriage, but she showed no interest. But now, a common man was lighting a fire within her belly, and she couldn't stop thinking about him.

Suddenly there was a loud thunder strike outside her window. She looked up, and, standing there in a purple haze, wearing nothing but white, was a tall, slender man looking at her from outside her window.

"Go to him, he needs you," she said to him, drying her eyes.

The man bowed, another thunder strike pealed outside, and the man disappeared.

Havovatch was sleeping peacefully, but above him there was the sound of thunder; the clouds turned purple and a white orb appeared above his head. He smiled to himself as thoughts of Mercury went away and he thought of happier times in his life.

Chapter Twenty
My Enemy, My Friend

Havovatch lay awake looking up at the sky; the soft grass caressed him, making him feel that he was lying on a natural bed. A cool breeze passed him, and he turned to see Buskull sitting on a rock with his back to him.

Havovatch could just see in his hand a small book or diary. Havovatch had not seen it before, and Buskull looked intently at his index finger running across the page as he studied the words.

Havovatch got up, and just as he did, Buskull put the book away quickly, as if he meant no one to see it. But, as he opened his satchel, Havovatch also noticed what looked like an old bottle of wine inside.

Feera and Hilclop were still asleep, Hilclop snoring and his legs spread out in a rather unconventional fashion.

Havovatch looked around and noticed something was amiss. "Where's the general?"

Buskull stood and rested on his axe. "He left; he told me to let you all rest."

"How? He cannot speak."

"He wrote it down."

"Did he give any other orders?"

"Only to continue west."

Havovatch yawned and stretched, and looked around the landscape to see if he could see Drakator, but, although he could see for miles around, Drakator had disappeared.

They spent the day walking at no particular pace. The day grew hotter and the terrain around them was hilly, making it hard to go any quicker.

Havovatch thought it strange that they had come across a small number of farms, all of which were abandoned ... no workers or livestock, with unharvested crops. There was also an abandoned village. They would usually have walked away from it, but Buskull sensed no one was there, so they went to investigate. The village had no signs of fighting ... the buildings were still in good condition and the doors locked; it was as if all the populace had left and closed up behind them.

Every hill they walked over led to more wilderness of continuing land, as far as they could see. The strange thing was that they found thousands of tree stumps, most full of decay. It was clear it had been a long time since the trees had been cut down. But the landscape was littered in stumps, as if a mass harvest of wood was needed.

"Stop! We need to rest," Havovatch said exhaustedly, as they came to the summit of a tall, steep hill with rocks on top, an easy viewing point to check the terrain.

Once they sat down, they could see all around them, but there was nothing to see that was concerning. Havovatch thought it weird to walk through a world they were technically at war with, yet they had seen no soldiers, forts, watchtowers or the sort of creatures they had encountered a few days previously.

He approached Buskull and Feera, whilst Hilclop slumped on the ground and began to undo his equipment so he could relax between two slabs of stone.

"How much supplies have we got?"

Buskull undid a small satchel from behind his belt, and produced half a loaf of stone bread and a handful of rice and oats. Feera shook his empty satchel. Havovatch looked into his to find it empty as well. He looked up at them again. "Water?"

"Mine's full," said Buskull.

"Have you not drunk anything?"

"I have more … rationed it, Captain."

"I'm not having that – make sure you get your fill, that's an order."

Feera shook his bottle; there were but a few mouthfuls in there.

Havovatch sighed. "Let's rest. We'll start walking when we have regained our breath."

The unit set about finding a comfortable place to sit, whilst watching out in different directions. Hilclop, however, sat with his legs and arms crossed and his eyes closed.

The others instinctively knew to watch out … it had become second nature for them. The last thing they wanted was to be ambushed because one of them was not paying attention.

Havovatch took his helmet off, resting it on a rock, and loosened his armour slightly to feel a bit more comfortable.

Despite it being late in the afternoon, it was still hot and his tunic was sticking to him from sweat steaming from within. He looked at the others: they all seemed exhausted as well, apart from Buskull, who never seemed to be worn out.

He consulted his map, but there was little detail on it as to rivers and towns in Loria. Camia was detailed with everything from a brook to a small hamlet and the city, but Loria was just an empty space with only the capital, Len Seror, marked.

A short time passed, and Havovatch's legs began to ache more than feel better; he rubbed them, trying to massage away the pain.

"We'd better move; it will be dark in a few hours and I'd rather just go a little bit further before nightfall. Look out for a river or stream, there has to be one nearby!"

Hilclop grunted at the request. Feera and Buskull were straight to their feet and redoing their equipment, whilst Hilclop stayed sitting in his comfy spot, with his helmet sitting loosely on his head, covering his eyes.

Once ready, Havovatch moved off down the slope, followed by Buskull and Feera, each kicking Hilclop in the side as they passed. They did not wait, and Hilclop, in a panic, sprung to his feet, still half asleep, in order to catch up with them, not realizing he'd left his bow and arrows behind. But, in undoing his uniform, Havovatch did not know that Undrea's handkerchief had fallen out ...

The grass almost died as a foul beast stepped upon it, its aching body worn and folds of skin flapping in the wind, but the beast felt no pain ... little could hurt it with the torment of its past.

It sniffed the air with its long, jagged nose, long black locks twisting in the wind. Skulls of different creatures were tangled amongst its hair and rattled together; a few new human skulls were also added for its trophy. The smell of sweat and testosterone was more than potent to the creature, almost like a scented path of the unit's movements.

It looked back at its own scouting party – five strong, evil creatures ready to do the most unspeakable acts for their own pleasure, as if the darkness of the earth had spat them back out.

Wrisscrass bent down, picked up Hilclop's bow and arrows and smelt them. He could pick Hilclop's scent out from the unit's trail.

"They're getting sloppy – it's not much of a sport," he chuckled unpleasantly.

"*We* won't fail in *our* mission," said Brin, the youngest of the group, who limped with a broken leg, but had not had it treated and carried on as he was, ignoring the pain as if it was nothing.

"No, we won't! Because if we do, the master will tear your soul out!" said Wrisscrass, with a scowl of evil.

Brin looked on nervously at his leader, and deep down he started to tremble at the thought. The only real sense of fear any of them had was their fear of their master.

"Wrisscrass!" said Scabb, one of the more senior scouts, who was used to his jests. He bent down, picked up a white handkerchief by the point of his sword and handed it to him.

As Wrisscrass took it, he felt calm strike him: it was so pleasant, he dropped to his knee as if he had been hit by a thunderbolt. Calm was an emotion he had grown out of, and his anger flared back inside him, snarling and bringing up what he thought were joyful images, his favourite being his first kill when he had been only nine. His father's face before his eyes, as he pulled the jagged blade from his heart, came back to him. His father would have been so proud.

He stood up to the confused faces of his unit, and suddenly heard talking inside his head. The telepathic link Wrisscrass held with his unit opened, and all heard the voice.

"You're not Havovatch. Where is he? What have you done with him!?"

There was a cruel, deep laugh from Wrisscrass. "*Your Havovatch is no more!*" The rest of the contingent started laughing over Undrea's sobs.

"But how can we have the link? How can you hear me?" Undrea shouted in confusion.

Wrisscrass laughed harder and held up the handkerchief in one hand. Scabb produced two small rocks from his pack – not normal rocks, but like black crystals.

"Because, my sweet," he said calmly, *"we have telepathic links."*

And Scabb banged them together a couple of times with the cloth between. The cloth's rich chemicals ignited, and the handkerchief burnt before their wicked laughter. Wrisscrass held onto the cloth until it had gone, his finger and thumb burnt, and suddenly he was content again. He turned to Brin.

"Go back and tell the army we are close, tell them to follow our trail, and we will succeed in our quest, much to the failures of our brethren."

A fist was thrown into the air and the pack moved off, Brin running with a limp in the opposite direction.

The sun was now setting in front of Havovatch. It loomed over in its pink state; the hills around were just a shadow of blue as the sun hit the horizon. They found a river to refill their waterskins, and yet again came across signs of civilization, but still no living person.

But, as Havovatch looked south, he saw what appeared to be the silhouette of a structure on a hilltop a league or so away; it was enormous. He pointed to it. "There! Let's move, but with caution!"

The unit proceeded. Hilclop still hadn't fixed his armour properly, and as he adjusted it he then realized something was missing. "Oh, no!" he muttered.

Buskull turned. "What?"

"I've lost my bow and arrows."

"Well, where did you have them last?"

Hilclop bit his lip. "When we sat down."

Buskull turned to Havovatch and quietly tried to call him over.

"What's the matter?" said Havovatch, keen to get to the structure.

"Hilclop has left his bow and arrows somewhere, likely where we made rest."

Havovatch gave a long, sharp stare whilst gritting his teeth. "For crying out loud, boy! Really, what is wrong with you?"

Hilclop said nothing; he almost acted as if he was used to looking like a fool. He just stared at the ground, waiting for them to dismiss it and move on.

"We should reclaim it, Captain," Buskull protested. "If Camion equipment is found by the Lorians, they may think we are invading."

"Agreed, you and Hilclop return with haste." He then pointed to a steep hill just north of the structure. "Feera and I will be there, studying the structure, and will wait for your return. Try to make it before nightfall, I'd rather not knock at the door at night, and I really don't want to wait until tomorrow!"

Buskull nodded, and hauled Hilclop up by the back of his tunic, as they set off the way they had come.

Havovatch and Feera made their way to the structure, trying to work out what it was. Lying on their stomachs, looking over the top of a hill, they squinted.

"I think it's a fort – I can see movement and torches being lit along the battlements," said Feera.

The pair kept, low and made their way towards the structure by using the ravine as cover. Eventually they came to the slope they wanted to get to. They were about a bow shot away from the fort, and could see clearly the battlements and the garrison manning it. They watched for some time, working out times for how long the guards would take to conduct their patrols along the parapet. They were not attacking the fort, but any information could be useful.

The fort stood about fifty feet tall, and comprised lines of solid trunks spiked at the top.

Watching intently, the pair ignored their surroundings. Hearing a noise behind them, Havovatch at first dismissed it as Buskull and Hilclop returning, but it became more ominous as the noise was louder and indiscreet.

Turning, the pair almost pushed their faces into a spear point, as eight dwarves stood there, fully armed. The dwarves looked at each other, and spoke in a rough tongue Havovatch could not make out. They stood but half the height of Havovatch and Feera, but they were well equipped, with solid helmets, chain mail from head to toe, thick body armour and, between them, a whole arsenal of weaponry.

"Captain, any suggestions?" said Feera, raising his hands to show no threat.

"Not right now, no. I have not really met dwarves this close before."

"Neither have I."

The dwarves then started to hit them with the butts of their spears, making them get up, and descended upon them to take on their weapons. Once these had been confiscated, they were hit in the back of the legs and escorted at spear point towards the fort.

Suddenly, from the left, appeared Buskull and Hilclop – Buskull with his arms raised, and Hilclop red in the face and gasping for air as if it were a scarce commodity. Clearly Buskull had pushed him hard, but Hilclop still did not have his quiver.

Upon seeing them, the dwarves started shouting, their language rough and hostile, and they almost charged at Buskull with the weapons, shouting "FRELLA! FRELLA!"

Buskull seemed to ignore their shouts and joined the unit. The dwarves, reacting angrily to his presence, kept talking to each other, pointing their weapons towards Buskull, as if they feared he would run away or act spontaneously, and paid no attention to the rest of the unit. Buskull just held out his hands, indicating he wasn't going to do anything.

They walked alongside the wall of the fort, when suddenly shouts could be heard from above.

All of a sudden, there were noises behind the gate as bolts were undone. It creaked opened loudly and out walked a thin, young man with three very nervous boys behind him, shakily clutching spears ... they could not have been older than fifteen.

The man was unshaven, tiny-framed and wearing a wolf's head over his own. He stood in front of the unit with his hands behind his back, trying to look official.

"What business do you have here? And who are you!" he spat.

"I am Captain Havovatch of the Three-Thirty-Third Heavy Infantry of ... Camia," he said with a slight pause, hoping it would not cause any issues.

"Camions?" he said as if it were a filthy word. "I did not think you ventured from your oh-so precious lands; what brings you to Haval?"

"We're on a mission from our king. These kind fellows captured us," said Feera, waving a polite hand at the angry-looking dwarves.

"Bollocks! What's your mission? And where is your permission to walk through my land?" the cantankerous young man shouted, growing more hostile.

"Our mission is our own business, I'm afraid. I cannot share it with you, but can I ask who you are?" Havovatch asked, politely.

The man's face grew long, and he took a step forward with his hand at his sword hilt. Instantly, Buskull produced his axe, and Feera went to guard. The dwarves all made ready with weapons and closed in, but did not engage. Hilclop stood with his arms by his sides, watching the situation escalate, but making no attempt to do anything.

Havovatch put his hands out to stop them, then turned back to the unfriendly man. "Look! We are not enemies today. If you will let us on our way, we will be no threat. We just ask for water and any food you could spare."

Before the young man could speak, an elderly man approached from within the fort. He was tall and broad, with a white beard; despite his age he seemed strong and well built, but wore evening clothes with an undone dressing gown. He walked over, put his hand on the young man's chest and pushed him to one side with little care.

Either side of him were two well-armoured knights.

"Forgive my son, Knights of Camia, he can be over-zealous in his ways. What do you want here?"

"There is nothing to forgive, my Lord. I am Captain Havovatch, but I'm afraid we are not knights, merely soldiers," he said. "We seek refuge in your village, and we will repay you in any way we can. Can I please ask that these fine dwarves lower their guard, though?"

The lord's son cut in, "No! They will point their spears at your arse until I say so!" he said, more whining than trying to sound authoritative.

"Shut up, Rembon!" barked the lord towards his son, who stood looking at the ground and shifting his feet nervously.

Havovatch was almost taken aback, that the lord's son shared the name of his nemesis during his training, all those jests and common assaults. He wondered if they were related.

Turning back to the unit, the lord composed himself and smiled. "Well, Captain Havovatch, we are technically at war, but I will honour your request."

The lord spoke in a rougher tongue to the dwarves, and they hastily made their way towards the confines of the town. But, in single file, they passed Buskull and spat on the floor before his feet. He frowned and watched them stroll away.

"Mercenaries! They can be hard to find, especially good ones; these dwarves, though, take little but do well. Shall we?" the lord said, gesturing with a hand into the town.

"Mercenaries, my Lord?"

"Yes – thanks to your king, we have a slight peace agreement under the terms of war: when the world is at war then we make a proper peace. Ironic, don't you think?" Havovatch did not really know what to say to that. "Our soldiers have gone to Camia to man the defences, so now we have no garrison and no soldiers to protect the land. I have dug deep and paid for these warriors to protect us, but we are slightly cramped here, with all inhabitants of the area in our small little town."

"So, that is why we have seen no one since the border?"

"Yes – they have not all come here, though: some went to the capital with all their livestock; meat will fetch a good price in times like these. Others went to distant families to keep away from the fighting, and what was left came to our little town. How did you get past the border, though? It's still manned."

"Ermm ... We do not wish to be a burden and will happily leave, my Lord. I just request some food and water?" Havovatch said quickly, his parched mouth longing for a gulp.

"Nonsense! It is a rarity for our kind to have peace, Captain, so let's dine as such: you and your soldiers will be given some quarters and new clothes, and eat with me tonight." The lord smiled, but eyed them incredulously.

"As you wish, my Lord."

The lord smiled, put his arm out to accept Havovatch's shoulder and led them into the town.

As they walked through the gate and into the town, they noticed that it was surprisingly big inside. There were about two hundred houses, tightly packed between the walls, spread over the hills within. Before them, as they entered, was a wide dirt path leading all the way to a grand villa at the centre. As they came to the main plaza on the other side of the gate, the residents looked at them in some anticipation and worry, obviously wondering who the strangers were.

The unit were led down the long path towards a villa.

It was very ostentatious. Mainly built of wood and painted white, it had a veranda and tall, narrow, stained-glass windows; each window was a different colour with patterns adorning it; it was three storeys tall, with the roof tiled red. It was very different to the other houses in the town, which had just a simple one- or two-storey wooden structure. Some even had small gardens in the front, growing vegetables .

The lord led them inside and sat behind a table.

"I am Lord Kweethos, the lord of the lands from the Port of Beror to Len Seror, and humble servant to the Queen Melina. Can I ask how long you require to stay?"

"Just for the night, my Lord Kweethos. We are used to sleeping rough, so we require little in shelter; we just ask for food and water."

"Nonsense! You shall have more than that. Take your weapons to our blacksmith; he will treat and whet them for you. You will be given decent quarters and new clothes. I'll even get the baths heated so you can refresh yourselves. I must say that you look battered and worn and full deserving of some treatment."

Havovatch grinned. "Your hospitality is greatly appreciated, my Lord, but I must stress that we cannot accept all of that. We are strangers, but are happy to have what you can spare."

"I will hear nothing of it!" he said, smiling. He snapped his fingers and a servant appeared; crouching low with his back to the unit he put his ear next to Lord Kweethos. Havovatch tried to hear what he was saying to him but the lord spoke too quietly.

"I understand you're trying to be polite, Captain," he said out loud as the servant scurried off, "but please don't be so rude as to decline my offer. Our village is yours."

Reluctantly, Havovatch accepted. Four chairs were brought in from the adjacent room, and were put behind each of them so they could sit down at the table, with a much larger chair for Buskull. Rembon stood in the corner, leaning against the wall with his arms folded, eyeing each of them and clearly not happy with their presence.

Havovatch ignored him. "Your generosity is greatly appreciated, my Lord," he said, before taking a long gulp of water given to him in a goblet.

Kweethos smiled. "I was once a soldier, and I know the hardships of being outside in the rough with little to keep you going. Do you mind if I ask why you are so far away from home whilst our armies muster?"

"I can only tell you that we are on a mission of great importance direct from King Colomune." The mention of his name seemed to change Lord Kweethos's expression.

"Yes ... well, I knew there was something afoot. We have not been given any information, but not too long ago a message from my queen said to send my entire garrison east to Camia. Nearly all of my military force left, leaving us defenceless."

Lord Kweethos stared at his glass, spinning it, as if he wanted to ask a question he did not think he was going to get the answer to. "What is happening in Camia, Captain?"

"I'm not entirely sure, my Lord," Havovatch tried to cover it up well. "I know that there is something afoot. Camia was in a state of panic before we left."

"I see. Well, let's hope all will return with haste!" he said, toasting the air with his goblet. "Now, let's not talk any more than we have to about business; we are men and as such we will act like men." He clapped his hands at the servants and they began organizing a feast.

"Now my friends, as we have some time before we eat, use this time to get yourselves ready. I will have my servants bring you some clothes."

"I hope not to insult you, my Lord, but I must stress that I appreciate your kindness but I have to have one of my men keep an eye on our equipment whilst it is being looked at by your blacksmith. It's our standard procedure, I hope you understand?"

Lord Kweethos boomed with laughter. "I would have it no other way. You are a soldier and your sword is the weapon of your trade, you will always want to know what is going on with it! I agree!"

Havovatch stood up, followed by the others. "I look forward to dining with you, my Lord."

They left into the warm evening air of the safe haven. Despite there being few unequipped soldiers on the battlements, it did fill them with some sense of safety. Havovatch thought it might have been because they did not have to keep watching their backs any more … although they were in an enemy territory.

They were led to a single-storey building isolated from the other houses; it was close to the wall, with flowered gardens around it. Inside was cosy and seemed to be made for nomads. There was a white washing basin in the corner, and spread out along the room were several beds. There were curtains on the windows and a small fireplace built into the wall. They each picked a bed and took time to relax. Buskull sat at the end talking to Feera, whilst Hilclop snored loudly in the corner.

"So, did you find his bow and arrows?"

"No, Captain."

"No? Well, was he sure he left them there?"

"He says so, but we searched the area and could not find them, but there was one thing I noticed ..."

"Go on," said Havovatch, stepping closer.

"There was something there before we returned, I don't know what, but there was definitely something there."

"A threat?"

"I don't know, Captain. All I know is that there was something there."

Havovatch sighed, fed up with these mysteries and unanswered questions.

Choosing a bed, he hid his dagger between the bed post and the wall. He saw a broken floorboard by his foot and lifted it up. He put his papers inside and then put it back down, making sure it did not look uneven.

"Can we trust these people?" Feera suggested to Havovatch.

"Yes, I agree, let's keep our guard but try not to be rude; they seem to be nice enough … despite the Lord's son!"

There was a sudden knock at the door, which took them all by surprise. Buskull answered it and was almost pushed out of the way by a very small fat man who was finely dressed, his long, black hair slicked back. He pushed his way past, with a manservant carrying four neat, flat sacks over his shoulders. The man walked with his chin up and free hand gracefully in the air, as he walked past them all without saying a word, and over to the other side of the room where he clicked his fingers at a line of hooks. The manservant hurriedly hung them up before bowing to his presence, then ran out of the room.

The man, in a squeaky and patronizing tone, raised his eyebrows with one hand on his hip and one finger in the air, pointing at Buskull. "I take it you're the big man?" he said rhetorically.

"This is yours," he said, pointing to the longest sack on the wall. "Please do not *tear* it, as I spent some time making these in the first place and it's some of my best work!"

Buskull looked at the large sack and stripped it off to reveal a large, red tunic. His face sneered at the horrible colour and the ugly design of the clothing.

"The same rules apply to the rest of you! Give or take a few inches, they will suffice for now." The man left, sashaying across the room as Havovatch and Feera looked at each other, puzzled.

"Oh, and his Lordship said that you can take your baths when you're ready. I'd ask that you wouldn't change into those fine gowns until you have one! Your bodies are not quite fit for such fine material. You will find the bathrooms in the second house to your right as you come out!"

Before anyone could say thank you, he shut the door.

Havovatch looked out of the window, watching the strange man walk away. "They haven't even got any guards watching us."

"If it helps, Captain, I don't feel suspicious about these people. I have been this way before and they're not known for their rudeness. It's their custom to look after guests," Buskull said reassuringly.

"Very well, I think we'd better freshen up, I don't want to be late for Lord Kweethos. Feera, once we have finished, take Hilclop and watch the weapons being treated. When they have finished, come and find us."

"Yes, Captain.

Chapter Twenty-One
Pleasurable Company

Havovatch and Buskull arrived back at Lord Kweethos's villa an hour later, fresh after a much-needed bath. Buskull even used the time to make himself more presentable by trimming his beard and shaving his scalp with his dagger. Havovatch had unsuccessfully tried to do the same, but left several scratches around his face and neck.

The scarlet tunic Buskull wore did not suit him in any way; no matter how many times Havovatch looked at him, he could not help but try to hold down fits of laughter, especially when Buskull first put it on. He particularly didn't find it funny when Hilclop was on the floor and Feera bent over a bed, with tears in their eyes, and Havovatch having to walk outside because he couldn't control himself.

Havovatch, on the other hand, had been given a wonderful emerald-green tunic. The fabric was excellent, very delicate on his skin yet tough and comfortable to wear.

As Feera and Hilclop left, giggling into the night, to check their weapons, Buskull and Havovatch made their way to Lord Kweethos's villa. They found him sitting at his table in the same way they had left him, goblet in hand and drinking wine as if he had an endless cellar below.

"Apologies, my Lord, for our tardiness; the other two will be joining us presently. They are just with your blacksmith."

"None required, Captain Havovatch, you have impeccable timing."

As Havovatch sat down, he noticed that there were no dwarves present.

"Are the mercenaries joining us, my Lord?"

"Ha! I doubt it; they don't favour your big man there," Kweethos said, pointing with his goblet towards Buskull.

Buskull frowned. He was used to people not liking him, but usually it was because he could always beat them in a fight, and he did not like it when someone unnecessarily did not like him.

They sat at an oval table. Before them was a feast of salads, fruits and bread rolls, with a stuffed pig on a skewer to one side of the room and a proud chef next to it.

Lord Kweethos gave him a nod, and he started to carve the roast beast. The smell was divine, cooked with a honey glaze, and each plate was given plenty. Kweethos delved straight into eating, whilst Havovatch and Buskull started more politely.

To one side of the table was Rembon. He could not stop staring at Havovatch with a deep and disdainful glare, which made Havovatch feel uncomfortable.

Soon, Feera and Hilclop arrived, and Havovatch was relieved to focus his attention on something else. He looked up at them in confusion at how quick they had been, but Feera just gave a shrug, with an impressed grin on his face.

Lord Kweethos was talking to Buskull about his enormous size and what battles he had fought in, so Havovatch leant over to whisper into Feera's ear. "You were quick!"

"They're masters of metalwork, Captain; he had all the weapons sharp within minutes. Oh! He thinks he has found a replacement for your throwing knives, he is putting them into your vest as we speak."

Just then, Lord Kweethos turned his attention to Havovatch. "So, Captain, forgive me for saying so but you must be in your early twenties?"

"Actually, my Lord, I am only eighteen," he said, curling the corners of his mouth into a proud smile.

"Well, I'll be damned, either your country recruits younger men these days or you have a superb talent!"

"I wouldn't want to say, my Lord. Our regiment was ambushed at Coter Farol. I was instructed by my captain to lead the army back to Cam in his dying moments. For that, my King promoted me due to my determination and bravery."

"Coter Farol?" Kweethos said frowning. "Forgive me, but isn't that a coastline? What on earth attacked you there?"

Havovatch froze with his goblet to his mouth in realization that he had said too much.

"Pirates, my Lord," Buskull cut in.

"Pirates? But they sail in no more than twenty Cut Men or so; you said you were in an army?"

"Yes, my Lord, but we think they were feeling rather lucky that day. Unfortunately, we were not a full regiment at the time; most of us were fresh out of training, and were sent on a scouting mission to learn our new roles as infantrymen."

"I see," Kweethos said, not entirely believing their story.

Rembon continued to stare at Havovatch as everyone spoke around the table, slowly tearing bits of bread from a loaf and sticking them deep into his mouth, caressing his lips around his fingers as he withdrew them. This performance made Havovatch feel slightly uncomfortable. He tried to connect with him in a friendly tone. "So … you have an impressive wolf's skin; may I ask where you got it?"

Rembon did not answer at first; he just kept looking at him until Lord Kweethos nudged him. "Wolves are native to my country!" he said abruptly.

Havovatch looked on incredulously. "Really? I thought wolves were native to Camia? Isn't your native animal the goat?"

"No!" he said sharply. "Wolves venture to me when I call them – they're mine."

Havovatch noticed Lord Kweethos rolling his eyes back and taking a long, deep gulp from his goblet, streaks of wine spilling down his cheeks as if he could not drink quickly enough.

"Haven't you got men to inspect?" he said after he had finished the wine.

"Actually, I have, so I will not waste my time eating with you rekons when my brave men sit in the cold, keeping you safe!" he said, standing up so quickly that his chair fell back as he stormed out.

Havovatch and the others politely stood up, but had barely got to their feet by the time he had gone.

"Excuse my son, he is … different," Kweethos said, with a regretful sigh.

"Nothing to forgive, my Lord," Havovatch said reassuringly.

As Havovatch went to sit down, he noticed the four stained-glass windows lining the wall. The setting sun was shining behind them; what he first thought were patterns in the window from outside were actually pictures.

The first on the right was red, with a man holding a sword high into the air on his outstretched arm, as he sat on a reared horse. Surrounding him were small horsemen, their faces stern and grave.

The next window was green. Crouching down was a woman, drawing a bowstring back as arrows sailed over her head, again surrounded by armoured men, each of their faces as grave as the one before. Between the green window and the next were the double doors to the room. The next window was blue, and stood on it was a pile of rocks, with a lone man trying to push a banner to the top, the banner worn and tattered, barely showing a muscular creature on it. Havovatch was amazed. *It couldn't be,* he thought.

The final one was purple. It had two men, one standing straight, staring out of the picture, his arms aloof holding a sword loosely in his hand, and again Havovatch could not help but feel he had seen that sword recently. He screwed up his face. *Where have I seen that*?

The other man in the purple window was showing his back. He was staring over his shoulder at the other man, his face grim and dark; his eyes seemed to tell a thousand stories.

"Captain?" Lord Kweethos said curiously.

"Yes?" Havovatch said, not tearing his eyes away from the windows.

"Is everything OK?"

Havovatch became alert. On the edge of his seat he turned to face Lord Kweethos directly. "Yes … my Lord, apologies, I was just thinking something over."

Havovatch was keen not to get into a conversation with him about the knights. He knew that the people in the windows were those who he was searching for, but could not give up the details of his mission. *But why are they here?* he thought. Next to nothing was known about them, and now they were standing in front of him.

He could see Kweethos eyeing him up suspiciously, and tried to direct the conversation elsewhere.

"I must say that this is a lovely place to live, my Lord. May I ask what you are doing so far away from anywhere, though?"

"We are the midpoint between Len Seror and the Port of Beror; we act as a lookout and guard the lands, assisting with trade and suchlike."

"I noticed that there are few woodlands around but a lot of tree stumps, most old and weathered," Feera said, trying to satisfy his curiosity.

"Yes. This entire area was once covered in trees, but when the great silk rush started a hundred or so years ago, trade became very important to Loria. And so, in the last century, all the trees were cut down to help build ships, ports, carts; you name it, it was made from it. The land around us suddenly turned into little more than an open plain; unfortunately we did not think to grow any more in their place," he said with a sigh of regret.

"So, your country specializes in fabric?"

"Everything, really – we put all our energies into anything we can trade as we make a lot of money from it. Quality fetches a fine price. You go anywhere in the world, across the South Sea to Durandas, over the mountains to the white regions in the north, or west across the desert, you will find wine, weapons, armour and clothes, all made in Loria," Kweethos smiled proudly. "We even used to make the tunics for the Camion military until the Cowards' War."

Havovatch suddenly cracked his knuckles, as did Feera. But Buskull kept his composure. They knew what he meant by the Cowards' War, whereas they knew it as the War of Savages.

When the island of Santamaz had attacked and killed all aboard a Camion cargo ship passing their region, Camia had gone to war against it. But the Camions had to go either by land or by vessel, and since Santamazz was a collection of islands in the Gulf of Pera, it had a skilled navy with a large and deadly fleet. So the Camions wished to travel by sea as little as possible, and tried to march through Loria. But the Lorians refused to aid them, becoming a hindrance, lining the sea with their ships and refusing entry for the Camions to cross their lands. They seemed to condone the savage actions of the Santamazians. The Lorians, of course, said that no such incident occurred, and that it was just an excuse for Camia to invade and force another alliance upon them.

But the Camions disagreed, and won the war by taking the longer, northern route around Loria. They attacked Santamazz, overwhelming the islands until their people surrendered, and forced them to swear allegiance to Camia. The Lorians took this as a sign of the cowardice of the Camions, thus from that day Camia was a place full of cowards.

Havovatch was a guest in Lord Kweethos's town and so remained polite, but fought down a huge urge to jump across the table and strike him. Referring to the War of Savages as the "Cowards' War" was saying that all Camions are cowards, and Havovatch knew he was far from that.

There was a long, uncomfortable silence afterwards. Lord Kweethos was so drunk that he did not appear to notice he had insulted his guests, and kept drinking into the night.

Havovatch looked around the room, trying to think of something to break the silence; seeing the green window, he suddenly remembered Hilclop's misplaced arrows. "My Lord, do your scouting parties venture far? It's just that we stopped a distance away to the east and we may have left something behind. When we went to collect it, it had gone. Perhaps you picked it up?"

"No, I'm afraid not. I have twelve knights, who stay by my side, and the mercenaries only scout the land around the fort. The rest of this town's guard are young men, not soldiers, and so they stay within the confines of the fort. But it does concern me that your item was taken. Few people pass through this part of the world, and if you say something is missing then that makes me feel uneasy," he said, his speech slurred.

"Apologies, my Lord, it was nothing important. I feel we probably left it way off somewhere else."

But he gave a worried looked at Buskull, who, too, wore the same expression.

Eventually, Buskull, Feera and Hilclop went to bed, leaving Havovatch and Lord Kweethos alone. The room was a mess of half-eaten dinner and spilt wine, with a musky, stale smell in the room.

Lord Kweethos stood up with his goblet in his hand; opening his arm out, he rested on the wall as he walked to the door. "Join me, would you, Captain?"

They walked out onto the veranda watching over the silent town. Kweethos sat comfortably, rocking back and forth gently on his rocking chair, looking up at the stars. Havovatch took a seat on a bench.

He looked up at Rembon on the battlements – hitting a young man around the head and shouting at him, pointing at the floor and telling him where to stand.

"Your son seems … ambitious?"

Lord Kweethos chewed on his pipe whilst exhaling smoke from his nose. The cool air seemed to sober him a little, too. "He's a nuisance. His mother died giving birth to him. He is a coward and does little in the way of helping others. Instead he spends his time sponging off my fortune and telling others what to do." Havovatch was surprised at the sudden enmity. "After our men left the town, he insisted on taking charge of the garrison, and for some reason I accepted, probably because I was drunk. And now he just walks around with that stupid wolf's skin hat, giving ridiculous orders. A poor excuse for a leader and poor excuse for a son."

Havovatch leant forward; he felt as though he should say something but was not really sure what, for he was no father. "My Lord, if I may? He is your son; he will always be your son, whether you want him to be or not."

Lord Kweethos took the pipe out of his mouth and looked aghast at Havovatch. "Do you not think I know that!" he shouted.

Havovatch withdrew, holding his hands close to him. "Apologies, my Lord, I forget my place."

Rembon saw that they were on the veranda and that Havovatch did not have his men with him, and so made his way towards them.

"Not so tough without your men now, are you Captain!" he said confidently as he approached.

Havovatch ignored the comment, but couldn't understand why he seemed to hate him so much; he could only think that it was because he was a Camion.

Rembon stood in front of his father with his hands on his hips. "Father, all are present and correct on the walls, nothing is stirring out there."

"Ha! From what I hear, this unit walked straight up to the gate before your men noticed them. They would not spot a flame in the night!"

Rembon straightened his arms in frustration and sucked in a huge breath. "Is there *nothing* I can do which will please you, Father?" he shouted.

"No, there is something! Burn that stupid wolf's hat and take a knife to your gut!" he shouted over him.

Rembon stood there in shocked surprise. He looked at Havovatch, who was trying to pretend nothing was going on, then ran off. Havovatch even thought he heard him crying.

"Excuse me, my Lord, I must turn in for the night."

Lord Kweethos just grunted and carried on smoking.

Havovatch made his way back to the house, letting out a long puff of air, relieved to be away from the tense scene.

The town was nice to walk through at night. It was peacefully quiet, and in the windows he could see silhouettes, against candlelight, of families and friends as they stayed up chatting. He thought they were probably talking about his presence. He would, after all, if he were one of them.

The small path he followed had neat stone steps leading up the slopes, and the grass was neatly trimmed. He stood for a moment and closed his eyes, listening to the quietness around him, and his body was filled with a feeling of calm ... it was nice to take a breath for a minute.

But, suddenly, he was struck by a heavy object to the back of his neck. He fell to the floor, as something heavy landed next to him. Reacting instinctively to a threat, Havovatch turned onto his back to see Rembon jump on top of him, holding a dagger downwards in his hand, his free hand outstretched around Havovatch's throat.

Havovatch was startled, seeing stars in his eyes, his head swirling. But as he looked up, he did not see the long, matted hair and slim face of Rembon. He saw the Rembon who had mocked him so much during his training, every joke, every insult, trying to trip him up when he passed by, making insulting comments whenever he could, and the loud jesting and laughter of his friends.

Havovatch gritted his teeth and punched up, hitting Rembon in the face with his free hand with little care not to cause too much damage, knocking him backwards. Havovatch sprung to his feet just as Rembon got up and slashed across Havovatch's stomach with the dagger. Havovatch jumped back, narrowly missing the blade, and then got in close before Rembon could bring the blade back around.

He hit up with his palm into Rembon's jaw, then struck his groin with an open hand. Rembon doubled over and met Havovatch's knee to the face.

The whole time, Havovatch's face was a picture of pure rage.

He took hold of his wrist. Putting his hand on top of Rembon's, he pushed down, forcing open his grasp and dropping the knife. Standing behind Rembon whilst putting him into a headlock, Havovatch pushed his knee into the back of Rembon's legs, making him double backwards. Havovatch was now in complete control. His training had taught him well, and every move was built into his muscle memory.

Rembon struggled under the strain, trying to get free and to breathe.

Suddenly, Buskull came sprinting towards them, shouting and bearing his battle-axe, with Feera in tow. Lord Kweethos and three knights came running up from the other direction.

"What's the meaning of this?" Lord Kweethos shouted.

Doors opened as the inhabitants heard the commotion.

Havovatch let go of Rembon, letting him land heavily on the ground, still grimacing at the initial knock to the groin. He gritted his teeth and screwed up his eyes, holding the injury to the back of his neck.

Buskull descended upon Rembon, and, holding the handle of his axe under his neck, he pulled him up to his knees. Feera picked up the knife and handed it to Lord Kweethos.

Panting heavily, Havovatch looked at Lord Kweethos. "My Lord, he jumped me and tried to kill me."

"You liar!" Rembon tried to shout, between pain and the fact that Buskull's handle was under his chin. "He attacked me! I was trying to defend myself!"

Havovatch showed Lord Kweethos the blood on his hand from the initial blow to his neck, and then picked up the bloodstained rock. "He hit me with this as I was walking back, my Lord. I acted out of self-defence only."

Rembon had nothing to say.

Lord Kweethos stepped forward and looked down at his son. Then, bringing his open hand up, he slapped him across the face; looking down at him, his jaw quivering, he hit him again, and again. Havovatch could see it in his eyes. He hated his son, probably because he took the love of his life away and grew into the man he never wanted. On some level, he felt sorry for Rembon ... but only a little.

Buskull released his axe, letting Rembon fall to the floor holding his face and crouched into a ball, Lord Kweethos nodded at his knights, two of whom rushed forward and seized an arm each, whilst the other held his spear at Rembon's trembling face.

"My Lord, I see that our presence upsets him. We will leave first light so that he can forget about us. I wish for no charge to be brought upon him."

"Nonsense – he attacked a guest! In this country, that would earn death. He will be dealt with in our way!" Kweethos said, looking at the floor. Havovatch usually would leave it at that, but protested. "I appreciate that, my Lord, but I must press that I am not of your custom, and the attack was upon me. If it pleases you, maybe he could just be held for the night; however, I am happy for no further action to be taken."

Lord Kweethos said nothing for a moment, but remained stewing over in his mind whether his son should live or die; eventually, he grunted and walked away.

Havovatch turned to Buskull, grimacing and holding the back of his neck. "How did you know I was in trouble?"

He leant on his axe as he always did. "I sensed it, Captain, and I must say that is a brave thing you did there. I don't think I would be so forgiving to a man who would so selfishly try to take my life!"

Havovatch thought that over for a few seconds, but it was not his way. Rembon and Kweethos obviously had some issues but he could not let a father kill his own son.

They turned and made their way back to the house. Hilclop was still in bed asleep, unaware of anything going on. Havovatch checked his orders were still where he had left them. They were, but he suddenly remembered: where was Undrea's handkerchief?

"Where did I have it last?" he muttered.

"What?" asked Feera?

"Oh, nothing. Just talking to myself."

But then he remembered. He had put it between his body armour and his tunic, but his armour was with the blacksmith. It must have fallen out when he took it off. He crouched down on the floor but could not see it. "Damn!" he muttered.

Buskull came over with a bowl of fresh water and a clean towel, and dabbed the soaked cloth on his wound, as Havovatch desperately tried to think where he had left it.

Buskull wrapped a bandage around his neck and gave Havovatch some herbs from what he called his 'Magic Bag', which seemed to numb the pain, and, lying down, he went over everything he had done that day, trying desperately to think of where he had last had it.

Chapter Twenty-Two
An Important Decision

Havovatch stood naked on a platform ... there were no walls, just a pentagon-shaped stone floor with the outline of dark-bricked archways at every other side, showing the entrance to staircases going either up or down.

In the background were pink and orange flames in the never-ending abyss, with a constant thumping echo ringing out of metal upon stone, as if footsteps approached.

Panting heavily, Havovatch desperately tried to decide which archway to take.

Then he heard the footsteps getting closer.

Panicking as to when the black creature would appear again, he began to cry, sobbing and unable to cope with the torment of anticipation, and ran up one of the staircases.

But the creature appeared behind him, not running, just walking aloof, constantly staring at him. It had a large, solid, square helmet, and broad shoulders under dark, thick armour.

No matter how fast Havovatch ran, the creature seemed to be gaining, even though it was only walking. Havovatch turned to see the dark beast slowly raise its arm towards him, but he tripped and fell against the stone steps.

Turning onto his back, Havovatch looked up at the creature, which was nearly on him, aiming for his throat with its outstretched arm.

Havovatch rolled off the staircase and fell for some time, passing other staircases as he went. It did not feel as though he was falling, but that the staircases were moving up around him in this cosmic nightmare. And, in the distance, as he fell, he saw – as if on a giant screen – the outline of the happy experiences in his life, but cast over by a dark shadow. He saw his friends and loved ones hanging from gallows, being flogged, disembowelled and tortured, inches from death. He shouted out, but no one heard; he just saw the grief on their faces.

The images vanished and he looked down to see a fast-approaching staircase. Havovatch brought his hands to his face to protect himself.

He did not remember landing, but, opening one eye, he saw he was lying on his front. He pulled himself up onto all fours and looked up, and just saw the black outline of the creature staring down at him from the staircase he had fallen from. It did not look very far, but he felt that he had fallen for some time.

Looking up the staircase he was on, he saw it was ever-continuing, with no apparent end in sight. He looked down: the creature was suddenly in front of him, and now bearing down on him; it put its hands on either side of Havovatch's head and began to squeeze hard.

Havovatch saw a purple haze appear in the background behind the demon knight, with thunder rumbling around.

He shouted out for aid, but nothing happened. He shouted again with all the might he could muster; then, as if there were an eclipse, darkness consumed the space where the light had once stood.

The creature on top of Havovatch started laughing cruelly, echoing and deep. Havovatch felt that this was his end; he felt pressure on the side of his head as the beast continued its torment.

But Havovatch felt a surge of power come over him, and, gritting his teeth, he pulled off the helmet from the creature, and lay there amazed, staring up into Mercury's face.

Havovatch sat up quickly, panting and bathed in cold sweat, but as he did so he winced at his throbbing neck.

He heard a moan from the other side of the room and saw Feera and Hilclop still sleeping. Buskull, however, was not there. His bed was made more neatly than it had been before he had got into it, and his axe was missing. The red tunic he had been given was hung neatly on a hook on the wall.

Havovatch got up and went to the water basin on the far side of the room. His neck was still sore; he removed the bandages and dabbed at it with a wet rag. The wound was still oozing from the blow; it was going to play hell when he put his armour on and started running again. But he still felt a sympathetic urge to go and see Rembon and settle matters. He was not even sure as to why he had attacked him.

He saw that their armour and weapons had been returned to them and were neatly put on the spare bunks, his once-empty sheaths full with black blades. He took one out, measured it, balanced it and tested the sharpness by rubbing his thumb along the edge of the blade; he did not want to admit it, but they were better than his previous set. He put his green tunic on and attached his belt. Drawing his sword to examine it, he noticed that it sounded sharp just taking it out of its scabbard, the ringing of the steel blade filling the room.

He stepped outside and smelt fresh bread cooking in the open air. Outside, the town was alive with people chatting, going about their business or working at their trades.

They noticed Havovatch's presence, and some went indoors, pulling their children close. He paid little attention to them; he would probably do the same thing if he saw a Lorian in Cam.

Looking around, he noticed that Buskull was on the battlements on the far side of the town, and made his way towards him. He was hard to miss.

Havovatch took a stroll through the morning air. He was surprised when one woman approached and gave him a large sandwich with runny fried eggs and bacon, but as soon as he took it, she scurried away, not looking back.

Havovatch joined Buskull on the battlements. He seemed troubled.

"How's the neck?" Buskull said, as if he could sense his coming.

"Sore."

Buskull carried his gaze over the hills. He was deep in thought, and kept squinting as if he was frightfully confused about something.

"You OK?" Havovatch quizzed.

"Not sure, Captain; I think there's something out there."

Havovatch gazed out. "You sense something?"

"No, well … yes," he sighed. "I'm not sure, Captain."

It was not like Buskull to be puzzled – usually he had a direct answer and got to the point. "Do you think we are being tracked?"

"I don't think it, Captain, I am sure of it!"

"The Black?"

Buskull just nodded.

"Why can't you sense them, though? Are you sure it is them?"

"I cannot sense them, but I am sure that they are out there."

"I am going to need more evidence than that, Buskull."

Buskull sighed and leant on the battlements. "There are no birds around. I can feel the grass: it feels as though it is dying, as if it has been touched by death. I don't know what, Captain, but something is coming, something large and dangerous."

Havovatch followed his gaze, and suddenly grew aware of an eerie silence before him.

Buskull turned and leant against the battlements, looking into the town.

"Captain, these people cannot defend themselves," he said matter-of-factly, with his arms folded.

Havovatch sat silently and watched on; smoke was pluming out of the chimneys as breakfasts were prepared or workmen went about their trade. Havovatch was also surprised to see a woman helping out in the blacksmith's. Her dark hair tied back, wearing a thick apron and with her sleeves rolled up, she had thick gloves on, and banged at a piece of metal on an anvil with little sign of fatigue. A large, burly chap behind her was doing the same, probably her husband.

Children were running around, laughing and playing, pretending to be knights and using sticks as their swords. Havovatch smiled to himself; they were just like him and Mercury when they had been that age.

He thought it strange that these people seemed so … normal. He was brought up to think that Lorians were savages, that they performed obscene rituals and treated their children like vermin to toughen them up – but, looking at them, it was far from the truth. He wondered why he had been so misinformed about them.

"What do you think we should do?" asked Buskull.

"We have a mission."

"Agreed, but if we leave, could you cope with the deaths of these people on your hands? Remember the village we passed! The Black will destroy everything in their path."

Havovatch chewed his lip. He did not say anything, but gave a nod, and they made their way off the battlements.

"We need to speak to Lord Kweethos; he must know of this threat."

"Yes, Captain, but he has no army and we are not numbered enough to protect them."

"I know; I want you to get all his men in the courtyard with what weapons they have. We will teach them basic hand-to-hand combat, teach them how to man the battlements properly, what to look for."

"Yes, Captain, but do you think it will be enough?"

Havovatch stopped and looked up at him, letting out a heavy sigh. "No, but it will sure be a lot more than they know now."

They made their way through the town and knocked heavily on the door at Lord Kweethos's villa.

Eventually an unamused servant answered. "Yes!" he said gruffly.

"We need to speak to Lord Kweethos as a matter of urgency."

The servant slammed the door in their faces; they heard walking around but were not sure if their message was acknowledged.

A while later, the door was opened again and Lord Kweethos stood there, looking tired and drawn. "You wanted to see me?" he said, rubbing his eyes and clearly suffering a bad hangover.

"Yes, my Lord; I'm afraid we have not been entirely honest with you, but things have changed and we need to talk to you about something ... something serious."

Suddenly Lord Kweethos was fully awake to their confession. He stood there for a moment looking at Havovatch, but then pulled the door open fully. He did not tell them to come in, but they entered, as he took his usual place behind the table whilst Havovatch and Buskull stood in front with their hands behind their backs and chins up.

"When you asked me last night if we knew the reasons why your garrison had been summoned to Camia, we said we did not know. Well, circumstances have changed so that we must confess. There is a threat from overseas, my Lord. We have word of a dark army attacking our shores. We personally fought them at Coter Farol and believe there may be an invasion of Ezazeruth. Your men have been called to protect the east coast from that invasion!"

Lord Kweethos just sat looking up at them, saying nothing.

"H-However, we believe the threat may be closer than we realized. Buskull here thinks that a group of them are heading this way, maybe following us. If you give us permission, we will gather and train your men ready to defend the town. We will stay as long as we can until it passes."

Lord Kweethos still said nothing. He was clearly not happy; with his chin sunk into his chest, he just stared up at them, with a stare that seemed to cut through ice.

Havovatch wanted to speak, but he had insulted him enough, and so held his tongue.

But Kweethos turned to a guard who had just entered the room. "Gather *all* our men in the town, have them meet in the courtyard and make sure they have their weapons!"

He then turned to Havovatch and Buskull. "You have insulted me. I accept you into my town, my *home*! Give you the food off my table and facilities that my own townspeople would not be subject to so freely, and you lied to me?!" Havovatch went to speak but Kweethos carried on. "And you bring this possible threat with you that could kill my inhabitants?"

They both held their position and said nothing, just waiting for him to finish his argument. He sat there, tapping his finger on the desk; he was not looking at them any more, but into deep thought of what to do. "But I cannot deny that we desperately seek your help and guidance. If you can get my men trained to where they need to be, we will say no more on the matter."

"We will do our best, my Lord," Havovatch said reassuringly. "Buskull here is a superb instructor; he has been in many battles and is very experienced. He will have your men fighting fit by the end of the day."

"You said you fought this dark army at … where was it? Coter Farol? Who are they?"

Havovatch tried to think of how to put it. Would he believe in fairy tales about creatures of myth?

"My Lord, they were nothing we have seen before. They are creatures, greyish skin, bad teeth, hideous things beyond description."

"Golesh?" the lord said.

Havovatch and Buskull looked at each other in surprise. "You know of them?" said Buskull.

"Ha, I know of your kind, Captain, but here in Loria we don't forget our history. I know of them, through songs and tales from my father and his father before him. We are not so easily dismissive of what you Camions think are just fairy tales."

Havovatch tried to steer the conversation away from Camia again. "We have had several encounters in the last month. They can be killed as easily as a human. We will do what we can with your men; we just ask that every asset you have will be available to us," Havovatch said.

Kweethos nodded. "You shall have it!"

They both saluted, turned and walked out through the door. As they walked through the town, Buskull followed behind Havovatch. "Go and wake Feera and Hilclop. I want them fully dressed ready for battle; then go to their armoury and see what weapons they have. Meet me in the courtyard as soon as you're done!"

"Yes, Captain."

It took longer than Havovatch wanted for the townsfolk to arrive. There were only eighty-eight of them, mostly young but all aged between sixteen and fifty. They stood in a huddle in the middle, talking to themselves and occasionally glancing over at Havovatch and then muttering some more. "I ain't being taught nothing by a Camion," said one, drily.

Not long after, Lord Kweethos arrived, with twelve well-armoured knights all columned behind him. He was still wearing his sleeping clothes, with a gown loosely covering him. When he stepped up onto a broken wagon to address the town, the chatting stopped and they looked up to hear what he had to say.

"My sons," he said with his arms outstretched. "We are in unfortunate times: war may be close upon us more than ever, and our soldiers may not this day be with us. A force of unknown creatures are descending upon our town. We don't know what they want or what they will do, but know this: they will attack this place and we will defend our town." He pointed down to Havovatch with an open hand. "And this captain from Camia will train you. I order you to listen to what he has to say and I want no questions! The fate of everything we love and hold dear, your families, your lives, everything within these walls rests upon *you* defending Haval!" Tears began to run down his face, but Havovatch could not help but think it was for dramatic effect. "I know some of you will take exception to this, but I command you, I *implore* you to listen to their orders! Separate we are nothing, but as one …" he said, with a clenched fist, "we are unbeatable!" he shouted, throwing his fist into the air. The young men were astonished; some cheered, throwing their hands up, whilst others fell to their knees, overcome with emotion.

Women all around drew their children closer towards them and fell to their knees, crying. But the chant was cut short when Rembon pushed his way through the crowd. "Father!" he shouted. "Father! What is the meaning of this?" He stood looking up at Kweethos standing on the wagon. "These are Camions – you cannot trust them; *we* are at war with them!"

Havovatch leant closer to Buskull. "How did he get out? I thought he was incarcerated?"

Buskull did not take his eyes off Rembon. "No one can lock up their own son, no matter how deluded they are." He spoke as if he knew the bond of being a father.

Lord Kweethos, with one leg up on the side of the cart, looked down at his semi-naked son, still wearing his wolf's head. "Don't tell me what I can and cannot do in my own town, boy; you will take up arms with the rest of my sons."

"Will you stop calling them that! I am your son! Me!!" He pointed at his chest, almost pleading.

Lord Kweethos stopped for a moment before getting down. He did not look at Rembon, but more down towards the ground, and, in a low trembling voice said, "You are no *real* son of mine!"

Rembon's eyes began to well up with tears and he ran away as fast as he could, crying like a pathetic child and pushing through the group of men.

Havovatch stood in the way of Lord Kweethos. "My Lord, I am grateful, but do you mind if I ask what is to become of these men with you?" He pointed to his knights. "They seem well armed and look battle-skilled, and they would be a huge asset on the walls."

Lord Kweethos was still emotional from the ordeal with Rembon, and, without a word, he nodded and walked away. His knights did not follow: they stood motionless before Havovatch, waiting for an order.

"For now, man the walls until further notice, I will come and speak to you soon." They immediately marched off. Just then, Feera arrived in battle dress, with Hilclop rubbing his eyes behind him. Parts of Hilclop's armour were not done up, and he yawned, Feera must have kicked him out of bed. "We have a situation. Buskull thinks there might be an imminent attack. We need to train the townsfolk on how to defend the walls. We are spread really thinly, but we may have a day or so before they arrive."

"How many do we have?" asked Feera.

"Eighty-eight novices, twelve experienced, the mercenaries, and us four … so one hundred and twelve in total."

Feera shook his head. "Spread thinly? We will have yards between every man on the walls."

"This is all we have. Lord Kweethos says that there are no other towns until the city or the port. You saw the hamlets along the way; everywhere else is deserted. He is about to dispatch a rider to inform them that we require aid, but we need to make ready in the meantime." He thought. "Feera, I want you to find any experienced combatants from the group and teach them how to melee using only swords and shields. They will be an assault squad and will plug any gaps during the battle. Hilclop, I want you being trained with them. Try to mingle with them and find out who the better ones are and what they think. I need you to win their trust!"

"What? No! I am already trained; I'll just sit back and watch."

Havovatch wanted to slap Hilclop across the face but, in mind of the novices watching, he thought it best not to. "No! You do as you're told.

I want you to get them onside, work alongside them and help train any who are not doing as well – that's an order!" he snapped. "Besides, you did not finish your training, so this will be an insight for when you do!"

Hilclop said nothing, bowing his head in acceptance.

"How many do you want me to train?" asked Feera.

"No more than twenty, any more than that and we will have no more men on the walls."

Feera left and pulled Hilclop with him. Havovatch turned to Buskull.

"Report on the armoury?"

"They have a small armoury with spears, shields, swords, a few decent helmets and body armour. Their helmets are visorless with just a nose guard. These people pride themselves on making good equipment, so the quality is excellent, but the quantity isn't enough. The blacksmith has asked that he have his two sons pulled back to help make more weapons and helmets."

"OK: do it. Feera's group will all need to be the best equipped. The rest of the weaponry will be distributed to whoever we have left. Arm them as much as we can! I want you to show them how to parry and thrust with spears. I think a distance weapon would suit them better than close quarters; do they have any bows or arrows?"

"No, Captain, their soldiers took all of their crossbows with them. They have no distance or ranged weapons of any kind."

"That's going to complicate things. But we may be able to improvise. I think we are going to need to go on a recce as well; we leave later on this afternoon, so be ready."

"Yes, Captain."

It was not long until midday. Feera had the twenty men he had selected lined up in two rows, and in a short time had managed to show them some basic sword defence drills –they were slightly out of place and out of time, but by the end they were all swinging the swords and jabbing correctly. The armour Buskull had found looked quite good on them as well. They had pointed helmets with a nose guard, chain mail with beige and burgundy tunics over the top, and circular shields with short swords. These men looked as though they could finally hold their own; he just hoped they could.

Buskull only taught small groups at a time. He had twenty-five doing laps of the town, whilst he showed another twenty-five how to hold their spears properly, and how to parry forward and take out an enemy quickly and efficiently. He was demonstrating on a nervous-looking young man with a spear, showing where is best to hit that would incapacitate or kill them. He taught well. As Havovatch passed him, he could hear him saying, "Don't be afraid to strike; it is better you stick them before they stick you. Remember, *they* will not hesitate!"

Havovatch smiled … he was enjoying himself, and in the meantime had temporarily forgotten his mission.

But his attention was cut short when he heard shouting, and turned to see the dwarves huddled at the front gate, Lord Kweethos with them, his arms out as if pleading. But they turned and left the town.

As a group of the novices did another exhausted lap past him, Havovatch walked over to Lord Kweethos. "My Lord," he greeted.

"How are we doing, Captain?"

"Very well; what's happened to the mercenaries?"

Lord Kweethos let out a sigh. "They do not like your presence, and after hearing that you are training the garrison, they have left; I could do nothing to stop them."

"Apologies, my Lord." Havovatch felt a huge pang of regret, for he had lost this town's only fighting force with the exception of the knights, and he felt he should run after them and try to plead with them.

"I would not burden yourself with worry; what's done is done."

"Yes, my Lord. I am just about to go out with my men and your twelve knights and check the surrounding area. We found some good weapons and armour in the armoury. Can I ask why it was not given out before we arrived?"

"You may ask. We are a small town, but over the years we have experimented to get the best results from our clothing, food and weapons. I did not think there would be a threat, and so thought there was no need to waste precious materials if they could fetch a good price – it's our most valued commodity. If I just gave it out to our novices, they would damage or scratch it."

"I understand. Has the rider gone?"

"Rider?" Kweethos asked inquisitively.

"The messenger, my Lord."

"Oh, yes, he has, but he is not riding – we have no horses. I sent a young man I know to be fit and a good runner. With any luck, in a week or so he should return."

Havovatch's heart sank, but he tried not to let it show. "Well, we will stay as long as we can, hopefully at least until some reinforcements arrive."

"I would appreciate that, Captain."

Havovatch fought down the urge not to sigh. He wanted to find the next commander, although he was not sure where he was going to find him. He gave a respectful nod and walked over to the main gate. Buskull had already aligned the knights into two columns with Feera. Hilclop was running with the rest of the twenty-five. He was actually in front and seemed to be taking it personally to do well, clearly not wanting to be outmatched by people who were not trained to be soldiers, even though he was not one either.

The rest of the novices were on the walls. Some were marching up and down, others parrying with each other, practising what Buskull had taught them. They had a different attitude from what he had seen the previous night. They had their chins up and shoulders back, and were making more of an effort in everything they were doing.

The twenty novices Feera trained were really getting into their roles. Their mothers had come down to see them and marvel at their young boys in their new look. Havovatch decided to call them the Twenty: there wasn't any time for fancy names, and it fitted. They constantly practised, over and over again, sword disarms or attacking manoeuvres on each other. Their morale was exceedingly high.

Havovatch secured his helmet tightly onto his head, and pulled his sword and knives out of their holsters to make sure they were loose enough to draw quickly.

Buskull sent the last of the novices to guard duty. He had told them to call out to each other whenever they saw the reconnaissance group outside the walls, and to practise the chant along the wall. He ended with: "Communication is the key – practise it!"

The knights were dressed more lightly now: only chain mail, their spears and shields. It was the first time Havovatch had seen them with their helmets off. All of them had long, neat beards, looking full of wisdom and war by the way they stood and acted. He thought how similar they were, in many ways, to the palace guard of Cam.

The gates creaked open. Havovatch stood at the front of the two columns. Buskull had his mighty axe in his hands. Feera stretched his legs as they prepared to leave. Havovatch took one more look at the unit, and then put his hand into the air and shouted, "Move out!"

Chapter Twenty-Three
New Beginnings

The reconnaissance team had been outside the walls for a couple of hours. Buskull could sense something, but just did not seem able to track it. He kept shouting, "The scent leads this way!" – getting more frustrated with every failed result.

They stayed within sight of the town in case they needed to return, with Feera continually looking back in case green torches were being lit along the wall as a signal; Havovatch was also impressed with how fit the Haval knights were. Running long distances up and down hills was the main part of the Three-Thirty-Third's training, but the knights had kept up well.

Havovatch eventually stopped giving them time for rest. They had now covered most of the surrounding landscape around Haval. "I think if there was a threat we would have found it by now; let's return, we'll do this again tomorrow," he said between exhausted breaths.

The knights shot each other a despairing glare.

They walked back a little more informally to the town, still keeping their gaze on their surroundings and marching over the hills rather than between them.

As they approached the town, they could see the novices on the walls. There was a distinctive change compared with what the unit had seen the day before. They could see a long column of figures standing to attention, with their spears straight, gazing out. It would add to the strength of the fort to have disciplined soldiers garrisoning it. If the Black had seen what they were like the day before, they would have already attacked. Havovatch knew from his reading that deception could be a strong ploy.

As they approached the town, a voice shouted out from the gate house.

"Halt! Who approaches?"

Even though the scouting party was known to the novices, Buskull had instructed them to treat them as strangers until they knew their intention and identities.

"I am Captain Havovatch of the Three-Thirty-Third Heavy Infantry of Camia, and with me are the twelve knights of Lord Kweethos of Haval. We return from our reconnaissance mission and ask for admittance to the town!"

"Very well, friend, enter our stronghold," the voice shouted back.

The gates opened and they staggered in.

The slightly older novices were given senior ranks to help keep the others in order, and the appointed lieutenant who spoke to them approached. "Captain, I hope you enjoyed your run?"

"Very good, thank you, Lieutenant. Any issues?"

"One of the Twenty cut his hand in training; he has been taken to see the physicians. We received twenty-nine accounts of seeing you out in the hills; nothing else was been seen in your absence."

"Good. Is the injured man out of action?"

"I'm not sure, Captain – hopefully not."

"Very well, attend to your duties."

"Very good." The lieutenant saluted and scurried off enthusiastically.

Havovatch dismissed the knights to rest. He knew that they were going to be working the hardest if it did come to a battle.

Buskull was instructed to check on his men. In the few hours they had been gone, a store house had been emptied of its contents. All ready and sealed in wooden crates, ready to send across the world, all sorts armour and weaponry had been taken and distributed amongst the men.

The soldiers on the walls all had helmets; some bore leather shoulder pads or manicas. All had a blade of some sort, a sword or a dagger. All of the novices marched along, with long, thin spears and shields. Most now wore the tunics made for them by their mothers, worn over their chain mail with a belt around their waist. The women had all gone for the same colour, a dark cream down one half and burgundy down the other.

Still, thick, black smoke was pouring from the blacksmith's forge as he and his wife hammered away all day to make as many weapons as they could. Havovatch worried, though, that it acted as a beacon to all around where they were. Outside the forge were racks of spears, lines of shields and small piles of swords, which one of the blacksmith's sons was sifting through to check their quality.

Havovatch and Feera took their helmets off and wiped the sweat from their hair. As they walked into the square, they noticed Hilclop had lined the Twenty up to practice new drills. Surprised at the scene, they were both impressed. Hilclop was demonstrating clearly if sluggish actions were seen, and the novices were picking it up.

As Feera approached, Hilclop without question formally handed control back over to him and then got back amongst the Twenty's line.

Havovatch stood for a moment and looked at the town. There was a nice feeling there that evening: the novices were chatting and laughing on the walls whilst on watch. Whenever Buskull approached they would instantly go to attention, clearly hoping that he would stop and speak to them about how they were doing. Havovatch remembered how eager he had been to be noticed when he had been training.

Feera's unit seemed to be really concentrating on what they were being taught; all were watching intently.

He walked on to find Lord Kweethos. He was outside, looking at the active town before him from his porch. He sat contentedly on his rocking chair, smoking his pipe with his feet up on the fence of the porch.

"My Lord," Havovatch greeted him.

"Captain – pleasant trip, I trust?"

"Yes, thank you. Buskull senses could not get an accurate fix but he was adamant the Black were there; I don't doubt his word."

"Then neither do I," he said, smiling back. "I certainly wouldn't want to argue the point against him," he chuckled.

Lord Kweethos pointed to a seat next to him for Havovatch. A moment of silence passed as they both sat and looked on.

"I have not seen this town so lively in years," Kweethos said, to break the silence. "We are very isolated here, even when the garrison was here. Most of the time we just grow crops outside the walls, drink within, go to bed, then wake up to do it all again. This, though, is something else. The town has come together in a way I did not think would happen in the rest of my days, I have you to thank for that, Captain."

"You're welcome, my Lord, but I fear that the reason for this activity is for the sake of the town."

"Yes, true."

"My Lord, where did you serve within your military?"

Lord Kweethos did not answer, almost as if he was too pained to speak about it.

"Royal Guard," he said at last, but left an eerie silence that Havovatch knew meant he did not want to be asked any more.

There was another long silence, and then the chinking of metal as the Twenty practised into the evening.

"Captain, there is something I feel I must ask." There was a long silence of apprehension before Lord Kweethos spoke. "What is your mission?"

Havovatch sharply met his gaze. Lord Kweethos spoke with much wisdom, and Havovatch knew he could not talk himself out of this one.

Taking in a deep breath and trying to think of how much he was betraying Camia, he sat forward uncomfortably. "I am to find three armies who have been summoned to fulfil an ancient oath to my King."

The pipe fell from Lord Kweethos's mouth as he sat astonished at what he had just heard. He did not bend to pick it up, but looked to see if there were any signs of lying within Havovatch's eyes. "A-Are you telling me! That you are raising the banner of the Knights of Ezazeruth?" he said in a low voice.

Havovatch said nothing for a moment. "Yes, my Lord. I have met one of them already."

Kweethos gasped, "Who? Which one?" he demanded, bordering between fascination and fear.

"If you don't mind me asking, how do you know of them? Virtually nothing is known about them where I come from."

"Ha, unlike you Camions," he said, "our culture does not forget our heritage. Scores of my ancestors went and joined the Xiphos, only to put themselves into exile because of *your* past king. They will not fulfil their oaths, Captain; they want only to be left alone."

"We have already persuaded the Oistos."

Lord Kweethos looked back at Havovatch incredulously. "You lie!"

Havovatch nodded. "Due to the loss of my best friend, they are currently making their way to Shila; we will go west to look for the next commander. But how do you know of them?"

Lord Kweethos ignored the questions; he looked on reflectively, as if remembering a moment in his life. There was another gap of silence, until Kweethos spoke. "I saw you noticed them in the windows within my villa."

"Yes, my Lord – who are the figures in the purple window?"

"Not too sure, the windows were put in before I came here. I know of the three armies, but I know nothing of those figures. I stare at them often, trying to work them out, but to no avail."

Lord Kweethos bent down and picked his pipe up. He sat up in his chair and tried desperately to relight his pipe for his fix of tobacco.

"How will they attack, Captain?"

Havovatch sighed, "I'm not too sure. If they use resources locally then they will delay themselves, but there are two likely methods: scaling the walls, or battering the gates down."

"What do you hope for?"

"Well, both are fraught with dangers. We have no ranged weapons, so if they batter the door down it will just be a frenzy until one army gives, and we have untrained soldiers. If they scale the walls, we are spread too thinly, but will be able to pick them off one by one rather than attack them all at once."

"I have to admit, I had my doubts, but you are a very wise officer, Havovatch."

Havovatch gave a nod, not really sure how to respond to compliments.

"What of the injured, my Lord? There will likely be many."

"Yes, well, in war you have to expect these things. I have three physicians and they have four aides. They will be on the ground floor of my villa, and the women and children will be locked in the cellar. The entrance is hidden, so if the worst does come about, they should be safe ... I hope."

After that, Havovatch sat back, thinking what else he could do to save these people. He wished he had Undrea's handkerchief, as he needed to speak to her – he needed her.

Sitting back, his thoughts spiralled into dreams, and he closed his eyes and went to sleep.

Rotting flesh, east, No! South, No! North! Oh, where the bugger are those filthy rekons?! Buskull stomped along the battlements in frustration. Leaning on the parapet, he looked out across the landscape. He looked into every crevice within the hills, every mouth, every gully. "Where are you?" he said under his breath. The stench was stronger now, but why could he not find them? His mind was full of questions, but no doubts. He knew what he sensed, and he was not going to change his mind; all he wanted to do was find some evidence to prove it to himself.

Suddenly, Buskull realized something he wished he had told Havovatch sooner. He turned and walked heavily, with some haste, back down the battlements, to go and find him. As he passed each novice, they stood to attention. It helped them to respect their seniors and to stay alert, and above all to keep discipline, which Buskull adored.

In the square below, he noticed that the Nineteen had now become Twenty again; they were all sitting on the floor, looking up at Feera, who stood on someone's porch, using it as a stage, demonstrating personal defence and attack moves with Hilclop. Ranged around them were women of all ages, watching as their sons learnt their new skills.

Buskull walked into the town. He felt relaxed for the first time in a while, despite the unpleasant idea he had just had. He did not like working things out in his head. In battle, he could use his strength, but when he thought things through, it caused doubt and apprehension, two emotions he really did not like.

As he came to the villa, he saw his captain sitting alone on a bench, with his feet up on the fence of the porch. A blanket had been put over him, and he was contently sleeping.

He was not going to bother him now; rather he would explain his theory at a more appropriate time. He knew all too well what Havovatch had gone through in the past few months, and he needed his sleep.

He walked over to Feera and Hilclop, and stood politely at the back of the group of women watching. Feera was holding out Hilclop's left arm and demonstrating how to easily trip his opponent over to give him the advantage. Not one of the young novices was talking; all were fixated on what they were being taught, and some were even mimicking the moves themselves.

Feera noticed Buskull's presence and beckoned him over. The women turned and parted as he strolled through, some gasping at his size now they saw him up close. Most showed that they had never seen someone of his stature before.

He walked over to where Hilclop was, and dismissed him to go and check the walls. Hilclop saluted, and scurried off to the stairs with a certain spring in his step.

Buskull stood in front of the group. Feera stood respectably behind him with his hands behind his back.

"In battle," he started, "there are two choices: you either live … or you die." He paused, letting the reality sink in. "If this threat comes to us, you will have one of these choices throughout the time you are fighting, and it is up to *you* which decision you want to make. Remember who you are fighting for, look out for your friends and don't retreat. Always hold your ground to the last man. This is a new beginning for you in your lives, and you should feel proud. You have a badge of honour upon your chest and a reason to fight in your heart; now go home. Be with your family, realize how precious the smaller things are in life, and tomorrow be ready for whatever may come."

The Twenty stood and started clapping, others patting each other on the back. Buskull just looked at them in defiance, being the proud man he was.

When they left, he turned to Feera. "I think they will attack tomorrow morning."

"Really? What makes you think that?"

"I can't say for sure, but I know we are being watched. They are probing us for weaknesses. I posted more men to the south to try to get them to attack the north. It's the strongest point and gives us the better advantage. But there is something distant in the air. I think we have just a few of them out there; more will be coming soon and they are probably waiting for them."

"We should tell Havovatch."

As they walked through the town, they kept their voices low; the morale of the town was high and they did not want to ruin it.

"Do you think they will be ready?"

Buskull waited as they passed a house with one of the novices smiling at them, before answering. "Honestly ... no, they're not warriors, and we are spread too thinly. We will have to do most of the fighting ourselves. Tomorrow will be a dark day for this town, so let's just hope it will be a glorious one in the end."

Feera said nothing. It felt as if their fate was already decided and everything he had taught them today was for nothing. He just wished he had more time to spend training them. It was a heavy burden to realize he could be training these young men only to die.

As they approached the villa, Havovatch was still asleep. Lord Kweethos saw them coming from inside and came out to meet them.

"You really are a gift to this town, my friends," he said with a grateful expression.

"Please, my Lord, it is our duty, but we suspect an attack to be imminent, maybe tomorrow morning. Can I suggest that, when the horns ring, out you barricade yourself with the women and children in your villa?"

"Yes, yes, of course," he said, taking in a breath.

Havovatch heard the talking and woke to see he had been covered and it was nearly night. He immediately got up, rubbed his eyes, let out a long yawn and sprang to his feet. "Apologies, my Lord."

"None required, Captain, you are only human after all."

Havovatch turned to his unit. "Report."

"Can we have a word on our own, Captain?" Buskull asked.

Havovatch looked at Lord Kweethos, who recognized they wanted some privacy and went inside.

"What have you got that's so important?"

Buskull motioned for a private audience, and started walking off as Feera and Havovatch followed. He explained what had been done whilst Havovatch had been asleep. Havovatch was impressed. Buskull had done things he had not even thought of. They were as prepared as they were going to be.

"... but, Captain, I do have a theory I am keen to share with you about these ... *Golesh* relating to our mission."

"Go on."

The trio huddled together in an isolated area behind a house. "I fear there may be a traitor back in Cam, someone who knows of our mission and is keen to stop us. They know where we are, where we're going, and why we are doing this. These *Golesh* that keep turning up, I don't think it is by accident. I think we are being hunted."

Havovatch frowned. "What makes you think that?" he asked, although he had had similar thoughts.

"Well, wherever we go we seem to run into trouble that is threatening our mission. We ran unexpectedly into those creatures that General Drorkon slaughtered, and then again at High Rocks, the sortie after speaking with the Oistos, and again when we were with General Drakator. And now we are in the middle of nowhere, and out of all places in Ezazeruth I can sense them again! This can be no mistake, they are tracking us and us only! And these ones are smart: they are leaving no sign or trace of their presence."

Havovatch bit his lip as he thought it over. "Your theory certainly does have merit, but why do you think someone in Camia is betraying us? For what reason?"

"Well, who else knows of our plans? Who else knows where we are going? There is someone out there who does not want us to complete our mission! But, for what reason, I do not know."

"I think I know," said Feera.

This drew Havovatch's attention, and there was a chilling silence amongst them.

"After we were attacked and Mercury …" he grunted, still feeling the guilt. "I found a brooch in the grass. I was not sure how it got there." He produced the brooch from his pocket and handed it to Havovatch.

Havovatch recognized it as Camion, a cavalry brooch perhaps, but as to which cavalry regiment, he did not know. There were hundreds of different ones.

"Whose regiment is this?"

"Colonel Sarka's." Feera met Havovatch's gaze intently.

Havovatch looked at him with a stern face. "Well, it would explain a lot, but why did you not tell me?"

Buskull stepped in. "Apologies, Captain, it was my decision. We would have done but you were grieved about Mercury, and we felt it not the correct time."

Havovatch said nothing, just staring at the brooch.

"We will have to find a way to send word back to Cam. But for now we need to focus our efforts on the town."

"What about Hilclop? He could deliver the message," said Feera.

"No! He is a deserter, remember – he would be killed, and they would not believe him over a colonel anyway. Besides, we need every man we can get, even if one of them is Hilclop."

There was a nod of agreement. "I want us doing rotating shifts of guarding the walls tonight. I'll take the first shift; make sure you have your horns on you at all times and that the novices have theirs. Rotate their shifts so they get adequate sleep as well."

Feera and Buskull nodded, and Havovatch walked off, still with the brooch, Buskull noticed his fist was red as he held it tight, and despite the bad news he knew it would help in the ensuing battle.

Haval was a silhouette on the hills it was built on. Wrisscrass peered over, monitoring the movements of the garrison, timing how long they took to do their patrols, probing for weaknesses. He looked down into the gully at Scabb and the rest of his scouting party.

"They have more men to the south, few to the north. That will be where we attack."

Scabb grinned menacingly.

"The rest are not far behind; I can feel them. They shall be here by morning," said Wrisscrass, closing his eyes and feeling the power of his brethren.

"What are our orders, Sergeant?" said Scabb, gripping his war hammer tightly, eager to let out his long pent-up anger.

"Kill them all!"

Chapter Twenty-Four
A Day of Blood

Buskull stomped up and down the battlements as the sun rose the next morning. The air was cooler, and the hills were shrouded in a dewy mist, but there were no birds singing; there was the same eerie silence across the landscape as the day before, but, somehow, even quieter.

The novices were tired, leaning against their spears yawning as they looked out, their faces long and drawn, their enthusiasm wavering.

Buskull looked out into the mist and scanned the area carefully. As the sun rose, the mist evaporated slowly, but as it cleared he began to see something.

As it parted, it revealed a contingent of creatures standing a league or so away. They did not move, but stood in formation, looking at the fort.

Buskull did not hesitate. "SOUND THE HORNS, MAKE READY!!" he shouted.

All the novices around him woke up. None of them had noticed the threat until Buskull had alerted them. Feebly, they tried to get their horns up, but nerves got the better of them, and they either dropped them or could not summon the breath to blow; it was clearly an amateurish operation.

Again Buskull shouted at them, demanding that they get their horns sounded. Eventually, the whole perimeter of the wall had horns ringing into the town, and bells rang out.

Almost immediately, doors opened and the men ran to where they were supposed to be; within minutes, the walls had fewer gaps between each man as clusters of soldiers scrambled to the walls. Down below, the knights and the Twenty gathered at their places in the yard in perfect lines, weapons drawn in readiness for the onslaught. Buskull saw Havovatch, Feera and Hilclop running out of their house towards his location.

As he looked down the line of the wall he noticed that reality was starting to hit the novices ... slowly, they were edging their way backwards, becoming fidgety and on edge.

He looked over at the one closest to him and smiled. "Follow me, laddie." The novice gave a nervous grin.

As Havovatch arrived, they looked down at the horde of black before them.

"There are about five hundred of them!" he said, stunned.

"Quantity does not give edge in a battle!" Buskull said stubbornly, with one foot up on the parapet, rubbing his thumb over the edge of his axe blade.

Havovatch and Feera looked at each other and grinned. They knew it was good to have a bit of humour before battle; it took the edge off it slightly, but Buskull was a natural warrior and he took his fighting *very* seriously.

Havovatch walked down the walls and put his helmet on. "Gather!" he shouted to the others.

"Buskull will be lead fighter, so follow him. When the signal is shouted to pull back, do so without hesitation. To your positions!" They all grunted in unison and ran to where they needed to be.

"You!" Havovatch shouted at one of the novices, "go to the pottery and get as many jugs, and anything that you can fill with oil, as you can; and then bring them to the wall quickly!"

Havovatch turned and faced the now gathered novices standing to attention, some closing their eyes and muttering prayers.

"Men of Haval," he shouted, pointing out to the Golesh gathering on the hill, "They will kill your sisters … your mothers … your whole family. They will burn everything you hold dear! *You*!" he said, casting his hand at them, "are the garrison of this town; *you* are the only thing standing in their way. Hold your ground, and don't falter!" He threw his fist downwards for more emphasis. "NOW LET'S KILL THESE FILTHY REKONS!!"

There was a terrific cheer from all around as weapons and fists were punched into the air, and for a moment the young men felt as though they could take on anything.

Wrisscrass smiled. So many of his fellow sergeants had died because of this unit in the last month. He, though, had a reputation for not losing, and being brutal beyond compare. He smiled because he was sure of his victory and the promise of his master to release his brother.

Havovatch quickly jumped up and down to make sure everything was secured tightly on him, and drew his sword; he had picked up a similar shaped shield to the one back in Cam from the armoury. Feera took his two swords from his back and started twisting and flipping them in his hands as he warmed up. Buskull swung his axe from side to side as he prepared himself. The novices tried mimicking them, but were not really sure what they were doing.

The novice returned with several women, all cradling clay pots; they dished them out on the floor of the battlements and then ran to the villa, the novice returning to the back row, cradling a spear.

Havovatch walked up and down, checking their armour and winking or whispering words of encouragement, telling some of them they were the strong ones and that they would have to hold the others together.

"Pray to the Gods," said one of the younger novices, looking out at the Black.

"Which one?" said Havovatch.

The novice looked up at him. "All of them!"

Havovatch pursed his lips. "Today, let's try Grash, God of War."

"How can you be so calm?" demanded the boy, hoping it was a secret that he could quickly tell him.

"Clearly you have not been through any infantry training," he said, with a slight hint of sarcasm.

Just then, he saw Lord Kweethos approaching. He wore a very fancy ceremonial suit of armour, chain mail covering his arms and legs, with a purple tunic, golden stitching sewn into the edges of his collar sticking out from the mail. He had a solid steel cuirass that still fitted him quite well despite his not needing to wear it for several years. On his elbows he wore guards with small spikes, and under his arm he held his helmet with a red plume of feathers sprouting from the top. Strapped to his hip was a long sword, with two short swords curved at the ends; Havovatch frowned as he noticed they were not as affluent-looking as the rest of him, but had holes and scratches where it looked as though jewels had once sat, and was horribly damaged around the edges, as if someone had had difficulty pulling them out.

Lord Kweethos patted his men on their shoulders as he approached Havovatch.

"My Lord, you look grand, but I hope you will now be retreating to the villa with the women and children?"

"Not to be disrespectful Captain … but shove it. This is my town, and this old boy has some fight in him yet," he said, thumping his chest with a clenched fist. He smiled through his white beard. "I want to fight next to my sons; and if this is how I am going to die, it will be a most worthy death!"

"As you wish, my Lord."

Havovatch walked towards the wall. This was it; there was nothing left to do now, and he paused for a moment, closing his eyes. The wind passed him; he balanced his sword in a loose grip as he thought back to what they had done to Mercury; his forearms tensed at the image of Mercury's face before he'd died. He gritted his teeth; in his other hand he gripped the brooch given to him by Feera.

Everything slowed down around him, and as he focused he heard Haval's flags flapping in the breeze, the heavy breathing of the novices. This was it!

Throwing his sword into the air and screaming, Buskull stood with his arms outstretched, letting out his monstrous war cry. The novices, looking at each other, then followed suit as they chanted along the walls, beckoning the Golesh on … and it was answered.

Wrisscrass held his hammer into the air. "CRISHTA MATA! The captain's mine."

The Golesh horde lurched forward like a ferocious tide, covering the hill face as they ran towards the town like a wave of black water against the shore. There was no organization to them, just sheer lust for blood.

They ran with tremendous speed, and their howling echoed in the hills all around like a high-pitched shriek. It was nothing like the townsmen of Haval had ever heard before and struck the novices hard.

As the Black got closer, Havovatch saw that they had long, crude ladders with sharpened, spiked edges.

The garrison took up defensive positions by bracing their legs and pointing their spears at the edge of the wall as Buskull had shown them. Kweethos stood with his sword drawn on the left flank.

Havovatch stood low, holding his round shield tightly to his chest, his sword tip resting on the top of the shield, ready to skewer the first attacker.

As the Golesh approached the bottom of the wall, one of the novices shouted, "LADDERS!"

They soon came up, the tops of the ladders standing over a man's height when they leant against the battlements. All that could be heard were the sound of wood clunking on wood as the ladders were heavily placed against the wall, and the noise of metal as the Golesh scurried up them.

Buskull passed his axe to the closest novice, who dropped it. He grabbed the ladder, and, tensing up, his huge muscles flexing, threw the ladder back the way it had come, just as a Golesh frantically scrambled to the top, squealing as it fell backwards.

But instantly there were more ladders either side of him. He retrieved his axe from the novice, who was still trying to pick it up.

He braced himself, licking his lips and letting out a grunt. Buskull was in his zone.

Soon the first Golesh jumped over the edge of the wall, but, before it could make its move, the novices were sprayed with blood as Buskull's axe cut it in two. Then, holding it above his head, he cut down into another one and kicked the body off the wall.

Havovatch leapt forward and put his might into hitting the edge of his shield into the first one in front of him. Thick black blood instantly sprayed over him, and the creature went limp and fell back over the wall. He raised his sword and stabbed into the gut of another. As a head appeared over the edge, Havovatch punched it in the face, before holding the back of it and slamming it down on the spiked tips of the parapet.

Feera was in his element: as three landed in front of him at once, he dashed forward, ducking under their blows and slicing at the weak spots in their armour, he ended up behind them as they all flopped to the floor clutching at their wounds.

Buskull screamed over the walls as he pulled his buried axe out of the head of a Golesh slouched over the battlements and swung it sideways, cutting another clean in half.

The novices were reluctant at first, but, brought on by the courage they saw, pressed forward and began jabbing their spears into the Golesh, pushing them off the walls. Some of the spears snapped but were instantly replaced by the novices in the second row.

Lord Kweethos fought ferociously, showing a tremendous skill in fighting which Havovatch did not expect. He defended well and cut hard, and before long he had an impressive number of creatures littering the floor where he stood.

Although they had the advantage of height and some preparation, the creatures were fighting harder now ... with more ladders being put against the wall, the defenders were struggling to keep them back.

"FIRE! FIRE!" Havovatch shouted behind him.

The novices in the second row picked up the clay jugs and pots, and threw them into the Golesh coming over the walls and tops of the battlements. Seeing this happen, Hilclop brought up the Twenty, all holding torches, and leapt over the novices, throwing the torches at the oil-stained creatures before pulling back to the bottom of the stairs, waiting until they were needed.

In blind panic, the creatures became disorientated and began beating the flames that suddenly engulfed them. They shrieked as the flames burnt into them; some leapt off the walls for a quick death or to get away from the fire.

The remaining Golesh on the walls became surrounded by novices keen to get their kill, and soon the walls were clear of living creatures, but the advantage was soon lost. The flames quickly burnt out on the cold, wet wood.

Wrisscrass became frustrated, and, throwing a Golesh who had begun to climb the ladder off, he lurched up with tremendous speed. As his head peered over the parapet, he saw a lot of his brethren on the floor of the battlements. They had killed about eighty in total; he did not care, for it fuelled his anger.

Instantly, the thin, young humans charged at him with pathetic spears. To his left was a bald giant, throwing ladders back; to his right was a bronze-clad soldier: he smelt him, that was his target.

Wrisscrass jumped onto the battlements, swinging his hammer. He took out three of the boys at once, their boyish shrieks satisfying his lust. As he made his way towards the bronze man, every spear that came his way he caught and snapped in his grip, before thumping his hammer home into the soldiers. As it looked as though his path was clear, he was met by a short, thin warrior with two swords, and skilfully challenged him.

The creatures jumped over the walls two or three at a time. Havovatch felt he was on the back foot as he tried to counter. Without orders, Hilclop ordered the Twenty and the knights to advance into the melee; some injured novices were ejected through the back lines, from where they made their own way to see the physicians for treatment.

But the Golesh still came, faster and heavier, and the defenders were being pushed back.

Havovatch had to order a withdrawal and regroup, but the light was shadowed as a monster that had landed before him. Larger than he had seen yet, it had two curved swords screwed into each of its forearms. It crossed them together as it confronted Havovatch, making a spine-tingling screech. A novice hurried forward, shouting, with a spear pointing forward the way Buskull had taught him ... the Golesh saw it coming and did not move, but took the stab from the weapon. Unfazed and leaving the spear in its thigh, it punched the novice, stabbing him in the shoulder with the crude weapons.

The novice collapsed to the floor and was dragged away by his brethren. Havovatch parried forward, getting in close; he knew the Golesh could not fight him with those weapons at close quarters. With his shield holding off one of the blades, he used his sword to hold off the other. He kneed the creature in the groin and, as it doubled over, then head-butted it in the face. He saw that he had broken its long, jagged nose as blood gushed down its front, and, sneering at Havovatch, the Golesh licked the blood around its mouth and cackled.

Havovatch went in for the kill. He drew back a step and spun around, bringing all his force to his sword, and went to sever the head off the creature's massive shoulders; but the creature blocked, bringing its right arm up, exposing Havovatch's back to the beast; he fought to pull the sword back. The creature kicked the backs of his legs, making him fall. Standing proud and smiling, it brought its other arm up and went to slice through Havovatch's neck; but there were novices there with him, and they frantically and fiercely jabbed their spears into the creature, each taking a slice. It yelled out as it tried to deal with the multiple attacks; Havovatch, rolling onto his back, kicked at its kneecaps, bringing it down onto his waiting sword. The heavy monster pinned him to the floor.

With help from the novices, it was dragged off, and Havovatch gave a quick nod of thanks.

He took a quick look around and saw they were being overwhelmed.

"Hilclop, take the Twenty and regroup in the square," he shouted, just over the chaos.

Hilclop shouted and grabbed his men and the knights, barking at them to pull back; he did not have much of a voice for authority, yet they still obeyed; some of the novices who were so overcome by the ordeal on the wall went with them.

"Prepare to retreat to the square," Havovatch shouted.

Feera was struggling with a tough creature – it countered every thrust, every slash, and drove him back. The beast was hideous, with long, dark hair and skulls tangled within it; wearing different parts of armour around it and the fur of some creature on its shoulders, it was a fearsome beast, fighting with a heavy hammer as if it weighed nothing at all. Feera ducked under a blow, then kicked it back and tackled it into the wall, sending it over the side.

The last of the novices left, leaving just Havovatch's unit and Lord Kweethos fighting on top of the battlements. Lord Kweethos was so enraged by these beasts, he did not seem to hear the order to retreat and carried on fighting alone.

Havovatch fought his way through the quickly gathering Golesh, and grabbed Kweethos by the back of his cuirass, pulling him down the stairs, struggling as rage took over and he kept trying to fight.

Buskull and Feera were the last to reach the stairs; walking down backwards, step-by-step they tried to keep the Golesh back, giving everyone time to form. The enemy hissed, howled and wailed at the small victory, and, with sadistic smiles, carried on their attack.

The knights formed into a solid line with their huge shields and thick spears sticking out; the Twenty did the same with theirs, and what was left of the novices formed behind them.

Overcome, Buskull and Feera pulled back and went around the side of the left flank before it closed up.

Wedged between two long houses, the soldiers, as one, held the line as the Golesh crashed into them.

Havovatch looked at the walls as Golesh went in different directions. "We're going to be surrounded! We have to fight off the spares coming the other way!"

They ran, leaving Haval's guard to fight the Golesh alone.

Wrisscrass was holding on to the parapet, his hand wedged between two logs, his blood trickling down the trunks before his eyes. He would have laughed if he were not so angry from his defeat on the wall. There was a ladder near him, and one of his privates tried to help him up, but he threw him off the ladder, pulled himself over to him and scaled up and down into the town.

Looking into the town, panting heavily and sneering, he looked for the bronze man; he could smell him but not see him.

He turned to the horde mustering on the walls.

"Hurry up!"

Fighting through the scattering of houses, the Golesh became easy pickings as the unit fought alone and ran in different directions; but, as they chased after them, they soon found themselves separated.

Havovatch hid behind the wall of a house, and, when he heard footsteps approaching, he threw his blade out as a Golesh ran into it.

But three more arrived; he threw his shield at one, threw one of his new knives at the other and stuck his blade into the next, all in quick succession. He threw another knife at the Golesh, which was rubbing its face due to the hit from the shield. He didn't want to admit it, but these knives were far better than his Camion ones – he did not think it was possible. They balanced well and were fiercely sharp.

Turning, Havovatch nearly fell backwards as a creature stood there, ready to stab him with a dagger, but its face showed anguish and its body froze, then fell to the floor.

Rembon stood behind the corpse, his arms bloody; with a malicious expression and smiling, he looked up at Havovatch.

"No! Of all moments, not now!" Havovatch pleaded with him, noticing the look of madness in his eyes.

Rembon dashed forward, slashing left and right, using no skill. Havovatch deflected the blade with ease … he could easily kill him but he just couldn't bring himself to do so.

Then, more creatures came charging towards them. Havovatch turned to face them, but Rembon carried on attacking and slashed at the back of his arm. Havovatch cried out as one Golesh pushed Rembon out of the way and went to kill him. Havovatch kicked at its leg and threw his shield up, hitting it in the face, and followed by putting his sword into its neck.

Rembon attacked the other in a frenzy, making a messy job but killing the beast.

Havovatch stood up and confronted Rembon. "Look! Your town is under attack – you need to fight *them*, not me!"

But his face said it all: he was not listening. He bent down and picked up the fallen creature's mace, and Havovatch raised his shield to block, his sword ready to kill. He had no choice now: *One life to save many others*, he kept telling himself.

Rembon raised the mace into the air with both hands, with a wicked grin on his face. Havovatch went to parry forward and kill him as quickly as possible, with his sword pointing straight at his heart.

But the blow never came, and he lowered his shield to see Lord Kweethos hitting his son with a wooden club to the back of the head. Rembon was knocked out cold and fell to the floor.

Kweethos was pained by his actions; Havovatch could see it in his eyes. Kweethos pushed Havovatch around and assessed his wounded arm, but it was not too deep.

"We'd better hide him, my Lord!"

Kweethos nodded. They picked him up, moved him into an alleyway and covered him with a sheet that was used to cover firewood.

Havovatch saw Buskull, Feera and Hilclop dealing with the last of the Golesh in that area of the town, and they all ran back to the square.

The knights and the Twenty did well to hold the shield wall, but they had edged their way back to the villa and the Golesh were pressing hard; nearly all were within the town now.

The novices kept jumping over and burying their spears into the creatures, quickly rearming themselves to do it again and again.

But they were now at the villa; the path opened out in front of the square and the flanks perished. Buskull and Feera arrived just in time to plug the gap by frantically hacking against the Golesh pouring through.

This was it now: the shield wall was broken; soon it would be a fight till the death, and Havovatch had to make sure that he took as many of them down as he could, to protect the women and children.

He stood guard of his own space and waited for them to come to him. He did not have long to wait: they came from left and right, and he was fighting alone with all the anger he could muster.

There were cackles of crude laughter from the Golesh, as they knew now they had the advantage. In the sheer panic, some of the novices fled, dropping their weapons; others sat on the floor, clutching their ears, screaming.

Only the knights and a small group out of the Twenty were still fighting. Havovatch looked over at Buskull, who had creatures clinging on to his shoulders and another on his arm, the mighty warrior surrounded. Feera was losing control and pinned against a wall.

Havovatch heard his heartbeat within him; he had done everything he could, but this was where he was going to fall. He closed his eyes, hoping that something would change, that General Drakator or Drorkon would arrive, but as he opened them all was still the same, and the last of the townsmen were being brutally attacked.

But then something happened: there was silence. The Golesh stopped what they were doing as one; some paused moments before killing their victims, and then he heard horns ring out in the background … at first faint, they then became clearer and more frequent.

The Golesh all retreated back to the walls, and there was a strange shriek ringing out amongst them, as though something had scared them.

Havovatch pulled his sword out of the gut of his attacker and looked at what was happening. Then he recognized the horns, as did Buskull and Feera. They ran forward, Buskull purposely stamping on the head of a dying creature, crushing its skull.

Havovatch was running behind them, when before him stepped one of the creatures. It seemed different from the others, and, holding a hammer, it attacked him. Havovatch was struck with surprise; he thought they had all retreated.

He fended off the attacks, but that was all he could do – the creature was too powerful and strong for him to fight against. It knocked him to the floor and quickly raised its hammer above its head to strike him.

Then, the creature was lifted up and thrown through a house, as Buskull stood behind it, breathing heavily. Havovatch, panting, nodded, still feeling slightly shocked.

He got up, they ran to the top of the wall, and there they were: the Three-Thirty-Third in advanced battle formation, heavily stomping towards the rearguard of the Golesh by the foot of the wall, the rear ranks and sergeants blowing horns. The front rows of the phalanx chanted with each step, and the bronze mass of shields, helmets and armour covered the hill. They marched forward with their thick spears sticking out as the eight-thousand-strong regiment approached.

"W-What are they doing here?" Feera said, astonished.

"I don't care at the moment – I'm just glad they are!" said Havovatch, relieved.

Buskull rested his chin on top of his axe as they stood there, watching.

The Golesh knew they had no room to escape. The Three-Thirty-Third formed a semicircle around those whose backs were to the wall, waiting for the Camions to attack.

The regiment looked impressive; they had the biggest and strongest men in the vanguard of the phalanx, tightly forming to engage. At the rear was a huddle of archers taking aim at the creatures, pinning them down, and, when they came within yards, the Camions lurched forward and obliterated the last of the Golesh sortie.

Lord Kweethos exhaustedly came to the wall whilst holding a wound to his shoulder, but rested his free arm on Havovatch. He did not take his eyes off the battle below. "I am indebted to you, Captain Havovatch … I mean it!"

Havovatch nodded in appreciation and put his arm on his shoulder, and together they watched as his regiment finished the last of the Golesh.

***

Wrisscrass woke up, dazed, and stood up snarling. He had not felt such anger in his life. The feeling about his brethren being cut to bits was tangible.

He lay on the floor in a small house; looking up, he saw a long, heavy cloak, and, getting up, he put it on.

Stepping back through the hole in the wall he had been thrown through, he saw that everyone was on top of the battlements to the north, and so made his way to the south side, up the stairs onto the wall, and threw himself over the side.

Lord Kweethos sat at his table, smoking his pipe whilst a physician stitched the wound on his shoulder. Havovatch and Buskull stood behind him, whilst Feera and Hilclop stood against the wall to one side.

Acting Captain Jadge stood to attention with his helmet under his arm before them.

"So why are you here, Cap— … Lieutenant?" asked Havovatch.

"I was sent … unofficially, Captain."

Havovatch stood motionless for a moment. "You mean to say you have gone rogue?"

"I was advised to, Captain."

"Advised? By whom!" Havovatch was humiliated that *his* regiment had done such a disastrous thing.

"General Drorkon, Captain – he told us to come here with haste."

Havovatch frowned. "Come here? You mean to this town?"

"Yes, Captain; shortly before we were asked by Commander Thiamos to escort Lady Undrea to Ambenol, General Drorkon instructed me to come to this place for this day with the entire regiment, for your sake."

The lieutenant lost himself for a moment and rubbed his forehead. "Look, I would never break my oath, and I told him that, but I had no choice. Something came over me, I couldn't control it. It was like something else was making me come here, not me. I have not questioned it until now. Come to think of it, no one has questioned it; I can't even remember the last few days. This morning, I was just looking around at the landscape, when we heard the sound of battle and followed it."

"When did he speak to you?"

"Two weeks ago today, Captain."

"That's impossible; we were dining with him on the edge of the Camion border two weeks ago today."

Jadge became frustrated and lost his composure. "Captain! I know what I was told, I know what I saw; I remember everything up until marching back from Ambenol; it's just a haze from there. I don't think we even stopped marching until we got here."

"We did not even know we were going to be here until a few days ago," Havovatch pointed out.

The lieutenant stayed quiet: he did not know what else to say, and at times like this he thought it better to say nothing.

Havovatch knew that this act had been in his favour, but all this superstition and foretelling made him quiver, and making Camia's best infantry unit leave at a time of war could prove disastrous.

When he next saw General Drorkon, he certainly had a lot to answer for, but again it was strange how he became part of this plan that seemed to work out in their favour.

Accepting all these events, Havovatch pressed no further. "Very well, Lieutenant; what are your instructions now?"

"Well ... I ... don't really have any."

"Well, you cannot return to Cam – you would be sentenced. How many riders do you have?"

"Two, Captain."

"Send one. I don't want him wearing anything that identifies him as from the Three-Thirty-Third though; he must dress like a peasant or farmhand or something."

"We can get the necessary clothing you need, Captain Havovatch," said Lord Kweethos between puffs of smoke.

"Thank you, my Lord." He turned back to Jadge. "He also must not take a paper message but memorize it, and he is to report to General Drorkon and him only. I don't want any information getting out to anyone else!"

Havovatch thought quickly of something else. "I also want him to spread a rumour through all the villages along the way to Cam that the entire Three-Thirty-Third has been destroyed."

"Y-Yes, Captain; what will the rest of the message be?" the lieutenant, said rather nervously.

"Ask him to come to me, and I will explain it to him directly."

"Very good, Captain."

Lieutenant Jadge left as the Three-Thirty-Third were assisting with the clean up of the town. Havovatch was risking everything by making people believe his regiment had all been killed. However, he couldn't let the traitor in the midst of the commanders find out about this; also, it gave them some much-needed breathing space.

Feera, Buskull and Hilclop left, leaving Havovatch and the lord on their own.

"What do you think, Captain?" said Lord Kweethos.

"Not sure to be honest, my Lord; there is more to this general than meets the eye. However, at the moment, that isn't my concern. I will press on, nevertheless, with our mission. We need to find the knights!"

"Agreed!" Lord Kweethos said. "My men can garrison the town now, Captain Havovatch, but if you ever wish to return, my home is yours," he finished in earnest.

"Thank you, my Lord, what of your son though?"

"I have decided that Rembon has lived too long without help … he is ill, Captain. I know of a sanctuary that will help people like him, in the mountains to the far north, beyond the realms of Leno Dania. He will go there and be helped. I'm sorry that he made two attempts upon your life; I can't tell you how happy I am that he did not succeed."

Havovatch just gave a nod of appreciation and stepped outside.

Feera had gathered the Twenty, and had a reflective moment with them. Buskull, too, took it upon himself to speak to some of the novices. They stood in huddles, with their arms linking over their shoulders or around their waists.

Buskull was in the middle, patting them on the back and congratulating them, mixing praise with advice.

Hilclop stood alone on the wall, looking out over the terrain. For the first time, Havovatch noticed that he seemed to be content.

As Havovatch walked through the town, one of his soldiers approached and handed him Hilclop's bow and arrows; it was Rembon from *his* regiment. "We found it amongst the dead creatures outside the wall, Captain, looks like ours."

"Very good; have it delivered to that man on the wall there."

Rembon looked up at Hilclop and let out a short laugh. "What, Hilclop the incompetent?" he asked, as if it were a title they had given him.

Havovatch turned to face him directly. "In the past few days, I have seen him do things that will always make him more of a man than people like you; now go and give it to him, and salute afterwards! I will be watching!" he hissed, relishing the moment.

Rembon, slightly taken aback, reluctantly turned and went towards Hilclop.

Things were fitting into place in the town now. They had been luckier than they realized, and miraculously no one had been killed. Some were seriously wounded, others would have to live on with a missing hand, arm or leg, but all were alive to spin tales to their children for years to come. The quality of the Lorian armour the novices wore was good, and it had protected them.

Havovatch knew that, when it came to war, injuries were inevitable; but it was better to be alive and tell the story than to be dead and the story not be told.

He felt strange at the thought. Camions always evolved and forgot their past, keen to move on with their future, but the further into his history he went, the more ashamed he became of his country.

But not this time: he was going to make sure people remembered his story. He just hoped he would live to tell it …

The town was alive with people celebrating – a joyous and cathartic occasion. Havovatch was proud of what they had done here, turning an isolated and dismal town into something that had pride and a mark in its history.

Soon a messenger approached Havovatch, and he took him to one side between two buildings, out of earshot of everyone. He spoke to him at length and without blinking. The rider kept nodding and seemed to be repeating back what Havovatch was saying. When Havovatch was content with the messenger's instructions, he then put the brooch into his palm, patted him on the shoulder and walked away.

The messenger then left the alley, immediately got onto his horse and rode up to see the tailor on the north side of town.

Buskull, Feera and Hilclop approached, all of them grinning widely. They said nothing; just stood there looking at each other. Havovatch broke the silence. "I wish Mercury was here to see this; I couldn't be more proud. We have done a great thing here, and this must not be forgotten." The others nodded their agreement.

"What now?" asked Feera.

Before Havovatch could answer, Lord Kweethos approached him and, taking him by the arm, guided him to one side. He leant in and whispered as he placed an object in his hand. "You will find the Ippikós in a desert city. Head south-west; just keep going until all around you is yellow. When you find the city, search there for their commander."

He patted him firmly on the back, and limped off into the town as if their conversation had never occurred.

Havovatch looked down at the object in his hand, to see a small, sharp knife with a green and golden handle, and he smiled.

Turning, he walked back to the others. "Well, I now know where we are going. We head south-west, and we have increased in size and security, but I will hand command back over to Lieutenant Jadge – he will follow us but we will carry on alone as a unit."

"How far south-west?" asked Hilclop.

"To the desert."

Havovatch noticed Buskull's face drop again at the mention of heading west. He did not want to pry, but he knew something about the words pained him.

"Anyone got any questions?" he asked, hoping that Buskull might bring it up.

He looked up, his eyes a bit more alert. "Oh … yes, Captain, I think I have some more evidence relating to the conversation we had yesterday evening."

"What conversation?" Hilclop asked.

Waving a dismissive hand at Hilclop, Havovatch asked Buskull to continue.

"Well, the Golesh give off a very distinctive odour. I can sense them and I should be able to sense them now, but I cannot, and they are right in front of us"

"Because they're dead?" said Feera.

"No, I can still sense them after they die. Their bodies give off a foul stench."

"So why can you not sense them now?"

He whispered, keen on no one else hearing "There is a moss – it grows high up in the mountains, and it can hide almost anything from my kind's scent."

"OK, so they climbed a mountain and got it rubbed on them maybe?" Havovatch said.

"I don't think so, Captain: the moss grows very high up and it's rare. But the only people who know of it are me and a few of our senior officers."

"Hmmmm," Havovatch said, thinking about it. "Have you found the moss on them?"

"No – to put it on and for it to be effective, they would have had to have bathed in it, or eaten it. It leaves no residue, but hides in their pores. Trust me: they would not have wanted to eat it, not even the Golesh! But I am adamant: there is only one substance that can stop my senses, and it cannot be found or used by accident!"

"Very well, I believe you. Hopefully we covered our tracks by saying we were wiped out, leading this traitor to assume that we no longer need to be sought."

They all nodded in agreement. "Rest tonight," said Havovatch, "we move out early tomorrow morning and we will be pushing hard."

The unit stayed one more night in Haval, while the Three-Thirty-Third camped outside the town with a perimeter around it, to give Haval a break.

The unit bathed and had their weapons seen to by the blacksmith again. The next morning, after Havovatch had got up and got ready, he stood leaning on the battlements, taking in the beautiful sunrise.

The others were amongst the regiment outside the town, speaking to old friends and explaining how they found Hilclop. The tents had already been taken down and they were just amusing themselves until it was time to leave.

Lord Kweethos approached, with his son behind him. Havovatch at first felt a bit apprehensive, absent-mindedly moving his hand to his sword hilt, just in case.

"Wherever you go, I wish you well, Captain Havovatch." They took each other in a warrior's grip. "I have been on many missions in my lifetime, Captain, and I have heard of the missions others have been on. But yours is by far the most arduous and difficult. I wish you all the best in your quest, and if you are ever returning this way, Haval is yours!" he said, bowing his head. Rembon stood behind, with a sneer on his face.

"Thank you, my Lord."

Giving a nod at Rembon, Havovatch then walked with his head held high, holding his hands out to the novices, and they patted him on the back. He made his way out of the gate and towards the Three-Thirty-Third.

As he walked parallel with the town, all the novices and townsfolk were on the walls, waving.

Havovatch, for the first time in a while, did not feel stressed, but happy and keen to get on to the next stage of his mission.

Havovatch gave a nod to Jadge, and he bellowed, "THREE-THIRTY-THIRD, TO-YOUR-DUTIES!!"

There was a raucous stomping as the regiment marched away, and suddenly, behind them, the crowd cheered into the air. Before the unit set off, they turned and gave one last wave.

Chapter Twenty-Five
Foreigners

Five days had passed since leaving Haval. Havovatch had left the Three-Thirty-Third far behind as the four of them paced on, and whenever they turned they could see dust thrown into the air as the regiment marched in the distance.

The terrain changed from fields to sand dunes, and the temperature became unbearably hot as they made their way south-west towards the desert. With every step, Havovatch got more agitated by the heat, continually removing his helmet to wipe the sweat from his forehead.

The desert was full of dried rock and sand, with nowhere for shade and few places for water. It was a wasteland, and those who knew the land would make their way from waterhole to waterhole, triple the distance rather than going straight to the their destination, but necessary to keep close to the source for survival.

Havovatch had heard little about the desert … few ventured this far from his lands, and he had never thought that he would come so far.

As they walked on, the unit stayed relatively quiet. Hilclop was, again, not very talkative, and did not seem to enjoy walking; he was constantly sulking. Havovatch just put it down to the intense heat.

Buskull was never a talkative person, but he seemed even quieter than he normally was.

They came to a ravine with a waterhole at the bottom; there was a touch of vegetation, and there were some rocks to sit against, shading them from the sun.

The day was fading, and stars were starting to peer through the blue sky as day turned to night. The one thing Havovatch did agree with: the pink sky on the horizon, fading to blue above him, with sporadic star constellations and the desert landscape shadowed, was one of the most beautiful sights he had ever seen.

It got much colder when night came, and he draped his cloak over himself as he started to shiver. Buskull sat up at the top of the ravine, with his axe handle buried into the sand, and leant against it, crossed his arms and closed his eyes. The sudden chill did not seem to affect him.

Hilclop and Feera started a fire and curled up on the floor with their own thoughts. It did not take long for them to fall asleep.

As Havovatch reflected on helping Haval, he found himself drifting off, his mind wandering, his body getting lighter; the pains he felt faded, and soon he was into a world of his own, dreaming of climbing mountains with ease and taking on battalions of Golesh single-handedly as if he were General Drakator.

But he woke a little while later to a noise in his left ear; it took him out of his trance, and he was immediately awake and alert, looking around. It was slightly darker but there was still a faint glow of light.

At first he just tensed up; he stayed quiet, pointing his ear in the direction from which he heard the noise.

He thought it was his mind most of the time, but then he heard the noise again. As he looked at the crest of the ravine, he saw the outline of a head slowly pop up. Without hesitation, his sword was drawn, and he dashed over the top of the sand dune to meet a startled young man trying to pull back.

He jumped on top of him and buried his knee into the man's chest whilst holding his arm straight at the stranger's neck, sword drawn back and pointing down at his eyes so he could see the tip.

The stranger's face was covered with a rag, just showing his eyes; he was dressed lightly and looked worn. The others came up behind Havovatch to see what was going on – even Hilclop was there with his weapon ready.

"Patience, friend," the man said, choking through Havovatch's grasp.

"Who are you? And what business do you have here?" Havovatch demanded.

"I was just hoping for some water, but when I saw you were camping I thought to check you out. I mean no harm." The stranger grimaced from the pressure on his chest.

"Then why are you armed?" Havovatch said, looking at the man's clenched fist, holding a straight sword with a bent handle.

Buskull knelt down, removed the sword and gave it to Feera. He then bent down, pulled the stranger up by the cloth on his shoulder and ripped the rag from his head, Hilclop pointing the tip of his sword at him.

He was a slender man: tall, with frizzy, dark hair, wide-eyed and clearly petrified. Holding his hands together at his chest, he looked at them individually, trying to smile nervously.

"If I may? Please allow me some water," he asked desperately.

The unit moved out of the way, allowing him to go to the pool. The man rushed forward, falling to his knees and, burying his head in the water, drinking as though he had never had water in his life. When he finished, he looked up at Havovatch and the others.

"What will you do with me?" he asked nervously.

"Depends what you're doing here," said Havovatch.

"I am no warrior! I am a mere adventurer; my name is Ferith."

"Strange, You seem to have battle scars. Not something an adventurer should be having," Feera pointed out.

"I am no soldier! I am from the north. I venture in the world rather than fight it. I was just passing by and saw the trees. I have not drunk in days, and when I saw the pool I wanted to get some water quickly, as there is a large army marching this way."

They all looked at each other and grinned.

"Hilclop, stay with him, don't take your eyes off him," said Havovatch.

Hilclop positioned himself a few feet away from Ferith, who sat nervously on his knees, looking back at Havovatch. The others walked a few feet away to deliberate.

"Well, what do you think – is he a threat?" Havovatch asked, once they were out of earshot.

"Hard to say. He is either a good liar or genuinely travelling the world from the north," put Feera.

"I know a few things about the north, Captain," said Buskull. "I fought there for five years. I'll ask him some questions."

They walked back over to Ferith. Buskull knelt down in front of him and took his hands; holding his wrists, he looked deep into his eyes.

"Where are you from?"

"Viror," said Ferith, drawing back slightly.

"They have busy cities there, don't they?"

"No – tribes," Ferith corrected, confusingly.

"Who is your king?"

"We have no king: we have a grand master, Reefgrag."

"What is your country's weapon of choice?"

"Bone hatchets."

"How long have you been gone from Viror?"

"Twelve months this season."

"And why did you leave?"

"I was fed up of hearing about the world and never seeing it."

"YOU'RE LYING!" Buskull pressed into his wrists. "WHY DID YOU LEAVE VIROR?" Buskull shouted.

"AHH! I slept with another tribe chief's daughter. Please, I only lied because I have a price upon my head!"

Buskull let go of Ferith's wrist, looked up at Havovatch and gave a nod of reassurance.

Havovatch stood with his arms folded. "Why are people hunting you?"

"They told me to run; they gave me three days, then the country's best trackers started hunting me down. It's a tradition when someone commits a crime in my country."

"Well, we could make a few coins out of him and help them out?" Feera said with a grin.

Havovatch stared at Feera, trying not to smile. "They're hunting you because you slept with some other man's daughter?"

Ferith shrugged. "It is our way. Unfortunately, I got caught this time."

Havovatch stood with his arms folded for a moment as he thought. He took the sword off Feera and approached Ferith, who drew back slightly in anticipation of what was to come next.

"Very well, Ferith of Viror." He handed his weapon back, handle first.

"We don't own these lands, but we sure as hell are not going to let strangers sit with us, so you will leave now, and if you come back we will kill you," he said curtly.

Ferith produced his waterskin, quickly pulling the stop out of the top, and filled it up. Then he ran away, and, before he could put the stop back, in he disappeared over the top of the dune.

Once he was out of sight, Havovatch turned to the others. "Well done – you worked as a team, especially you, Hilclop. I feel I could leave you alone with someone to stand guard if the time comes for it."

"Thank you, Captain," Hilclop said, a bit taken aback at the praise.

Havovatch was finally glad he had mastered what rank to call him.

"Get some sleep, Feera – you're on watch next."

They all sat back where they were, and the quiet sounds of the desert were all that could be heard around them.

Chapter Twenty-Six
The Busy City

As Havovatch walked over a sand dune, he saw a large city towering into the sky, much higher than Cam but not as grand to look at.

It looked as if its founders, when building it, tried to build higher and better than those below them, as if there were a competition, until they ran out of room; going up and spreading outwards.

Surrounding the city was a tall wall with battlements and archery towers; it looked disused and worn, with huge chunks missing and heavy damage from sandstorms.

As they approached, Havovatch saw a long trail of people walking towards the main gate.

"Buskull, what do you think?" asked Havovatch.

"Well, there's clearly not any military power; civilians are coming and going; the defences look as if they have been abandoned. I'd imagine that it is a merchants' city."

"So, it should be pretty easy to get in?"

"I'd say so, but we should approach with caution ..." Buskull stopped, frowning deeply.

"What is it?" Havovatch asked. They all stopped to see what was wrong.

"I can sense the Golesh, Captain, but not like what we have previously encountered."

"OK – everyone be vigilant!"

They joined in the queue approaching the city. No one paid them any attention: around them were people dressed in all colours, most draped in cloth from head to toe; some affluently dressed men were being carried on carts pulled by skinny porters, while others had guards clustered around them.

One large man guiding a mule was leading several carts laden with all sorts of goods: furniture, cloth and cutlery.

As they approached the gate, Havovatch noticed that the line was not really stopping; and, as they came in sight of the arch, it became clear why. There *were* guards there, but they were not stopping or checking anyone in the queue, no matter who they were or how much they had.

The guards looked shabby and unprofessional at best. They wore cheap, thin armour, and some were leaning against the wall, with their spears resting out of arm's reach. Many people were walking in and out, but the guards did not stop or speak to them, or even seem to look at them. Havovatch thought one of them was even asleep; he wondered why bother with them if they weren't going to do their job. They were very undisciplined, but maybe this would go in their favour: it would look unusual with four elite warriors with no papers and not really much of a reason for walking into an entrepreneurial city.

Before they entered, Havovatch turned to the unit. "Remove your helmets, carry everything loosely and act casually."

Buskull turned the dagger on his belt to the front. "If I may, Captain, this place looks like somewhere that has professional thieves, the sort who could walk right past you and steal something without you ever knowing."

"OK – keep your hands on your swords, tuck everything else away."

They walked through the gate without an issue. It was arch-shaped, with a portcullis at the top, but it looked old and rusted, as if it had not been dropped in decades. On the inner walls to the gate were archery holes that had filled with sand and rubbish.

On the other side was a large plaza, but the fast-moving pace of the merchants made them funnel down a narrow street to their right.

In front of them, buildings towered above, higher than the walls, and there was as much sand on the street as there was outside in the desert. Every doorway was open, selling pretty much the same things as its neighbour. The street was packed with people: some women stood on crates by the walls, flaunting their bodies for a penny and offering other services, whilst a man stood on the side of a statue, preaching about a religion.

They half-drew their swords at seeing a Golesh shambling round the corner, but something was amiss. It was hunched over, with its knuckles rubbing on the floor like an ape. It wore a black, torn rag over one shoulder and around its waist; and it had a shackle around its neck, with a chain linking it to another man, who was holding it like a pet for a baron. They relaxed their stance slightly, but, as the movement of the crowd took them away, they could not help but look at it until it was out of sight.

Around them men, women and children were walking around, going about their own business. Their presence did not seem to attract much attention, but Buskull received a few quizzical looks.

One person approached Feera and grabbed him by the arm; half-startled, Feera instantly put his hand on the hilt of his sword.

"No, no, no, my friend," he said, with sour breath. "I've got a proposition for you, say half a coin for the knife." He smiled obsequiously, showing few teeth, all of them yellow and black.

Feera ripped his arm away, but the stranger did not even seem to see this as a rude gesture, but more of a challenge. He stepped forward again, grabbed his arm even tighter and tried to pull him closer. Feera grew impatient at the man's persistence, but before he could do anything, Buskull stepped into the man's space, pushing him back. "We are not selling anything, now go!" he said, with a low voice and deep eyes telling of much anger; just for extra measure he half-drew his dagger from his belt. The man spat on the floor in front of Buskull's boots, and merged into the crowd.

"Where are we going to find the Ippikós?" Hilclop shouted over the noise and rush of people. Unknown to them, a hooded figure raised his head sharply at the mention of the name.

They continued to walk down the busy street, keeping a firm grip on their kit. The last thing they wanted was their stuff going missing, but it was so cramped that they kept getting shunted in every direction, except for Buskull. Anyone who shunted into him seemed to bounce off, and eventually a path was created around him as he walked through the crowd.

When Havovatch turned a corner into another street, he noticed an empty alleyway. He pulled the unit in, and they huddled around him. "Anyone heard of this place?"

They all shook their heads.

"Has anyone been this way before?" Havovatch asked, eyeing Buskull particularly.

Again no one responded, but again Buskull's eyes frowned as if troublesome memories had surfaced.

Havovatch waited for a minute in case Buskull said anything, but he stayed very quiet.

"OK, first things first, it looks as though we are going to have a lot of searching to do; I think we'd better find somewhere we can stay, ditch our uniforms and blend into the crowd."

"How will we pay?" put Hilclop.

Feera pulled out a dagger from his belt. "This should fetch something – it has a golden handle."

"Dose it not have any sentimental value to you?" Havovatch said, taking it.

Feera shrugged. "No, not really. I bought it during my training. I was young and thought it looked good on me, but to be honest I never use it, just have it on me in case, but I have a better dagger than this now."

"Very well, if you're sure."

They did not have to walk far before they found a tall, thin building with a red door; above the door, it said *'Tavern'* in italic, red lettering. Feera entered on his own, leaving his weapons and armour with the others.

He soon returned. "We have been given two rooms for three nights, that's all the knife would fetch but we do have two meals a day with that as well!"

"Good," said Havovatch.

"And the meals should keep Buskull happy, anyway," Feera jested.

Hilclop sniggered, whilst Buskull gave him a rather unamused expression.

As they entered, there was a counter, with a rotund woman, wearing more make-up than they had ever seen, sitting behind it. She looked rather shocked at the appearance of the group before her, but said nothing and focused on them until they had gone upstairs.

They piled into the same room and started to take off their armour; it was the first time since leaving Haval, and all had dark sweat stains on their tunics where their armour had pressed against their bodies.

There was very little in the room: two beds, a small wardrobe, a stand with a bowl on the top, and a tall but narrow window on the wall.

Buskull looked out ... he was always security-conscious, but everything seemed to be normal, apart from a robed figure leaning on the wall at the corner of a junction. Buskull could not see his face, but he got the impression he was looking up at him. He bore it in mind but did not worry the others.

Hilclop helped himself to a bed. He put his hands behind his head, crossed his legs and closed his eyes. Feera turned to Havovatch. "Captain, I don't think we can leave our armour here unattended. If someone comes in, then they may tamper with it or take it."

Havovatch looked around the room. "Yes, I see what you mean, but there is nowhere to hide it."

"We could leave one of us here; I'll volunteer," said Hilclop, with his eyes closed.

Feera and Havovatch shot him a sharp look. "No – we cannot split up," said Havovatch, who then looked up at the ceiling. "Buskull, is that the upstairs floor?"

Buskull raised his hand and touched the ceiling. His arm was still bent as he reached up, giving it a knock a few times before studying the wood. "It appears to be hollow. I think there is a gap between the ceiling and the room above us."

"Good – if you can loosen any of the planks, we can leave our armour in there for the time being."

Feera moved a stool over to the side and helped Buskull knock a few of the beams out; then, bit by bit, they put their armour, helmets and weapons into the narrow space between the ceiling and the next room above.

"Keep at least a dagger with you, though, we need something to defend ourselves with, just in case."

Hilclop had decided to fall asleep, but the rest stood there in their tunics with a belt around their waist apart from Buskull, who had no armour to remove, standing there with his grey vest and dark brown trousers.

Hilclop was forced to wake up when Buskull tipped the bed over, and they all walked back downstairs. Feera gave a friendly nod to the woman as they passed, and they walked back out into the blistering heat of the day's sun.

Nothing had changed outside: it was still hot, and as busy as it had been before they had gone into the tavern.

They stood in front of the door and huddled back around Havovatch. "Right – we'll split into pairs. Buskull, you go with Hilclop; in one hour, return to the room and check that our armour is still there; in two hours Feera and I will return; after three hours we all meet back to here to debrief."

"What are we exactly looking for?" said Hilclop, rubbing his shoulder after his rude awakening.

"Well the only info we have is to head to this city. There, we will find a clue as to the whereabouts of the Ippikós. Look for warhorses, statues, well-groomed soldiers; look for anything of detail, and stay together! Do not split up!"

Buskull nodded and turned to walk down the street; Hilclop followed.

As Buskull strolled off, he took a quick glance back at the corner where he had seen the robed figure … it had gone, but he still felt that uncomfortable feeling of being watched.

Havovatch and Feera walked the other way.

As soon as they were out of sight, the hooded figure came out from an alleyway and walked over to the tavern. He walked inside and closed the door behind him.

As they walked through the packed streets, Buskull towered above everyone. He could clearly see everything in his path that he wanted to see. Hilclop tried to keep up with him, but his attention kept being distracted by the flaunting women and other goings-on in the city.

Buskull kept pulling him close, getting more abrupt every time, frustrated by him not paying any attention. "Remember why we're here, boy!" but Hilclop just nodded and carried on looking around, captivated by the wonder of the city.

The city had some sort of watchmen walking around, looking disgruntled. They seemed lazy, not really paying attention to anyone. Everywhere Buskull looked, he saw thieves making their moves. Some victims would stop and shout "thief!" as someone ran off, but the watchmen did not seem to notice or care. They just walked around with an indolent expression on their faces.

Buskull then noticed that Hilclop did not have his dagger to his front. "Boy, turn your dagger around."

Hilclop twisted his belt around to reveal an empty sheath. Buskull rolled his eyes and stroked his mouth. "Is there any hope for you, laddie?" he said despairingly.

Hilclop stayed silent and looked at the floor, waiting for Buskull to forget about the situation.

But instead Buskull looked around and noticed a small stall, which appeared to sell weapons. "Follow me, and don't look back!"

Buskull then turned and waded through the crowd. As he passed the stall, he looked in the opposite direction, put his hand out casually and took the closest knife to him. The owner did not notice, too busy haggling as he was.

When they turned a corner, Buskull turned back to Hilclop and gave him the knife. "Lose this one, and I'll put the next one somewhere far more secure!" he said, in a deliberate tone. Hilclop swallowed and put his hand on his backside at the thought.

Buskull then carried on walking, shortly followed by Hilclop who was trying to fasten the new dagger to his belt. Around them were irritating merchants, displaying sheepskins, fake silks and unusual vegetables. One elderly but persistent baron kept trying to get Buskull to be his gladiator, saying he would split the winnings with him.

But Buskull said nothing. Hilclop noticed how focused he was on his surroundings, so much so that he did not even think he noticed the baron speaking to him.

Then, suddenly, a sword was thrust in front of Buskull's face, which took him out of his trance.

"The finest steel in all Ezazeruth!" a merchant said, smiling deviously.

Buskull let out a long breath and looked at the man blocking his path, then along his arm and at the sword. He took it, and the merchant smiled with his hands clasped together, thinking he had made a sale; "Ohhh, yes, you warrior, you know a good weapon when you see one?"

Buskull spent little time examining it. "On the contrary," he began, "this blade is iron, not steel, it has not been beaten long enough and it's rusted at the hilt ... soon it will bend. In cold, wet weather it will rust, and it's so loose at the hilt that the moment you swing it, the blade will probably snap off the handle."

The merchant tried to keep his smile and waved a finger at him. "No, no, no, you're mistaken, I am a businessman, and I only seek the finest in the land!"

"Then I am afraid you're being conned." Buskull threw the blade against the wooden support holding up the merchant's canvas, and the blade snapped and fell from the hilt, clanging on the floor.

There was a burst of laughter from a small crowd that had gathered to see what was going on. Not changing his expression, Buskull simply handed the merchant back the hilt of the sword and pressed on through the crowd, whilst Hilclop, stunned, raced to keep up with him.

The merchant was left pleading with the crowd around him that he had been double-crossed, but the wealthier of the gathering started throwing small bits of copper down at his feet in pity at his humiliation.

Havovatch and Feera were getting frustrated; it had been a long afternoon and they had found no evidence of the Ippikós.

They found a square with no statues or fountains; there was graffiti on the walls, but nothing resembling a horse. Havovatch was not sure how long they had been looking, but, irritated by the day's poor results, he tried to find somewhere to cool off.

As they walked down another street, they found an outside bar shadowed from the sun, and, passing two people leaving, they quickly took their seats.

"What are we going to do?" Feera asked, with a sigh of despair.

"Order two drinks and have a rethink," said Havovatch. Feera cracked his fingers and looked around, just hoping that he would find something out of the corner of his eye that would jump out at him.

A young girl approached them with a tray and a rag in her hands. "Anything I can get you two gentlemen?" she asked, flirtingly, her attention caught on Feera.

"Two of whatever you have that can quench our thirst in this damned heat," Feera said, with a smile and a wink. The young girl smiled back at him. "Anything?" she said with a sweet tone and rushed off to the bar.

"I think she likes you," said Havovatch. Feera at first did not take his eyes off her, then looked back at Havovatch with a face that said: 'did you say something?'

"How are we going to pay?" said Feera, realizing they had no money. Havovatch looked down at a baron sitting adjacent to him; he had his back to them, but tied loosely on his belt was a small pouch.

Havovatch drew his dagger and cut the thread holding it to the belt. The man was so drunk and in fits of laughter he did not notice – he was talking loudly about some merchant being conned with false blades. And caught by the biggest giant he had ever seen.

Havovatch ignored the conversation and tossed the pouch over to Feera. "This should cover it!"

"This is not in our nature, Captain," Feera protested.

Havovatch leant forward. "I know, but in this city we need to survive, and, to be honest, it seems to be the norm here. And don't call me Captain – we don't want any prying ears listening in."

Feera sat back. "Very well, *Havovatch,*" he said, mouthing the words slowly.

Havovatch shot him a glare, but Feera just smiled.

The young girl returned with two large flagons, with white froth spilling over the top. She gave Feera his first, and then gave Havovatch his without taking her eyes off Feera. She tried to act professionally and maturely, pushing her chest out in front of him. "Thank you, my love, thank you very much," he said, and then gave her a small, rusted coin from the pouch.

Havovatch rolled his eyes.

She smiled, then walked back to the bar. Feera thought for a moment, then turned to Havovatch and got up. "I'll be back in a minute."

Havovatch raised his eyebrows and toasted after him, "Don't be too long." Feera smiled back and disappeared behind the bar.

Havovatch took a long gulp of his beer and then tried to relax in his chair for a moment, rather than feeling that he was on a mission.

He sat there for some time contemplating what was going on, then his mind turned to Mercury. He missed him; he hadn't had time to grieve yet. Many thoughts kept crossing his mind, such as what he would say to his parents – they must still have thought he was alive. It was a conversation he knew he had to have, but he was not looking forward to it.

He was thinking of how he was going to approach the subject when he noticed a presence in front of him, and the sound of someone pulling up a chair, the metal legs clinking loudly on the stone floor of the bar.

As he looked up he noticed that it was not Feera ... it was a tall, thin man, well-groomed and dressed in black; he had grey hair and a neatly trimmed beard, and piercing, blue eyes fixed on Havovatch.

Havovatch gently put his hand on his dagger, obscured under the table. Behind the man stood two burly men dressed the same way, but carrying long swords at their waist. Havovatch studied as much about them as he could in a short time, to see if they were a threat. He noticed that the swords were so high up that drawing them would prove difficult in a hurry.

The stranger said nothing; he just sat back in Feera's chair, looking directly at Havovatch. Then, taking the wooden mug, he took a small sip, but winced at the taste.

"Let me guess: you're more of a wine drinker?" Havovatch mocked.

The man said nothing; he just looked menacingly at Havovatch.

Eventually, Havovatch got bored. "What do you want?"

The man paused for a while before speaking. "You are not from around here, are you?"

"I don't see why that should concern you," Havovatch said curtly.

"Well, many people come to this city every day, but they don't come far. Do you mind if I ask where you have come from? Or why you are here?"

"Do you mind if I ask who you are and why the hell you want to know?" Havovatch did not blink as he met the stranger's gaze … the man clearly getting increasingly frustrated that Havovatch did not seem to fear him.

"Well, you obviously come from very far, not to know who I am."

"I can say I haven't had the pleasure," he said sardonically.

The man let out a long, exasperated sigh between clenched teeth. Then, taking in a breath, he composed himself and crossed his legs. He held out his hand to one of his men, who gave him a wooden box, and, without looking up at Havovatch, he began to remove some tobacco and poke it into a pipe. "I am Lord Ammos, I own this city, and I don't care much for people like you coming here. Therefore, I demand to know your business. I demand to know where you come from, and I demand everything you possess." To enforce his tone, he clicked his fingers, and his two henchmen stepped closer; then he looked up at Havovatch confidently. "And I always get what I want!"

Havovatch did not look at them, but kept his gaze on Lord Ammos. "My business is no concern of yours. I suggest you find someone else to harass."

Ammos's face started to turn scarlet; the men behind him became fidgety and volatile.

Eventually, Ammos composed himself, breathing heavily but forcing himself to slow down, putting his hands on his stomach and taking deep breaths; he was clearly not used to people answering him back. "I will give you one more chance," he pointed at Havovatch. "Tell me who you are … now! Or I will make life *very* uncomfortable for you!"

But Havovatch's expression did not change, and, after a long pause, he said, "No," slowly mouthing the word.

Lord Ammos looked up at one of the guards and nodded. "I'm sorry about this," he said, brushing some dust off his trousers and pretending to look in the other direction as if nothing was going on.

The tall guard pushed a man sitting between him and Havovatch out of the way.

But before he could do anything, Havovatch threw his beer into his face and jumped up, drawing his dagger. Holding it downwards in his right hand, keeping his left palm out, he stood in a defensive stance. The bar fell silent and passers-by stopped to see the altercation. It was not often they had seen someone stand in such a professional manner, and the bald henchman took a dubious look back at Ammos, who just gave him a nod to carry on.

He drew his long, half-rusted sword, and held it in both hands, pointing it at Havovatch's face, "You're not going to do much with that, my friend," Havovatch goaded the man. "You will have to raise it up to use any force, and this knife will be in your gut seven times before you can bring it down!"

The man quivered, again looking back at Lord Ammos for guidance. Ammos, sitting on the edge of his seat, now looked back at the other man, but he did not appear to move. As Havovatch looked up to see what was wrong with him, he noticed an arm around his neck: Feera stood behind him with his dagger at his throat. "Do we have a problem here?"

Lord Ammos jumped to his feet, looking at both his men. As the guard in front of Havovatch turned away, Havovatch quickly stepped forward, disarmed him and stood behind him with his knife at his throat, the same way Feera had done with the other.

They both stared at the lord, waiting for a response; he looked clearly stunned and confused.

"You won't get away with this!" he bellowed.

They edged back slowly, step by step; Feera then turned and threw the guard's face-first into a wall, knocking him out. Havovatch tripped his man up and knocked over a stall by kicking its foundations over him. They regrouped and ran down the street, as Lord Ammos could be heard shouting at his men.

As they ran, they made as many turns as they could, to try to get away from the men, putting distance and a maze between them, and after a while no one could be seen in sight. Stopping, they bent over, panting heavily, trying to get their breath back. "I'm glad you had fun whilst I was being set upon," Havovatch moaned.

Feera shook his head. "No, you don't understand – I was flirting with her and she gave me some information."

"Really? What kind of information?"

"She said that there are horse lords who visit this city every now and again; it's rare, but they come and march through the city as if they are looking for someone, or something, and then they just leave. No one knows why or where they go."

"Well, it's not much, but it's a start. Come on, we must get back to the tavern – it's about time we headed back anyway."

As they reached the tavern, everyone around them seemed to be rushed. They had seen glimpses of who they thought were Lord Ammos's men searching the area; they were going into every shop and building, and throwing their contents about. Meanwhile, Lord Ammos stood close by, with his hands behind his back, monitoring their progress.

Havovatch and Feera stuck to the back streets and went most of the way undetected; but, as they went to head out of the alleyway near the tavern, two large men wearing black, just like Lord Ammos walked casually around the corner.

They were not the ones they had fought earlier, but they all stood looking at each other, confused as to why two men were standing there and looking at them in anticipation.

But, before anything could happen, Havovatch and Feera punched them both in the stomach, before kneeing them in the face as they doubled over, finishing by holding them in headlocks until they passed out.

They were very large men – mainly fat rather than muscle – but were dragged behind a wooden box, deep in the labyrinth of streets. The job done, Havovatch and Feera casually walked off, looking around to make sure no one was following them.

As they approached the tavern, they stood to one side and scanned around them; nothing was untoward so they entered.

They nodded pleasantly at the woman, who had not moved from her seat; again she stared at them with fascination as they made their way upstairs.

When they walked into the room, Havovatch saw Buskull and Hilclop kneeling on the floor, with their hands bound behind their backs and white rags over their mouths. Before Havovatch could say anything, a dark object swung from his right and knocked him out. Feera was set upon by a group of men who were hiding in the other rooms off the corridor.

Buskull and Hilclop sat watching, completely unable to do anything.

Chapter Twenty-Seven
Contest

Havovatch awoke in pain: his head throbbed and he couldn't open his eyes. His hands felt numb, and he could feel blood running down the front of his face. He groaned with the pulsing agony as it came and went. As he tried to open his eyes, his head hurt more and he shut them tightly, trying to tense the pain away, but every movement he made just seemed to make everything worse.

He was sitting upright on a chair, with his arms bound tightly behind his back. Close to him, he could hear someone talking but all he could distinguish was the muffled sound of a man's voice over the tinnitus in his ears.

Seconds seemed like minutes, but he was starting to come round, his vision blurry, and he looked up to where he thought the light was. He could sense light in the room, but, everywhere he looked, the light kept flickering.

Suddenly, he jumped and gasped, as cold water was thrown over him. It cooled him slightly but was still unpleasant. However, things seemed clearer now. Before him he saw the outline of a figure sitting with their hands clasped together on a table.

"What do you want with me?" Havovatch said, groaning.

"Yo'll know in 'ime," the stranger's voice said in a slovenly manner.

"Where are my men?" Havovatch demanded. He could hear Hilclop screaming like a girl in the background.

"They're fines."

"It doesn't sound like it!"

"They ares, we haven't touched 'em, his ben like tat tince we tided 'im up."

"Then untie him!"

"I don't 'hink you understand her situation you're 'n!" the voice laughed.

"And I don't think you know who you are dealing with!" replied Havovatch, between clenched teeth.

The unknown man uttered a nervous laugh. Havovatch's vision cleared and he saw the stranger more clearly. He was dark-skinned, with short hair and two large scars running down either side of his face. His chest was bare, and he wore clothes that didn't match or even seem to fit him, as though he had just picked out a pair of each item no matter what colour or dress occasion they were for and put them on.

He had no apparent weapons; he just sat there looking pleased with himself and staring at Havovatch.

Ignoring the man, Havovatch started looking around the room, thinking back to his training – what he was taught to do when captured by the enemy. *Firstly, assess the situation. Can you get out? Any available weapons*? He knew that a weapon did not have to be a blade: it could be a table leg, a chair, anything to inflict pain or injury on someone. But the room he was in was small, about eleven feet long by six feet wide, and had only one studded door to the side, no windows. There was a small table between him and the stranger, with a torch on the wall. There was no possible way for him to fight his way out.

"Fine," Havovatch said reluctantly. "Let's talk like men – what do you want with me and my unit?"

The stranger's grin widened and looked unpleasant, as if he already had a plan for them. "Twell, first, as gentleman, let me tel' 'ou who I am, my name if Cofus."

"Captain Havovatch of the Three-Thirty-Third Heavy Infantry of Camia," he said officially, although assertively.

"Good, tee? We tar getting along tike brothers."

Havovatch ignored the remark.

"Now, I em 'urious to tee ha ya could all come inta ma city and tart asken question 'bout 'orsemen?" Cofus then bent down under the table and picked up a severed head. As he held it by the long, blonde hair, the head spun around slowly, revealing the face of the waitress Havovatch had seen in the bar.

"We don't 'ike pople like tat, they're up ta na god," Cofus grinned.

"Oh, you sick rekon," Havovatch said, tearing his eyes away from the gruesome sight; he gritted his teeth and clenched his fists, trying to pull his arms apart from the bonds. Despite the pain, every part of him was tensing up with rage, desperate to get his hands on this man's neck.

"Y'r bound and in a woom deep underground with only on' way 'n, yr beta giv' me somting as t' why yr 'ere."

Havovatch felt the bounds around him; he couldn't move, and, reluctantly, he felt he would have to play Cofus's game ... for now.

"We're looking for someone, but we're not here to cause trouble; and what do you mean – *your* city? I met Lord Ammos this afternoon; he claimed it was his."

"Yeah I taw, he won't 'ike what ya did to his men, but I was impressed with ta 'evel of skill ou used, I 'av' me own plans to tee 'ore," Cofus grinned, and Havovatch knew that he would be spending the day fighting at that point.

"Tis is ma city; I am in charge of the underclass, the thieves 'n' 'obbers."

"It's *your* city? Why do you live underground in the filth and not up top on the throne? Sounds to me like you give yourself a title you don't deserve, to make yourself feel important!" Havovatch said defiantly, trying to antagonize him, his anger helping to dull the pain. Cofus gave him a long stare ... it seemed to hit a nerve, but Havovatch met his gaze whilst blood dripped past his right eye. "What's the matter? Mummy and Daddy didn't love you as a child?"

"SHUP!" Cofus slammed his hand flat on the table, but Havovatch did not jump. He stared across at him and smiled.

Just then, Havovatch heard Buskull's war cry in the background. Cofus turned quickly in his chair to look at the door, but he fell silent.

"Very impressive your mon, defiant, strong, I 'ave me own plans for 'im. Whats his namd?"

"Giant."

"Strang name."

"Try whatever you want with him. If I don't kill you ... *he* certainly will." Havovatch mouthed the words. He could see in Cofus's face that he was starting to feel weary.

Havovatch started to hope that General Drakator or Drorkon would burst in any moment and rescue then, but he had to assume they wouldn't, and that it was up to him – after all, he had lost Undrea's handkerchief; how would they know where he was?

"We better be going toon, I don want ya to miss ta big event."

"What event?"

"You'll tee."

Cofus stood up, left the room and took the torch hanging on the wall with him, leaving Havovatch in the dark. He left briskly, as if the novelty of Havovatch had worn off, but he had a slight haste in his step as if he feared him.

In the dark, all Havovatch could hear was his own breath echoing off the dry stone walls; his body relaxed with exhaustion, and, closing his eyes, he succumbed to sleep. The next stage when captured: *When you can rest, take it, for you don't know when you will sleep again*. He suddenly felt like a Knight Hawk ... normal infantrymen did not often get involved in Shadow Ops.

He was not sure how long he had slept when two men burst into the room. As he opened his eyes, he could see their outlines with the light from the hallway behind them. They heavily lifted Havovatch from his chair and, with a man either side, dragged him through the labyrinth of underground tunnels. But, when the light from the torches touched on their surroundings, Havovatch noticed that they were not walking through tunnels, but streets: underground streets.

Soon he could hear chanting; it sounded as though he was underground. Deep underground. The chanting was muffled, the walls vibrated and dust fell from the ceiling.

One of the guards noticed his curiosity, and spoke with better language than Cofus, but only just. "This used to be the city, but built upon more and more and 'ow this is underground."

Havovatch didn't reply; it was a strange sight, seeing cobbled streets with doors to houses, and broken carts to one side, but no daylight highlighting in its usual colours; everything seemed to be so grim, dark and eerie.

Soon he came to some stairs leading up, steeply pitched; and at the top was light. As he ascended, he noticed the light was coming from an arch with curtains draped in front, the sun shining through the parting down the middle. As it was pulled aside, he was dragged through and stood on a balcony that looked over a small arena. In the centre of the balcony stood Cofus, whilst around him sat what appeared to be very wealthy barons, all finely draped in colourful cloth.

Cofus turned to him. "Arrrrr, young mon, I tort you weren't gona make it! I hop' me men were rough with ya!" he grinned, followed by haughty laughter around him.

Havovatch looked around ... below them was a sand pit, stained with blood-smeared patches. "I've heard of these places – they've been banned!" he protested with disgust.

Everyone around him paused for a moment and looked at each other, before bursting into laughter.

Cofus was crying with laughter and slapping the side of his chair, as he tried to speak between catching his breath. "'ou really don't 'ow where 'ou are do ya?"

Suddenly, horns rang out and the laughing died down; everyone turned to look down at the gates to the side of the arena below. As they opened, out walked Feera and Hilclop, both dressed in just a rag around the waist and covered in yellow paint; each of them carried a rusted sword.

The crowd went wild at them, shouting abuse and throwing rotten fruit and other missiles. Feera, taking charge, took Hilclop into the centre of the arena, out of the way of the crowd, with his sword brought up ready and surveying his surroundings, calming himself for what was to come.

Becoming outraged at this situation, Havovatch turned to Cofus. "These are soldiers of Camia! You cannot treat them like this – it's an act of war!"

Cofus did not look at Havovatch – he just glanced around, enjoying himself. "But ya are not in Camia, plus ya need two countries to have a war, and we are in no country, so tit back and enjoy. I 'ave a good on' set up tor tem to tart tings of." Cofus looked up at Havovatch with a wide smile. "And don't 'orry, if 'hey do die, it will be a god death."

A horn rang out again, and another gate opened to their left. At first, nothing came out, but something could be heard: heavy snorting and the tramping of an uncontrolled beast from within and, after a few moments, a loud noise was heard: the sound of something flat and hard hitting skin. Then, a huge, grey monster stepped out.

"A Gracker?" Havovatch said in horror.

"You tee? You tee wat a mean? God death!" Cofus said, with one finger raised.

The Gracker was gigantic: it stood on four legs, its giant belly rubbing along the ground, with scaly skin that seemed to change colour in the light. It was green, with patterns of blue as the sun hit it, with large, red eyes, a long tail, and spikes running along its spine from its head to its tail. It was a beautiful monster in many ways. Havovatch had never thought he would see anything like it in his life.

The beast raised itself slightly and, opening its mouth, howled at its bloodlust, making the crowd go wild. Havovatch saw its teeth: they all looked exactly like the one that his father had given him. There were three layers, all sharp, and it appeared to have been fed, with blood dripping thickly between its fangs.

But he then saw the shock on Feera's face and tried to find a way to help.

He looked around his surroundings: none of the barons were armed apart from the two guards standing next to him. The guards had short swords on them, but they were both on the other side of Havovatch's reach. *Just what I need! In this unorganized mess, the two men guarding me just so happen to have their weapons on the wrong side*! he thought in frustration.

But even so, his hands were so tightly bound behind his back that he could barely move anyway.

There was no pause, and, on seeing Hilclop and Feera covered in yellow, the beast charged. Feera seemed to be the only one keeping a cool head. Hilclop was panicking, his hands brought to his chest, with tears streaming down his face.

As the Gracker charged towards them, Feera pushed Hilclop out of the way at the last second. Hilclop fell with a thud, dropping his sword. Scrambling to his feet, he ran to the other side of the arena, desperately trying to scramble up the wall, trying to get away from what he thought was his impending doom.

Feera stood in the centre, crouching low, with his left hand out for balance and his sword drawn back, pointing at the beast.

The Gracker charged again at Feera, and, just as it went to collide, Feera pivoted around and the beast went straight past him; as he spun, he slashed as hard as he could at its scaly body, but it was so thick the sword barely scratched it.

The Gracker, seeing Hilclop ahead of it, continued its charge straight for him. Hilclop curled himself up into a ball, staring with horror at the onslaught.

Havovatch shouted, "Hilclop, jump, reach for the spikes!"

His voice got through and Hilclop looked up; on the wall were wooden spikes lining the arena.

Quickly jumping, he caught the spike, just as the Gracker approached … he lifted his legs to his chest and it slammed head-on into the wall. The wall shook slightly, with the crowd above it going silent for a moment; then, when they knew everything was all right, they burst out laughing, and started pelting Hilclop with tomatoes so he would fall to his death.

The Gracker was dazed for a moment, seeming to sway from one side to the next; it then shook its head and looked around. Feera came to its blind side and tried to hack away at its scales, but it was just too solid … even with his own weapons, he would not have been able to cut through. The beast turned and hit Feera side-on; Feera fell and the Gracker went to trample over him.

Hilclop looked down, and, in a moment of impulse, he landed next to the beast. He hit its eye as hard as he could with his fist and ran for his life to the other side of the arena.

The Gracker pulled itself up, put its head into the air and howled; small bits of frost came from its mouth. Havovatch had heard they could breathe ice, but this one obviously was having trouble, probably because it was not in its natural habitat of the icy north.

It crouched low and followed Hilclop. Feera quickly jumped up and sprinted after it, but the Gracker caught Hilclop and knocked him into the air; he landed with a heavy thud. He just lay there, caressing his stomach in sheer agony. The beast again went to trample over him, but Feera arrived at its head; and, raising his sword, he struck the creature's eye. The Gracker withdrew, snatching the sword out of Feera's hand. It howled in pain, throwing itself around, trying to stop the agony and rubbing the side of its head on the floor, the sword still embedded in its eye.

Feera rolled over to Hilclop's sword and then ran back to the creature. He raised his arms, holding the sword downwards in both hands; bending at the knees, he brought the blade down heavily into the top of the creature's skull.

The blade went through, snapping at the hilt, sending shards all around them; the Gracker's body went into a spasm and fell to the floor.

The crowd were astonished; the entire arena was deathly silent, apart from Feera's heavy breathing in the centre as he fell to one knee to catch his breath. As he looked up, he saw Havovatch, and they both gave a relieved nod.

"It appears you have talented men. I hope they fare as well in the next match, for the audience look impressed," one of the barons said.

"You see what they can do? I have eight thousand more just like them sitting outside your walls and they will come and find us soon!"

Suddenly there was silence on the balcony. They had obviously been informed about the approaching army, and all had serious looks on their faces as they stared at each other.

Cofus looked around and noticed that this was not doing his business any good. "Please ma friends, we are saf', I can assure you of tat, tets enjoy the next round." He clasped his hands together, whilst throwing Havovatch an angry look.

The gates opened, and Feera pulled Hilclop to his feet. He was still holding his stomach, but they braced themselves for what was next.

Feera handed him the sword from the Gracker's eye and held the broken sword for himself.

Out of the shadow came ten creatures, and Havovatch stood amazed. "Golesh!" he said with disgust, *so that's what Buskull sensed*!

But they were not like the other Golesh he had fought over the last few days: they were smaller, their skin shaded a murky green instead of the cloudy grey, and they doubled over like a hunchback, their knuckles brushing on the ground, much like the one he had seen when entering the city. They were lightly armoured, some with a helmet, others with shields, and all carried one poor weapon, either a mace, a sword or a barbed spear.

"Where did you find them?" Havovatch asked.

"They are tound in ta Misty Desert."

"Let me join my men!" Havovatch demanded.

Cofus looked up, and, eager not to let Havovatch say anything else that could upset his customers, he gave a nod to the guards.

Havovatch was dragged back downstairs to the gate. As his bonds were undone, he was handed a rusted iron sword. He tried to hold it, but the feeling took some time to come back to him. A sweating, fat, semi-naked man hoisted a chain, and, as the gate opened, Havovatch staggered out towards his unit in the centre.

"Right," he said, as he made his way to the others. "They want a show? So let's give them one. Attack triangle, centre on, rear turn and draw away – let's see how we go!"

Feera nodded, understanding the battle tactic jargon, but Hilclop, who had no idea what he was saying, stood with his sword loosely by his side, staring around in confusion.

"Remember we have killed these creatures before!" he continued. "And Feera, try to swap that weapon!"

"Now?" asked Feera.

"NOW!" Havovatch shouted.

The Golesh were circling them. However, the three of them ran towards the gate they had emerged from. Only two creatures stood there, whilst the others were spread out around the arena.

Holding just a mace each, they were set upon by Havovatch and Feera and beaten down.

Swapping their measly swords for a mace, Havovatch and Feera turned head-on to see the rest of the Golesh closing in on them.

Feera went left and Havovatch went right, leaving Hilclop standing behind them with his sword in both hands, quivering.

Feera bent over, sending a charging creature flying, before shoulder-barging his way into the rest.

Havovatch did the same, going for brute strength rather than tactical skill, a trait they had picked up from Buskull.

Hilclop stood alone. Two came towards him, one holding a spear, the other holding an axe, but, in their desperation to fight, they barged into each other. Hilclop saw his moment, and, stepping back with a sudden impulse of rage, he forced the sword into the face of one of the creatures; ripping it out, he then deflected the spear away before slashing the other Golesh's leg, resulting in a deep laceration, pumping blood all over the ground.

He had a sudden surge of confidence flowing through him; the crowd were chanting at him, spurring his confidence higher.

Suddenly, a Golesh broke away from Havovatch's fight and charged at Hilclop, waving its arms and shrieking its war cry. Hilclop stood there, his chest heaving, his arms straight, as he frowned and looked up out of the corner of his eyes at the creature. Snarling, and mustering a fresh breath of air within him, he raised his sword and ran at the beast, screaming. It was hardly a manly shout, but it did the trick.

The Golesh felt the attack coming towards him, and, as Hilclop ran towards it, it turned and retreated across the sand for its life.

But the Golesh was not looking where it was going; it tripped over a loose helmet and fell, with Hilclop lunging on top of it, punching it repeatedly in the head as it tried to fight back, and as it lost its guard he brought his sword down into its chest.

The creature went limp and Hilclop came back to reality, the bloodlust inside him vanishing. He looked around in wonder at what had happened. As he stood up, Havovatch and Feera were approaching with a nod of impressed satisfaction, having already dispatched the others.

Hilclop's entire body was trembling; he felt light, as if he could fly, and suddenly he did not feel fear – it was as if he could take on anything within that moment.

"Not bad, not bad at all," said Feera.

They all stood together, looking up at the balcony in defiance.

Then the gates opened and some scruffy guards stepped out. "Drop your weapons!" one of them barked.

Reluctantly, seeing no other option, they did so, and at spear point they were escorted back through the gates whilst the crowd cheered them.

Havovatch was re-bound and escorted back upstairs. When he got onto the balcony, Cofus stood up; he did not look entirely pleased. “Com, we ’av ta special event,” he said, sulking, as he headed straight past Havovatch without a second glance.

All the men followed; one gave Havovatch a pat on the back as he passed.

They headed deep into the underground labyrinth of streets. Eventually they came into a large, underground room. In the centre was a small square ring with a small fence, about chest height, around it. Surrounding it were opulently dressed men, all with hands full of gold coins and bags, shouting and waving them around.

But, as he entered, all went silent. Cofus and the barons with him sat on a platform, slightly raised to clearly see the ring; Havovatch stood just behind Cofus.

Cofus gave a nod and the crowd parted out of the way to one side, then Buskull was led in. His hands were chained together; a metal brace was around his neck, with four chains linking from it, with a man on each end pulling him into the arena.

Buskull did not struggle, and, walking with his eyes fixed in front of him, he almost seemed relaxed. Havovatch tried to catch his gaze to let him know he was there.

Buskull stood in the middle and was made to face the platform. Havovatch gave a nod. He knew Buskull had seen him, but he made no gesture back, appearing to be meditating.

The chains and brace were undone, and Buskull stood there with his arms aloof.

“It cannot be!” said one man as he stared at Buskull in astonishment. “He is an Algermatum, a warrior race from far away from this world. It is said that before they are born their child’s spirits are dipped in a lake of blood from all their warriors who have fought to the death, and that they come back as fiercer and stronger warriors.”

Havovatch listened intently, wanting to know more, but very few were listening to the man; the crowd started cheering louder as the doors on the other side of the arena opened, and an enormous, dark man walked in, the crowd giving him pats on the back and chanting “Emios”.

He was not as tall as Buskull but he was far larger in size: his arms were huge, his stomach hugely rotund, and, as he walked, the beams of the floor could be heard creaking under his heavy weight. He had long, black, plaited hair going down behind his back, and no guards stood with him. He stood alone, staring at Buskull's side, snorting heavily.

Buskull closed his eyes and bowed his head in prayer, murmuring to himself.

When he had finished, he turned and gazed at Emios to his left, with a stare that could have cut through iron.

Cofus stood up and put his hands in the air, and the room fell silent. "Gentlemen, 'tis is our special event!" There was loud applause from the merry crowd. "Long has it been since our young Emios 'ere has needed a 'orthy opponent, and 'ow, we have just tat. Known to his friends as Giant." Havovatch swallowed, noticing the twitch in Buskull's eye. "I present to you, the Beast … from the East!"

The crowd cheered again, and Emios, not taking his eyes off Buskull, sneered, revealing that he had few teeth.

In the background, a tall man in a black hood, unseen in the mayhem of the crowd, stared at what was going on. He left briskly, no one seeing him, or even noticing.

"Begin!" Cofus shouted, with an open palm cutting down through the air. Emios tilted his head back and opened his arms out, shouting into the air he charged at Buskull.

Buskull stood there, not changing his posture. Saying nothing, he stood with his arms loose by his sides; then, just before Emios could hit him, Buskull raised a clenched fist and punched him in the side of the head, then, hooking his arm underneath Emios's, he lifted him over his shoulder and brought him down heavily onto a wooden support.

Emios spat out what teeth he had left and staggered to his feet, desperately holding on to the wooden fence for balance; then, raising his fist, he went to punch Buskull. Buskull caught his hand in the grasp of his own hand and squeezed; knuckles could be heard breaking, and Emios bowed down before him, crying out in pain.

Buskull let go and kicked Emios in the stomach; then, with one hand on his shoulder and the other on his groin, Buskull heaved Emios above his head and threw him into a beam supporting the ceiling.

The beam snapped as Emios fell through it, landing on some of the patrons behind.

Then, part of the ceiling caved in and buried them. All that could be seen from the debris was Emios's arm sticking out ... at first it tensed up, and then it went limp.

Havovatch let out a sigh of relief; the entire room fell silent – most stood with their jaws dropping at the sight of what had just happened; even Cofus was on the edge of his seat, stunned into silence. He had lost not just his star fighter, but also a number of his customers.

Havovatch looked back down at the guard's sword. The guard must have switched sides and was not paying attention to him. He turned slowly and gripped the sword hilt; the guard did not see him.

"Buskull!" Havovatch shouted, and then spun as quickly as he could, throwing the sword out of its scabbard and towards him. Buskull leapt forward and took hold of it. Several men jumped over the fence to stop him, but he smacked and kicked at them and hewed the blade into their torsos, with little time for mercy.

Cofus ran for the exit as all hell broke loose. Havovatch ran beside him, tripping him and then kicking him in the head as he did so. The guards tried to grab Havovatch, but, with the crowd leaving in a riot and rushing past in every direction, they could not get a proper hold of him.

Havovatch leant against the fence, hauled himself over and landed on his face on the wooden deck.

As Buskull fought off three men at once, he turned quickly towards Havovatch, and slicing downwards, cut through his bounds without injuring him. His arms now free, Havovatch punched a guard in the face, then drew the sword away from his grasp before sticking it into his chest.

The arena was now empty, with the last few patrons desperately trying to get out. Havovatch and Buskull jumped over the fence together and ran out of the doors that Buskull had been brought in through, and continued up a spiralling staircase.

When they got to the top, two guards came running down. Havovatch put his sword into one, and Buskull leant over and pulled the man into the air and threw him against the sandy wall behind him. It caused it to collapse, and earth filled in the corridor blocking the way to anyone chasing them.

When they got to the top, Buskull ran in front of Havovatch and barged through a large door. Once they were back outside and on the streets again, everyone stopped and looked at them before running in panic.

"We must find the others!" Buskull shouted. "You go that way, I'll go this way!" Havovatch did not bother arguing – he just did as Buskull suggested, or rather told.

Running down an alley, Havovatch found a cowering baron whom he had seen on the balcony. He grabbed him and put his sword against his throat. "Where are my men? The ones who killed the Gracker!"

The baron was too scared to answer, just quivering in terror.

Pushing the blade in slightly, Havovatch lost patience. "Tell me now, or so be it your head will part from your body!" he said, showing a rage he did not know he possessed.

The man, shaking, pointed to a large, green door at the other side of the yard. He began to wet himself … clearly this was the first time he had been threatened in his life.

Havovatch pushed him away and ran to the door, banging the hilt of the sword on the heavy gate. The door was opened by an elderly man who looked annoyed by the loud interruption. Havovatch grabbed the back of his head as it appeared, and heaved it against the gate before throwing him out into the street.

Inside, the room was slightly illuminated by small candles on alcoves in the walls. Along the room on either side were beds, some occupied by gladiators spending their winnings on women.

Havovatch ignored them and ran to the door at the end, as the big, heavy doors he had just come through burst open and a dozen men came running in, holding an assortment of weapons. Havovatch looked at the disorganized mob. "Do you even know how to use those?" he mocked, before going through the door at the other end.

He closed it hard and wedged his body against it; then, seeing a torch on the wall, he pulled it off and jammed it into the handle and the lock in the wall. There was a heavy banging from the other side from the mob chasing him, but he knew it would give him some time before they could get through.

He ran down the narrow corridor, kicking every door down. "FEERA, HILCLOP!!" he shouted along the way.

He stopped; he could hear something – muffled voices – and he ran to where it was coming from. It led back underground, down another spiralling staircase. As he went, a guard was walking back up, investigating what was going on. Before he could react to seeing Havovatch, a slash immediately cut through his throat. He grabbed his neck as blood streamed out between his fingers, and dropped to the floor.

Havovatch carried on and eventually reached a dungeon. "Feera, Hilclop!"

"Yes, Captain, over here!" Havovatch saw them waving their arms frantically out of the cell door window; he grabbed them in relief.

"Good to see you, friends! Stand back – I'll try to kick the door in." He put all his might into kicking it, but it was solid and would not budge. He tried again, but it was still shut tight.

As he looked through the cell window, he saw they were not alone, but another figure emerged from the shadows. As he focused, he noticed a familiar face: it was Ferith, just standing, looking as battered and bruised as the others.

Just then, the men who were chasing Havovatch caught up. They burst into the wide corridor and stood panting, disgusted that they had to run for a change.

Havovatch stood in the centre of the room and held his sword out, ready to defend himself.

"You are about to attack a captain of Camia. Your actions will cause war between our nations!" It was pointless saying it, more an impulse than a threat, but he was used to saying it under these circumstances.

Some of the men laughed nervously; some started to strut forward. Havovatch braced himself – he knew he was a good fighter, but there were a lot of them, and he started to think he might not get out of this one.

But, before anything could happen, a group of hooded men barged in behind the attackers and slew them where they stood. The attackers did not even have time to react. Havovatch looked on in shock and confusion at the sudden rate of death that had played out in front of him. *Now, who are these rekons*? he thought.

Two of the cloaked men ran over and battered the door down with battle-axes; two others grabbed Havovatch and disarmed him. They put a hood over his head, and each took an arm, locking it behind his back. He felt himself being dragged again; he was getting fed up with this, no matter where he went, he always seemed to be heavily manhandled.

Eventually, he knew he had been taken into the street, as he could hear crowds around him and the natural noises of the outdoors. Then he was back indoors and placed firmly on a chair, and the hood was removed.

He looked around. Buskull stood in the corner, holding his battle-axe; Feera, Hilclop and Ferith were placed with him.

Feera and Hilclop were given their uniforms by one of the hooded men. Ferith stood rubbing his arm, trying to understand what was going on.

Across the room sat Cofus. His hands were bound behind him, blood was running down his face from a small cut to his head, and he sat there quivering, making pathetic, pitiful sounds.

"What's going on? Who are you?" Havovatch asked the captives.

"You are to be quiet until the commander arrives!" a man said in a deep voice, whilst standing by the door.

These men stood very tall and broad. They had huge cloaks dragging on the floor, with hoods over their heads and black scarves covering their faces just like the Oistos. Havovatch wondered if they were the Ippikós, but how had they found them?

A short time passed, the doors were opened and a tall man strolled in, followed by a dark, cloaked man – the tall stranger's hair dark and short, his face long and battle-scarred.

He stood in front of Havovatch first, then turned and looked at the others individually.

"Well, Captain, I believe you have been looking for me. Can I enquire as to why?" he said, turning his attention back to Havovatch.

"Can I assume you're the Commander for the Ippikós?" he said, looking for confirmation.

"That has yet to be decided, now talk," he said curtly.

Havovatch sighed. "I am Captain Havovatch of the Three-Thirty-Third Heavy Infantry of Camia. I have orders for you, but they seem to have been misplaced."

One of the guards stepped forward and handed the commander the pouch holding his orders; he took them out and read them all very quickly.

"Hmmm," he mused, putting the parchments back, and pointed at Havovatch with the pouch. "You have some guts, coming here and demanding this of us!"

The sudden outburst changed the atmosphere of the room, with the guards suddenly tensing and becoming hostile.

The commander walked over to Cofus, grabbed his hair and pulled his face up. "I knew your day would come – a filthy little maggot like you just cannot keep out of trouble. I thought you would have learnt your lesson from when you took *my* men."

Cofus started to whimper. "Please, I am a businessman, I can get you—"

Before he could finish, the commander produced a knife from under the cuff of his sleeve and sliced Cofus's throat. The body fell. It happened so quickly that Havovatch just stared in dumb shock at the act.

The commander turned to the guard at the door and spoke to him in a language Havovatch found vaguely familiar.

The guard turned to Havovatch. "You are all to come with us, so get your uniform on!"

One of the men approached and gave him his uniform, neatly folded. It did not take long. Once he had finished, he brushed some dirt out of the crest of his helmet and proudly placed it on his head.

They all left the room together; as they looked outside, they squinted through the reflection of the sun on the white, sandy walls. In the street stood about fifty mounted men, all cloaked in sandy-coloured hoods that covered their faces. Four of them led spare horses, which Havovatch and his unit were instructed to get on.

An order was shouted, and they all cantered off down the street.

The streets soon cleared for the cavalry, despite their bustle; they went round every corner with haste and did not stop for anything.

Havovatch rode near the front, alongside the main wall of the city. He saw Lord Ammos in front with about fifteen men standing behind him. They purposely blocked their path, and Ammos showed the palm of his hand for them to stop.

But the cavalry did not slow down. Havovatch went to draw his sword, but, before he could, a small fraction of the riders behind him charged ahead and rode them down. As Havovatch looked beneath, he saw Ammos's bloodied face on the floor, but he could not see his body.

This is no ordinary cavalry unit, he thought, a shiver rushing down his spine at the thought of what company he was in.

They approached the main gate, and the horses went into single file. The horse Havovatch was riding seemed to file in with the others on its own without any command. Havovatch did not feel in control; he just accepted where the horse was taking him, and once against cursed the beasts.

They left the city into the blistering heat. Havovatch was glad to be away from the place, and, at a strong gallop, they went south.

Chapter Twenty-Eight
The Council

General Drorkon sat near the centre of a long table in the Great Hall. At one end was Commander Thiamos, whilst to his left sat Duchess Imara in all her glory on the King's throne, and somehow Lord Fennell was at the meeting, sitting opposite him. Drorkon wondered how the manipulative snake had managed to get in. He had no ability or experience whatsoever in running a city, yet here he was advising on what was best for the country in the King's absence.

Drorkon felt that there was little use in being there. Though he advised against the bad decisions they always made, he was often ignored or voted down.

The decisions usually meant that the rich at the top of the city had all they wanted, whereas the lower classes were ignored and had nothing to protect them except the militia. These people thought little of other people, and he detested them.

As thoughts came to him of how Havovatch was getting on, he smiled and knew that somewhere, someone in the world was doing something right. He had received the message from the messenger and was keen on bringing the traitor that Havovatch mentioned to account, holding the brooch within his grasp.

He was just waiting for Lord Fennell to stop speaking about a military strategy that made no sense whatsoever, so he could bring up this urgent matter.

"So, I think, by removing the higher classes of the city to a safe haven within the forest, surrounded by all Camion military personnel to protect them, we will trick the Black into thinking we are in the city and safeguard those who are important," Lord Fennell said, standing up and addressing the council, with an out-of-date book about military tactics on the table in front of him. There was a huge round of applause as he finished, and he stood with a stern face and gave a nod of appreciation, with one hand behind him and the other tucked between the buttons of his jerkin.

Drorkon seized the moment to cut in before someone else did, although he had to overcome the huge urge to point out the failing in Lord Fennell's plans, which was that the lower class would be defenceless and alone in the city, even though he was sure that was the general point of this tactic, making him feel even more disgust for the higher classes.

"My Lords, Ladies, Sirs, Gentlemen, and all that I hold in such high regard." He had never quivered so much at saying something so wrong in his life, but he thought speaking to them in the manner in which they understood would assist him in getting his goal. "I bring a message of devastating tidings which I feel compelled to share with you." The room fell silent, as all eyes were on him, eager to hear what he had to say. "I was given word yesterday that the Three-Thirty-Third, the regiment that went rogue, was annihilated a week or so ago in Loria, but the message bears further burdens. It appears that there is a traitor within our midst," – there were gasps and quiet chatting amongst the council – "and, before we can do anything else, we must find the leak and plug it, before any more misfortunes can arise."

"And where is your evidence of this ... treason?" shouted Lord Fennell, jumping to his feet in shock that Drorkon could mention such a thing.

Drorkon looked around at their eager eyes, and, digging into his pocket, he went to pull out the brooch.

"I have sources that have brought me direct evidence of who is involved." He clasped his hand around the brooch and went to pull it out. "And we must stop him!"

"THAT WE MUST!" a male's voice shouted from across the hall.

Drorkon halted and looked up in alarm to see Sarka appearing from behind a curtain. How long he had been there? He must have got in here before the meeting had started.

"Colonel Sarka? What a splendid surprise, but I was not aware you were invited to this meeting?" Drorkon said, pursing his lips, sensing something was wrong.

"That I am not, but I am a patriot of my country and I feel the need to protect it, especially from a traitor!" he spat, staring intently at Drorkon.

"Then you have news of this matter?"

"That I do, Drorkon!"

"Colonel Sarka!" Drorkon said sternly. "I am a lord, a general and one of the highest-ranking officers of this state, and certainly this council, so please address me by my title!"

"I would, Drorkon," he said, clicking his fingers with a raised hand; and then, from every entrance, one of Sarka's guards stood there, menacingly. "But I do not use the titles of traitors."

There were more gasps from the council, as all stared at him open-mouthed; and, suddenly, Drorkon felt outmatched. Twitching his fingers, he desperately thought to try to better the situation.

"And what is your evidence?"

At another click of his fingers, a group of men were brought forward and bowed before the council. "My Lords and Ladies, these are witnesses to some of Drorkon's treason, and, chilling as it is, we have no other understanding as to how deep his treachery has gone."

The first man stepped forward. He was a seasoned man with a white beard and scars over his face, and well dressed in ceremonial uniform. "My higher people," he addressed, "I am the watch commander of the town of Persa, west of Cam. A group of drunken soldiers maliciously assaulted several of my citizens and were seized by myself. But they were released by force and my staff assaulted at the command of Gen… of Drorkon!" he said, pointing at him.

"Those men were on an important quest directly fro—" began Drorkon.

"I am sure we are going to hear a good speech to clear your name, but the fact is that you ordered a watch commander to release criminals who assaulted his people?" Sarka interrupted.

Drorkon looked on sternly; he had nothing to say, but his hand was still gripped around the brooch, and he was waiting for the right moment to reveal it.

The next witness stepped forward. He was a vagrant, he smelt repulsive, his face was unshaven, his clothes dishevelled, and he spoke in a squeaky tone. "Me Lords and Ma'am's, tat man assaulted ma friend; poor old Grimble has a broken finger, and feels even more depressed than he was." Sarka grunted for him to get to the point. "Oh, tes … he well, we followed tim you tee, after ter assault, and he went into te Tree-Tirty-Tird barracks, I sat on old Grimble's shoulders and tooked and listened to twat was going on—".

"Due to the circumstances, I have pardoned him for this matter, as his evidence outweighs his crime of spying," Sarka interrupted, before nodding for him to continue.

"Tes, and we heard 'im telling an officer tere to go rogue after they had escorted te pretty woman Undrea, who old Grimble and I have a tight crush on," he grinned.

"You are mistaken," Drorkon protested. But his challenge was clearly not believed; with everyone glaring at him, he could see it in their eyes that they had already made up their minds that he was guilty. He knew it was a matter of plotting an escape, but, with a guard at every exit, he had only a slim chance of making it out. Reluctantly, he let go of the brooch, for it seemed meaningless now.

The final man stepped forward. "My Lords, Ladies, and those above me – I am a strategist, and the officer of my team. I must point out that we have more than compelling evidence to suggest that Drorkon's heavy cavalry regiment, the Two-Twenty-Eight, went to the far east, where a village was brutally decimated under his watch – men, women and children, all killed – and yet somehow? Drorkon appeared at King Colomune's last meeting whilst this happened, when he should have been protecting this area, so what *were* they doing?"

Lord Fennell quickly interrupted. "I can confirm this, as I was there!" he said, deliberately trying to get his voice heard, then sat back comfortably in his chair, looking up at Drorkon with a slight grin from the corner of his mouth.

Everyone looked towards Drorkon for an explanation, but he knew it was futile. *Well played, Sarka,* he thought; he did not even see this one coming. But he couldn't help but notice that all the witnesses wore brooches of the Two-Twenty-Second cavalry unit ... Sarka's unit. The same brooch that was sitting in his pocket. It all began to make sense: the leaked information, Havovatch always being dogged by the enemy. He cursed himself for not having seen it earlier.

He clasped his hands together in front of him. "Well, there certainly appears to be a witch-hunt, doesn't there?" Stepping to one side, he pushed his chair in neatly.

Duchess Imara stood up, and, in her arrogant and slimy tone, she said, "Thank you for bringing this to our attention, Colonel Sarka; your courage, dedication and loyalty to the land will be rewarded!"

"Thank you, my Lady; if I may arrest the assailant?"

There was a nod of agreement from the council, and Sarka nodded at his men. They all drew their swords and strode towards Drorkon.

"Well, I bid you all good day," Drorkon said, before hastily striding towards the corner of the hall, followed by Sarka's men, thinking that he had nowhere to go.

He turned as he reached the corner, saluted the crown above the throne and, with a tear running down the side of his face, pushed through the brick wall and stepped out.

The guards ran to the spot as the wall closed; they pushed at it but there was no give. "QUICKLY, LOCK DOWN THE CITY, DON'T LET THE TRAITOR ESCAPE!"

Drorkon ran down through the streets as quickly as he could, but everywhere he looked Sarka's men were at every corner of the city. Sarka had clearly taken every precaution.

He went down the hidden paths and through secret doors and levels of the city, as cautiously as he could, but eager to get out of the city before it was locked down.

He knew his time was short, but, as he rounded a corner, he stepped into full view of Sarka's guards, blocking the path with their horses. He stepped back quickly, and was fortunate not to be seen. However, to get to the other side of the street he would have to risk being noticed.

Closing his eyes, he muttered some words under his breath and, placing his hand out around the corner of the building, he went to see if Sarka's guards had seen him.

One casually glanced his way, but did not notice him, and he slowly peered out further. Despite him being in full view, none of them saw him, and he ran to the other side of the street and back into the confines of an alleyway.

He continued down through the city at a run and eventually came .

It was not far – he was going to make it. The watchmen at the gate saw him but did not react. Clearly they were not aware of the lockdown or the order to arrest him.

"STOP!" he heard behind him, as several of Sarka's guardsruffians came running around the corner.

He pretended not to hear them and carried on, but, as he went to go through the gate, two of Sarka's men stood in front of him, holding swords. The watchman, unsure what was going on, stood hesitantly between them.

The guards approached him and he drew his sword. With superb skill, he outmatched the two cavalrymen and, parrying away their weapons and running his blade through them, he killed them both, before going through the gate. Turning to the watchman, he shouted, "SHUT THE GATE! LOCK DOWN THE CITY! SARKA'S MEN MUST NOT LEAVE!!"

The watchman nodded rather shakily, but shouted for the gate to be shut, and the emergency bell rang out.

There was a sudden rush of watchmen funnelling out from the watch-house and down towards the gate and Sarka's men.

Drorkon ran down the road, and, as he looked further, he saw four horses and three riders. They galloped over to him and he mounted, and, as fast as they could, they went west to find the rest of his regiment.

Chapter Twenty-Nine
The Horse Lords

Havovatch pursed his lips as he rode on the uncontrolled beast. He was not sure, but he thought that the horse knew he did not like riding, purposely jolting over mounds in the everlasting desert.

They had been riding all day, in two columns, with the front riders bearing a ruby-coloured flag with a centaur waving in the wind. The heat was intense, and he kept trying to take his helmet off to wipe the sweat from his forehead, but held a firm grip upon the reins of the horse. Every time he went to let go he felt that he was going to fall off, and so had to keep his legs compressed around the horse's body, bending over to keep his head near the horse's mane, praying that the journey would end soon and that he would not fall off.

He could not see the others; the horsemen were quiet and had ridden along in silence for the majority of the day.

Havovatch rode next to a man not much younger than himself, with soft-looking skin and short, dark hair. His eyes were dedicated and focused; and, staring in front of him, he made no effort to communicate. He was a slender man, with a long, red cloak, leather body armour and a collection of swords on each hip, varying in size.

"Can I ask something?"

The young man said nothing; his face did not even change to acknowledge Havovatch had spoken. Havovatch began talking in a firmer tone. "I have a regiment of men outside the city! I need to speak with them!"

Again the young man said nothing.

Havovatch knew it was futile to try to get his attention – from what he remembered of the information given to him by General Drorkon, the Knights were stubborn and uncooperative. So, he tried to take his mind off the torment in his legs and spine by assessing the area where they were riding.

There wasn't much to see. He was in the middle of the desert with tall sand dunes around him, the sky a piercing blue with no clouds in sight.

Eventually he saw the leading banners dip down, and the columns in front of him descended onto the terrain. As he went down with them, he almost lost his breath, his heart leapt into his throat and he suddenly felt that he was going to fall a thousand feet.

What lay before him was a long canyon deep into the ground, and spanning the bottom of it were thousands of buildings of all shapes and sizes. There were wide-open plains of verdant grass surrounding the small city. Running around were grazing horses, left free to do as they wished. Rivers ran through the city, all leading to a great lake in the centre. But what struck Havovatch most was the lake's colour … not the blue of the sky above, but a haze of purple. He looked up and almost fell off his horse. The sky was no longer the piercing blue of the ocean as it had been moments before; it was now a haze of pink and purple, with waving patterns of changing colour like the Northern Lights, stars twinkling in parts of the sky.

With the lush grassland below, the sand yellow of the canyon walls, the dazzling sky above and the beautiful lake, it was a tropical paradise; suddenly, fear drained from him, as he was taken into a world of peace and harmony. There was nothing to fear about the sight before him.

Staying in two columns, they rode across a precarious narrow ledge, zigzagging down to the valley below. Soon they were at the bottom, the horses slowed down and the riders dismounted with ease, tethering their horses to a long pole with a trough full of water below.

The horses delighted themselves in a long, satisfying gulp. Havovatch gritted his teeth as he slowly lifted his leg over to dismount. As he did so, his legs gave way to the numbness and he fell down, wincing as he lay on his back looking up. There were a few laughs from the other riders. The horse he had been riding absent-mindedly made its way to the trough and started drinking.

A guard or knight – he was not really sure – approached, and, as he held an arm out, Havovatch took it and was hoisted to his feet. What he had at first thought was an act of good manners turned ominous, as the guard or knight pushed him around and made him march to an opening in the cliff.

They went inside, and he was sat down on a step carved into the stone. He was instructed to keep his head down; if he did not, he was going to tie his head to a hook on the floor before him.

Naturally, Havovatch obliged without question. He had had enough of being tied up and being mistreated over the past few weeks. Parts of his body were still sore and aching from the fight at the bar when they had first started their mission.

Although his eyes were shut, his ears were still listening to what was going on around him: the shuffling of armour, laughter from children outside, the noise of horses moving about and snorting.

He felt slightly conscious but noticed that he was snoring slightly – either that or breathing heavily; usually he would have snapped out of it, but, after what he had been through, his body needed a break, to shut down if only for a few minutes, so he welcomed it.

Soon he was into a deep sleep and started to dream; he felt his body completely relax despite sitting on a step with his head bowed.

His dreams took him all the way back to Cam, lying on his bed in his chambers looking out the window at the clear, blue sky – he had a feeling of comfort as his mind remembered the sounds of the city and men training in the yard.

But, suddenly, he was shoved. At first, he did not move. He intended to wake up and castigate the intruder, but then the shoving came stronger, and he immediately roused and looked up with tired eyes at a tall, heavily clad knight before him. He could not see his eyes, but he wore the same armour that Garvelia and the Oistos had worn when they had emerged after Mercury's death.

"Follow me!" he snapped.

Havovatch stood up and picked his helmet up from next to him, and, with his free hand, he rubbed his face hard, trying to relieve the stress.

As he was led deeper into the cave, he saw Hilclop sitting on the other side of the cave, head down. And, spaced along it, was the rest of his unit in the same position.

The cave grew darker as he went further in, but torches lit the passageway. The cave walls appeared to be have been carved by man, with torches immaculately positioned every ten feet.

Soon, they came to a fork in the cave and took the left passage. Surprisingly, there were doors down the passageways, and they stopped outside a big brown set of double doors fixed onto large hinges.

The guard made an unusual knock on the door, and it was unbolted and opened from the inside. Havovatch was escorted into the room, and the door was locked behind him. With every crank from the lock, he twitched, feeling just a little trapped.

He tried to distract himself by looking around the room. It was full of artefacts and souvenirs. Strange suits of armour hung like empty warriors in the corners of the room, and ancient weapons hung on the walls; shelves were crammed with scrolls or parchments, and, at the back of the cave, Havovatch was surprised to see a window letting in some natural light. The room was surprisingly large, and, sitting before him, behind a grand oak desk, was the man he had spoken to in the city.

The desk was strewn with hand-sculpted animals and warriors. The warriors stood tall and proud or in combat stances, as if re-enacting past battles. The commander sat quietly, writing; the guards around him stood to attention silently, not moving a muscle; there were four of them standing upright, each holding a long spear.

Eventually, the commander put the quill into a pot, sat back in his chair with his hands on his stomach, and looked up at Havovatch. He tried to stand to attention, hoping that some respect may go in his favour.

"How old do you think I am, boy?" the commander said drily.

"Apologies, Sir, I do not know," he said formally.

"I will be two thousand and sixty-eight years in a few months." Havovatch almost rolled his eyes, clearly not impressed by what he already knew from the Oistos.

"I see you have managed to convince the Oistos to gather at Shila?" he continued. "Their commander was always weak!" but Havovatch felt by his tone that he did not mean it.

The commander put a hand into the leather satchel, which held Havovatch's orders. And pulled out the small piece of paper between two fingers which was marked 'X'.

He read it out loud, his voice making Havovatch shiver. "You are to fulfil your oath!" he said contemptuously.

He held it in both hands and then looked up at Havovatch. "Tell me, Captain, why should I?"

"Sir, my men and I are but messengers – it is our King you need to speak—"

"I am speaking to you, boy! Many years ago, Agorath mustered his armies and descended upon Ezazeruth. We pledged our lives at a moment's notice to stop him, and, against our wishes, a king – *your* king – made us live beyond what is natural. I remember that day, boy – oh, yes! I remember it very well. So, I'll ask again, why should I?" His voice was fierce, with two thousand years of built-up anger.

There was a long silence; Havovatch thought very carefully, not wanting to insult him. "Sir, I have no answer to what you ask. All I can say is that many have died, one very close to me, as a result of this dark shadow. If I could find a way to put your curse to an end, I would, but it was a king of many years ago who cast it upon you. I ask that you do not chastise the people of today for his doing."

Havovatch felt almost content, thinking that he had said the right thing, although he did not even know where it had come from. The commander looked up at him almost in acceptance, but then he burst out laughing.

"You think you can come here with your poetic ways and convince me? I'll tell you something, boy," he said, pointing his long finger, "I took up an oath with my brothers, after the curse was bestowed upon us, that we would never fight for the land again, and I will not break it!"

"You broke your last oath, Commander," Havovatch said plainly.

The commander sat back in his chair, almost taken aback by the remark. "You try living for as long as I have. I have had thirty wives … THIRTY! Throughout that time I have seen them perish, as I live on. I don't dare have children as I could not bear to bury them! So, don't stand before me and speak as if you think what I am doing is wrong. I have been through much pain at the hands of your past king, whilst he rests in peace. *I want my peace*!" the commander said, hitting his chest with his fist.

"Sir, you are bound by your oath; once you fulfil it, you can have your peace."

"Huh! Do you think that if we defeat Agorath we will just have the curse removed? We can only die by being killed in battle! Your king took my life, and I will not let him take my honour!"

"Then may I ask, Sir, what are you and your *honour* waiting for?"

The commander sat in silence for a moment. Havovatch had triumphed. All this time, all these years they had hated the east, it was true – but they were hating something and doing nothing about it.

"I understand where you're coming from, Captain, but you're obviously too young to comprehend. I can't even believe that you are old enough to be a captain. What are you – fifteen?"

"Eighteen."

The commander grinned. "So, your people are recruiting boys to do a man's job? What is going on? Are you bred to be a fountain of knowledge at a young age or something?"

"My Lord!" Havovatch said angrily. The commander had hit a nerve, and he was getting annoyed with people making assumptions about him because of his age. "I was promoted for acts of valour by my King, so I would appreciate it if you would not insult my rank or my age. Now, if you have nothing else for me, I have another message I need to deliver, and then my country needs me … Sir!"

The commander's face went stern as he looked up at him; he was turning red and he could see his fist clenching tightly. "Get him out of here," he said between clenched teeth.

Havovatch thought that he had wound up the guards as well. When the doors opened, they took hold of an arm each and rather angrily took him back the way they had come.

Havovatch was put into a tent outside. It made a change from a cell or being tied up. The walls were of colourful cloth, dark purple, reds and oranges; to one side lay a bed made of thin bits of wood, but was very sturdy. There was a basin of fresh, clean water to the other side. He had to relinquish all his weapons before he went in, but he was not locked in. The entrance had just a flap of thick fabric over the canvas. He tried to take a peek outside, but could only see the metal of a guard's cuirass in front of him. As the sun shone down, he saw the silhouettes of giant knights, holding spears, all around the tent.

The tent did not block out the noises, though; he could hear people speaking in the familiar tongue of the Oistos.

The tent was cool. He stripped down to just his underwear and lay down on the bed. Putting his hands behind his head, he finally relaxed, and, letting his legs hang either side of the frame, he went to sleep.

Havovatch lay smiling to himself as visions of Cam appeared, feeling as though he was flying, looking over the city.

Suddenly, he swooped down and through the streets, zigzagging between markets before shooting up again, higher and higher; the Acropolis now below him, the smoke of the Heat Pit soaring high into the sky. He spiralled around it and then stood motionless, hovering above the clouds, looking on through the transparent mist of the green hills of the world and ever-continuing landscape.

Something caught his eye – off in the distance a light shone on, a familiar light, and a calm feeling about it pulsed energy towards him.

Suddenly, his body was flown away from the city and below him he saw the land become blurred as he went.

He passed the village in which he had been arrested, and then flew over the woods where they had found Hilclop. Soon he appeared over the burning village, with plumes of black smoke rising into the air, and then onto High Rocks and the forest where he had met the Oistos. In every location he passed, he kept seeing figures, too high up to make them out, but he got the feeling he was looking down upon himself and his unit.

He passed through the Forbidden Passage, and then past the waterfall and through the lands of Loria. Soon he was above Haval, seeing a Black army gathering, moving towards the north side of the town.

But he did not stop; still soaring, he saw the land turn from green to yellow as he came upon the Busy City, and circled around and then up its high towers tearing into the sky. And then he stopped, and was facing south.

Far into the distance of the desert, he saw a crease of white light on the horizon. It was sparkling, and in some way different … there was a red tinge to it, and then the light turned as scarlet as blood, and he got an overpowering feeling of dread and suffering.

"No!" he shouted out into the abyss. "I can still do this!"

But the light turned redder, as red as it could be, before turning black; then the sky turned to thunder, with violent lighting strikes like he had never seen, before cascading down to the ground around him.

And he began to fall.

He tried to flap his arms frantically to fly, but nothing happened. He screamed as he descended, the burden of failure looming over him.

He awoke lying on the floor, with his face buried in the sand. As he lifted his head up, he noticed that he was covered in a stale sweat. How long he had been asleep, he did not know.

He brushed the sand from his face and got onto all fours. Breathing heavily, he sobbed as a feeling of anguish ran through him.

He turned and sat awkwardly, feeling that he had to be uncomfortable … whether it was to keep himself awake or to punish himself, he was not sure.

But, as he looked around the tent, he noticed that it wasn't the same tent he had just been just in. A white sheen seemed to envelope the entire area and everything seemed so … holy, as if he wasn't worthy of being in this place. A sense of peace washed over him as he took everything in. As he continued to look around, he sensed a presence, and at the entrance he saw a tall, man standing with his hands in front of him, smiling pleasantly. He had short, dark hair, like stubble, with a receding hairline. His features seemed vaguely familiar, too.

"Rise, my son," he said, holding out his hand.

"Where am I? Is this Heaven?" Havovatch asked, before taking it.

"That will come in time ... meanwhile, your destiny is not yet fulfilled."

As if it were a movement not of his own, he reached out and took hold of the stranger's hand, and was raised to his feet. Again, the man smiled at him, and, with an open hand, he beckoned towards a glowing orb by the tent flaps.

"Follow it, Captain, and fulfil your purpose in this world. We will help you as much as we can, but it is down to you," he said softly, but his face was serious. Then the stranger started to disappear, and appearing above him were purple outlines, like large skeletal creatures looking down upon Havovatch. The mysterious man did not take his eyes away until the last moment.

When all had cleared, Havovatch looked at the orb, and slowly it passed through the tent flaps, not parting them.

Havovatch went forward, and, as he reached out to move the flaps, his hand passed through too. He withdrew it and examined it with interest, and then, with a spring in his step, he pushed his entire body through.

Before he knew it, he was in front of the guards at the front of the tent, but they did not seem to notice him. Outside, there was an unusual atmosphere. There was no one running or playing, no sounds whatsoever: no wind, no smells – the area was tranquil and silent.

The orb hovered next to Havovatch and then, slowly and delicately, moved off through the town.

Havovatch inquisitively followed it. He soon noticed why the town was so quiet and still. Everyone was frozen in the last movement they had made: children jumping through the air, others talking or walking through the streets, two horses with men riding them playing some form of game, the particles of sand kicked up from the ground but keeping still.

The orb then moved to the base of the zigzag path that led up out of the canyon, and slowly it began to follow the path to the top.

Havovatch, still following, tried to work out if he was in a dream. Everything felt so real, but then again he had had several similar dreams recently.

Eventually, the orb got to the summit. It was night now, and Havovatch noticed that the sky still had the same purpling in the air but was much darker, with more stars.

The orb moved to the edge of the cliff and then stopped.

Havovatch stood looking at it, and then it slowly started to disappear.

He watched as it turned into nothing, and, as it vanished, the world below went back to normal, and movement began all around, with noises, as it once was.

Then, to his amazement, he saw the commander sitting with his feet dangling over the edge of the cliff where the orb had disappeared. He was smoking a pipe, looking over the city, alone and reflective.

"Good evening," Havovatch said quietly, still taken in by the strange spell he was under.

The commander turned quickly and, upon seeing Havovatch, jumped to his feet and drew his sword.

"Guards!" he shouted over his shoulder, his voice loud and rugged, but no one below responded.

He shouted again, but still no one responded. With his sword still pointed at Havovatch, he turned and sidestepped towards the path, and once again shouted for help, but none came.

Havovatch stared at the sword and noticed that it was similar to Garvelia's, but the hilt was ruby red; with the same unusual large design in a spider-like shape, but with only four legs instead of eight.

As the commander went to move down the hill, he seemed to knock into something, but there was nothing there; yet he was unable to move past this impenetrable, invisible wall.

"What have you done?!" he said, staring at Havovatch, horrified.

"Nothing, Commander! To be honest, I have as many questions as you do."

Feeling trapped, the commander raised his sword and went to slice down at Havovatch. His arms went down, but his sword was stuck motionless above him. He turned in shock and looked up, but as he reached out, the sword raised further out of his reach, as if an invisible force was taking it from him.

He looked back at Havovatch in a new light. "Fine! Do what you want with me, warlock!" he said, his arms raised and closing his eyes.

"Commander, please! I am not here to hurt you; I'm not entirely sure how I got here."

The commander opened his eyes and put down his arms, looking at Havovatch inquisitively. "Very well – so, what do we do now?"

"I don't know."

There was a long pause, but the commander was the first to speak. "Captain, I don't know what is going on, but I don't like it. If you have anything to do with this, please stop, and I will hear your plea."

"I have no control over this and no idea what is going on! But since we are in this situation, I feel, as gentlemen, we need to act like them. You know my name, what is yours?"

"… Avron."

"Fair enough; I won't pretend that I know what you are going through, Commander Avron, but all I will say is this: you can continue to live this strange dream of yours," he said, casting an arm over the city below, "or you can finish what you have long waited to do. The Black were the ones who attacked this world, the doing of Agorath, who you swore to defeat. He is now coming back, and you will need to fight him, because no one else knows how."

Avron said nothing, standing there biting his lip and taking in what Havovatch had said.

"As you say, Captain, you don't know what we have gone through."

"There are still things worth fighting for within this world, Commander, things I have yet not seen. But, within this last month, I have seen things I would rather forget. I have seen children dead, animals killed, I have seen an assortment of crimes that are so heinous I dare not speak of them again, and this is all at the hands of the Black!" Havovatch fell to his knees. "I beg, if you do not stop those who have done these terrible crimes, then I ask you end my life now, so that I will see no more pain or torment, and that I can forget what a cruel world this has become."

Avron looked down at him for a long moment; he did not move, but he met with Havovatch's weeping eyes and saw conviction in what he said.

Bowing his head, he gave a nod.

Havovatch awoke back in his tent, with his arm slumped over the bed. His head hurt, as he had had such a deep sleep. Sitting up, he rubbed his face and wished for cold. Reflecting on his dream, he wished it could just have been as easy, but with a newfound confidence he went to get dressed and march back out to try again.

He pulled the tent flap away and walked into the city. It was alive: men were saddling horses, and spears were being put into columns in the ground. Knights queued up to get swords sharpened; children stood cradled by their mothers, and both wept; and banners were raised, loosened from their knots to sail in the breeze.

There were no guards in front of his tent. As he looked across, he saw the commander, now in the same type of armour that the Oistos wore when they went to war, but with his breastplate ruby red, and a centaur emblazoned on the front. Upon seeing Havovatch, he approached. "You're finally awake, then?"

"Sir? What is going on?"

"Are you mindless – don't you remember last night? We are taking up our oath, so smile! We are going to WAR!" he shouted, throwing his fist into the air, followed by a raucous chant from his men. Havovatch was taken aback – so it hadn't been a dream? He shook his head, shocked at the revelation.

Turning to Havovatch, Avron drew him in close and whispered into his ear, "Captain, I don't know if you are aware, but the laws state that all must be at Shila …"

"In order to complete the oath – yes, I know, Commander; one more to go."

"Yes, Captain, but did you also know that you have one month and eight days before the last commander must be at Shila, or we are forsaken, and will vanish into nothingness, our souls with the wind, never to experience death, nor peace?"

Havovatch swallowed. *Garvelia missed that bit out,* he thought, but then realized he had not given her much of a chance to tell him.

"We now leave this sacred haven for war. One part of our spell is broken, and it is up to you to get the last army to Shila. My men will escort you back to the city. Can I suggest that you muster your regiment around you and get yourself to the Xiphos? At this moment in time, you are the most important man in the world."

Avron patted him hard on the shoulder. "Oh, and Captain, the next commander will not be so easy to convince. He is a cold, hard man who has suffered more than any of us. You will find him and the Xiphos at the base of the northern mountains. That's all I know of them. All I can say now is good luck!" With a wrapped hand to his chest, he made a slight bow with his head and turned back into the city.

Suddenly Buskull, Feera, Hilclop and Ferith were standing staring at him. Horses were brought forward, and a lieutenant approached. "Captain, we will take you back to your regiment. I suggest we make haste!"

Chapter Thirty
The Beginning of the Invasion

King Colomune stood proudly on the quarterdeck of his galleon, near to the rear squadron of the fleet, with hundreds of ships in front and around him. Below him on a desk was a map, with a course plotted out, with little statues for the main ships.

Atken sat behind him, his face as plain as it always was.

It was a clear, bright day, and they had been sailing for just over two weeks. It was easy going, with calm seas and little in the way of trouble.

Colomune felt positive. He stood in his finest burnished armour, with his helmet under his right arm, gleaming as a beacon to his men, an air of confidence around him, smiling and taking in the sea breeze. He was in a good mood, mainly because Colonel Sarka was not there to tell him what to do; in the last two weeks, he had so grown in confidence that, when he returned, he was going to have him arrested. He had already told Atken to arrange it, so when the time came he would not lose control and become weak again.

He felt calm and closed his eyes, taking in the sounds and feel of the open sea: men tightening ropes, sails flapping, the ships pushing through the waves, the feel of salt spraying against his face.

As he stood with his eyes closed, he grinned at the thought of his statue standing higher than those of any of his ancestors in the Great Hall; his name being mentioned in songs and rhymes and chanted by children, hailing him as a hero; and portraits put up over the city of Cam in his honour. He felt a warm sensation in his stomach as he thought more and more about it; in the last week he had thought of little else.

But he woke from his trance as he heard shouting from the stern of the ship; he looked across as the first mate came running towards him. "My King," he said, saluting in the sloppy way that was custom amongst sailors.

"Report!" King Colomune said, trying to sound official.

Atken grunted at the dramatic act.

"The scout ship reports land ahead; what are your orders?"

King Colomune took a few moments before saying anything, trying to make himself wise, but the first mate was not a patient man. "My King? Did you hear what I said? The Admiral needs to know your orders."

Colomune, slightly taken aback, looked down at the map and back up at the first mate.

"Just answer the damned man," Atken said, fed up with this masquerade.

"Prepare for landing!" Colomune said a little sheepishly.

"Very well."

The first mate put a clenched fist into the air, signalling to the sailors at the front of the ship. The sailors started gesturing with different coloured flags to the other ships, and they began tacking. Soldiers started to go to their battle stations, preparing to beach, horns and bells ringing out around the ships; on every deck, there was a commotion as the soldiers got ready.

Colomune clicked his fingers at an aide, who produced a blank sheet of map paper and figurines of regiments, and began to sketch out what he thought the coastline looked like and where best to moor, ready for King Colomune to monitor the battle when they beached.

Colomune did not notice at first, but the clear, blue sky grew slightly dark, as if night was rushing forward. Then a black cloud appeared.

Then, Colomune's attention was drawn to someone shouting, and he looked up, noticing the change in atmosphere.

The commotion stopped, and there was an eerie silence from most of the troops, all fixed on looking at the strange ambience around them. Then, in the deathly silence, he heard: "ATTACK FROM STARBOARD!"

His heart skipped a beat and he looked to the right, but could only see the mass of white sails and ships in his way.

Then he heard a thunderclap – it was loud and echoed across the open water. Suddenly, looking up, he saw the black clouds seeming to expand from nothing; they got bigger and more sinister-looking, soon taking up every available blue gap in the sky. There were purple rumbles of thunder between the clouds, and suddenly night was cast over the fleet. The purple thunder escalated, and huge strikes came tumbling down around them.

"ATTACK FROM PORT!" shouted someone else from another ship. Looking left, again all he saw was masses of sails with the deafening sound of thunder.

The water became choppy, and the boat swayed heavily with the waves; some ships started to collide into each other, as they were too close together and could not cope with the rough current.

Colomune gripped onto the side, as did all of the crew on board as the waves became more violent; most of the men on the ships fell over, with some falling overboard, screaming as their armour dragged them into the water.

Turning to an aide, he went to shout, when he was interrupted. "ATTACK FROM THE PROW! ATTACK FROM THE STERN – WE'RE SURROUNDED!"

Chapter Thirty-One
The Final Stretch

Havovatch was escorted back to his regiment by fifty cavalrymen – man and beast heavily armoured, the knights carrying thick spears with a wavering, ruby-red banner on each one. Despite their burden, the horses moved with superb speed and agility, he felt quite intimidated being around them and was glad that they were on his side.

When they came back into view of the city, its towering steeples upon the horizon and soon the huge surrounding walls, they saw that the Three-Thirty-Third was encamped outside, with columns of white tents pitched on a flat surface of the land. The city seemed strangely eerie, and, as they got closer, it became apparent why.

Guards dressed in blue and bronze were manning the front gate. Soldiers could be seen patrolling the ancient walls, and people entering or leaving the city were being searched.

As they approached, Havovatch saw three figures standing to one side, monitoring the goings-on, and saw that one of them was Captain Jadge.

The war riders saluted and broke away, leaving Havovatch and his unit to approach his men. "Well? You've been busy," he said, regarding what was going on with clear bemusement.

Jadge turned almost in disbelief to see him, as did the other two officers.

"Captain … you're alive?"

"Well, I had Buskull with me," Havovatch said casually, too exhausted to be surprised by anything seen or said.

Jadge looked at the other two officers, who wore the same expression. They stared at Havovatch as if he were a ghost, their skin pale and their bodies frozen.

"We heard you had been taken captive and died in an arena fight. We shut the city down, trying to find your bodies in order to prove it," said one of the officers.

Havovatch let out a slight laugh. "Really? How did you hear we were dead?"

Jadge grunted, getting his composure back. "Yesterday morning, we reached the outskirts of the city. I sent some scouts in to blend with the crowd and see if they could find you. There was a lot of commotion at the time; we found trampled dead bodies on the floor, and everyone was running around in panic or looting. One of the scouts reported that he had heard people shouting about a giant gladiator escaping an arena and going on a killing spree." Havovatch stood, poised, listening to the story. "I then sent the Three-Thirty-Third in and took control of the unrest, and began questioning people. We found clear descriptions of Buskull and put two and two together, but the rumour was that you had died."

Havovatch knew he should explain, but was too exhausted to. "Well, we are not, and we need to be moving by morning. Have the men leave the city and prepare to march tomorrow; have them well fed and watered. We have a long way to go, and this will be the making or breaking of our mission!"

"Yes, Captain!" Jadge said officially, then turned away, clearly annoyed with his captain's bluntness after all he had done to find him.

"You did well, Lieuten… you did well, Captain," Havovatch quickly added, noting his discomfort.

Jadge gave a nod of appreciation, and, taking the moment in for a while, he then snapped to attention, and set about getting the Three-Thirty-Third out of the city and accounted for.

Havovatch turned to his unit and noticed Ferith standing aimlessly next to them.

"How much do you know?"

"What ya mean?"

The unit surrounded him so he could not escape, and Ferith held his hands up to show no threat.

"You have, unfortunately, followed us on a secret mission, Ferith of Viror. I am afraid that we cannot trust to leave you alone, at least until we complete our quest."

Ferith started to panic, visibly shaking and going wide-eyed. He stepped from one foot to the next. "P-please, I am no threat, I merely got caught up in something I wished not to be."

"How did you end up in the prison cell?" said Havovatch.

"Spies from Viror found me. They paid a price for me to be kept locked up whilst they stayed a few days in the city, and were going to return me to Chief Erash."

Havovatch thought it over, looking with narrow eyes at him. "Well, that's as maybe, but we do not know how much you know, and your word is not enough."

"Listen! Please! You have my word!" Ferith said, bending slightly and opening his arms out.

Havovatch shook his head. "I cannot trust that – too many people rely on me." He clicked his fingers at Sergeant Metiya, who was passing by.

"Sergeant, this man travels with us. Have two scouts and two archers posted with him at all times. Confiscate any weapons he has, and, if he runs, they may shoot him."

Metiya, without question, pointed his spear at him.

"Ferith, we are but a few weeks from the end of our mission, and you will be treated with the hospitality of my regiment, but that will change if you show any sign of threat to our mission. Do I make myself plain?"

Ferith, shaking frantically, gave a nod, and was led away by Sergeant Metiya.

"Couldn't we just kill him?" said Hilclop.

The others all shot him a look of disbelief.

"We do not just kill people, soldier!" Buskull said firmly.

Havovatch looked at him sternly. "I am shocked you could say such a thing. To take a life is not an easy task and clearly something you need to learn about," he added.

Trying desperately to gain some credibility, Hilclop persisted. "But he could put our mission in danger. Now he is just dead weight."

"Were you any different?" Feera pointed out. "We thought the same things when we found you!"

Hilclop stood startled for a moment, shocked into silence and almost sick.

Havovatch looked down upon him like a judge. "I brought you on this mission to help you grow up, Hilclop, to learn things that few others would have the chance to know. But I hope you start to wonder about the preciousness of taking a life, because that is what this mission is about, sustaining the life and freedom of Ezazeruth!"

Havovatch turned his back, the others following, leaving Hilclop to contemplate their words.

Over the following days, Havovatch marched north, with the regiment clustered around him. They progressed little by day, only managing about ten miles or so, with some men lagging behind. Usually, they would march at the pace of the slowest man, but Havovatch knew he needed to get to the Xiphos, and soon.

With the knights' lives at risk, Havovatch felt that he wanted to save them more than summon them, and took it personally.

As the regiment approached rivers, they would march through them and refill their waterskins, but they ate little; some lackeys ran amongst the ranks with salted meat or bread, or dried fruit. One time, they found an orchard and pilfered the apples from the trees. Havovatch knew that the owner would not be best pleased, but with eight thousand mouths to feed and the world at stake, there were more important issues at hand.

As he marched, he was reminded of his training all over again. Despite being nearly starved and marching almost constantly with little rest, with the threat of being attacked, and walking into the unknown – and despite the exhaustion – Havovatch enjoyed it.

Time wore on, and the northern mountains finally came into view, with their snowy peaks visible. After another seven days, the Three-Thirty-Third approached the foothills of the mountains. Havovatch looked behind him and noticed a long, blue stream of figures struggling to keep up. They had been lucky not to encounter any threats in the march from the Busy City. Well, he thought they had not; prying eyes may have been on them without their knowing, but, with the might of the Three-Thirty-Third, few would attack them.

Havovatch raised a clenched fist into the air, and the exhausted regiment came to a halt. Most men collapsed to the floor, as their numb bodies could finally rest. Jadge approached him. "Your orders, Captain?" he said tiredly, his face drawn, barely showing any energy.

"We rest, let the trailing soldiers catch up, send the fitter men to the rear and assist them. I will take the unit and go from here."

"But, Captain! You said for us to stay with you!"

Havovatch had told Jadge about their mission and what was intended of them; he had obviously told others to keep their spirits up, and everyone knew they had a purpose: to protect their captain.

"You have done all you have needed to, Captain Jadge; it is now time for us to continue alone."

Jadge looked a little crestfallen. "Very well."

"Your orders are to account for the men lagging behind and set up an encampment here until we return."

"And if you don't?"

Havovatch shot him a glare, but the reality of what he said was right, they might not ...

"OK, stay here for seven days; if we do not return after that time, march back to Cam and report to General Drorkon – he will account for your desertion."

Jadge nodded. "Very well, Captain … good luck!" he said, putting on his finest salute.

"Thank you, Captain." They clasped each other's forearms, then Havovatch walked through the ranks of his men with Buskull, Feera and Hilclop.

As they left the perimeter, they walked alone towards the foothills of the mountains; clouds above them turned dark, and the dreary mountains of the north loomed before them, the snowy peaks hidden by the clouds. Suddenly, to the unit, it seemed an impossible challenge.

***

Havovatch shivered in the bitter cold, his teeth chattering, and he clasped his hands under his armpits to try to keep warm and get the feeling back in his fingers. Snow blew into him from every direction, and, no matter what he did, he got colder and colder.

They had been climbing for three days and were over halfway up the mountain, the track long behind them, with Buskull leading the way.

The rope linking Havovatch to Feera behind him, and Buskull in front, kept snagging whenever one of them stumbled.

Eventually, Buskull found a small cave in the cliff's edge, and they piled in. Naturally, they clustered together to share what warmth they had. Buskull seemed like an oven, though; he was still only wearing his vest, and his giant arms and shoulders were bare to the cold, but he seemed undeterred.

"What do we do?" Hilclop begged as his teeth chattered. He visibly looked worse than the others, not being as fit.

"Buskull, how are we doing?"

"Hard to say, Captain – we are still a good distance from the summit."

"Our waterskins are frozen, Captain," said Feera.

Havovatch reached down to his, and felt a solid lump.

"We … could … try to eat the snow, t-t-that is water, isn't it?" suggested Hilclop, too cold to speak clearly.

"I wouldn't," Buskull interjected, "it will use your body warmth to melt the snow and you will get colder, but we do need to drink, otherwise you could get hypothermia."

"How are we going to drink?"

"Give me your waterskins," he said.

Each one of them took a shaky hand, tried to undo the clasp on his waterskin and handed it to Buskull. Buskull took them all and cradled them against his chest.

Soon, he reached out and gave them their skins back, with a wet patch on his vest from the melted water.

They each drank, and it was warm; they could feel it trickling all the way down their throats and into their bellies, like warm honey straight from the hive.

"Empty them; I'll then fill the skins with snow and melt them again," Buskull shouted over the wind hitting the cave's entrance.

Perplexed at finding out that Buskull's body could cope with the temperature, they downed their skins, and giving them back to him, they pulled their cloaks tighter against themselves, went to the back of the cave and lay on the floor, cradling each other.

Buskull approached the entrance and poked snow into the skins until they were full; again, hugging the skins against himself, he used his immense body heat to melt them.

They lay there for some time. Buskull sat up against the cave wall, looking out at the entrance whilst his huge arms embraced the unit. It did not seem strange to them, although it looked as though they were hugging a big man like a child's toy ... it was survival, and the heat emanating from Buskull was helping them to get the feeling back in their toes and fingers. Not long after that, Havovatch stood up, at a stage where he was comfortable enough to take the cold, and took off his armour. He readjusted everything so that it was more comfortable, and his cloak was now underneath his armour.

The armour pressed against his tunic, and the cloak kept in his body heat; the only issues were his bare fingers on the frosty snow and his cold, metal helmet on his ears.

Ironically, he kept thinking back to the Heat Pit and how he wanted to go back there.

The others, once they had warmed up, mimicked what Havovatch did, and the morale was a little higher, but it was getting dark outside. "It will be suicide going out there at night; we'll stay here until tomorrow – the wind may die down and we can start again," shouted Havovatch.

They resumed hugging Buskull as the night wore on, and they were left in darkness, with the constant winds outside the cave blasting the entrance.

They awoke the next day to calmer, but still bitterly cold, weather.

As Havovatch stood up and went to the entrance, he saw the precarious path they had been following: barely a few feet wide, with a sheer drop down and nowhere to grip on the cliff's edge. He wondered how they had made it that far.

But, as he looked ahead to where they needed to go, it did not look any better, and the path continued up, with the summit out of sight.

Buskull heated their waterskins again and they took a belly full each; feeling revived and warmer, they again linked a rope between them and Buskull led the way up.

It was much steeper that day, making the journey hard going. Every time he looked up, he could still not see the summit, just the looming cliff edges. There were no clouds about; the sky was a piercing blue, and cool winds swept past their faces, making their skin red and dry.

As Havovatch looked down, he realized how far they had come up. He had to grab onto the cliff and pull himself against it as he took in the overbearing view. But, after a moment, he calmed himself, and, looking out into the world and its beauty, he was suddenly awestruck, wondering how a place so beautiful could hold so much pain and suffering. But a tug on the rope snapped him out of it, and, following Buskull, he carried on.

Something changed in the air. Before he could look around, he felt something land on him; he turned his head and saw a robed figure, and suddenly he was bent over the cliff's edge. Not wanting to fight in fear of falling, he gripped tightly onto a rock, and felt the pressure as he was pulled back onto the path, but his face was pushed into the snow.

His heart stopped when he heard two echoing shouts disappearing over the edge of the cliff, and he hoped that it was not his men!

Suddenly, he was forced onto his feet and his helmet was removed; he had little time to see anything as a gag was placed in his mouth and a hood over his head. He did not remember what happened next, but blackness followed as he was hit on the back of the head.

Chapter Thirty-Two
The Stubbornness of Man

Havovatch awoke to swirling shapes. He made out that he was in a red tent, and the sun shining outside clearly showed the outlines of two figures before him.

Seeing stars circling his eyes from the hit to his head, he tried to shrug it off, but, as his consciousness revived, he felt his hands were yet again bound behind him, and very sore. Being tied up so much recently was starting to cause permanent scarring to his wrists.

His vision cleared, and in front of him stood a slender man. He was finely dressed in long robes and did not look like a warrior or battle-worn – more of a politician or diplomat.

His hair was dark and neatly trimmed, with a receding hairline, and he stared at him with malevolent intent.

The other figure was heavily dressed in warm clothing and wore a metal helmet with the visor up, and a scarf covering his face. Havovatch could only see his eyes, and they were just like those of the other man: *enraged.*

Havovatch could not be bothered to be diplomatic any more, his patience worn thin with exhaustion and his tolerance gone. "Let me guess, you're the Xiphos?" he said wryly.

The masked man approached and slapped him hard around the face with the back of his hand.

Havovatch spat a mouthful of blood and looked back up at them for a long moment.

"Well ...? Are you going to speak? Or shall we see who blinks first?" Havovatch mocked.

The masked man again approached, but the slender man jabbed a hand in front of him and spoke in a language Havovatch was starting to find familiar; and at that moment he had no doubt that these *were* the Xiphos.

The large man left, but shot a contemptuous look back at Havovatch before he did.

The slender man stood presentably, with his hands behind his back. "I am Commander Duruck," he said formally.

"So you are the Xiphos?"

Duruck ignored the question. "I have seen your orders. Strange that two others appear to be missing?"

"That's because they have seen what is right in this world and have chosen to protect it."

"You come across very ignorant ... not a good quality for a soldier, or a captain."

"I'm more of an artist!" Havovatch said drily.

Duruck smiled slightly in the corner of his mouth, but not because of the gag.

"So, let's get facts straight ... you have one order for me, you are alive, you look beaten and unwell, and your attitude speaks of fatigue and dread, so I can safely assume that my two cohorts have done as you say, and that you have gone through hell to get here. So much so that you have lost someone ... someone close, I am guessing?" he said, bending at the waist, looking into Havovatch's eyes for a reaction.

Havovatch said nothing; he was just frowning, with his jaw quivering.

Duruck stood up and drew a dagger. Havovatch took a deep breath as he approached.

He stood in front of him, twisting the blade in his hand, then bent behind him and cut his bonds.

Duruck walked over to a desk and sat down neatly, pushing the tails of his tunic under him as he did so. He put some glasses on and took a quill, then began reading paperwork as if Havovatch were absent from his presence.

Seeing a jug of water next to him, Havovatch swigged the contents down. He then sat for a few minutes, tending his wounds on his wrists with a wet rag torn from his tunic. They were so sore they were oozing all sorts of fluids. He winced as he doused them, trying to clean the wounds, but his body was stiff.

The entrance was directly ahead of him, with the flaps waving as a breeze passed by, and it suddenly occurred to him that he was climbing a mountain – why was it not cold? It was actually quite warm.

With Duruck ignoring him, Havovatch stood up and stretched, then strode towards the flap. "Did I say you could go?" Duruck asked, not taking his eyes from his quill.

Havovatch ignored him and went to walk out, but, as he did so, two huge guards appeared. Havovatch's face nearly hit their breastplates, they were so big, and he noticed a minotaur embedded on them.

He looked over at Duruck, who was still ignoring him, so he turned and stood in front of his desk. The guards automatically left as he did so.

"Well, are you going to write or are we going to talk?"

Duruck did not answer.

Havovatch sighed heavily, and slammed his fist down on the table, making several objects rattle.

Duruck did not flinch, but he stopped what he was doing to look up at Havovatch's fist, and delicately pushed it off and carried on writing.

Havovatch was astonished. *What in hell is going on*? he thought.

He went back over to his chair, made himself comfortable and sat looking up at the ceiling of the tent.

It was nearly dusk outside, and Havovatch was sitting with his legs spread, slouching in the chair with his index fingers to his lips, deep in thought.

Due to the light getting darker in the tent, Duruck had lit a candle on his desk, but otherwise he had not regarded Havovatch – he had just kept reading and writing.

Eventually, he stopped and sat back looking at him. "I hope we can talk as men now? And that your manner is less ... rash?" he said calmly.

Havovatch conceded that he had insulted him, and stood up before him.

"My apologies, it has been a ... rough few months," he said, as if he were addressing one of his own commanders, desperate not to have the silent treatment again.

"Why do you come?" Duruck asked.

"Because I was ordered to."

"You come only because of your orders?"

"My orders told me to come, and I have taken an oath not to fail."

"Then I guess you are going to come out with some magical reason as to why we should accept?" Duruck said, shrugging his shoulders.

"You swore an oath to accept."

"Why should I and the blood of my people be sacrificed to the world? What has it done for us?" Duruck spoke very calmly. After the warning Havovatch had received, he expected shouting and aggression, but Duruck was far from what he'd expected.

"If you do not, the Black will still get to you."

Duruck shook his head. "We are well defended here!"

"A part of the curse has already been broken; the other armies march for Shila and within a month they will be scattered to the wind."

"... They knew what they were doing, and they knew of my thoughts towards it."

"And you will abandon them?"

Duruck said nothing.

Havovatch felt dread inside him ... he was not getting anywhere, and hoped that the magical light would soon appear. "Please, you were right – I lost a friend getting to you, and many other innocent people will die too."

Duruck shook his head. "I have lost loved ones too, Captain, it is part of life, and they were not sacrificed to my cause."

"I know of your story, and I am sorry—"

"Sorry!" For the first time Duruck became abrupt. "Sorry that my men have lived for over two thousand years? Sorry that I have watched wife and child die one after the other? Sorry that for all that is good within this world, *we*! – the very people who swore to protect it – had our freedom ripped away from us? You may be sorry, Captain Havovatch, but only for your own sake, not for ours."

Havovatch was taken aback by the sudden hostility; he was not too sure how to respond.

"To be quite honest, Captain, I don't give a care for what happens to this world – as far as I am concerned, I have forsaken it long ago!" Taking his quill, he carried on writing.

Havovatch seemed taken aback by this. This man really didn't care what happened to the world! "Well I'm *sorry* to have *disturbed* you, Commander," he said abruptly, before turning away.

Then he remembered he had heard the shouts of someone falling off the mountain during his capture. "If I may, are all my men accounted for? There were four of us."

"And there still are," he said, not taking his eyes off his work.

"But I heard shouts – someone fell?"

Duruck looked up. "Yes, two of my men fell to their deaths, thanks to your giant."

"I'm sorry, but they will be at peace surely?"

"I thought you said you have heard of our story? We are not invincible, Captain, we are immortal. We can still die at the blade, and we can get broken bones. We still feel pain and suffering, but a curse wears on us, never to age or die of disease or infection. If we do die, though, our souls can never rest in peace."

Havovatch felt a sudden chill pass through him at that, and tried to think of their souls roaming the blackness of nothing for all eternity.

Duruck once again got his head down and carried on writing, and, conceding, Havovatch went to leave again, his mind empty of ideas about how to progress.

Putting his hands into his pockets, he wondered where Undrea's handkerchief was. He touched his face where she had kissed him, and he was overcome by a feeling of love, not calm. But then, the thought of the Black arriving took hold of him; she was at Ambenol and too near the east coast – he was failing her.

He turned and looked at Duruck, with a feeling he could not describe rising within him, his hands shaking and his face turning into pure rage. "With all due respect, Commander, I have come to the end of what I can cope with: your kind's sulking ways, and betrayal of your morals and honour."

Duruck ominously stood up, disgust written over his face.

"You swore an oath," Havovatch continued, "an oath to protect people, and many innocents will die, who deserve to live, because of your dereliction to duty; and I tell you now! That I swore an oath to get you to fulfil yours, and I shall not leave here until you accept it!"

Duruck walked around the desk and stood toe-to-toe in front of him, and then grabbed him by the scruff of his tunic. With impressive strength, he threw Havovatch against a beam of the tent.

"YOU-DO-NOT COME HERE AND TELL ME WHAT I MUST DO!"

Havovatch too grabbed Duruck and pulled him closer. "THEN IF MY WORDS DO NOT PENETRATE THAT SKULL, MY SWORD WILL!!"

Duruck kept a firm hold and, snarling, he pushed him back, taking a long, wrapped object that was hanging on the wall and storming outside.

Havovatch stood up; with adrenalin rushing through him, he followed. As he walked out into the open, he saw Duruck standing in the middle of a stone plaza, his sword drawn, facing him. The sword was the same as those of the other commanders, with the large spider-shaped hilt of four legs, but his was sapphire blue.

A large knight approached Havovatch and gave him his. He took it and pointed with it at Duruck; it was much shorter than his.

"If I win, your armies are under my charge-"

"And when I win you and your men will die!" Duruck responded coldly.

Havovatch suddenly saw Buskull and the others tied to a pole buried into the ground, looking on, concerned. There was nothing they could do – a thick rope covered them from the neck downwards, and guards surrounded them.

Taking a breath, Havovatch raised his sword and charged at Duruck, but Duruck merely stepped out of the way. Havovatch swung back in his direction, Duruck ducking under the blow. Havovatch pushed towards him, but, with every move he made, Duruck passively disengaged and refused to fight back.

As Havovatch quickly became tired, Duruck struck. Almost like a dancer, he parried forward, deflecting Havovatch's blade and easily getting under his guard, elbowing him in the face.

Havovatch felt one of his teeth being dislodged and his mouth instantly filled with blood, but he stepped forward and, catching Duruck's blade with his own, he swung with his fist to hit him. Duruck spun around and punched Havovatch in the face, again making him stumble, but there was no mercy. Duruck hit him in the stomach, in the kidneys, a knee to the thigh, a slap to the face, followed by another knee to his skull, making him full backwards.

By now a crowd had gathered, chanting "Duruck! Duruck!" Havovatch's morale lessened.

Clumsily, he got up, trying to show defiance, but he stumbled and was unable to wield the blade properly due to the shock and pain.

Duruck was barely worn out, and again Havovatch pressed forward.

Duruck was clearly more masterful with the blade, anticipating every move Havovatch made before he did it, toying with him.

Then, as if he had become bored, Duruck slashed at the inside of Havovatch's leg.

Convulsed by pain and shock, he fell, clutching at the wound. There was no remorse. Duruck kicked him in the face and slashed at the inside of his other leg.

Havovatch cried out and heard Buskull shouting in the background. He clung to his sword with his bloodied hand, but his head felt light. He gasped for air that did not seem to appear, and the world around him started to spin.

Duruck kicked his sword away and stood blocking out the light. He pointed his sword at Havovatch's eyes. "You should never have come here, Captain … my face shall be the last thing you will see!"

He brought his sword up, and, in both hands, maliciously heaved it down into Havovatch's chest.

Havovatch gasped. He looked down at the blade within him, feeling the sticky, crimson substance pouring from his wound and the cold metal within him. Suddenly, he came into contact with his own mortality. The light faded from his eyes, and the last thing he saw was the malice and crazed look on Duruck's face, looking down upon him.

ABOUT THE AUTHOR

I love writing, I truly do. But I never thought that I'd write a book. I always knew that I was slightly different, but I could not put my finger on the reason, and I have never really told anyone this until now …

Growing up, my mind was always somewhere else, usually exploring a world of my own. I remember that, when I was in year 3, I was always looking at a picture book of Romans fighting Celts, and I would imagine what the next sequence of actions on the page might be. In year 5, I drew and wrote my own magazine, called *Rocket Mouse*. When I went to secondary school, I liked to pretend my pens and pencils were spaceships, and often woke up from my bored and playful trance to see everyone around me working; I had no idea what we were doing. This was often the day-to-day activity of my life, and it was, in many ways, frustrating, because I could not understand why no one else was doing the same thing.

At the age of seven, I was recognized and treated for dyslexia; I knew what it was but often chose to ignore it, as I was happy to live in my imagination, so I just did not see it as a problem. But I have always told people about it, as I am not ashamed and I do not see it as a label!

My love for fantasy began when the epic story *The Lord of the Rings* came to our screens. My mind went wild with Middle Earth, its characters and the wonderful tale that John Ronald Reuel Tolkien created.

After that, I came up with my own world and spent my time visiting castles and woods, drawing scenes and making notes. And so, I decided to become a film director and put my plans into action. But, halfway through my college course in Media Studies, I decided to change my career and become a … police officer (talk about a career change, eh?), because I did not think I had what it took to follow my dream; that's all I saw it as … a silly dream, and not what *normal* people do.

At the age of twenty, I joined the police, but after two years of service I chose to leave, due to irreconcilable differences. During that time, I forced myself to stop daydreaming, and I left my imagination in the past.

But it was going through that career which caused me to write, for the person I was before I joined the police was very different to the one I was when I left; and, near the end of my short career, my imagination came back, almost as if it were meant to.

But, since leaving, I had been in a bad state; I had to see a psychiatrist and was dosed up on medication. But the best medicine was writing – being able to place my imagination into another world was the real saviour of my life.

And so you have the first finished instalment in my trilogy, and there is far more to come …

If you want to follow me, check me out on Facebook, Twitter or www.thomasrgaskin.com .

Thomas R. Gaskin

Lightning Source UK Ltd.
Milton Keynes UK
UKOW02f1857290516

275162UK00002B/50/P